More Praise for

Safe in America

"A penetrating study of loss. . . . Intimate, unsparing and psychologically profound." —*Publishers Weekly*

"A bittersweet look at family life. . . . Hershman is a talented writer with a gift for bringing the reader into the everyday world of her characters." —*Chicago Tribune*

"Hershman is a spellbinding storyteller." —*Booklist*

"Deeply poignant and compulsively readable." —*Cleveland Plain Dealer*

"A heartbreaking book, about a family so richly realized I had to remind myself, like a child watching a movie, that they're not 'real.' . . . Marcie Hershman has written a remarkably moving and timely story about love, family loyalty, ambition, loss, and finally, the courage to remain hopeful even in the face of history's cruelty and the body's fragility." —Rosellen Brown

"Powerful. . . . The emotional power of the novel lies in that turbulent 1940s world Hershman is so brilliantly making her own literary preserve." —*Boston Herald*

"Recommended reading." —*The New Yorker*

"Hershman has again vividly rendered a world in which no one is safe from terror and loss. . . . Her power comes from clear, accurate writing that often prompts a painful jab of recognition." —*Bay Windows*

"Hershman confronts us with family crises that teach us much about the chaos of the world." —*Miami Herald*

"No writer I know makes humanity's great questions more personal; no one makes individual questions seem more universal. *Safe in America* is a spiritual journey of importance to us all."
—Christopher Tilghman

"Hershman does a masterful job of shaping human beings who readers can care about."
—*Jewish Review*

"Uncannily intimate. . . . By placing a totally genuine diorama of an age gone by within the rougher framework of an uncertain present, Hershman helps to illuminate the relationship between that time and our own."
—*Boston Sunday Globe*

Safe in America

ALSO BY MARCIE HERSHMAN

Tales of the Master Race

Safe in America

A Novel

MARCIE HERSHMAN

HarperPerennial

A Division of HarperCollinsPublishers

A hardcover edition of this book was published in 1995 by HarperCollins Publishers.

HarperCollins books may be purchased for educational, business, or sales promotional use. For information please write: Special Markets Department, HarperCollins Publishers, Inc., 10 East 53rd Street, New York, NY 10022.

First HarperPerennial edition published 1996.

Designed by Alma Hochhauser Orenstein

The Library of Congress has catalogued the hardcover edition as follows:

Hershman, Marcie, 1951–
    Safe in America : a novel / Marcie Hershman. — 1st ed.
        p. cm.
    ISBN 0-06-017144-8
    I. Title.
    PS3558.E777S24 1995
    813'.54—dc20   95-5737

ISBN 0-06-092734-8 (pbk.)

96 97 98 99 00 ❖/RRD 10 9 8 7 6 5 4 3 2 1

For Phyllis and Eugene Hershman
and for Robert, Cliff, and Dan

Acknowledgments

I am grateful to the Mary Ingraham Bunting Institute of Radcliffe College, the Corporation of Yaddo, the MacDowell Colony, the St. Botolph Club Foundation, and Tufts University for residencies and grants that sustained and encouraged; to the American Jewish Historical Society, Waltham, Massachusetts, for use of their immigration files and archives; to the AIDS Action Council, Washington, D.C., for the vital work they do; and for the support of so many friends who came through for me in ways I never knew I would ever need—and did need. My heartfelt thanks especially to Ellen Levine, Robert Jones, Jill McCorkle, Dan Wakefield, Eileen Pollack, and, always, Rebecca Blunk.

Acknowledgments

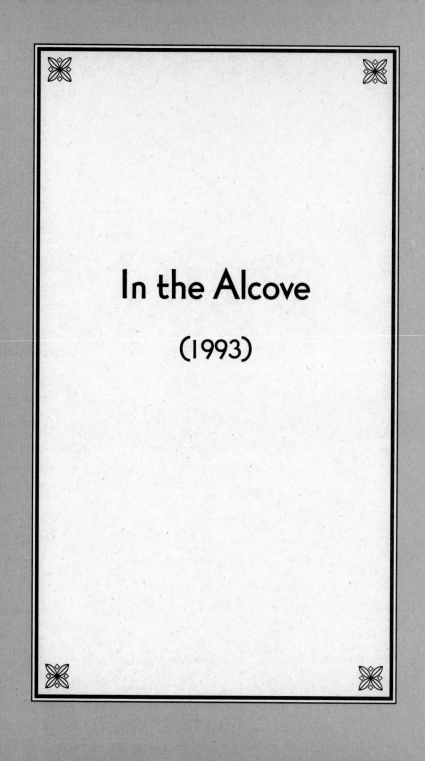

In the Alcove

(1993)

None of them ever really knew their grandfather. Of course they couldn't have. They were thin-legged, silly little kids, and he was a quiet man, elegant in his white-on-white shirts, his French cuffs, his gray suits and black smooth-grain leather belts. His hair he combed straight back from a high forehead, and each morning he shaved with a cup full of lather, a barber's brush, and a straight-edge razor. When he was in his prime in the first half of the twentieth century, adults dressed more formally because they knew they were adults, no longer children. Only children dressed in play clothes. Oh, sometimes the ladies did wear light, frivolous patterns and fabrics, but still there was something about the dress or slacks that aged the outfit. Something about the folds that gave the person a little dignity. Fashion was how he made his living: he had a store in Cleveland, Ohio; he and their grandmother did. At Buckeye Shopping Center they sold clothes, retail.

Now the children have grown up, and they also dress the way their peers do. All of them like toddlers in sweatshirts and sneakers. Big ones wanting their bodies to be taut and free as the little ones'. As if life is really about staying young. Though they don't admit it aloud, they expected that the time of dark responsibility, of making a series of quick, small, and irreversible decisions while the world spins away beneath them, had gone the way of their grandparents. In other words, they wanted to believe the time for adulthood is dead.

That's adulthood as Vera and Evan knew it, with all its struggles against those larger forces that you know, of course, can't be stopped. Vera was the true storyteller of the pair, and once she was gone too, they held on to her stories as they would, as they could. They held on because in a way that's uncanny their brother Hal has always looked almost exactly like Evan. And because from early on, it seems they felt that as soon as Hal began to age, they'd get to see their grandfather again. Only this time they'd stand eye to eye, through Hal's changed, matured body. And then, in a manner of speaking, Evan would talk to them. Maybe tell them all that he had to face, those stories about the family that Vera couldn't bring herself to fully confide, no matter how much they'd begged. Funny, the treasures you believe another's life will bring you. Funny, the easy acceptance of such gifts you also assume so safely will be yours.

With a shake of her head, Joy turns from the sight of two of her three grown children, sleeping. She gazes down the long silent hall, then once more at the slight glimmering of the hands on her watch. She accepts that she's here, waiting in an alcove for news to come to her again. She accepts that now, in so many ways she can barely enumerate, she sits where her mother, Vera, once sat.

Of course Joy accepts it; and doesn't want to believe it.

ONE

Coins in the Fountain

(1967)

Nineteen-six-oh-six Van Deusen

Everything we're frightened of, Vera once said, starts out small. Even the most terrible things—and this she knows—happen as part of our day.

First, Evan's left arm stiffened, though he hadn't been sleeping on it, at least not that he knew; he'd awakened on his back. Slowly, he raised the bare arm above his head. No pain, just the cool air bathing it. Second, he began kneading the area that didn't hurt, his neck and shoulder. As he worked these muscles over hard, the few hairs on the back of his hand caught the low light in the room. The day had only just started; the creamy slats of the venetian blinds were edged pink. Evan was then sixty-seven years old, and of course he knew what to do with his own body's aches and pains. Third, lowering his arm, he slipped his hand just under the sheet, where the best heat was trapped.

Vera was sleeping on her stomach. When he ran his fingers along her spine, the silky nightgown rippled. By habit she turned toward him, eyes still closed, and sighed. She didn't yet know that during the night mostly everything had unraveled. The tiny crossed swords of her black bobby pins had slipped from the curls she'd hoped to keep coiled; a piece of the tissue paper wadded to support the waves of her hairdo now beat loosely against the pulse in her neck. Her disarray and abandon were full of trust. He watched her, breathing. He cuddled into her and could smell part of the secret between them: the warm skin on her neck, the beautiful Vera-is-here perfume. How long did he stay like that? Fourth, his chest tightened with a fierce warmth. It was true, nothing hurt him.

Later, she stood before the mirror in her bra and half-slip. She had just pushed down the red button on the can of hair spray when his knees buckled. He had just knotted his tie. Windsor knot. The radio was playing the first strains of "Three Coins in a Fountain"—the early-morning show's theme song. The wet hiss of the Aqua Net seemed to go on and on as he turned. His mouth fell open and nothing but pain—a tight, breathless gasp lost in the loud upswell of a popular song—came out.

Evan's tie clasp, its gold bar V-ed apart, bounced from the toe of his right wingtip onto the new bedroom carpet. He tried to grab one of the handles on the new bureau. It was seven drawers high, a man's upright dresser. On top of it, rising above him in an oval frame, was their first formal portrait: the two of them young and thin in the sepia shadows, one vase of brownish flowers stiff with life at their elbows as they smiled at a letter she held up to the window—what was it?—he reached for it; bright Polaroid snapshots of their children and grandchildren in three different frames; the blue sapphire cuff links he'd just pulled from the drawer rolling back and forth like crazy eyeballs; they all slid past him.

He had no breath. A long rag was being forced down his throat. It filled his chest.

"Evan?" Vera turned in the doorway.

How frightened they were at that moment to see each other. In that single moment when she stood half-dressed in the bright bathroom and he let himself keep going down, they took in and understood everything. That in the lit doorway she was a silhouette. That the ash dresser, stocked with his clothing, was stronger than he.

"Try to breathe, it's all right." Her fingers were at his collar. *Nimble*, he thought. Nimbly they unbuttoned, gently, quickly tugged on the tie with its just-perfected knot. She was kneeling on the floor, straddling his chest. She was talking. Her own breathing was shallow and fast, her breasts rising together in the brassiere. What words she said he had no need to listen to, because he already understood them. Fear. Placation. Fear. Placation. The same way she had once spoken to the babies—but different now, because she was also somehow demanding, as she wouldn't have of only a child: Yes? Isn't this going to end up just fine? Tell me it will.

His head in the pink weave of the rug, Vera's sixty-six-year-old fingers pulling at his collar, but pulling really at *him*: Breathe! Stand up! Get up! "No color in his face," she muttered, angry-sounding. She stared down at him with all her will. Her eyes, no longer one surface, were sharp and cutting through everything that was visible, invisible. Her broad face was full of effort.

How lonely he felt watching her. So much desire. Does anything in life prepare you for this? His arms and legs went numb. He shut his eyes.

"Look at me!" She slapped his face. A second time, a third, with her open palm. Even then, her skin was familiar to him. The radio announcer's flawless American voice came into the room. It was 7:00 A.M. From the radio a choir of factory whistles blew—the station's trademark—signaling the start of the new program. Seven A.M. exactly. Fifty-two degrees at the edge of Lake Erie. One degree warmer right outside the 'RLS studio in downtown Cleveland.

The water of the deep lake would be cold. Nearing the bottom, it would have to be very cold.

"Stop," Vera said from above, "please stop. Evan, please." She lunged forward, pressed all her weight on his chest.

The pain was something he could not believe. In the dark lack of breath, through the hundred shadows of his own lashes he saw her naked arms working strong as a peasant's, the dimpled flesh quivering as she rocked back and tugged. "One—and one," she muttered; her hand closed over his nostrils; "and—and two." She bent down and kissed him, covering his whole mouth. He wanted to cry as in her air came. "Two and three," a moment later he heard. Again, up she sat; again, moving and pushing down on his chest; again, pinching his useless nostrils; again, her lips covering his; again: a rush of her breath forced inside him. "One, and one." She pressed harder. Up, with that quick yank away, as if pulling hand over hand. Down, with a kiss. His eyes flooded with tears and he gave up seeing clearly. He heard, "Two. And." Nothing would end; it would always be her weight, her kiss, and the pain, over and over.

Then something yellowish-white came between them. Evan saw this filminess flowing right out of his face. When Vera pulled back in a blur, his whole body convulsed.

"It's all right," she muttered, furious. She pounded his chest with her fists. "It is all right now."

He turned his head in one huge shudder. Bile spurted to his lips and onto the wool rug. He was breathing. Vera started to cry. But she wouldn't stop: leaning back on her haunches, she kept pulling the winding cloth, the rag, the linen shroud, out from the cave of his chest, out of his arched throat, out of him.

What were the things of the world he'd seen pass between her hands? What were the things she'd held on to, caressed, dropped? Sixty-six years she had in her then, and forty-seven years he'd had to see what she did. Not long. Then again, very long. Vera's hands: with them she gripped what she could; made quick work of that which served no good purpose; cut off or soothed this one or that; waved: *Hello!*; waved: *Good-bye!*; waved: *Good-bye!*; and waved: *Good-bye! Good-bye to you.*

The two of them had been immigrants, two of the lucky ones; both were young and excited leaving the Hungarian part of Czechoslovakia. She'd left the town of Szacsur, and he close-neighboring Nagymihály. Then, fifteen or so years later on the first side—the old side—of the ocean, everyone they loved back there began screaming and dying. Hitler got hold of them. What then could they do? In this big, free country they tried many things. Oh yes, to be safe, and know that those you love are failing.

Do you want to walk with me? Vera would ask them—the grandchildren, not their own children. Not their own youngest, Joy, not Teddy, and not even when he was still with them, their eldest—Hankus, their Hank. As the years went on, Vera found it difficult to speak about Hankus aloud. She'd be telling the grandchildren some little story that included him and suddenly she'd grimace and stop. Maybe in those moments she saw him not as the teasing, joking boy who threw his arms around her but instead as the son she'd lost. No, that child she couldn't bear to bring close. But the grandchildren were different. She'd call: *Abby! Hal! Ricky! Hurry to me—all of you.* They'd run right to her and she'd open her arms, even her ten fingers stretching open. *See,* she'd say, her arms full, her expression triumphant. *See, Pop, the energy? These quick little ones—your very own.*

"We're going to put you on the stretcher, Mr. Eichenbaum." From behind him two white-trousered knees straddled his face. Two dark thick-wristed hands swooped close; they worked themselves in under his shoulders. "Ready with your side, Frank?"

The other ambulance attendant, also a black man, squatted down in front. As if already doing the hard work, he grimaced as he cupped Evan's calves in his palms. "Man, you remember I'm protecting my neck."

Evan still lay on his back, on the carpet, head near the base of the bureau; he saw that the girl had vacuumed beneath it; there were the indentations made by the Hoover's wheels and the ruffled, reverse-nap trails left when the dresser got shoved back to the wall. Though he could smell his own sweat and vomit, and to his surprise the sourness of his urine, he couldn't stop staring at this low, clean place, where so much effort had been expended just to get rid of dust.

"One, two—"

"Careful," Vera's voice floated in. "Please."

"—three."

Up Evan went, face to the ceiling, then as slowly down onto the wheeled trolley. The moment the men's hands slid out from under, he panted, winded. As exhausted as if he'd levitated himself. The trolley wasn't tall; he lay at the level of their thighs.

"Fasten the straps," ordered the man standing behind him.

"You know which hospital?" Vera asked.

"Sure. Got it under control."

Frowning, the attendant kept untwisting the cloth belts. He laid one with a tin buckle on Evan's stomach, then he threaded another through it and gave the brown cotton a slight tug.

"Wait," said Evan in a voice full of breath.

A long, bony, clean-shaven face—a sad face—bent over him from behind. "Need something, Mr. Eichenbaum?"

Suddenly Vera pushed into view. "What? What do you want?"

My arms, he wanted to say, but ashamed, turned his head.

On the open door of the closet was his belt rack. The rich dark strips of leather hung down by their metal buckles. When he'd stand in front to select which one to wear, the whole row would click and sway: cowhide, calf, alligator, lizard. The lizard belt, shiny black and expensive, would slip through his pant loops with a pleasurably fast flick.

"This young man tied"—he was breathing too hard—"my arms."

"Well, sure! It's procedure. We got to keep you safe with the traffic and all."

Evan closed his eyes.

Vera was gripping his hand. "I'll stay with you, *tateleh.*"

"Nope, missus, sorry, you can't. No riders in the van."

"But I have to!"

"Sorry." There was a *clank* and the gurney jerked as the attendant released the brake on the wheels. "No riders. You call, we haul, that's all."

Bastard, Vera swore in Hungarian. *Kiss my ass.*

"Company regs—regulations."

"So, go," she snapped. "Take him into your ambulance."

"Usually the wives, they follow in a car or someone comes to drive them."

"I'm taking the car, Evan. I called the kids already to meet us there."

Queasily, eyes still closed, he nodded. The gurney rolled backward, then began going forward.

On his way now. In his mind, Evan was seeing the tracks of the Hoover, how like herringbone they ruffled the pink wool fibers around his dresser. He was leaving their apartment. The rubber wheels of the trolley were rolling quickly: through the pink-carpeted bedroom, through the beige-carpeted living room, then—

with a jiggle—over the jamb and into the common foyer for the building's third floor.

"My God," the neighbor cried. "I didn't hear a thing. What's wrong with Evan?"

"Sally—" Vera faltered.

"But what is it?"

"Damn! What's with *you*, lady," the younger attendant burst out as Evan's eyes flew open. "Not now, okay?"

"Frank, quiet, the regs—"

"What, she can't wait? You can't wait?"

"Don't you threaten me! I was only—my dog's been cooped up all night and needed to"—her Pekingese began barking, high angry yaps. "Oh, get in, Ginger, in. I'm sorry, Vera. Get in!" The dog howled; she must have kicked it. From behind the closed door came a burst of recriminations. Her husband Walter's voice: *Stupid, you know that? A nosy gossip, a dumb—*

Vera took hold of Evan's hand.

After a moment the elevator's door clicked and smoothly slid back. He was rolled over the threshold.

In the cramped, silent compartment, Vera and Evan's eyes flickered to and away from each other. If only the descent to the lobby would go faster. If only it never would end.

Vera bent over the attendant's arm to kiss Evan's right cheek. As the door began to open, she said: "Evan." Taking a breath, she repeated in Hungarian: *Ivan.* And had to step behind the attendant again.

"Missus, hold the door open, so we can take him. And listen, don't you try to keep up with the van. Don't try; you drive careful."

Vera pressed her palm against the red "Open" button. After Evan—gray-faced, strapped down—was wheeled out, she punched the blue one. As always, it took the mechanism a moment to start closing. The internal parts rumbled as if debating the order, but then the steel slab edged out of its slot and drifted left. Vera took a step with it, to see if they'd reached the front alcove yet.

"Watch it," Frank was complaining. "*Lift* over the stairs, man! Don't give me all his weight. Didn't I say my neck's bad?"

Vera was cursing the slowness of everything familiar. She should have gotten out and taken the stairs down to the parking garage in the basement, but now the door was just about closed. Overhead, the "down" arrow lit up green, and still the elevator didn't move. If only she could reach the oily metal cords in the shaft and pull them herself, as the priests had pulled the bell ropes in St. Stefan's. *Everyone!* At the bells' deep Sunday sounds on a Tuesday midafternoon, she and her sister Irina and their school friends, searching for tadpoles, looked up. The girls' and boys' arms were wet past their elbows; their shoes and yarn stockings were back in the pile near the teacher. *Everyone!* All the children in their groups up and down the bank looked up from the reeds. *Come running. Everyone—Catholics, and you few Protestants, and you still fewer Jews. Everyone who can hear: Russian soldiers are attacking our neighbors in Nagymihály. The Cossacks are stealing from them whatever they want. Wheat, horses, wagons—people, listen to us—*the great bells were rolling, were almost upside down—*save yourselves.*

But Vera didn't have a graceful iron bell swinging over her head, only a gear-toothed pulley the size of a large crystal fruit platter, which although given a signal still hadn't turned. Under her breath she recited her sisters' names. *Irina. Sara. Margret. Rose. Etel.*

Save yourselves, the bells rang out again.

The teacher screaming. Barefoot, Irina began again to pull Vera, Vera pulled Irina; behind them, sobbing, ran Margret, and Etel, and stumbling Sara. Far on the other side of the bridge, in her black skirts Mother was coming for them; she was waving both arms over her head. Not for a minute, running, did Mother stop waving. As if full up with fear that her own children wouldn't ever be close enough for her to touch again. Waving she ran, silent, mouthing their names.

Hankus, Vera said abruptly. And flinched, furious all at once in a terrible rush at Evan, for making her remember.

Then furious at everyone. At everyone, from back then, and now.

The sealed chamber was moving, but quietly; her breath echoed. Eyes on the closed wall of the door, Vera put her ring hand on the cold steel railing and waited for the moment she could hurry out.

There was sun on his face and a cool breeze. Evan opened his eyes to yellow leaves overhead. A few fluttered down onto his chest and blew off. The clouds were gray, very excitable. Birdless black wires dipped from street pole to street pole, and each one was full of electricity. Such a wonderful thing, electricity, when you stopped to think about it. He hadn't always lived with it. Not until he came to this country. But America was strung with electricity; it was lit up and jumping. One step over here and he'd felt the current. One step in America and he knew he would work—work fast like electricity and prosper. He would make his life good.

"Don't stare," a woman spoke sharply.

"Jesus, Mom, you don't have to yank my arm. I'm not bothering him."

Slowly Evan turned his head.

Over her shoulder, the woman looked back at him guiltily. She was maybe twenty-eight, twenty-nine, with big dark eyes and a pretty face. Right away he saw she was frightened of him. Probably no one else had done this terrible thing to her yet—the terrible thing she thought he was doing: dying in public, where no one ever should. He tried to smile, but she wrenched herself around. Her son, although sullen-shouldered, was an obedient boy and didn't look back. The two reached the driveway just as the garage door to the building began to lift. From inside a horn blatted a warning, and they hesitated. Evan saw the shiny front grille of their Chevy. Their car had no scratches or dents. Its huge perfect body was a source of pride.

"Okay," said the tall attendant, angling the gurney—"in you go."

Evan winced. He looked up at the attendant, the underneath of his jaw. "What is—" His breath wouldn't come, no more than a thread. "What is your name, please?"

He was tilted. The gurney began joggling up the metal ramp. The stink from the rattling tailpipe floated up with them.

"Name's John Fuller." Curving his back, he ducked his head and edged into the ambulance. A clank, again against the legs of the trolley. He must have put some kind of restraint on them.

Evan moved his caked lips: "Thank you for telling—"

"Don't waste yourself talking. No oxygen tank here—only in the hospital. I could learn to work a tank, you know? Damn, I'd like to learn *some*thing. But the doctors make those regs." He hauled up the ramp, slammed the back doors. Then he bore down on the long handle, locking it. "Okay," he yelled, banging on the side of the van, "all set, Frank. Get going!"

The siren sprang to life in one burst, then the motor. It was awful. The attendant had one hand clutching a bar on the ceiling, the other balanced flat-palmed and bouncing on Evan's chest. They were watching each other; Evan couldn't rip his own eyes away. Two turns, then a straight headlong—the van was going very fast, faster than was safe, and the long loud wailing never moved any farther away. It just would not slide off. No matter what was happening out there, or how hard the man pressed down on the pedal, the *waa-oo, waa-oh* kept on. Inhale it was, and exhale. In. Out. In and out—the panicked cry stayed right above Evan; the driver was trying; but it wouldn't slip off. *Was this it?* Evan stared at the bobbing, somber face: *Was this his time?*

The attendant shouted, "Listen, don't use yourself up trying to talk. Save it."

Eight hundred and three South Hampshire

Traffic sped onto North Park with its glorious wine-glass elms and thick oaks. Behind the trees, serenely bricked mock Tudors and Colonials sat back on their lawns in a final burst of gentile graciousness before the suburbs—with a downward swoop of the beautiful hill—gave way to the city. After that, traffic crossed into Cleveland proper. The road surface became less smooth, the pavements lined more closely with the low brick storefronts and the squat clapboard and asphalt-shingled homes of the city's early-to-rise workers. Many of the steel mills were still fired up and running back then.

In the midst of the congestion, a siren-winding Allen-Berks ambulance and a 1965 Chevrolet bearing license plate HW 214 shot through the yellow traffic lights. All the cars in front, behind, and pulling quickly away to the curb were American-made: heavy, solid, big-motored. Perhaps a couple of German imports cruised by, but none of the vehicles had molded lightweight fiberglass or plastic panels; and there was nothing yet that even hinted of Japan and the East's coming prominence.

The Central and East Europeans—the Poles, Hungarians, Czechs, Slovaks, Croats, Russians who made up the bulk of the workers at the big industrial plants like U.S. Steel, Republic, Fisher Body, and American Steel and Wire were already on the morning shift when Evan had the first of his two heart attacks. On the sidewalks in front of the workers' homes, children were carrying lunch boxes and schoolbooks. On the porches of the houses, calling out last-minute instructions, or at the bus stops, heading toward their own jobs, were the women who'd hinged their lives to the shift workers, to the children.

A number of the women boarding the public buses would ride them into suburbs west and east of the city, where they worked as domestics, cleaning houses and engaged in what would later come to be more formally called child care. The woman who worked for Joy and Leo Buckland lived even farther down in the city in Hough, the black ghetto, the site of the previous summer's awful, useless riots. She had a car, but at five minutes to eight on that October ninth she hadn't yet arrived at the Bucklands' house, and in the large, turquoise-and-white kitchen Joy was moving quickly, her usually fluid movements jerky, unappealing. She was slapping together tuna fish sandwiches so she could get the three kids off to school as quickly as possible.

"Leo, I'm almost done," she called over her shoulder. "Should we leave a note for Esther?"

"*Of course* leave a note!" he shouted from his study, where he was rummaging noisily through his desk. "Otherwise, she'll turn right around and go home. Leave her a key in the milk box. We're not getting a delivery today, right?" He slammed another drawer closed. "Joy! Are we getting a milk delivery?"

"No. Milk's on Tuesdays and Fridays."

"Then leave the key in the box for her."

"You do it, please, I'm busy. Help me." She gathered up three big-bottomed Bartlett pears and one by one dropped them into the three open sacks. From under the long counter she took out the roll of waxed paper and, fingers shaking, tore off a sheet. She placed a sandwich in the middle of it.

"Could you make triangles at the corners," Hal said, looking up from his sixth-grade social studies text resting on the kitchen table. "They hold better than just the folds."

"And use rubber bands around them too," Ricky piped up. "Okay, Mom?" He whispered something in his older brother's ear, and obligingly Hal opened his mouth, his teeth wound in braces. "Hey, Mom," eight-year-old Ricky said, "need some rubber bands? Hal's got four of them, but they're wet."

Jaws wide, Hal gave a lion's roar.

Joy looked at her first son with the glittering metal wires in his tender mouth and abruptly stopped working. "You look just like my brother."

His jaws snapped shut. "I do?" His cheeks flushed pink. "Really?"

"No, he doesn't," Abby protested from the other side of the table. "Besides, they didn't have braces in the old days. So Uncle Teddy couldn't have worn them, could he?"

"Well, I'm not talking about Ted."

Abby frowned. "Uncle Hankus is who you mean?" Carefully she tucked a long, heat-straightened strand of blond hair precisely behind her ear; she hated being fourteen and still having to let her mother correct her. "Hal takes after Pop, everyone says that."

"Well, I'm talking about something different than appearances. Hankus could act silly to make Mom—Nan—laugh. Isn't that just what you were trying to do, sweetie, for me too?" She nodded encouragingly at Hal.

"Sure, Ma." He flipped his hand back in that loose-wristed way that bothered Leo so much. "I want to make you happy all the time. Like Hankus did for Nan."

"Me too," said Ricky.

"Ahh-ooh-ah-ooh-ah!" Hal pounded his chest; he gave it two good thumps, right over his heart. "Me Tarzan."

All at once Joy started to cry, emitting small, painfully constricted gasps.

"What's wrong?" Hal exclaimed.

As her three children looked up in horror, she tried to pretend she was laughing. How could she explain that his playful, hollow thump-thump meant something more? That she was frightened about how much could happen?

"You kids," she said, wiping her nose with the back of the hand still holding the waxed paper. "Sometimes everything you say just cracks me up."

Not five minutes later she and Abby were alone in the kitchen. Nervously, Joy pushed a wave of frosted hair off her forehead and whispered, "Listen, Pop's not feeling well, sweetie. Come home from school right away. If I'm not here, I want you to look after your brothers."

Abby picked up her lunch sack from the counter. The brown paper bag was heavy and off-balance because of the pear; she refolded its mouth so it wouldn't rip. "Will Pop be okay?"

"Oh. Oh, I hope so. Yes."

"Let's get going, Joy," shouted Leo from the hall. "And Abby, you go on to school." The outside door slammed.

Joy continued through thin lips, "Pop's getting good care.

But your brothers are younger and don't understand these kinds of things very well. You're fourteen now, it's different for you, isn't it? You can help me out. Do you get what I'm saying?"

"I won't tell Hal and Ricky."

"Not a word. There's no reason for them to know." She leveled her gaze. "And you won't let your imagination rush away with you, will you? Imagining bad things?"

Abby shook her head. In a low shaky voice, she replied, "I won't do that."

"Well. Well, that's good! If Hal picks up on something, because he's that way, alert to slight changes, try not to—"

"Mom," Abby said, drawing her thin shoulders back, "you don't have to keep harping on it. I said that I get it. Don't worry." She exhaled, and her face hardened as she tried to erase every bit of childishness in her. "Please?"

It made no sense, but Joy saw not Abby standing inside at the living room window, watching as the electric garage door folded upward in rigid thirds—she saw herself standing there. A blurred girl behind a window. She herself seemed to be watching as the long ice-blue Buick Electra backed out with two shadowy figures in it. It was thrilling how the car didn't back out cautiously but accelerated in a quick swing backward—as if Leo were really somehow out in front dancing the jitterbug and he had just spun the Electra as if it were his partner, spun that car out, loose-armed and laughing—it was his pretty, light-hearted girl—swung it out in order to swing it again forward, to him. Leo, in leading, could do whatever he wanted.

The Electra hesitated in the back jog of the driveway. Then its big tires turned a few degrees, straightened, and the car zoomed away down the black drive.

It seemed, looking back, as if Joy stood stock-still and watched all that happen. As if she were allowed to stay home, in just that one place, and they—the other adults—were the ones having to race across the city because a relative was in danger. These two miraculously *other* parents were moving swiftly and easily, almost romantically, to help. From behind the window in the quiet, expensive suburban living room with its blond Scandinavian furniture, she stood watching as the car carrying a miracle couple sped past the sweatered children who were swinging brown lunch sacks and drifting in straggly twos and threes to school; it sped by Hal, waiting to cross at the far corner.

Through the windshield, Joy knew that Leo's face and next to it her own made two familiar if blurred pale ovals. Then the reflections of the overarching oak branches were streaming across the glass, submerging both faces, like stones.

Emergency Wing

Vera kept it in front, that siren a towrope whipping her back and forth into the waves of traffic. Most drivers pulled over to let the ambulance pass. But there were those who glanced in their rearview mirrors and saw an opportunity speeding toward them. They'd step on their accelerators and swerve in behind the van. Twice Vera was cut off. When a battered yellow Corvair, trunk plastered with U.S. OUT OF VIETNAM: NOW! decals, fishtailed in and missed her car by inches, she fell back for good. She watched the ambulance signaling right, flashers pulsing.

The hospital came up more quickly than she expected. She pulled into the drive and then, muddled, stepped on the brake all the way. Immediately a guard waved her on, and as if on its own, the Chevy drifted around back to guest parking.

But the moment she stood outside of the heat-radiating car, the keys bunched in her hand, Vera woke up. She began to run. This was the rhythm she had to get used to: the oblivion of concentration, then simple, limb-rigid rush.

With her first step on the black rubber mat, the glass doors to the emergency wing swung apart slowly. A long-fingered white hand was waving her forward in a friendly way, as if the man were simply rising from behind a restaurant table and, spying her, recalled he had, oh, some little story about someone they both knew he wanted to share.

The rows of orange molded-plastic chairs separating her

from the doctor were maybe half-filled. For the most part, the people waiting in them were quiet, passing among themselves only a few words, the briefest of eye contact. A drifting layer of cigarette smoke hung from the ceiling. A nurse slid back the window in the admittance station and leaned out. "Mr. Vincenti? Mr. Vincenti, please."

"Vincenti," shouted a man with little joy, "finally!"

Vera crossed the flecked linoleum squares. "Where is he? You saw him? Dr. Kessler's office said he—"

"Mrs. Eichenbaum, please, it's all right. Stop and take a breath. I'm standing in for Dr. Kessler today. Mark Rivchin. Uh huh—Mark Richards now, remember me? Harry's boy?" He gave her a tentative smile.

"Sure, I remember," she said shortly. "From the old neighborhood." Atop the gurney's pallet lay two cotton sashes, crumpled, spineless. "I'm not senile."

"Let's talk," he said, taking her hand.

She let him squeeze her fingers. "Where's my husband?"

"He's here, on this floor. I've ordered the full battery of tests."

"Is it his heart, you think? Is that it?"

He lowered his gaze. His sharp wedge of a chin fell into itself, doubling in a thick sternness. "Well, I'm not about to jump to any conclusions. I'm sure Dr. Kessler wouldn't either. Chest pain can also come from something wrong with a gallbladder. Or it could be an inflammation of the lungs, what we call pleurisy. He's on oxygen, of course, and IV—that's a glucose solution intravenous. I've called for an ECG, an electrocardiogram. Then a chest X ray, which will show the heart's size and—"

She couldn't bear how carefully he was speaking. As if she were some dummy who didn't know English! As if she hadn't faced things already in her own life that he couldn't even dream about, they were that bad. All she wanted to get from him was the answer to what she wasn't asking: Would Evan walk out of this place?

The loudspeaker crackled: "STAT. Dr. Hammer, to room six-oh-three. STAT. Six-oh-three. Dr. Hammer."

She had to ask.

"A pay phone's down the corridor. Is anyone coming to sit with you? Your sons?" He cleared his throat. "Sorry. Your son. I can't recall your daughter's name."

"Joy. And Leo's coming too, her husband." She glanced at his hand on her arm. No ring. Never married, she'd heard. Good-looking enough and nice. But shy socially. Still living, was he, with that boyfriend, also from the medical school?

"I'm glad she's coming. I'll talk to you again after we learn more." Nodding, he stepped back from her.

"But if it's the heart—how long—"

"If it *was* a heart attack, he needs to get through the week. Seven days is the most dangerous period."

The nurse slid back the window and called out, "Miss Polaczek, please."

"He'll be all right if he gets through the seven days," she said as he began to walk away. "Is that it, what you're saying?"

The two ambulance attendants came out of the swinging door of the admittance station and stepped to the side. She wanted to ask again, to make sure that she understood that all might go well. But where were her words?

The doctor hit the swinging door with the flat of his palm; he was through it, was gone.

The senior ambulance attendant said, "Excuse us, missus."

Vera reached for the gurney. "Don't take it." The sheet was damp. The folds and rills mapped out how Evan had lain: his back, back of thighs, calves, heels, his belted-down arms. Closing her eyes, Vera saw again the back window in the ambulance. That dark glassy square had offered her nothing.

"How is he?" She held on to the rail.

"Well, he got here just fine. Just fine."

"You were with him?"

"Frank drove." He jerked his chin toward his partner, who seemed not to be listening as he picked with a comb at his hair. "I was on watch, you know, in the back. A smart man. Not the type to talk and bring more complications down on himself.

Some of them do that, despite what you tell them. Gives a man a helpless feeling."

"He's all right now, do you think?"

"Oh, sure, do just fine. Here they know how to do things for someone in his condition."

From the corridor a woman was moaning, "No, not my son, not my son."

"Missus, they hook him up to an oxygen tank, and in a few seconds he's breathing easy again. Excuse me, please." The attendant took hold of the gurney.

Vera unsnapped her pocketbook. "Let me give you something, please, for helping my husband."

The two men exchanged glances.

"Against regs," John said. But when Vera looked up, billfold in hand, he muttered, "We just hauled him, you know?"

"Please, I want to."

Frank slid the Afro pick into his trousers pocket, against the thin leather square of his wallet. "Fine with me," he said. Because it wasn't something he'd asked for, he was letting her put her hand out first, with her money.

"This is for my husband. For getting him here so fast."

The taller one leaned forward, grimacing as if something pained him. "Okay, missus. All right. Good luck to you." And fast as possible put both hands back on the gurney. The edge of the ten-dollar bill was flicked up against the pallet as he shoved past.

From back in the admittance station the nurse called out: "Miss Polaczek, if you do not make yourself known immediately, I'm skipping to the next name on the list."

The doors, hit with daylight, swung open. Before he stepped into the glare, the one who'd ridden with her husband turned and gave Vera a strained, bitter smile.

She raised her hand. She waved: *Good-bye.*

First they unstrapped his arms. Then they lifted him onto a second gurney. Again he lay beneath the gaze of strangers. "Am I—"

"Don't try to talk," ordered a voice, sounding too girlish to be in charge.

From over his head, spread like a slingshot, came a clear plastic cone. It was put over his mouth and nose, and then a strap was tightened around the back of his head. "Now, breathe," he was told, "in and out. Take it easy; don't force it."

She bent over him. A face nothing like the voice. Middle-aged, and all her features worn and rounded—the chin, the tip of the nose. A crown of curls streaked gray. "You can do it, can't you? Sure you can." And to show what she meant, the nurse exhaled, her lips making a circle.

"The mask won't fall off. Let go, please." She tapped the back of his hand. Shoving up the white shirtsleeve, she turned his arm hairless side up and rubbed two fingers up from his wrist to the bend of his elbow. "How nice, you have wide veins."

Behind her an orderly tore the sheath from a hypodermic needle. "Coming through for blood samples, Marie."

"I've got to put in this IV first."

"Hello, Mr. Eichenbaum." A man's voice coming at him from the other side. "Mr. Eichenbaum?"

Evan gasped as pain shot through his left arm.

"His shunt's in." The nurse taped the tube to his wrist.

"Hello, sir. The pressure in your chest, we're going to allevi-ate it if we can, right away. Orderly, ready to connect?"

The boy who was hanging a filled clear glass bottle on to a metal pole said cheerfully, "Just about, doctor."

Evan closed his eyes. Far down in his throat was a wild jig-gling, like his heart was a whole egg he'd managed to swallow but couldn't keep down. "Wait—" he said into the mask; but the word got lost. He started to shake.

"Mr. Eichenbaum, try to stay calm. Your anxiety is an afteref-fect, understand? I'm going to do everything possible, just like Dr. Kessler would do."

"I can't—" He opened his eyes, stared blindly into a bright light; shut them again.

The nurse said, "Lidocaine's almost connected."

"Not—" Evan's breath loud and fast, the sound rebounding from the mask and into his mouth. Everything was pushing for room into and out of his throat. He couldn't tell anyone, that's where the pain was.

"Sedative," he heard. Then: "Nurse, swab the area."

A cold wet lick of alcohol, and then, in the middle, the tight pinch of a hypodermic needle pressing in.

"This will relax you."

After a moment, Evan looked up.

A man's face smiled at him. "Evan? Better now? Remember me? Mark Richards? I'm attending you today."

Weakly, Evan nodded.

This doctor was just Harry Rivchin's son. Harry Rivchin's smart boy. The one who took an American name to get into college under the Jewish quotas that forced good boys to be even better and, if they were to succeed, to knock each other out of the few slots. He was his own Hankus's age, same age. But something about this thought was getting tangled. Evan saw the face, but it was wavering above him.

Was standing up, far away. Was talking about X rays and taking an inside look. About electrodes. Monitors. Evan hardly heard him; the mask of air was so loud. Getting louder.

"Did you see him this afternoon?" Evan called.

"Who?" the boy yelled back, over the wind.

Evan shouted, cupping both hands to his mouth. "My son. Did he stay late at the high school, Mark? Is that why he didn't come home? I keep telephoning to check, but he doesn't answer." On the sidewalk in front of the store stood the rack of women's cotton dresses—forty pastel sleeves making hallelujahs, pleated skirts swinging open like bells. A storm was coming in off the lake. You could smell all the big water stirring about. Smell the drops in the air, almost ready to burst. The sun just over the roofline of Rivchin's Pharmacy was glowering a sick green; it was already smeared by the first of the clouds, the thinner gray ones. The huge black clouds would tumble in next. As with everything, the strong shove the weak to go before them. So

when the storm arrived in all its force, it would sweep the whole
street. It would lay claim to everything: the sawdust-sprinkled
threshold of Heller's Kosher Butchers, the brick facade of Wein-
stock's Hardware, the red-and-white-striped pole revolving above
Lou the barber's sign. And anything small but not fastened
down would be seized. Already the long banner—BUY WAR
BONDS! DEFEAT HITLER—tied high between two lampposts over
the middle of the block was flapping like crazy. Where the wind
punched, the black-painted words twisted and bulged.

Turning, he checked the sign over his store: BUCKEYE SHOP-
PING CENTER—not even one shiver. Behind the huge plate-glass
window, the salesgirls were busy with customers, factory workers
off the second shift. This was one of the year's biggest sales. It
was almost the Easter holiday for them, the customers. Easter
1943. Through the window he saw Vera showing off a man's
white shirt; she was unbuttoning it down her own front, its
empty collar tucked under her chin, her hands working in front
of her. Her head was tilted to the right and she looked very serious. Talking. Nodding. A good saleslady, she really was.

"What?" the boy called again from the doorway of his
father's pharmacy. His high school letter sweater slapped back
with a gust and the whole street darkened. "What did you ask
me? You want me to tell you about Hankus?"

Evan waved. "Never mind! Take your father's newspaper rack
inside before the rain starts. Save his stock, Mark." Just then the
cold needles drove down. All at once pounding everywhere, over
everything, like an attack. They stung, trying to go through him.

"Mr. Eichenbaum!" Taller, Mark must have raised himself up
on his toes; he was shouting over the storm, still trying to talk to
him. "How can I know? Hankus never liked me. I don't know
how it happened that he didn't come back."

Eyes streaming, Evan heard himself sob that all he wanted to
hear from Mark now was one thing: he was going to be fine. He
would get him out of this terrible place soon, one hour, two,
maybe three. He would not even have to stay the night.

• • •

The smoke from her cigarette rose to the ceiling. Vera walked to the far side of the room, where a line of paintings hung against a white wall. She barely looked at them, all landscapes—just there to give the illusion of having someplace to go. Slowly she paced between the spindly rubber plants set in the corners. After a while, she stubbed out the cigarette.

"Mom?"

Vera turned. Seeing Joy rushing toward her made everything inside hurt in a fresh way. Shaking her head, she raised an arm between them, the palm outward. Wanted this last bit of distance.

Joy just stopped. Her face, already flushed, composed itself; she was struggling to obey, trying to please. She swayed a little and said, "How's Dad?" Her hands fell awkwardly to her sides.

"I don't know!"

"You didn't talk to the doctor yet?"

"Sure, I talked. But Dr. Kessler's away. It's only the Rivchin boy."

"Mark Richards, well. Well, he's a doctor now, Mom. He's got to be good or Dr. Kessler wouldn't be working with him." Joy paused. "Didn't he tell you anything?"

Nodding, she pressed her lips together. If she let it slip out, it would be uncontrollable.

As Abby had, Joy tried to keep her voice flat. "He's going to be okay, isn't he?"

Vera unsnapped the metal clasp on the pocketbook. The two tiny ball-tipped brass prongs separated; she snapped them shut—and open again. Close. Open. Couldn't she talk to her daughter, tell her anything?

"Okay. Okay, Mom. We'd better—let's just wait for Leo to finish parking the car. Do you want to sit down?"

Vera nodded at Joy. She was five-foot-five, triumphantly average in height, slim and athletic. She kept trim from golf and tennis. An American girl, after all. The olive-hued skin that marked Vera as somehow foreign, on Joy seemed more the underbrush of a nice tan. Now she was wearing a navy V-neck sweater, a red shirt, lightweight jeans. Like her own kids.

"Over there?" Joy slipped an arm around her.

After a few steps, Vera whispered, "He has to make it through seven days. That's what the doctor said. See, this next is the dangerous time."

The nurse called from the admittance station: "Eichenbaum! Evan Eichenbaum, to the front, please."

Vera twisted away from Joy's grasp.

As Vera pressed forward against the ledge by the station window, Joy couldn't move. "To the seventh floor," she managed to overhear. The nurse indicated the bank of elevators.

"Wait!" Joy cried, voice tight.

Vera turned in midstride. Her eyes swept the room as if uncertain where exactly to stop and settle.

"Can't I come?" said Joy. "You don't want me to?"

Vera hesitated. Her girl's face stared back, pinched with anxiety.

Leo was maneuvering irritably through the rows of the waiting area. Tall and burly, of course he'd seen his wife right away, but his gaze was fixed on his mother-in-law. His jaw was set. Tucked under his left arm was a bulky cardboard box. A portable file. Filled with forms and papers he could sort through, for hours if need be.

"Come," Vera said brusquely. To the two of them.

Leo grabbed on to the edge of the closing elevator door and shoved the slab back. "What floor?"

"Seven." Vera hurried in. "You didn't see Teddy yet, Leo?"

"Not in the parking lot. Nope, Mom."

"On the phone he said he'd be—"

"Teddy's probably on his way," Joy said, cutting her off. She punched the button on the panel.

"*Seven, Joy!*" Leo reached across her.

"That's what I pushed." Then she whispered into his ear.

"No," he muttered. "That's what he said? Seven?"

Joy glanced over at Vera, but she was staring straight ahead. At nothing. At the closed door. There was no real sensation of the elevator's ascent, only its sounds.

"Almost there," said Leo edgily. Shifting the cardboard box under his left arm, he moved forward, chest out, as if someone had challenged him to stand his ground. He put himself squarely in front of where the door would first slide back. A bell pinged.

For the first time, Vera felt herself shake. Evan would be standing there, waiting for her. *We made it to closing time, yes?* he'd say. He'd roll the white shirtsleeves back down over his forearms—the same slow way he did it each day after work; he'd take his time because, now at this quiet moment, he was the last one in the store he had to please—and he knew exactly how to do it. Pulling the sleeve straight, he'd refasten the cuff links and say, *I checked the back. We can unpack the new merchandise in the morning, first thing. The storeroom's locked, with everything nice and safe. Lights off, Mameleh?*

Sure, lights off. I want only for us to go home and sit down. But this she didn't say aloud. Now the door opened to a long white corridor, and the air smelled dead.

She stepped out. The silence of the ward seemed too raucous. Full of clickings she couldn't quite hear, movements she couldn't quite identify. A silence of slow breaths, of rubber-soled shoes and trays of medicine bottles, of panels of tiny, neatly blinking lights; the long hallway a sieve leaking from its half-opened doors.

Joy and Vera stood by the single couch in the alcove while Leo went to speak to one of the nurses. When he returned, he kept his gaze from wandering into any open doorway. "They've got him listed as being in two different rooms," he muttered. "This nurse says he must be in the other ward, over in the other building. A stupid clerical error. It's seven-nineteen, but in the intensive care ward in North Hall."

Vera blinked. "They already took him somewhere else?" All the energy went out of her. She took a few steps in a half circle, then turned to them. "Where is he now?"

"Room seven-nineteen. North."

Vera began to cry. "I can't find him, he's waiting for me.

Everything we went through together for so long, see? Now I can't find him. What if I can't reach him?"

"That bent sonofabitch," Leo burst out, "he should be here talking to her. He must get his kicks from leaving wives hanging. Where is he?"

"Leo," Joy said.

He glared, his face red. "What?"

"Mark spoke with Mom. He could be in with Dad now, trying to help him, you don't know. Don't add on to this. Please."

"I'm *not* adding on. I'm asking if he explained things."

"Well, he did. Briefly. Where's North Hall?"

He put the box on the couch and sat down. He didn't look up at his mother-in-law. To staunch her crying, she had the flower-embroidered hankie crumpled against her mouth. Where the thin cotton was wet, it was almost transparent. "You have no sense of direction at all, Joy," he said, half under his breath. "You're unbelievable; I have to show you everything. Go back, past the elevators, then turn left. That's north. Take the elevator down and—"

"You aren't coming?"

From a doorway to the left came a faint series of groans. Grimacing, Leo shook his head. He jiggled the cardboard box on his knees. "I have papers to look through for him. Besides, only one visitor at a time." He paused, sickened at himself for knowing right then how much physical misery he didn't want to face. Mumbling so that only she could hear, he ducked his head. "If you need me to—but hospitals—and your dad hooked up to—"

"Leo," she said quietly.

Eyes damp, he lifted his chin. "I'll come if you need me," he repeated.

Looking quickly away from his face, she nodded, choosing to believe. "Leo's going to wait, in case Ted comes here first."

Vera wadded the hankie into her pocketbook. "You can take me to Daddy? You won't get lost?"

Joy gave a slight laugh. "I can always ask for help."

Intensive Care

A penlight shone into his eyes. Mark Rivchin moved it from one of Evan's eyes to the other, and back again to the first; he was searching in him for what? Bending over, the boy was trying to stare inside his pupils. *Soon will come Halloween,* Evan would tell him when the moment was good.

He meant by Halloween the oxygen mask he was wearing. Wasn't it like a disguise? He meant this was October, 1967—not that other time. Not that mixed-up time from '41, '42. And that egg clogging his windpipe! That constriction in his throat was gone. He knew what holiday was coming up in real life, yes? That's what he meant. He was now in his right mind.

The little penlight clicked off. "Slow down the IV rate, nurse. It's dripping too fast."

Not Easter coming, he would say as a joke, *but Halloween.*

"Connected, nurse?"

With a curt nod, she snipped another piece of cloth tape and patted it over a wire already secured in three places to Evan's chest. A few of the hairs had gotten tugged up together.

"Good, we're about done." Flipping the paper back over the clipboard, the boy slipped the pen into the chest pocket of his white coat. Against the white fabric the blue pen looked jaunty; it was instead of a handkerchief. So now as a doctor he was very well dressed! The round metal ear of the stethoscope, he slipped that in the chest pocket, too. A boutonniere, almost.

"Uh-huh. See this reading, nurse?" Leaning over, he was now studying some gauges. "That's too low, understand? I want to get it raised another degree."

Gone was the authority that earlier had edged her girlish voice as she said, "Yes, doctor."

Evan sighed. In America they had both Halloween and Easter. In Hungary, there was only Easter. Of course, the Jews didn't celebrate that holiday, not back there and not here, either. But in America at least he didn't have to stay locked up inside, out of sight of the gentiles. Back there, if they saw him out on the street on any of the Christian holidays, there could be trouble. They'd come after him, shouting all kinds of things. *Filth! Christ-killer! Blood-drinker! Vermin!* Why was there always so much trouble between people? So much hating and lies? So much beating and running? To live like that, always out of breath. He was once a boy and then he was a young man, and he did not want it—not for one more year, not for one more month, or one week, not even one more night or one more morning. That's why he'd left. He couldn't know that what would come would be worse. He didn't abandon his family; he'd tried to save them. He loved them, he did; he could almost still see their faces, what they used to look like. It was all years and years ago.

The nurse plumped a pillow beneath his neck. "Why are you working so hard," she chided. "Take it easy. It's only in and out." She cranked the top half of the bed, until he was sitting propped up like a toy.

"It's coming," said Evan into the oxygen mask's blowing wind. "Halloween."

She came around to his side. "What?"

He told her again.

She turned away. "I'm not sure he's making sense, doctor."

Evan was tired of everything suddenly. Weakly he gestured toward the plastic cone of his mask. The smell coming into it was cold and as bitter as quinine. The boy leaned forward. Dark-browed—like his father.

"Halloween." It took all his strength to say it. But what he thought would call up a laugh, instead brought a dead look to this poor smart boy's eyes. Ghosts, Mark thought he was talking about. Ghosts and not masks.

Straightening, Mark said something to the nurse. She kept tossing the soiled bed linens into the metal hamper in the corner of the room. She kept the splattered woolen pants and silk tie and stuffed them into a half-filled plastic bag. Then she drew the blinds across the window, which he hadn't yet had time to look out of. She left with the bag of his clothes in her arms.

The boy stayed where he was. "Okay. First, you appear to have had a heart attack. But that's over now, understand? The situation has stabilized. I've given you a relaxant, which should kick in soon." He smiled a little. "After that, we give the chicken soup."

At the door, a knock. Ignoring it, he went on, "You have one big job to do now, and that's to try to sleep."

"But what if—" Evan was too breathless to continue.

"You need to trust me. I promise I'm doing everything possible. Your regular doctor would do exactly the same."

He shook his head slowly against the pillow. "What if when I'm sleeping, something happens?"

"Uh-huh, that's why you're hooked up. The machines can alert us to any hint of danger. Understand?"

The nurse stuck her head in from the bright hallway. "Dr. Richards, his wife and daughter are here."

He waved her back. "Tell them to wait a minute."

The door shut.

"I'd like to be sure you understand what I just told you."

For the first time since he'd failed to hold on to his bedroom bureau, Evan felt his hands tremble. He gripped the muslin sheet the nurse had unfolded neat as a dinner napkin across his chest. His arms had been strapped down for too long, and now he was so tired he could barely crumple this sheet. But Vera was here now, Vera of the hands that could help and hold his, and this *pisher* said she should wait *a minute*. He wanted to take him by the scruff of the neck and shake him.

"I promise you, sir, you don't have to worry." He glanced down at his clipboard.

Vera was here, so what was he talking? What was this boy talking?

Evan did not want this. Not now. Not for one more moment. The door did not move. He knew who he wanted to come through it.

What was he talking?

Would he talk forever?

Vera should wait. A minute.

Silently Vera and Joy watched the nurse turn from the door. It usually is quiet in this type of ward until there's a STAT, an emergency. Then personnel come racing down the hallway. When you only see doctors at bedside as they stand over someone who can barely lift an arm, someone who requires at this time in his or her life—in his or her confinement—to be carried from one place to another, then it's frightening to suddenly see them come flat-out running; shocking to see the white coats lifting away from their bodies and the black stethoscopes wildly looping out of their pockets. Their feet then seem fragile and somehow anachronistic. How is it that with all the technology it's their feet that must, with speed, with haste, with need, take them to the bedside? Their faces, also, seem to push forward. At such moments they are as much about the limits of flesh as is any patient in the wards. Will they get there in time? To stand over that face? And which room is it this time? Can anyone remember? Seven-fourteen? Seven-nineteen? Seven-sixteen? Seven-fifteen? It will always be one or the other or the other. The numbers of need change, despite logic.

"I'm sorry," the nurse now said, approaching them. She quickly touched the tiny gold cross with its ruby-heart center that hung about her neck. "The doctor's still talking with Mr. Eichenbaum."

"You mean Dad's—" Joy gave a small sob. "My father's awake?"

"Awake the whole time, yes."

"Excuse me, miss," said Vera, and leaned closer, "but what is under your arm?"

The nurse's worn face flushed as she shifted the clear bag with its awkward bulges.

"Are those my husband's clothes?"

"Mom, what's wrong?"

"I want to know where she thinks she is taking them," Vera said sharply. "What are you doing with his clothes, please?"

Marie Wadja drew herself up. "When clothing is fouled, we get it laundered. It's a courtesy to our patients." She paused. "The cost gets added to the bill."

Vera held out her arms. "Please."

"For heaven's sake, Mom, they have a system. If Dad's clothes are soiled, let her take care of it. You want to bother with washing now?"

"I want them."

"Listen," said the nurse, "it's fine. I'm certainly busy enough."

Vera brought the bag in close against her. It all weighed something. You could tell the slacks were made of good substantial material; though they were crushed into the other articles, they weren't nothing. None of Evan's clothes came to nothing.

"No more?" she asked hoarsely. "Didn't he have shoes? I think he was wearing his brown ones."

The nurse was half turned away, checking the tag on the metal cart left out in the hall. "He had on black shoes."

"Black," said Vera slowly, "I see."

"There's a closet in the room. They're in a paper sack on top of the shelf."

"I see, thank you."

"Are you okay standing, Mom?"

Vera stared past her. "Sure. Why not?"

"May we wait right here, nurse?" asked Joy.

She said it'd be fine, then to the white-coated orderly exiting three doors down, she called sharply, "Paul! Take this cart back. And check the inventory against the slips. Be sure we're not missing any meds."

Joy whispered, "Everything will be fine, Mom. Dad's going to pull out of this. We're lucky, that's what you always told us, remember?"

Vera watched the orderly bend easily to the lower shelf of the cart to replace a small bottle before pushing away. "What did you say to the little ones?"

"About Dad? Well, not much, I guess." The moment she said it, she felt a pang of guilt. "I had to get them off to school. I wanted to get here as fast as I could." She hesitated. "You never told us that much either, you know."

Vera stiffened. "When?"

"When something bad was happening. When I was a kid. I always could tell—I'm sure Hankus and Teddy could, too," she said. "But you know, well, I guess, oh, this is silly, but as the youngest, I was afraid you'd be angry with me. You could be pretty terrifying back then."

"Back then was different."

"I know." A prickle of the old panic crept along her spine. "I didn't mean you were—Mom, that was stupid. I was just remembering as a kind of guide for what to do now, with my own—my kids. I know that you were protecting us. Trying to pretend everything with the family—" Joy stopped, looked away.

In the pit of her stomach, Vera felt sick. Someone had to come right now and help her. Someone had to tell her what to do with herself. It wasn't the same, what was happening with her husband. Evan was here with her; he was safe. And they were in their real lives now. Not like back then, the two of them caught between—and always waiting for the news. The news that took a long time, and even a longer time, always the longest time to arrive, and then ended up wrong. But she couldn't compare such events; everything is always just enough different, the one from the other. A person couldn't say that she knows what to do, she knows now what will happen, she knows finally the world, because *that other thing happened before, so it shows what this will mean.*

"I did tell Abby Dad's ill," Joy was saying, "but I didn't mention his going to the hospital. Bring up something not part of her normal experience, well, as I remember about myself at her age, well, it could start her thinking that maybe now everyone she loves—" Joy stopped; she shook her head. "Anyway, I didn't tell the boys yet." Again she paused, and saw Hal's sweet horror, his imagined-ferocious Tarzan war cry cutting off at the onslaught of her sudden tears. Joy plucked a black thread off her blouse. "Well, you know kids frighten so easily." She looked up all the way. "Mom, let me hold Dad's clothes now."

Vera shrugged. Lightly she said, "No trouble for me."

"Don't be silly, you'll get tired."

"So I'll get tired. I've been tired before."

"But I'd like—I just think you should save your strength. You don't know how long we'll be waiting."

Vera stared past her. The hall was empty, and every single one of the doors was closed. She shut her eyes; when she opened them, she saw the same silent stretch. "Where is he? He said he'd be here by now. Maybe something's gone wrong for him."

"The doctor?"

"No."

Joy's mouth tightened. "Teddy."

"Maybe he thinks we're at another hospital."

"He knows where we are," Joy said coolly. She glanced at her wristwatch: 9:31. She would almost bet that he was outside on the pavement, grinning caustically at no one and everyone because he wouldn't make himself walk up to any of the hospital's entrances. Thin-lipped, she said, "Ted's a big boy, Mom. He's not in any trouble, you know that."

Weary all at once, Vera set the plastic bag down on the floor. "So. Done." After a moment, she took out a few cellophane-wrapped hard candies from her purse. "Darling, you want?"

Mark Richards stepped into the hall, pulling the door to seven-nineteen shut.

With what mixture of relief and dread they went toward him. A distance of only a few yards. Suddenly, both Vera and Joy felt the need to whisper, felt that they were in fact already whispering, although neither had so much as said "Hello, doctor," or "Hello, Mark," or "Tell me how he is. Right now!"

He had a clipboard pinched under one arm, a hand slipped quickly into the side pocket of his trousers. It was possible to hear him jingling a mix of keys and coins.

"Ladies." Mark withdrew his hand to reach over to Joy. "A long time," he said, squinting curiously at her face.

"Yes, right. How is he?"

"Tougher than I first thought. But it was a heart attack, and not too mild. Let me explain some of what—"

"I'm going to him," Vera said, turning away.

"No. *Vera, stop.*" He reached for her. "You can't go in, Vera, I mean it!"

Both women groaned. That his arm shot straight out like a traffic cop's wasn't what startled them. It was his use of Vera's first name. It alone seemed to signal the new world that, because of illness, they'd just entered. Mark Richards, the familiar stranger, was their guide. He launched into a quiet recitation of medical terms that was chilling.

They tried to hold on to everything. Vera kept nodding at him, the young man whose mouth was moving in his face so easily, who was pronouncing so carefully and insistently a string of horrifying words.

"Uh huh. And in a condition such as your husband's, after the original assault, there's often a second one, a second attack. Often this comes sooner rather than later. As I said before, if he makes it through the next seven days, you'll have your husband." Here he coughed, or maybe it was just a way to cover his mouth. He had to know what he was saying to her.

Vera knew his mother, of course, May, a quiet little woman; she had known too his father. Harry had died of a heart attack, only a few months after his retirement. Gone in a snap of the fingers after a long, careful life. A man who'd chewed everything until there were no lumps to disturb his throat but who always insisted that the plate set before him first be brought to the table full, piled high. The little woman was always scurrying back and forth, righting the balance between pot and plate, and between insistent father and reticent son. May scurried still, but at Harry's old place at the white enameled table now she herself sat, the air wheezing sadly out of the red seat-cushion when, finally exhausted, she let herself rest. Vera heard that she now volunteered for everything, every Sisterhood activity at the temple, every Ladies' Auxiliary meeting. If it was on Monday or Wednesday, Thursday, Friday, Sunday, what did she care? Sure, she could help. She had all the time in the world now, didn't she?

Joy said, "What can—" She didn't want to have it happen, but she was crying.

Furiously Vera squeezed her fingers. "Enough," she warned, her lips barely moving. The girl hadn't learned that yet, that crying did no good? That you had to keep on?

In a low voice, Mark said, "He's getting the best care. I wish you'd believe I know how to do my job."

"No, not you." Joy lifted her chin. She didn't glance at Vera, though it was her mother she was addressing; with a steadier breath said, "What can I do? For him?"

"All right, first off, no matter what, be calm. Smile. If he asks you anything, don't blurt out whatever comes to your mind. I'm the one to answer his questions. Your job"—and here he smiled in an instructive way—"is to go on being his family. Support him. Distract him from himself."

He glanced at his clipboard. "Okay, last point: minimal visiting. One at a time, and for no more than ten minutes during regular hours. And no children under twelve."

"He's alone," Vera blurted. "He's alone now."

"That's not quite true. He's being monitored by incredibly sensitive equipment."

She snorted, and waved that reply away.

He gave a tight smile. "These machines *do* give him an edge. Well, now you can go in, but no noise from you, Vera. Mrs. Eichenbaum. Not one peep. I don't want him woken up."

"I wouldn't wake him, I wouldn't!"

"Honestly, Mark, my mother knows how to behave."

He flipped his wrist in a loose way, a gesture at odds with the sternness he'd been projecting. "Please don't misunderstand me," he said, coloring. He shoved his hand into his trouser pocket. "I want him to get well, too. He was always nice to me, don't think I don't remember that."

Vera pushed that reply away also. But she was shaking inside in earnest now. He thought he knew Evan. Because of some slight friendliness shown in the past, he thought he knew him enough to feel the loss. But this boy who didn't even like girls couldn't be expected to understand what it could mean. To be losing a dear one. Oh, her sweet *tateleh*. Her dear Evan.

"Mark said you can go in now, Mom," she heard.

Vera glanced at the bag slumped by the baseboard. "Fold Daddy's clothes. To leave them on the floor like this isn't right."

Joy bent down, and spoke louder, "Everything will be fine. Don't worry, we're lucky, remember?"

Vera half turned. Eyes wide, she took in both of them, looking not at each other, but straight ahead, at her. Familiar strangers, these two grown-older young ones. With a shudder, she saw they'd wait there, against the white wall, for their own turns to go in.

"I am worried, darling." Vera grasped the cool doorknob. "It's like back then."

TWO

The Gun Goes Off

(1935 forward)

Two-six-oh-two East Trainor

She truly wanted to be with her children all the time, Vera once said, but she had to work in the store. At three forty-five each afternoon she'd call and ask the hired girl: Were they home from school yet? Joy was? Okay, put her please on the line. Oh, that sweet little voice. That little voice saying: *Don't worry, I'm all right, Mommy. I'm okay.*

Hankus returned next, opening the front door really fast. So, this time, too, he'd outraced Teddy! To show his younger brother what success meant, he whirled about and slammed the door between them. Contest over. Done.

The brass hinges squealed and again swung wide. "No fair," cried Teddy, bursting in. He tried to tag Hankus in front of the small fruitwood table, but Hankus dodged, and by mistake Teddy's fingers brushed the stack of foreign-stamped envelopes, scattering them. Three thin sheets of notepaper slid out. Nearly black, tensely covered in writing, even the margins had been filled, sideways and upside down, with long lines of multisyllabic Hungarian words. Not an inch given over to waste.

"Watch where you step," Hankus warned. "You'll rip them."

"You pick them up, not me!"

The boys' leather soles pounded wildly along the waxed oak boards, getting louder as they passed through the foyer.

"No running," said Joy under her breath. On tiptoe she slid her snack plate off the kitchen counter; with both hands she started carrying it to the table. She was wearing the blue cotton dress that wouldn't be hanging in her closet much longer because it had started to pinch under her arms; it was already short at the waistband. Joy's face back then was round, the disguise of childhood. And she wasn't really pretty.

"You're dead! Hankus, fall down."

"Stop cheating; you have to let go of my book strap."

The kitchen was at the rear of the house. On this late fall day both windows had been cracked open a few inches above the suddenly mum-heavy flower beds of the backyard, where the golden blooms were waving triumphant as fists atop the dark stems. Staked in a twisted line beyond them were tomato plants, veterans of a long summer, a few still supporting the last slow-reddening globes. A pumpkin sat on the ground. Corn stalks, stripped of shadows once slick as torpedos, were straw men already. The garden tangled at the windows. It was their father's yard, really. He loved working in it when he didn't have to be at the store. His country farm, he called it in jest.

Joy, pulling out a painted wood chair whose legs bumped backward along the linoleum, saw none of it. Neither did the boys racing toward her. Now that the children were in two-six-oh-two, they didn't look at what was outside. Game over. Done.

The white-and-black enameled Glenville stove stood against one of the kitchen walls, and against another stood the hard-wood-topped chopping counter and the double-deep porcelain sink on steel legs. The icebox sat between the pantry and the back door. A room of a few clean, efficient, practical surfaces. Just as their mother wanted it. There was not one padded thing in it, excluding the pudgy little girl who ducked her head low to her plate as the boys burst in.

Joy the Baby sat, back to them, at the red-oilcloth-covered table. Suddenly, the air smelled buttery and sprinkled with cin-namon. At six-thirty that morning, before leaving for the store, their mother had put a kuchen into the oven. Though the coiled pastry had been cooling on the counter since they'd left for school—away the day long, keeping their noses pointed down at cursive sheets, citizenship essays, geography maps, arithmetic and spelling blanks—here in the kitchen, where chalk-dust erasers had never once smacked, the air still smelled good.

Joy chewed, sending the incongruously long Shirley Temple curls bobbling over the blue cap sleeves of her dress. The boys tugged off their woolen sweaters and tossed them onto the hard-wood counter. The black lunch pails clanked down into the sink for later washing.

"Hi-dee-hi-dee-hi, Joysie." Hankus was breathing hard. "Guess you won, you beat us."

"I did?"

"Well, did anybody else get here before you did?"

"Hey, come on, she isn't in this with us. That's nuts."

"Why don't you be a good loser?" Hankus asked. "Of course Joysie's in it." He gave her a natty salute.

"I didn't even try," she exulted, grinning back. Hankus could make her the winner, just by his saying so. Turning to the thinner, darker boy who blinked at her from behind rimless spectacles, she said, "Hi, Teddy."

He scowled. "It's ho, stupid. When someone says: Hi-dee-hi-dee-hi, you say: Hi-dee-ho. It's from a song; that's the chorus." Teddy tucked the shirttail back into his knickers. The knickers were to be his last pair; as soon as they wore out, he'd get to wear trousers like the other boys. He went to where Hankus stood, head bent over the pages of a newspaper.

Fringed by sandy wisps of hair, Hankus's neck was stem-white and smooth, still a child's; only Teddy didn't think of Hankus as a child, because no matter what, Hank ended up staying older than he himself was. It burned him to have just another child lording it over him. Thirteen to his not yet eleven. He didn't think of himself as a child compared to Joy because she was nothing. What was the baby, six? Five and three quarters? He didn't even know. But Hankus, already three inches taller and heading upward with a determination that seemed like it might never stop, was a different matter. Hankus's just standing there poring over a newspaper made *him* into the baby.

Teddy looked down at the paper and saw Hebrew letters. Yiddish squiggles. Thick impossible words. But there was a photograph, although half of it was hidden under the fold. "Hey, I know what you're reading about. I know that from civics."

Hankus looked up. Even his face was good. A broad, open kind of face. And with a sprinkling of freckles across the bridge of his nose. "What do you mean?"

"That article's about the New Deal. Works Progress Administration."

"You understand Dad and Ma's newspaper?"

Teddy shrugged. "Sure."

"You think a photo of a man painting over the name of a building has to mean W.P.A.? This paper's about Europe, I think—Poland, Germany, places like that."

"Well, that article's about the W.P.A."

Hankus laughed. "You can read Yiddish? Joysie, guess what Teddy knows now?"

She looked up, her lips buttery with kuchen crumbs. "What?"

Hankus did a little silly dance. "Ya da oy. Ya ya sprenish, ya ya boom. "

"Ooooh," she said, giggling. "Ooooh-vey."

"Wait, I didn't say I could *read* Yiddish," Teddy protested. "I just know how—"

"Ix-nay, ix-nay, Eddy-tay," said Hankus, wagging a finger. "Iddishe-yay oy-bay."

"Don't. I don't know any of that old-country junk, why would I? Americans read English."

The corners of Hankus's mouth drew down, darkened abruptly by grief. Shaking his head, he said in a mock-bass voice, "Ow-nay ou-yay elong-bay i-nay he-tay ld-oay ountry-cay."

"No I don't." He paused. "I-ay on't-day."

"Es-yay!"

"O-nay, ankus-Hay. I-ay—"

"Stupid," Joy said flatly. The word surprised her, and she pulled back a bit against the chair. A second later she tried it again, that ugly sound. "Stupid. You are, Teddy." Then looking at his wide, startled eyes, she ducked her head and started to weep. She hadn't meant to call him that, but she didn't under-stand the game. She just wanted to stop it from going on and on.

"Eh," he said, with a shrug, "what do you know, Ho-ho?"

"I know some things."

"Yiddish? You better. You're going back to the old country, Ho-ho."

She caught her breath.

"Yes, didn't you know they're waiting for you? Everything's old there. The people are ghosts."

"No," her voice quivered, "you can't make me."

"Op-stay," said Hankus, sounding more like himself. "She's getting scared."

"Hi-dee-ho, Ho-ho. You're going. Off you go to the ghosty old country, Ho-ho."

She beat the table with her fork. "Stop saying that!"

"Ho-ho! O-gay ack-bay, Ho-ho."

"*Sha!*" the hired girl called out so forcefully from the rear entry that the three of them jumped.

The back door clicked shut. Karla Wojdynski's footsteps came quickly toward them. At once the children seemed to scatter, though Joy still sat at the table and Teddy still stood (now half-turned away) at her side and Hankus began slowly to fold the newspaper back into a neat rectangle, the small photo innermost.

She set down the wicker laundry basket. "Well?" she asked, hands on hips. They avoided looking at her eyes, a cooled Christian-blue, one set slightly higher than the other.

Fishing their mother's embroidered hankie from the jumbled pile, she shook it out in front of Joy's teary face and pinched the thin cloth with its lingering scent of Fels Naptha to the girl's nostrils. "Blow."

Her fist crumpled the moist hankie. "Never get done," she muttered. "Always clean everything twice. So, why must I hear this uproar? Why fight with family?"

"We weren't fighting." Hankus lifted his chin. "Not really."

"Why yell then?"

"It was only us trying—it was about—" He stopped, his face hot. Everything had made sense when it was happening, but now he wasn't sure. He didn't know how to answer, not for himself, not for Teddy and Joy. But he needed to; he was the eldest.

"Oink! Oink, oink. Like piggies in a barnyard you sounded. Suddenly you don't open the mouth? Theodore?" As she pronounced the name, its *Th* burst apart as a single sharp *T*. She waited, but Teddy only looked down and moved behind his father's empty chair. "Nothing from you? Joy, then, can you tell about the ruckus? Explain to me how you act?"

"Op-stay i-tay," Hankus said under his breath.

Karla shook her head sadly. "Who knows how to talk about this fighting, please? Nobody?"

Teddy looked up from the flat pages of his homework and out the parlor window. There, in the waning sunlight, his parents appeared, walking along the front pavement. And it was only seven o'clock, more than an hour earlier than they usually got back from work. Quickly he ran to the radio and turned off the dial. The anthem to Hudson High faded in the middle of the stirring exhortation to *raise the flag high, boys.*

Hankus's head popped up over the top of the horsehair sofa. "Hey, that was Jack Armstrong."

"No listening while doing homework, that's the rule."

"Don't be like that, it's not hurting us. Besides, we don't have to tell them."

Teddy smiled. "They're back early. I saw them outside."

"Movie night!" Hankus threw his pen into the air. "I bet we go to the Lowell for the new Baby Leroy movie."

"I bet the State. They have the best newsreels. Time," Teddy boomed, "marches on. Here we see Deutschland, where people like bratwurst. They like having a good ol' time. But not every-one's happy. The Yiddish papers say what's going on for—"

"Stop it." Hankus cut him off with a tightly nervous laugh. "That's not funny." He paused. "Bet you're right."

"About what?"

"We'll probably go to the State."

Grinning, Teddy brought his fingers up to his nose. He could smell himself, his own smell, and a little of the kuchen he'd eaten for a snack, after Karla had relented.

"Take your hand down. Licking your fingers. God!"

"I'm sniffing." He waved his hand under Hankus's chin. "Not licking."

He shook his head. Walking away, Teddy looked like a piece

of taffy that had been pulled an inch too long, sort of loopy arm-and-legged. His muscles just had no real punch or snap to them, only a slow chewy elasticity, like he would bend and bend and bend before anything would really happen. Exactly like taffy. Taffy Teddy, that was it, the all-day sucker.

"Listen," Hankus said, "if they don't come in soon, I'm turning Jack Armstrong back on."

Teddy was watching his parents from the desk. They were still standing under the Dutch elm with the house address nailed to its trunk. A few yellow leaves calmly floated down. His mother, who wasn't any shorter than his father, only wider and quicker in her gestures, fell silent; her head bent and the blue ostrich feather on the hat swooped forward, trembling a little in the breeze. His father was speaking; he stepped toward her. The brim of his pearl-gray fedora caught the tip of the feather, arching the thin spine between them. Then his father stuck his hand inside his suit jacket, up near his heart. He paused, not yet removing his hand; his mother spoke then, jerking her head fiercely. What did Dad have in there? All of a sudden, Teddy watched his mother burst into tears. The sight of her face contorting was so awful, he lurched to his feet. Outside, both parents—he saw this too—paused. Had they noticed him behind the glass? Seen that they'd frightened him? Tentatively, he waved. And they turned their backs, faced the curb. Heads bent, continued talking. "Oh," he said, as if gut-punched.

"What are they doing out there?"

"How should I know," he grumbled, sitting back down, "I'm in here, not there."

The radio hissed on. "Jack! Jack Armstrong, you come home right now," shouted Mrs. Armstrong, sounding both amused and agitated. "I mean it now."

"Aw, Mom!" Jack's voice was prickly with the static that meant he was far away. Something scuffled: footsteps. Obviously he was headed up the walk. Hinges squeaked; the door was opening wider, letting the boy—bright-eyed, square-jawed, blond-haired—back inside his home. "Mom?" In the pause, Jack's voice echoed as if he'd just entered one of the receiver's glowing tubes, though of course he was standing in the mirrored entry of the Armstrongs' own house. "Hey," he whispered, finally. "What's going on? Where is everybody?"

"Surprise!" Whoops and titters from a whole bunch of girls and boys.

"What?" gasped Jack. "I—I—oh, gosh." There was a loud thud against the floorboards. Then the slow circling tinkling of a coin.

"Fainted!" Mrs. Armstrong moaned. "Oh dear, this isn't what I expected! Someone, please, he needs water." A door slammed.

The door slammed.

Evan called out, "Where are you? Who's home?"

Scrambling over the arm of the sofa to shut off the radio, Hankus shouted, "Hello, Dad!"

But it was Vera who walked toward the front parlor. Without looking up, she dropped a wadded-up handkerchief into her leather pocketbook and snapped the tiny clasp closed. "Everything okay here?"

"Why not?" Hankus grinned from the middle of the sofa. Math book, notebook, sheets of paper were all strewn about him.

"Such a wise guy," she said with a slow smile. "Who taught you to answer a question with a question?" Glancing to Teddy, who hadn't turned around, she took off her hat, quickly running her fingers along the feather to smooth it. Then she touched her hair, impatient with the brown strands that had fallen away from the well-spaced waves of the permanent. There weren't that many lines in her face back then, just the two that went from nosewing to the corner of her mouth; the mole on her upper lip was yet not too noticeable.

"But why not answer a question that way, Ma? Why not?"

"Oh, again a question? You know, Chaim my father would do that too. But he wore black suits and had a long beard—he acted very dignified, so you didn't expect him to joke. That made it funnier." She paused. "You won't have a beard like the old Jews, will you, Hankus?" She tugged at the air below her chin. "Bits of food get caught in it. These days people don't like how that looks, they don't think it's so nice. Daddy uses a razor. You should take more after him and be modern."

Hankus's smooth cheeks flushed pink. "Sure," he said, "I'll shave my beard like Dad."

Furious, Teddy stayed working. A few minutes ago his mother had scared him by crying over something in Dad's vest pocket, and now she was telling Hankus how to shave. As if Hank could ever look like some old rebbe. Well, he didn't want to hear any of it. Couldn't there ever be anything simple, without some worry attached? Teddy scowled at the last gray words he'd scrawled on his lined paper: *without the.*

"Where's my little Pride-and-Joy?"

"Up with me, Mr. Eichenbaum," Karla shouted, "helping put away laundry. Soon I will be done here for the day."

"She is working?" he said, pleased, halfway up the staircase. Then, sharply: "Joysie! I don't want running in the house. You must walk slow and careful. Especially on steps."

Hankus leaned forward from the couch. "Can I listen to the end of Jack Armstrong, Ma?"

"No listening when your brother is studying. He's applying himself."

"Hah. Taffy isn't working."

Vera smacked her palms together; and both boys jumped. "Don't call names," she snapped. "No names ever, you hear?"

Teddy bent lower to the desk and kept writing. That uncoiling rasp, the *sst* of lead against paper, told anybody with ears that he was probably writing something very complicated, even if he didn't actually have the ideas yet, just the sound for them—and just the covering-up action of his hand. Anyone with eyes could see he was thinking hard about something, if they happened to look.

Voice gentle so as not to distract her scholar too much, Vera said, "What are you studying, darling?"

"Gold standard," he muttered. "FDR. How he wants to change things."

"Fine, you keep studying what President Roosevelt does. He's good for the Jews."

"Ma," said Hankus, "why are you home early?"

The ceiling shook above them: Evan, walking across the bedroom floor.

On the bottom step Joy stood tugging at the waistband of her dress. She wanted her mother to turn around on her own and see her, so she could ask about helping with dinner. But she was still talking to the boys. She wouldn't ever stop, it seemed.

"Are you home early because of the State?"

Vera's chin jerked up. "What are you asking?"

"Well, I guessed we'd go to the State, the one in our neighborhood." He twirled the fountain pen between his fingers. "Teddy guessed the Lowell."

"My smart boy," she said, after a moment. "The two of you. It's movie night, you're right."

"Sha-zam!"

"Sam, Sam," breathed Joy in the foyer. She called into the boys' cheering, "Can I set the table by myself, Mommy? Karla said to ask."

But Vera came so swiftly toward the foyer that Joy took a step back. "So all right," she was muttering, mouth set. She glanced ahead, and saw Joy, but from under her breath came a curse, that long one with the string of *oo*es and *ish*es—Hungarian.

"Mommy?"

"Joy, go in with your brothers."

Vera walked brusquely past and up the stairs in a house that at five-thirty that night had yet to smell of dinner's warm spiciness. Up the staircase, one navy leather midheeled pump after another; each varnished oak step a six-inch rise; thirteen steps until the second-floor landing. Joy turned her face upward, watching her mother. Her mother's familiar shape, her mother's quick certainty.

"Joysie, come here."

She let Hankus wave her into the front room. As soon as she wandered near enough, he seized her hands.

"Let go of me," she said glumly.

"But I want to dance on movie night. Do you know how to spin? In a circle with me, can you?"

She caught her breath. "How fast?"

"Real fast. Can you?"

She paused. "Yes."

He gave a slow chuckle and pretended to twirl one end of a long mustache; he stroked a beard, dangling unruly, invisibly from his smooth chin. "All right, we'll spin," he half sung out, raising an eyebrow at her. "This won't be *davening*."

She giggled.

"Guess who's got you next?"

"Spin with me? He won't do it."

"Right, I won't."

"Too bad, you two," Hankus said. With a sharp tug that she quickly planted her feet against, he leaned backward and, squeezing her fingers, shockingly closed his eyes. His face was all inside now, all quiet, toward himself. For one moment, Joy could stare past him, to Teddy. Then Hankus shouted: *Try to hang on!* The room turned to spinning and spinning and spinning.

Evan turned from his dresser. The bureau, made of pale inexpensive pine, had small brass pulls. On top of it rested the formal photographic portrait taken fifteen years ago—not that long, it seemed to him—in the first months of their marriage. There was something in it he couldn't quite figure out, a secret stillness he loved. "What?" he said, seeing the anger in Vera's face as she walked into the bedroom.

She shut the door and said, "The kids think we're taking them to the picture show."

"Oh?" Evan's brown hair was slicked back from his forehead. There were bags under his eyes, and his beard stubble was rough. He looked tired. "Why do they think that?"

She kicked off her shoes. Karla was at the linen closet in the hallway, folding the last of the laundered towels; Vera kept her voice low. "Because it's Wednesday—dime night. When Hankus asked me about the State and why we came home early, I was so stupid, I thought he was talking about us going right away to the government. So stupid! The child doesn't know the pressures we have. But when I figured it out what he was really asking, I just said, sure, movies."

"That's not so bad." Evan massaged his left shoulder through the cotton undershirt. He'd already hung up his shirt; the belt he'd taken off too; but not the pants, which were only unbuttoned at the waist. In black-stockinged feet he crossed over to the bed. "We'll go to the movies and have some fun, yes?"

"How can we? We have to talk about Solly's letter. Tomorrow you'll be in New York City. Seven days. You want to wait seven days to talk?"

He patted the mattress beside him. "Nothing is going to change too fast. Sit a minute."

"Usually you're the one who gives in to them. You're the soft one. What was I thinking? I was still upset. We'll go to the movies another time."

Evan shook his head. He took a fresh pack of Chesterfields and matches from the drawer of the nightstand.

Vera unzipped her navy blue dress and pushed it slowly over her hips to step out of it. In her slip, she sat down next to him. "If we are going out, I should keep these on." She plucked at the brown top of the silk stockings where they fastened to the garter belt; she fingered one of the snaps, the size of a dime. "But it's not right to go."

He lit the cigarette and offered it.

She made a V with her fingers. Squinting against the smoke, she inhaled.

"Togetherness first," Evan said. "Then we can talk about when my brother and your sister should come to us, yes?"

The State

It was Teddy's turn to take the money. Dollar bill in hand, he ran to get into the line. When finally he reached the cashier cage, he slid the dollar just under the glass window. "Two adults, please, three children."

"How many you say?" The old lady's fingers tapped against the glass.

Someone prodded him from behind. Surprised, he turned.

His father smiled at him. Maybe he'd been watching him the

whole time, not trusting he would do it right. "You should go right up to the window, honey. Speak near the hole." His father touched the brim of his hat to the cashier.

"I know that," he said, and got as close to the glass as possible. A moment later, victorious, he held a jointed streamer of blue tickets in one hand and the loose change in the other.

"Move out so others can buy," his father instructed.

"I know. Where's Hankus?"

"He met some friends and went in. Mommy's in the lobby already, too." He touched the back of Teddy's neck. "Stay close to me."

All the noise in the neighborhood was getting made right in front of the movie house. The quiet, elm-darkened streets the family had crossed in the fifteen-minute walk from East Trainor now seemed as far off and exotic as the idea of sleep. Here people were strolling about. Electric trolleys rumbled down the center of the avenue; many of those who disembarked hurried to join the line in front of the theater; others paused at the corners flanking the building to speak with the unemployed thin-suited men who had set themselves up selling fruit: one round Depression apple for a nickel.

The new State Theater was built to last. It had a spotlit marquee, colorful posters, a gilded cashier's booth, four brass-trimmed glass doors, an ornately carved stone facade topped by the gentle swell of a cupola, and a drawing power no other building in the immediate neighborhood could match. It was as tall and impressive as Central Synagogue. The nine-year-old synagogue stood on a busy corner, too, and it also was a fifteen-minute walk from the house on East Trainor, though in the opposite direction. The majority of its congregants were Hungarians, and most of these were observant Jews, but not at all Orthodox. They remained most faithful to those religious customs from the old country that, familiar and restorative, didn't impede the pursuit of life, liberty, and happiness—those *broches* or blessings that they knew to be part of the sacred ceremonial rites of the U.S. of A. Each week, Evan and Vera attended services, drawn by a proud and sweet mix of religious obligation

and social nostalgia to a synagogue that seemed as much lands-
mans' club as hall of worship. The same pull as for most everyone who walked in the door. Of course, yes, they had come from
elsewhere, but under Central's beautiful, vast, and echoing
dome they sat also as American citizens now.

Evan and Teddy entered the State Theater's lobby. It was
packed, as if whole other neighborhoods had found their ways
in. Still, people were keeping to their own kind. Hankus was
standing near the popcorn machine with Harvey Oppenheim,
Buddy Stein, and Marky Rivchin. The boys' parents were milling
about on the red carpeting and talking only with one another,
picking out familiar faces from all the rest. Mr. Rivchin, posture
erect as it was when he stood behind his pharmacy counter, was
proudly pulling a silver cigarette case from his jacket pocket to
offer a smoke to Mr. Stein, who with a twitch of his fingers waved
it away. In spirited conversation with Billie Oppenheim, Vera
kept shaking her head; she was wearing a flat brown hat now, not
the one with a feather that would annoy anyone sitting behind
her. She also had Joy the Baby by the hand. In a contented daze
brought on by feeling tiny but taken care of in the very midst of
a congenial crowd, Joy clutched a red-and-white-striped cardboard box to her chest. Perhaps there would still be popcorn left
inside it after everyone took to their seats. Often the flimsy bottom flaps gave way and the kernels poured out.

Evan leaned down and took all but one nickel from Teddy's
palm. "Tell you what, go buy a second popcorn for us. Tonight
we will have more than we need."

In the crowd of boys Marky Rivchin was saying in his new
stabbing green stick of a voice, "But that science test was easy.
Honest, I thought Foster was going to make it much harder. I
thought it was a cinch."

Hankus and the others scoffed.

"Uh-huh," Marky insisted, pushing out his chest. "I'm posi-
tive. Besides, I have to get a ninety-five. My father says that's my
bottom limit."

"How much do you bet you fail?" Buddy demanded. "How
much says, Rivchin, that I beat you?"

By the time the girl took the nickel from Teddy, nearly everyone had begun drifting toward the propped open doors to the main room. His father, though, wasn't going anywhere, still *keeping an eye out,* as he liked to say.

"Over here!" Vera waved at them from inside the door.

As usual, they went toward one of the smaller side sections and not toward the center with its double-length rows. They stayed in the rear of the theater, going no farther than the last third. "See? You always make sure to be near two exits," Evan said, as usual, as they filed into the row. "Just in case."

They settled in amid the hubbub, voices in loose conversation, feet shuffling along the red carpet, chords rippling from the piano set below the edge of the stage. A few moments later, at exactly five minutes past seven, the overhead lights dimmed and the ushers' flashlights blinked on. The velvet curtains at the front parted. As the huge white screen spread wider, glimmering blankly before them, the audience hushed. The piano chords got quieter, quieter, until they were inaudible. And still, latecomers scurried down the sloping aisles, pausing every few yards to point at a seat. "Empty?" they whispered, then turned to signal one another through the dark or sometimes just slid ahead into the row with a smile that said to those already settled and whom they were now disturbing: *So sorry for this!*

Twice a week on average, people went to the picture shows. Over the years the newsreels showed them President Roosevelt sitting behind the welter of microphones, forehead beaded with sweat under the harsh lights and speaking forcefully once again a few lines from the same fireside chat they heard not that long ago, when they'd leaned over their radios at home and fiddled with the dial; showed how the black blizzards of topsoil swirled through the sky from Texas to Montana; how the convicted kidnapper-murderer of dear innocent Charles Lindbergh, Jr., turned his narrow face from the cameras as he was taken from jail; showed them how the tiny features repeated, shockingly alive, in the infant faces of Canada's Dionne quintuplets; the way medals gleamed on the chests of the FBI agents who had ambushed John Dillinger, "Public Enemy Number One," as he exited a Chicago movie house—where he, too, had been sitting in the dark, facing a screen; and how the *Morro Castle* burned off Asbury Park, New Jersey, while throughout those days and nights the tourists and residents crowded together to watch; and the way crowds in Germany marched in rows to salute Hitler, who with Hindenburg's death had made himself Reichsführer—that they sat and watched too, uneasy in the collective dark, shoulder to shoulder in the plush seats, with the main entertainment, the fantasy, the drama, the well-constructed comedic sequences and glamorously tragic images yet to come.

Hankus was sitting, legs sprawled, in the chair on the aisle; Joy sat next to him, her head already drowsing to the armrest between them; then Evan; next, a chair piled neatly with their sweaters; then Vera; Teddy occupied the innermost position, a box of popcorn on his lap.

Look at the audience sitting in the dark. A resonant male voice orating; the air booming with narration and on-and-off-again symphonic chords; the stream of dust-moted light untunneling images and seamlessly spilling sense—edited, perfectly timed, well expected—across a reflective screen. Marches on. Time. Marches.

On. Time. Marches.

Time.

Marches.

Marches.

Rising out of his seat on the screen, and once more larger than life, Babe Ruth was pleased to sign autographs for the fans crowding about him. As the Babe waved a huge pale hand for the camera and finally settled back in the spectators' stands—for he's two months by then into his retirement, the images changed. Suddenly the players were dressed in white dress shirts and white slacks, and the batter was positioning himself near a small upright post instead of home plate. The bat he bounced in the air over his shoulder was odd.

"No, it's cricket," a woman in the row behind replied to her companion's mumbled question. "British." Time marches.

Vera leaned across the armrests and whispered, "Make her little head comfortable."

Evan turned his glitter-eyed face to hers in the dark. Marches.

"Her *kepelleh*," Vera mouthed, jutting her chin at the sleeping child. "Put it down."

As the cricket players leaped and raced on the screen, Evan took a sweater folded atop the pile next to him. This he propped like a pillow beneath their daughter's neck. He brushed away the awful corkscrewed Shirley Temple curls so they wouldn't get caught and pull at her scalp if, in the plush public chair temporarily hers, Joy tried to turn in her sleep.

In this short time Evan missed seeing the last few black-and-white images, with their shift of focus to the British ambassador greeting FDR behind a guardrail; he missed the long last shot of the two countries' flags waving together against the cloud-studded sky; the gray whiff of smoke leaving the barrel of the starter's gun; the astonishingly organized melee the gun had released: the dark fierce stretch of numerous thoroughbred legs, necks, spines, manes, tails, and the hunched-over, pale small men riding atop them, the great beasts, till only one in the next shot stood still, wreathed in victory. Then the music came up, and Evan did see the curtains begin pulling closed from the sides of the stage. The heavy drapes made just the gesture of closing; a third of the way in, the gold velvet folds swung back and again glided apart. It appeared they were opening more fully than they just had for the newsreel. It wasn't so, of course. The new extra width to the screen was an illusion, accepted by those watching, all of them quite eager now for the fantasy of the evening to start.

The applause filled his ears. Hankus loved his hands. He loved the full sound his palms could make, pocketing the air between them. That buried wide explosive sound—a man's sound—he could make it happen just by bringing both slightly curved palms together. Had he been able to clap like that even this past

July, this past August? He couldn't remember. Probably he still had hands like Teddy's back then. Small. Too boyish.

Now he couldn't imagine ever getting over the surprise of being able to make a sound like this. Secretly he knew that by applauding just before the fade-out of the movie and continuing on through the words *The End* as they floated over the Marx Brothers' three surprised, vaudevillian faces, he was also in a way applauding himself, this lanky, smooth-skinned boy who had been given such an astonishing gift. He could have this power in his own body—he brought his palms together hard, fast—for the rest of his life.

Hankus jumped to his feet as if never had he found himself more entertained, more captivated, more moved. And by what? A low comedy? A plot that had the madcap brothers still trying to jimmy their way into a life of ease? Where Groucho went to a society party as Captain Spaulding an African explorer and thought he was getting called instead *schnorrer*? Simple silliness, he knew, with the brothers getting their usual comeuppance at the end, everything around them a shambles. But now, with a wide grin, he couldn't be happier. He looked about; really, wasn't it *great*?

With a moan Joy wrenched herself out of a dream and pushed herself upright. Her right cheek and eye stung, chafed from pressing into the jackets' wrinkled woolen sleeves. She looked up at the shadow she knew to be Hankus, saw how his arm movements kept blurring, and, confused by the sharp report of his palms, the wider waves of sound swimming up from the rest of the audience, and by the flickering light, started to cry.

"It's only a movie, yes?" Evan whispered, patting her shoulder. "That's all this is, Joysie. Remember we're in a theater?"

She knew what he said was so, his breath warm in her ear, waking her. But the reassurance wasn't enough to staunch the flow of what had already begun inside her. "He has to be still," she sobbed. Her whole body trembled. "Hankus has to be still."

"Okay," Vera spoke firmly, "enough clapping. Sit down a minute and be quiet. You're scaring her."

Hankus felt his cheeks grow hot. "I couldn't do that," he said almost angrily. "It's just—I just really liked it." He glanced down the row, at the four faces, each ghostly, watching him. All around them people were starting to gather their sweaters and coats. It was almost over for now. Suddenly, standing where he was, third row from the back in the right-side section, Hankus put two fingers to his mouth. With a defiance born from an enthusiasm for his own best intentions, Hankus filled up his chest; and with a rush, a thrilling release, sent out a shrill whistle.

Two-six-oh-two East Trainor

Evan sliced another bruise from the tomato. Prodding the paring knife further into the center, he searched for the heart of the spoilage.

"You couldn't wait until morning? You had to go to the garden and get that tonight?" Vera stood just inside the kitchen, looking at him with an expression that wasn't really a smile. The slight gap between her square front teeth made a dark line, even with distance. "So tell me," she said, pulling out her chair, "is it any good?"

He sliced off a red oval, offering it to her on the flat of the knife. "Good enough. By morning, there wouldn't have been anything here to save. This was on the ground. It was too long on the vine, maybe."

"I wouldn't mind letting one rot. We only have bushels of them, Evan. I don't want to spend my Sunday afternoons canning."

"It's better to have plenty." He took the last piece for himself. "They're in bed?"

"Sure." She pulled off her chunky celluloid earrings. The clock atop the Glenville read 9:43. Either she should start making the dumplings and slicing vegetables now for tomorrow's dinner or get up before six and do it before work. "How early tomorrow morning does the train leave?"

"Five-ten. Adolph will drive me to the station at four-fifteen. I'll bring back some good buys for us, you'll see. And we'll have a better year in the store, maybe."

"Good. I hope so."

"When the children are older, you'll come to New York, too. We'll make a little trip for ourselves. Business *and* pleasure."

Vera put an overseas envelope on the oilcloth. "We have to talk about Solly's letter."

"Here's what we should do." Evan sat back. "We tell him to come to America. We bring him over now, since no one else except your sister is asking to come. And for her we already filed, yes? Let it be Solly's turn, then."

"Sure, we filed. What we heard since then is nothing."

"The government will reply, don't worry."

"Listen, *tateleh,* you think they're going to say yes to everyone? Maybe no one else wants to come from your side, but from my side of the family they do."

"So far only Irina—"

"No, all my sisters want to come. Everyone on my side wants to. Only they don't know it yet."

"Oh?" Slowly he smiled. "And you're going to tell them, yes? They're just as stubborn as you are."

"They're coming." With the heel of her hand Vera daubed up the drips of red pulp from the oilcoth. "I planted some little seeds in their heads."

Evan was silent. "Not everyone in Europe wants to be an American," he said finally.

"You never scrubbed clothes on a board; that's what they have over there. I have a washing machine and clothes wringer, I told them. I said I threw out my scrub board. I don't ever want to live like that again, to have modern thoughts but no modern conveniences." She paused. "I miss my family, Evan. At the holidays, we sit around only the one small table. Only us and our three little ones in this whole country."

"You don't see? Exactly what I mean! If we start now to bring over Solly, he also can live here. I know he'll be a big help to us. And once he learns English, he can have a job in the store. He's a good-looking boy. What do you think? We apply for him now, too?

"Well?" He waited. "Well, what do you say?"

She pushed the envelope a ways toward him. "I remember he has big ears."

He laughed. "Oh, not really big!"

"Pretty big," she said slowly. "What was he, Hankus's age, when we left? Did he ever say one word to me back then? You don't know how he's turned out. You can't say you really do. In the photo he still looks like a closed-mouthed yeshiva boy. Quiet, slow—same as your father. Not much for working then, and probably not much for it now."

Evan sat rock-still.

She shrugged. "But maybe when he comes, he'll take his nose out of the books and work his way through the world."

"Don't worry, yes? He writes how he wants to be an American."

Picking up the used saucer and paring knife, she went to the sink. The children's lunch pails were draining upside down along the counter. No matter how much soap she used, the insides of the metal containers always gave off a faint milky smell. Wetting a washrag, she began to wipe them out again.

"Volkmann from the stationer's," said Evan, "has relatives he's trying to sponsor. Germans, though. Every few days he goes to the Red Cross, he goes to the government agency, goes over to the Jewish Foundation. Then he tries with the Hebrew Immigrant Aid. The German problem can't last forever, I tell him." Lightly he rapped his knuckles on the table. "We don't know how lucky we are with our families. Czechoslovakia is what it always was, no better, no worse. It's that madman Hitler. Everyone else in Europe has only the usual problems. I feel bad for him, for Volkmann."

"His wife is Alma, a skinny woman? Always stands a little too far away from you when she talks?"

"That's her."

Vera wrung out the dishrag. "I think we need to wait until Irina's application is approved, and *then* put in one for Solly."

"Why?" he spoke sharply. "For what reason? You think we're asking for too much? I hear the stories, too. But we'll qualify as sponsors, Vera."

"The store isn't doing enough business to—"

"No, it can turn around. We're hard workers. This country likes hard workers. So if we promise to support Solly when he gets here, what harm can it do?" He paused. "Irina and her two little ones you want on the quota list right away, yes? Today you even cried to me about not getting her forms back yet."

Vera rested her hand on the faucet. "I love her, Evan. She has to come here. She needs the chance to start her life over. It hurts to think of her as a widow now, all on her own to raise those two girls."

"Your sister," he said quietly, "is dear to you, well, so too is my brother to me. I want to know him again. I want to give him his chance, can't I do that? So no more bothering about it, all right? We'll find a way to bring the both of them. After all, we got here. We're not the only lucky people, yes? So let's keep to the sunny side, the good side, and not to the other."

Vera looked over her shoulder. "What? What did you say about your mother?"

"I didn't say about my mother."

"You should." Turning the knife under the tap, her fingers skimmed along the sharp, watery blade. "I bet *she* will have plenty to say as soon as she learns where her youngest son wants to live. Everything in America is unclean—it's *trayf* to her. Only the money we wire over to her family each month, that's kosher." Vera shook off the knife. "Oh, yes, she will have plenty to say. I can almost hear her."

"Ah." Chilled, Evan massaged the muscles that suddenly tightened in his left shoulder; for a few moments he worked them over in silence. "I will write to her then."

But even after so many years away, a mother is not reduced to a piece of paper, an envelope, ink, a dried postage stamp. It might be easier to think she may be so reduced, but that's not the case. The voice locked in our heads, the voice that spirals through our dreams, the voice born both too early and too far off to be carried through telephone wires, the voice that comes only from the shaken cords in a human throat six thousand miles away, is full, is real, is *embodied*. And despite distance and hidden desire, it will not easily play dead.

So at once Evan, brown hair falling back over his brow, stretched his arms over his head and said, "I'm going upstairs."

So immediately Vera, her round face flushed and smooth, replied, "Yes, go. I'll be up in a minute."

After the kitchen and bathroom faucets were turned off, and the lights were clicked off, and the windows closed against cold drafts, and the sheets on all the beds were pulled up to all the chins, and the children's eyes stayed racing beneath their closed lids, and the police car turned the corner of East Trainor and continued to the next elm-silenced street, and the clouds, still white, drifted across stars and the quartered moon, and their casting of light and shadow rippled the dark gambrel roof of two-six-oh-two, and rippled the roofs of the houses on either side and those farther along—and then farther along, the waves of the ocean shifted and a half hour passed, the voice of the woman whose first name would be lost to her only great-grand-children—the frightened woman who thought she had given up only one of her sons, *Ivan*, to America—was that night in her small house at dawn in a far rural country, going on and on very loudly.

She was talking hopelessly and angrily to her youngest son, Sol. Her Yiddish phrases sounded desperate, ragged, raging. All of what she said to Sol then, the singular fate she was prophesy-ing for him if he left, she would soon enough learn to be terribly wrong.

Vera's and Evan's hands reached suddenly out, their bodies pressed together, their mouths opened, soft, rushed and hot with whispers: *It will be fine, it is all right, it is all right now.* They could imagine what Evan's mother was saying right then—she was always real to them, certainly they knew her name, her face, her own particular tone and touch—but still they hoped they weren't really able to hear her. They hoped they weren't sure of her voice. Because Evan didn't have a brother in the whole of

America, and he was lonely for one. Because Sol, little Solly, had been a child when Evan turned his face from Nagymihály, but now Sol wanted to join him. So Vera and Evan tried not to hear his mother shouting: *You can't leave here, can't leave me and everyone you love—not you, my good son!* Instead Evan wanted to hear himself say: *I've secured your passage; you can come to us now. Dear brother.*

Vera hoped that she might hear Evan say that, too—but only after her sister and nieces had safely arrived. They both wanted to believe they could hear his mother's voice only when enclosed in a letter. They both hoped this would prove enough for her voice. Because a thin sheet of paper can be folded. And that night, Vera and Evan made their own breathing loud; they reached for each other and allowed their own wordless breath and greedy touch to take over, lead them. Their breaths came faster and faster and became more urgent; and for that short wonderful while they could hear only themselves. And always, they stayed quiet enough so their children wouldn't hear them, and wake, and cry out.

Immigrant Aid

The Hebrew Immigrant Aid Society's door, fronted in frosted glass, stopped her. It was nothing but a door, but still Vera hesitated before putting her white-gloved hand against it. She could picture the dark oak counter, the stacks of paper, even the pencils the other applicants had fingered and laid aside after saying a little prayer under their breath or quickly and quietly rapping their knuckles against the edge of the counter. Knock on wood. Wood like her head. A dummy, that's what she was, someone standing in a hallway, imagining what was going on inside, instead of someone who opened a door as if inside was where she belonged. When she'd telephoned the agency about Irina's paperwork, she was told to come by in person. Well, in she was about to come—only just in one more minute. All that was in front of her was just another transaction.

Vera took out her compact and caught in the round mirror

her wide eyes, then her grim mouth: the coral lipstick was still on all right. She wiped a smudge of the pink stain from her front tooth, then pressed her lips together as if she'd actually applied more color from the tube. Snapping the compact closed, she cursed at herself: *Go in, dummy!*

The door shut behind her. At once it was clear that she wouldn't have to take a chair against the wall and wait, because a gentleman was just turning away from the last clerk in the row. She watched him come toward her.

Walking, he barely glanced up from the sheaf of papers in his hands. Yah, missus, he muttered, yah, sure he was done. *Goose is cooked,* he added, and snorted unhappily into the gray bristles of his mustache.

Vera hurried past the backs of the five or six other people bending over the counter. They were discussing, discussing, discussing their cases with the clerks on the other side. The clerks bent forward only slightly from their necks, but those on the public side of the counter pressed their stomachs against the edge of the wood; concentrating every bit of their energy and will forward, they hunched their shoulders.

From the end of the dark counter the free clerk smiled and waggled her fingers. "Come," she said, "dear." A telephone gave a half-ring from the back of the room.

"Now then." She lifted a powdered moon of a face. Her black eyebrows were drawn on, carefully arched in a design of eternal surprise, and the dyed-black hair was arranged in a style popular back in the twenties with the flappers. She wasn't at all as youthful as she'd appeared from farther away. "Is it still drizzling out, dear?"

Vera shook her head.

A lady two positions over started crying, but very quiet. Couldn't it be relief, just as well as something else, making her sob? "About my sister," Vera said, pressing against the counter. "Her application."

The clerk had a piece of foil-wrapped hard candy in her hand and offered it.

"Not for me, thank you." Vera shook her head. "The notification card—I know this is important to start the immigration process, but we still haven't received it in the mail. We filled out all the forms through this office. They were to go on to Washington, D.C. But it's been two months, and we have heard nothing."

"Two months isn't long," the clerk replied. "It only feels that way. Okay, I'll start at the start and see what's what. You have an accent, dear. You're naturalized, I hope?"

Vera stiffened. "You think I don't know I have to be a citizen to be a sponsor?"

"Oh, everyone gets insulted by that question because I sound native-born. The truth is I was born in Berlin, but my parents left when I was a baby. So"—she flicked her wrist—"no accent for me. But then, no one notices her own accent, do we?" The clerk stabbed out a cigarette burning in the tin ashtray to her right. "Okay, now tell me, dear, you're a naturalized citizen?" She waited, her gaze wide open under those hairless eyebrows.

Vera drew herself up. "I have been in this country since 1920. The U.S. citizenship test, that I passed in 1931. The certificate I got in 1932."

"Now we're getting somewhere. So you filled out form five seventy-five, and sent it in to the Department of Labor, I'm sure."

"Form five seventy-five, yes."

"Okay. And you didn't receive a card that looks like this in the mail?" The clerk produced a flat green postcard stamped *Form 576*. She flipped it over. "'The issuance of immigration visas is exclusively a function of United States consuls,'" she read. "'Determination of whether immigration visas will be issued can be made only by the United States consul to whom the prospective immigrants apply for visas, and all communications regarding the matter should be addressed to him.'

"Well?" She looked up.

"That—that we didn't get."

"Okay, I see. I'll go check your file. Your name?"

"Eichenbaum. Vera."

"What nationality is that, dear? Not German."

"Hungarian," said Vera, "when I was growing up. But after

the Great War they gave our village over to make the new republic, to make Czechoslovakia."

"That's where your sister is now, still in Czechoslovakia?"

"Yes, but no longer in Szacsur, where we grew up. And her name now is different."

"Well, of course it is." She smiled in an odd, slanting way. "You did say she has children."

"Osvat her name is. Irina Osvat."

"I'm Miss Stein, if you need to call for me. Back in a minute."

While the clerk went to the files set in a smaller room at the back of the office, Vera tugged off her white gloves and put them into her pocketbook. The telephone shrilled—two and a half rings. The lady who'd been crying was no longer making any sound that rose above the general murmur. Out of the corner of her eye, Vera saw her bending over some papers, a handkerchief clutched in her fist. The clock on the side wall read 11:14. Soon she'd have to go back to the store. Business picked up when the factory workers came in. They came in to find something to remind them how they felt and looked when they weren't exhausted. Between eleven-thirty and one o'clock, Buckeye Shopping Center's mirrors were full of men and some few women holding clothes up against their bodies and squinting at the reflections as they turned this way and that. Mothers and children came later in the day and usually used the dressing rooms. The shift workers couldn't take that extra time, not unless they came in on Saturday. But of course the store was more crowded then. As crowded as it could be in a bad economy. People chose carefully what clothes they wanted, if they were able to choose to buy at all.

The clerk came back, holding nothing. "Okay," she said, perching herself on a stool. "This sometimes happens. The paperwork was a little delayed."

"How, delayed?"

"It wasn't sent in. Well, it was mailed to Washington, but something happened. It was sent back to us instead. By mistake, it then got put back into your file." She coughed. "We did send it off again to D.C., but I guess I'd have to admit that didn't happen until, well, just about yesterday."

Vera gripped the edge of the counter. "Two months of waiting and nothing is started?"

"Nothing *yet*," the clerk amended. "Please, dear, really, the paperwork's on its way—but only a bit later than you'd thought. I'm truly sorry."

Biting her lip, Vera just shook her head.

"Okay. Maybe you should know the numbers we can bring in from Czechoslovakia are actually quite low. By law of the Johnson Act—do you know this?—a foreign country's immigration quota is limited to at most *two* percent of its ex-citizens living in this country back in 1890. From Rumania, for example—and this is in my head because of Mr. Mantz, the gentleman here before you—even if ten thousand people apply, only seven hundred forty-eight of them might be allowed in. That's the maximum. And even then the government might decide not to fill all the slots. Well, it seems not many Rumanians were living here in 1890! Now, for the English and so-called Nordic types, millions of slots are kept open. Unfortunately, these people don't appear to be applying." Again her smile went slant and she bent her neck forward. In a quieter voice she added, "Believe me, it's worse for the German Jews."

"What happens," Vera whispered, leaning in closer against the counter, "to my sister's turn now? With the limits, others from her country have gotten ahead of her."

"Now it's more complicated than you or I can really understand. A very complex governmental process."

"Hurry up, please!" a man called from the front of the office where a line had formed. "Some of us can't lose our jobs." There was a sudden outbreak of coughing.

"But I want to know," Vera persisted, "if it's like a contest, if the quota pits from the same country one application against another for the same slot."

"I can't say it's quite like a contest, no. You can't really think like that. Dear," said the clerk, "wouldn't you like one of these?" She shoved a piece of hard candy across the counter. "Okay.

You'll get your five seventy-six card in the mail, notifying you of your suitability to be considered a sponsor, and then we'll take it from there. Meanwhile, you can begin to gather the required personal affidavits, and the number of financial statements and such. The government doesn't want to let in anyone liable to become a public charge, which means without funds or ongoing financial support. You have to prove you can not only financially support the people you bring in but that you have an obligation to do so. The government is very strict on this."

"I know. The lady from before told me."

"Do you need an instruction sheet to take home?"

"Please, yes." Shaking, Vera unwrapped the foil on the candy and put the sweet in her mouth. The taste of sugared coffee spread over her tongue. "One more thing." She paused. "I need forms for another family member. My husband's brother. He wants to apply too."

"From where does he want to apply?"

The telephone shrilled. One ring. Two.

Vera tugged the thin black strap of her watch down to where her wrist was more narrow. "He lives in Czechoslovakia. Same as Irina."

"Ah," said the clerk, "yes."

"My husband says we should apply all at once, for everybody. I think we should get one over first, and then go ask about the other."

"Well, everybody has a theory." The clerk sighed. On top of the instruction sheet she put a packet of forms, stapled in the left corner. "Okay, you're caught up now, Mrs. Eichenbaum. When you complete your brother-in-law's forms, send them in, just as you did with your sister."

"No difference?"

"None at all."

"Thank you," Vera said. Head down, she studied the top sheet of the packet as she walked away.

"Excuse me?" A young man, maybe only twenty-three, twenty-four, stopped her. "But, please, are you done with your problems here?"

She took note of his accent. Polish, probably. Maybe still only a greenhorn, and not a citizen.

Behind her, Miss Stein called out, "Next."

The candy was thickly sweet in her mouth. "Yes, I am through, sir."

"Come, dear," she heard the clerk say. "You may come over here to me now."

Two-six-oh-two East Trainor

"You liked that?" asked Sandor Belak. He leaned expansively back against the couch. "So listen to this."

"We're listening," Evan said, with a nod to the little ones to stop fidgeting.

Sandor rubbed his hands together. "One night four men are sitting around a cafe table in Munich, and they're having some of that good hot *kaffee mit schlag* and a little piece each of strudel. One man takes a bite of the strudel—it's apple—and gives a long, mournful sigh. The one to his left begins rolling a napkin, very nervous, between his palms. The third one stares into his coffee cup and gives a short groan. Suddenly the fourth man throws down his fork. 'For heaven's sake,' he cries. 'When will you people learn not to discuss politics in public?'"

Evan laughed, but he kept looking at Vera out of the corner of his eye. Though she hadn't been quiet with her guests, she hadn't been talking much to him. He'd just returned from New York, and they hadn't had so much as five minutes alone together. On the bed his heavy leather suitcase lay open, with only one side unpacked. The train hadn't been late getting into town, but Adolph's Plymouth overheated as they were driving up Euclid Avenue. When Evan opened the hood and waved away the steam that seemed to pour out from everywhere, Adolph bent down for a look; the engine block, he proclaimed, was cracked; so the two of them pushed the car over to the curb and locked it. Finally, he'd gotten home by streetcar, walking in the door not fifteen minutes before the Belaks knocked. They'd come over for dinner and a nice game of cards.

"You like that, *boychik*?" Sandor Belak asked Hankus while fitting a cigarette into the long black holder that he used as a filter.

"I guess."

"But you don't really get it, eh?" He struck a match. "What about you, Master Theo? The little girl I won't bother with asking, so young, what can she follow? But the boys—"

Teddy shrugged. "I get most of it."

"Fibber," Hankus whispered, poking him, "Fibber McGee."

"The boys have no need to think about such things," Evan said.

"Fibber and *Molly*," said Joy, picking up on Hankus's whisper and looking around for approval.

"I see my wit is wasted on the young." Sandor sighed and reached—fingertips only—into the dish of salted nuts his wife, Lili, stood holding above his ample stomach. "Thanks be to God."

Evan glanced at Vera; again she was smiling only at their guests, not at him. For the past week, the two of them hadn't spoken. No one they knew telephoned long-distance just to talk; it was too expensive. Telegrams covered the miles quickly but were almost always reserved for emergencies or bad tidings. People were supposed to be patient about being separated. Distance was distance.

But he could see she was angry at him now.

"Sandor," said Vera, "do you know any more jokes?"

"I have plenty. In the insurance business I hear more jokes in one week than that big *macher* Will Rogers does in a whole year. But this one I think I'd better tell in Yiddish." He nodded toward Hankus, Teddy, and Joy, who sat swinging their legs on wooden chairs dragged into the dining room from the kitchen. "Because of *der kinder*."

"Oh, not that one, sweetheart," Lili moaned. But her long-jawed face was red because she was already attempting to suppress her laughter.

"Ach! Such *narishkayt*." Sandor wagged his head.

One minute later and all the adults were roaring.

• • •

Evan had come home tired and expectant, ready for the familiar smallness of his life to overtake him again. In New York City everything felt crowded together and yet also far away, the one from the other. Each activity, each building, each street, each face, each prospective deal seemed—once he managed to get up close to it—huge. For five days, from morning till night he met salesmen. One by one, full of moxie or earnest and dour, they lugged their black sample cases to his hotel room or to the midtown coffee shops where they'd meet up because these places had booths where they could spread out their wares. Other times, alone, he faced the long ironwork flights to the garment-factory showrooms.

As he climbed, he couldn't forget how far he had come from the boy who labored below, on the ground floor. At the top of his climb, he pushed aside the tall grillwork door, the door to an immense cage. He straightened his suit jacket. He took off his brown hat and pinched it at the crease. He smoothed back his hair. He'd started as a greenhorn in the garment district, punching holes in belts, fastening on the buckles. He went on to the line—making spats, then clothing. Now, he was the one buying all that. Of course, he needed to get a good price on this trip, because sales at home weren't too good.

Some people thought it was foolishness not to let the salesmen come to him in Cleveland; they argued salesmen were already riding the rails. But Evan had to see with his own eyes all that was out there for purchase. He had a plan he hadn't even dared mention to Vera yet: in a few years he hoped to open a second store. A second would cement the reality of the first; it would secure everything for his family. But to get to that store, what he offered the public every single day until then had to be good. More than a value, it had to be something people would remember and want enough to walk across town to buy. Something not only good but different. There was nothing wrong with difference. Changing the way people looked and looked at themselves—that's what fashion was. Was it a plus if his store only fit in with all the others? He came to New York City because he wanted his store—his stores—to be always just a little bit dif-

ferent from everyone else's. A bit of difference suited him. It's
how he always felt. Never, in old country or new, was he a fish in
water.

"In New York now," he said to the guests at his table, "on one
street you have Tiffany's, on the next an open lot where stands a
Hooverville. Diamonds on one side, cardboard shacks on the
other."

Lili put down her fork. "That sounds terrible."

"In the city I went everywhere; I passed everything. I saw it
all over."

"You couldn't pay me enough money to go back there," Sandor said. "Those tenements and factories were miserable places.
Bet you a nickel they're miserable still."

"But they gave you a start, yes?"

"What they gave is a kick in the *tuchis*. I'm a happy man now
that I landed here, but let's face it, I'm not doing such good
business that another little kick in the *tuchis* can't come my way
again. Or maybe in my *kishkas* I'll get it." He waved his fork
loosely over the table. "Then I'll really go flying."

"Sandor." Lili reached for her glass of seltzer. "The children."

"What, it's a big secret the economy's no good? I should pretend I don't know it, too? I'm in insurance. I have to look right
inside the lion's mouth." He raised his eyebrows. "I'm supposed
to look after it's eaten."

Evan laughed and glanced over to Vera; her body was angled
away from him. "Remember Morris Grosz?" he said. "I also ran
into him. Now he owns a place in Brooklyn. A triple decker, he
says, with everyone in the family together. His parents live
upstairs with his sister's family, and his brother and his children
live down. He's in the middle."

"Eh, Morris Grosz in the middle, what's new about that?"
Sandor popped a piece of brisket in his mouth. "The man could
move anywhere he wanted—anywhere!—the mountains, the
desert, could come to Cleveland and be with us, even. And
where does he go when he finally gets his money saved from
working for years in that *farshtinkener* sweatshop? Over the
bridge to Brooklyn."

"People like what they already know," said Lili. "That's not so unusual."

"True, it's why I like you, sweetheart."

"Excuse me," said Hankus, trying to force his way in. "But what did you do in the factories in New York, Mr. Belak?"

"You're curious? I thought you're supposed to be a wise guy; I'm not right? Master Theo is the one with the answers, so we're hoping for a big scholar. And the little girl will be pretty one day, I'm sure. But maybe I'm wrong about everyone. How old are you, *boychik?*"

Hankus shifted in his seat; he put down his fork and knife, crossing them. "Thirteen."

"That's right. I should have known because I heard you read your Torah portion for your bar mitzvah last summer. What a warm, warm day that was. Well, you did very nicely." His gaze flickered over to Vera, asking should he go on with the subject as Hankus wanted, or just drop it.

She and Evan didn't like to mention those years around the little ones very much. They wanted the children to be hopeful, not always to be imagining the struggles that were gone. Sweatshops, ugliness. Breathing in, Vera suddenly smelled not the rich broth of oniony gravy and brisket, but cotton dust flying up from the frames of the hot, oily looms. All over again she could feel a sticky pelt covering her fingers, arms, and neck, her face; could taste the lint clotting gritty and dry in her mouth; eyes watering, couldn't blink the fibers away from her short lashes. One day it'd gotten so bad, she'd hurried out of the factory on lunch break and was startled to see small pieces of herself peeling away in the wind. Gray flakes. Her skin; but not. Just more of the debris that had to be carried off by the gusts that slowly shook themselves out above the misty waves of the East River.

She'd been a greenhorn back then, one of the stream of girls who worked with nimble fingers and a closed mouth, who was dead determined to accomplish all she'd set out to do. She had a life to start with Evan; his earnings they saved for their own business; hers was to pay the daily costs and to wire to their families back home. She stored this money in a red-stamped tin canister that had originally held brown leaves of tea. Every time she lifted out the folded bills, they smelled rich. When at the end of the month she wired a sum home to Szacsur for her mother and the girls, so they could eat, Vera imagined her mother's darkly beautiful, intelligent face in the steam, the kettle wrapped in a white tea towel and still pouring, her sisters talking and laughing, grazing hands at times as they passed the cups (as she herself remembered doing when she too had her place), a clear bowl of sugar on the center of the lace doily. She'd been the mischievous one in that family. The joker, you could say, and much loved. When she told them she would leave and go with her Evan to America, what moaning and sadness arose from that circle. In the beginning, she carried that strong emptiness in herself. It was no joke.

Look, she was also no dummy. She knew the bills her mother and sisters received on their end of the wire were not the same ones she'd brought to the bank here. But when she opened the tea canister and the rich scent drifted out with the cash, that's how it seemed. Throughout those first years, working at the factory in the day, or drifting off curled next to Evan at night, she took this secret pleasure, thinking how her money warmed Mother, Irina, Rose, Etel, Margret, and Sara, and brought them all together, laughing, at the one table.

Sticking her fork into a small piece of brisket, she nodded at Sandor. "Fine," she said. "A little bit tell him."

"Okay." Sandor slowly leaned back, resettled his weight on the chair. "Well, so I was fifteen; and I was six and a half days a week working in a tannery. See, I had this skill my father taught to me back in the old country. It paid better than some other jobs. Only in dying animal hides, you'd also get your own skin dyed, too—blue, black, sometimes brown, all the way up past your elbows. And the stink with it—*feh!* But I saved from my pay, a little here, a little there, because I was living with my cousins. We would sleep the three of us in one cot." He slid the index finger of his left hand between the second and third fingers of his right. "Look here, Hankus. Here's how we slept, head to foot. One in one direction, two in the other."

"All of you were squeezed together in that space?"

"On one cot?" asked Teddy, not to be outdone in the interest department. "Not on a bed?"

Sandor nodded.

"That sounds like fun."

"No, it doesn't," Hankus said, irritated. "He didn't do it because he wanted to."

"You're right, *boychik*," said Sandor, "it wasn't fun, not one bit. My cousins didn't like it much either. Don't try it; I don't recommend it."

Joy looked up, a little piece of potato on her cheek. "We don't have any cousins, Mr. Belak. You don't have to worry, because we can't try it."

"What are you saying, Joy?" Vera snapped. "Of course you have cousins." She slapped her hand down on the table. "I tell you about them, don't I? Don't I read to you from the letters? You think they're only made-up stories?"

Joy froze.

"You have six—no, *eight* cousins, you don't know that? You think you have no family, *meshugge*? Eight little cousins you have. And just on my side. Am I talking only to myself about them? My own daughter doesn't listen if I try to tell her?"

"Vera, *sha*," murmured Evan. He picked up the salt and shook some onto his cooked green beans. "Long day," he said.

Teddy, glancing at Mr. Belak, said, "I know all our relatives live over in Europe."

"Listen, Joysie," Hankus whispered, "they're in Szacsur. Sound familiar? Szacsur?" The way he said it soothed her; it sounded like her own secret password.

"Okay," she mumbled, "I remember."

"Nagymihály is where your father's from," Sandor put in, heartily instructive. "Me, too. It was some place, all right, it lacked for"—he raised his brows—"eh, what *didn't* it lack for? But lots of good people are still there, in Nagymihály."

Evan said, "Mommy is frazzled, because all week long she was taking care of everything without me. I don't even know yet all she had to do. She's tired is all; she didn't mean to shout at you, Joysie."

Vera pushed up from her chair and leaned over the table. "Look at all this brisket. Who needs more? Or potatoes?"

Joy's voice caught. "Mommy? I didn't mean it. I wasn't paying attention. I remember everything now."

"Don't say that," Vera groaned. "It's not right." Ashamed, she made herself look at her girl to see the small face red and frightened by having disappointed her. But she knew the truth: she was the one who'd disappointed. One day Joy would be old enough to see how it had gotten mixed up, all that was inadequately exchanged between them; she would be able to sort things out, as they should be. This thought stung her the more, and deepened her embarrassment.

"All done," she said carefully. "Everything okay." And paused. "You want more potatoes, darling?"

"No, thank you," the girl's voice lightening with relief at hearing the change in her mother's tone. "I have enough."

"Well, good. Eat up what you have, then."

Lili cleared her throat. "May I have something, Vera? I really shouldn't have another bite, but the meat's so moist, I can't resist one more little piece."

"See what she's like? My Lili always waits until it appears she's doing someone else a favor to ask for her seconds." Sandor reached over to pat his wife's hand. "If it looks like something is only for her, well, she doesn't do it. To her mind it's not right unless it's for someone else's benefit."

Flashing a toothy grin, Lili said, "It's true! I do that."

"She gets everything she wants this way, especially from me."

Evan let out a breath. "Everything she gets that way from you, Sandor?"

"You sure you want to know about this, eh?"

"About the everything? Sure, sure."

With the serving fork, Vera poked a piece of brisket and laid the thick brown strip across Lili's plate. She was already starting to smile.

"Well," said Sandor, lowering his voice. "It's true. All her seconds—that kind, too. Of course you know she asks me then only for *my* benefit."

"Why are they all laughing again?" Joy whispered across the table.

"One thing," said Vera, getting into bed, "I want to do tomorrow."

"Yes?" Evan tugged the sheet over her shoulder, bare save for the strap of her nightgown. There was a white fleck of tooth powder dried on her chin. He put his finger to it, wiped it off.

"Tomorrow's Sunday, so no store to open. I want to drive out to the country and have a picnic with the children. Too soon it'll be cold."

"Okay, we'll do it." He got up on his elbow. "One thing I also want to do. But I want to do it right now."

"Oh?"

"I want to see the application you got for Solly. Is it different from Irina's?"

"The same."

"So let's see it." After the Belaks had left, he heard about the mix-up with her sister's application. Accounts out of order, it unsettled him. Or maybe he was just overtired from traveling, from worrying about Vera's anger, from joking with guests all night, from playing those games of five hundred rummy. He wasn't a drinker, but he and Sandor had each had a shot of peppermint schnapps after the fourth hand—there was that in him, too.

Holding a sheaf of papers, Vera got back under the covers. When he reached for them, she held them away. "No, *tateleh.*" She shook her head. "This is your bedtime story. I'll read it to you." She flipped the top page of the pile. "Just one section I'll read. That's enough for tonight. So, this first one is called 'Information and Instructions for Preparing Affidavits.'"

He wedged his pillow against the headboard. "I knew Sandor would agree to make an affidavit swearing that Solly's my brother, that he knew my family in Nagymihály. I bet Oppenheim will do it, too. He wrote for Irina, didn't he? We need more. Who else can we get?"

"You want to hear this now, Evan, or you want to talk?"

He waved a hand.

She read, "'Persons filling out affidavits on behalf of prospective immigrants must submit up-to-date proof of their financial assets in *duplicate*. This proof should consist of the following:

"'One. A letter from employer indicating length of employment and average weekly wage. If in business, a certified public accountant's statement indicating worth of business, and income from same.

"'Two. List of U.S. bonds and notes indicating numbers and maturity value, duly notarized.'"

"Maybe we should save to buy some," he said. "What do you think?"

Shrugging, she read, "'Three. Letter from banks indicating savings, etcetera.

"'Four. Copy of latest income tax return.

"'Five. Cash surrender value of insurance policies.'" She paused and looked over at him. "Why do they need to know that?"

"Just go on." He wasn't drowsy yet from this story; instead it was making him anxious all over.

"'Citizens sending for wives, minor children, husbands, and parents must also file Form I-one thirty-three in *duplicate,* which requires two American citizens as witnesses.'" She scanned the page. "'Further, affidavit forms have to be made in *four copies,* all duly notarized, answering all information required therein.

"'A memorandum setting forth the nature of the corrob—'" she hesitated, "'the corrobor—corroborative financial evidence to accompany these affidavits, to be obtained in *duplicate*.'"

He said, "Duplicate, again! Irina's paperwork took me so long. I made a mistake and everything stopped. And if the carbon paper slipped or tore, something else was a mess. It's not good for me to use more than two pieces of paper at once in our machine. Maybe we should ask the Schneider girl to come in this time; she's trained in typing."

Vera paused. "Maybe, Evan.

"'After completing the affidavit,'" she read, "'all copies duly notarized, kindly forward the original and duplicate together with the supporting financial statements, in *duplicate,* directly to your relative or friend abroad for presentation to the American Consul.

"'In addition,'" her voice wavered, "'in addition, send this agency a copy of the affidavit, so that we may communicate with our European office for purposes of assisting in obtaining a visa for your relative or friend—'" she stopped. "Huh. That's where we can get in trouble with Irina. Affidavits last for six months only. If the paperwork isn't completed, or the visa doesn't come through, we have to get new ones from everyone, all over again. You think Sandor will do it twice for Irina?"

"Go *on,* Vera," said Evan.

"'—and also so that we may assist in arranging transportation as soon as such becomes the case.'" She stopped. "End of the bedtime story. Bottom of the page."

"And we have all the other forms we need to fill out? Nothing is missing this time?"

"Nothing was missing last time. It was a mistake in the sending, that's all. All the papers for Solly"—Vera showed him the forms drooping over her wrist—"are right here." She put the sheaf back on top of her nightstand. Two pages fell under the bed. She'd have to remember to get them in the morning.

"So," he said, "we know how it will go."

She bit her tongue from replying: *What do we know?*

Sighing, Evan reached out and turned off the white-shaded lamp. Night snapped to the walls. They kissed quickly and settled into the darkness.

Rolling Hills

It was the sunny side he always told them to look for. It was the sunny side not of just the street, like in the song, but of the whole golden field. An almost Indian-summer day. The air was a melody of wings and scent, and the haze in it was made up of small life—bits you couldn't see unless you squinted very hard: seeds that might one day be trees, pollen drifting away from the centers of flowers, insects too busy tipping the last grasses to sting. And that sky! Everything about its horizon was blue, blue, blue.

Making their way through the field, each of the Eichenbaums carried something useful. Evan had the wicker basket usually used to tote laundry, now filled with the food, knives, forks, glasses, and plates; Vera carried the jug—water and cider—mixed; Hankus had the big navy wool blanket rolled under his arm; Teddy, sweaters if it got cold; Joy, a paper bag with cloth napkins and the dessert spoons. In addition, they were bringing the things that might give them pleasure, that would more simply *pass the time,* would let them *while away the day,* would allow them to *daydream,* would help them *enjoy, enjoy.* Among them they had a shoe box of photographs, a magazine, paper and crayons, a baseball and bat. They were climbing to the top of the second of three small rolling hills.

Halfway to the top, where the ground was dry and the grasses neither too long nor too prickly, Vera stopped. Her little ones had begun sagging under the endless ten-minute responsibility of carrying their loads. Evan, who had been warning "Don't run! Don't run!" from way back by the roadway fence, was panting. His face was red, and a trickle of sweat inched down from his temple to his jaw. What was supposed to be a grin looked to her more like a wince. She saw now she shouldn't have packed the potato salad in the glass bowl; she should have kept things lighter. She should have used a tin. Or left it out altogether. Or carried it herself.

"Here," she proclaimed. "All done."

"This is our spot?" Teddy said dubiously at her side. "Where the grass is brown and dead?"

"This is it."

"Hankus," he shouted ahead, "too far!" He turned, "Mom, tell him."

"Let him go. Why shouldn't he run a little, if he wants?" She was busy. She wasn't watching her eldest child disappear, as he would in her dreams in the countless years after, over a bare hill that kept rising. "This is a good place. Everything sits flat." She set down the water jug.

Joy came running up. "Here, Mommy," she shouted, just as the bottom of the paper bag in her arms gave way. In one bright, noisy gush, spoons, bouncing end over end, disappeared into the weeds.

Teddy groaned. "Why did you do that?"

"I didn't mean it, I didn't. I was helping."

Walking back down the hill, Vera just laughed. She was wearing loose slacks and a blowsy smocked peasant blouse, and comfortably she knelt down. "Why cry? You know how you can fix something like this?"

Sniffling, Joy looked at her.

"Don't you have napkins? You take a napkin out of the broken bag, and when you find a spoon that fell, you just give it a good wipe. See? A good wipe and it's not dirty. No more mistake."

"Watch out below!" Hankus shouted. He was waving to them from above, swaying a little, balancing both feet on the bald pate of a smallish rock. "I'm taking off."

"Don't crash into us," Teddy yelled.

Hankus leapt, holding the blanket so it would unfurl above and behind him. The wool's weight was just enough; the heavy dark fabric streamed backward, slapping furiously at the ground he'd just passed. "I can't stop! I'm flying."

"Stop!" screamed Joy and Teddy, both shivering with delight. "Hankus, stop. *Stop!*"

Evan watched his eldest child sail past. With a grunt, he set down the wicker basket. "What do you say, everyone? Ready to eat?" He stood again, licking the sweat from his upper lip.

"And this," said Vera, picking another photograph from the shoe box, "is also someone very special. See your Aunt Irina?" The children didn't know anything about Irina's trying to immigrate. It wasn't time yet.

Teddy pushed up the wire glasses sliding down the bridge of

his nose. He squinted at the image in his mother's hand. "She's tall."

"Think so?" Vera looked at him. Hankus, sitting cross-legged, was still studying the last picture she'd passed around: a portrait of Irina's two little ones, Lily and Miriam; the photograph was fairly recent. The girls, sweet-faced, were dressed in peasant skirts; they held their arms overhead and had their toes pointed. They were probably dancing, Vera'd said, on some kind of town holiday. Irina was a good dancer, light on her feet and willing at the pull of a bow against strings to smile and sway, so why not her little girls, too? Hankus's hair fell over his forehead so she couldn't see what details he kept studying so hard; he was so absorbed. Probably he was looking for a connection between their faces and his. He would be disappointed; with cousins there wasn't always something visible in the way of family resemblance.

"I think Aunt's tall, too, Mommy." Joy leaned in from the other side, not quite touching her.

"Let me see again," said Vera. In the decade-old photograph, a twenty-year-old Irina, oval-faced and thin-framed, leaned against a cherry tree, its shadows falling like a shawl over her shoulders. It looked like a pretty day in Kassa, the town where Irina and Andras had moved as soon as they were married. There was a corner of their house visible beyond the tree. Vera had never seen any more of the structure than this one sun-bleached stucco section—and then only in photographs; it seemed to be where the Osvat family stood for photos. From under the fruit-laden tree, Irina stared quite openly back at her, her closest sister—and yet the only one of the sisters Vera hadn't seen married because by then she was long in America with Evan. Irina's chin was lifted and her lips were parted, almost pursed in a kiss—perhaps she was in the middle of saying something: "Not this close!" or "Not yet!" or, most doubtfully for a young woman who had a camera pointed at her, "I'm ready." Her hands held her pleated print skirt down against her thighs. You could just see the wedding band on her finger as the skirt blew up to one side. So, there had been a breeze that day.

Vera said, "My sister is not as tall as Daddy. He's not a very tall man." She glanced over at Evan, asleep a few feet away with a *Fortune* magazine shading his face. A customer had given it to him, and he'd brought it home. While the children were flinging a paper airplane into the air and chasing after it, careening in nearly as many loop-de-loops on the ground as the airplane made, higher up, Evan had read her a new national survey. He had read a little too quietly, given the children's shouts, but she'd heard him nonetheless: more than a third of those asked said that Nazi policies against the Jews didn't matter at all; 15 percent said these policies were good—a benefit for Germany. Evan had glanced over at the children, who were jumping with arms straight up in the air; they were yelling at the toy riding the breezes: *Lindy, land here! Hey, Lucky Lindy, we're down here!* He'd commented, "Well, at least half of them does think it's wrong, what's happening over there." He paused as the children's shouts for the aviator got louder. He'd heard how Lindbergh had begun to make comments in some of his speeches, praising the Nazi government. Evan couldn't understand how he could do that. Lindbergh was his hero too, as an American.

"Daddy's not tall for a man," said Teddy, uncrossing his legs. "But Irina is tall because she's a lady."

"Aunt Irina," Vera corrected him. "For respect, you don't call her only by her name."

Hankus laid Lily and Miriam's photo on the center of the blanket, uneven from the clumps of grass bent underneath, and gazed at it as it slid a bit. "Where's their father?"

Ignoring him, Vera gave Irina's photograph to Joy. "Don't bend the edges." Again she glanced over to Evan; he was snoring. The air was still.

"Where is he, Ma, their father?"

"He died, Hankus."

"Did he die a long time ago?"

"Not very." She kept her voice short. He'd asked Sandor last night about the factories, and now he was asking about this. Too grim for the boy. She didn't want to encourage anything further.

She should sift through the photos in the box, find something else to distract him.

But he lifted his chin, being stubborn with it. "Why did he die?"

"Hankus, he went away to work. When he was away, you know, he got sick."

Teddy of course picked up on it now. "What did he work at?"

"Well. Well, he was good with his hands." Gingerly she took Irina's picture from Joy and placed it next to the image of the two girls. A fly landed nearby; she shooed it away. "He fixed things. See, he was someone who liked fixing things, making them work right."

"Like automobile engines?" asked Teddy.

"Maybe."

"The old country has cars?" Joy said, incredulous.

Vera smiled. This was better. "Some people have cars—people in the city, sometimes in the towns. They're modern over there too, Joy." For a second time she waved off the insect. Fat and slow, made drowsy with the end of the season, the fly rumbled away from her hand. "See, to us it's the old country, but not to them. Because they live there, it's not old, it's only where they have always each day lived. Home."

"Why didn't Uncle just stay at home and work there?"

"That's enough, Hankus. You don't need to learn always the answer about everything."

"But I think maybe he wouldn't have gotten sick then," he said. "Because, really, it's sad about Lily and Miriam. They don't have him with them anymore. So I was just wondering why he didn't just work near home."

"Yes. Well, see, sometimes you have to go away. You get sent by someone else."

"A boss," said Teddy.

"That's right."

"Daddy had to go to New York City for work," said Joy. "But he didn't get sick, did he?"

Vera held her tongue. "What happens here is different."

"Why is it different, Mommy?"

She sat back. "Let's talk about something else. Let me find a picture of someone from Daddy's side of the family to show you, all right? Somewhere is a picture of his youngest brother."

"Dad has older brothers too," Teddy put in.

"He has both, yes, older and younger. But I want you to see a picture of his youngest brother. He's a boy—well, he's a man now, I suppose. He's another uncle you have. I want you to tell me about him. Tell me what you see in his face."

"You mean if he looks like Daddy?" asked Teddy. "Or if he looks goofy?"

"Uncle wouldn't look goofy," Joy said, very solemn. She had to pay close attention; last night her mother thought she didn't know anything about the family. And that town that sounded like a secret, she had to remember it too; that's where their relatives still were.

"All right." Laying down the photograph of a young man, Vera said lightly, "So, between Aunt Irina and Uncle Solly, who would you like to live with?"

"Why, Ma?" Hankus tilted his head up from the girls' photo. "How come you want to know that?" The tips of his sandy hair lifted in the breeze.

"Oh, it's just a game, like a contest."

"Why?"

"Don't be like that, a question with a question. There's nothing wrong with what I asked. It's only a little game." But she hurriedly slipped the photograph back in the box.

Joy squealed, "A baby!" She held up a print of a little boy in a velvet suit, clutching a ball. Although the photo wasn't hand-tinted, the child's cheeks seemed to hold a pink blush, and his smile was impish and unforced.

Quickly Vera turned the image over. She saw her sister Margret's spiky handwriting on the back and laughed in sudden recognition. "It's your cousin Emek, from when he was two years old; the date is 1928, see? On his birthday. I could eat him right up, just look how sturdy his little legs are!"

"I'm older, right? Emek isn't even ten now." Teddy took the

print. He held himself over the image as he would over a text-book, back rigid, head slightly bent, not a muscle moving, study-ing his cousin with all his might. In that pause, Vera flushed with embarrassment for what she'd just asked from her children. And she'd done it to Solly, who also was trusting of her, who couldn't even suspect she might be as small and selfish as she just acted.

Teddy flipped the square over. "But I can't read one word of this writing. This says it's our cousin Emek's birthday and he's two? Is that what it says?"

"Yes. My dear older sister Margret wrote it." Vera paused. "When we were girls, she helped me get good at sewing. We laughed the whole time! If I close my eyes, I can still see us embroidering that tablecloth. See, your Aunt Margret is very nice, besides being smart. You'd like her, she knows lots of sto-ries."

"Wait, we have an Aunt Margret, too?" Joy said, looking scared at how the list of their family kept growing.

Vera nodded. "Yes. Margret."

"You know, Ma, about Uncle Andras?"

"Okay," she said. "Enough, Hankus. No one can change what already happened."

"I'm sorry about him." Her eldest child looked her full in the eyes.

Close-lipped, she shook her head. And *still* he held his gaze steady.

"Ma?" He was staring at her as if it was a fresh loss.

"Thank you," she said, and right then understood how she had just accepted, in the middle of a picnic, a condolence. Vera turned her face away from the boy; she'd felt it, it hurt terribly. It just hurt.

Later, a cold wind sprang up. As the sun left the field a chilled gray, no longer gold, they packed themselves into the car. Soon the children were drowsing in the backseat of the automobile, too tired even to glance at what scenes rolled past their windows. That's when she whispered to Evan that she'd almost told Han-kus the truth about what happened to Andras. How Andras was pulled off the street and arrested one afternoon after teaching his biology class at the *gymnasium* and that he was right away sent off to some prison; that there he died after not even two and a half weeks; that against Jewish burial custom his body had been cremated immediately by the prison authorities and so who knows how or why he died, let alone why he'd been arrested. And that was that. That her sister Irina was heartbroken and close-lipped and stubborn, and that she wanted to bring her darling little girls to America where they'd be safe, that, too, Vera almost told Hankus. That he might get to stare at his cousins' faces for real to see what he could see. That they might dance, the two girls, one day in the front room to the music on the radio or to a record on the Victrola. That he might one day hear their heels clicking, their laughter rising. That he might teach them good English. That they might have a very full house for a while, what with Uncle Sol too, if his application—oh, her relief at this!—they'd sent in, finally. That one day when Irina and her girls and Solly were ready, they might leave them. That they might then go live wherever they wanted; that she hoped they would choose to stay in the neighborhood, their own neighborhood.

"But you didn't tell," said Evan, under his breath, eyes on the road ahead. No streetlights, so far out in the country, so far away from the city. No traffic light at this point where the hills they'd picnicked on were still now and then visible as wavering smudges in the rearview mirror. Ahead the sky was gray, streaked with the last orange beams from the sunset. They were driving west, to two-six-oh-two, in the round-backed black Chevrolet—a Chevy, not a Ford, because in every newspaper he could, that bastard Henry Ford had said Jews murdered Christian children in secret religious blood rituals. Now, along both sides of the road, the land lay open. The few gauges in the Chevrolet's black dashboard were unlit, and so early in the twilight, headlights wouldn't make much of a difference, although Evan had switched them on after he'd started the engine. The Eichenbaum family would be home in about forty-five minutes.

"Did you tell," Evan repeated, "about Andras?"

She said, no, of course not. She couldn't tell her child that. She could hardly bear to think about it herself, so how could he? What could he do with it?

Two-six-oh-two East Trainor

The little girl looked back at the house but saw no one framed in the doorway or windows. She'd thought she heard someone calling out to her very faintly: "Joy!" But it must have been a stranger's young, faraway voice, because she hadn't immediately thought: *Oh, Hankus!* or *Teddy, oh!* A glance at the Kleinmans' house next door showed the same silent stillness: only glassy windows, a closed front entry. And no one.

Joy was wide awake and excited by how she'd gotten herself up and out as she had. She'd told herself she could wake at the sun's rise, and she'd done it. Quickly she'd pulled on her clothes and sneaked down the stairs. She was propelled by a strong desire she couldn't explain: she had to say good-bye to her father. He was taking the train to meet someone, a man in Akron who wouldn't come to the store with his samples—that's what she'd overheard. But Joy saw how empty East Trainor Road was, how there was only the puff of her own breath in the chilled air. She hadn't been quick enough. She'd missed him. This time, she couldn't kiss her father good-bye. She shivered, standing out on the porch, alone.

Still, it wouldn't be long until Joy would forget everything about this first of her many efforts to bid farewell to someone she loved; forget the way the night's shadows pulled back from the trimmed bushes and pavement and dragged along the house walls to cede back to new cold light the familiar street on which she was born; forget too that she'd come outside at all for this good-bye; forget herself ever being this young. It happens to most children, this infant amnesia, where nearly all the babyish activity up until age six or so, they just somehow forget. Memory begins for most then, all over again. In a way, they enter a new life; move freshly into their next sense of themselves; and keep moving forward.

Quickly running down the steps and into the yard, her heart pounding, Joy whispered, "Daddy?" She pushed back the long brown curls from her face. Cupping her hands about her mouth, she called again, even more quietly.

All at once, snowflakes swirled down. Tiny gifts, given early and unexpected. With a turnabout skip, Joy stuck out her tongue to catch one. She was giving her tongue an airing, that's what she'd say if anyone saw her. Excited, she ran after the flakes, or she stood in place waiting, or she hopped, or dipped from her knees. A lacy gust spun about her. Then one flake landed, cold-hot, the tiniest pinprick of a nearly nothing, and melted wetly on her tongue's tip. When she looked up, the sporadic white swirl through the lindens' yellow leaves was dizzying.

Slowly, ungloved hands out at her sides for balance, Joy started spinning in her own circle. On the pudgy cheeks, the rounded chin, the long dark eyelashes, the not-yet-refined features, cold silent kisses.

"Hey, you! Little Eichenbaum!"

Joy stumbled, a hand and knee going down on the flecked grass. She peered through the branches of the evergreen bordering their front walk.

The newsboy stood there, his palm slapping the blue bulging cloth bag hanging off his shoulder. "What are you doing out so early?"

"I'm giving my—" she said, biting her lip. "It's not early. I was just walking." Slowly she got up and came around the side to face him.

"Hey, are you crying?" Marky Rivchin said. "Is something wrong?"

With the back of her hand, Joy wiped her wet cheeks. "It's only snowflakes."

He flushed; his ears pinkened. "Uh huh. Well, sweat too much in cold weather and you can overheat. What about polio?" Then he glanced over to the front porch and said, "Better duck."

"What? What, Marky?"

With a windmill windup, he heaved the morning edition, rolled tight and wingless, just over her head. Then he walked away with his own head down, as if releasing that single paper hadn't lightened his load at all. For a moment it looked like he was about to turn and wave at her from over his shoulder, but instead he dug into the bag and drew out another paper.

"I'm not Little Eichenbaum," she screamed after him. "I'm Joy, *Joy*. Little's not my name."

Despite herself, Vera burst into a laugh as she opened the screen door. "Why are you yelling at that nice boy? He gets yelled at plenty already at home, I'll bet." She stopped, shook her head. "And who said you could go outside by yourself? Wearing only a sweater, no coat."

"I wanted to tell Daddy good-bye."

"You can't. He's gone already." It wasn't even six o'clock yet; Vera kept her voice low. Not everyone had to be awake at such an hour. Across the street an upstairs light was on in the Arnofskys' house—and two lights on, too, in the keep-away-from-us-if-you-please old Richardson sisters' place. Beyond these isolated brilliants, nothing but a long sleepy dimness filled the neighbors' windows.

"It's so quiet," Joy whispered, rapt.

Caught herself by the chill and hush, Vera nodded.

Windlessly flakes spilled out from the clouds. The sky was the gray of Evan's fedora, and the sky covered everything. In this stillness the footfall of a forty-eight-pound child coming up the front walk sounded loud. But the *whomp!* of a newspaper against a neighbor's front door seemed like a muffled bomb. At another time she might have not heard it in just this way; but this morning she awoke to Evan half-sitting on his side of their bed, dressing hurriedly in the cold dark. To see him rushing like that, without a glimmer of light on, it hurt her somehow. He shook out a long black sock. *Careful,* she'd murmured, using what was his phrase for love. Drawing her arm from beneath the covers, she touched the curve of his back; ice-cold from the air was how the cloth undershirt felt.

Whispering because of the children, he'd said, pulling the sock over his foot, *Why are you worried? If I don't like the man's samples, so I won't buy the line.*

"Mommy, can I stay out here longer?" Joy asked, eyes on her. "Please?"

Suddenly the hall window opened upstairs, and Hankus's voice sailed down, "Hey, Joysie!"

Before Vera could say anything, her daughter was running backward, away from the porch and into the middle of the yard, her bare, cold-reddened legs snapping back and forth quick as scissors. Grinning hugely, chin lifted, she stopped and waved up to the second story. "I see you up there. Hi, Hankus, hi."

"What are you doing? Hey, are you eating snow for breakfast? I'm coming down, Joysie. You beat me again."

"This is crazy," crowed Teddy. "Let's go eat snow!"

In a voice just loud enough to carry up the stairway, Vera called, "You boys listen! You stay inside and get yourselves ready for school." Then: "Joy, I have to go early to open the store, get to work. Don't make me wait longer for you."

Another thud, up the street—fainter. Vera bent over and picked up their own paper from the porch floorboards. There would be no time to read it, not even to glance at the ads. Shivering, she said, "Come in with me, this moment."

The little girl stood stock-still on the step. "I hear Daddy's train whistle now, Mommy."

"You can't hear that. He's too far away."

Snow! Hankus and Teddy were singing inside, their voices strung high with excitement, *snow, snow, snow!*

Corner of Salisbury

The boys decided at the last minute to take Salisbury Street. Joy had left earlier and was already walking on Davis, as usual. Salisbury was the shorter route to school, but they rarely used it. Maybe it had something to do with what happened every December, how each house on the block displayed a Christmas tree and decorated many of the live bushes out in the yard. No one ever discussed it; Salisbury was fine, of course. But when that morning a snowball streaked from out of nowhere and flew right over their heads, Teddy shot Hankus a true-blue look and whispered, "Les run."

"Not me." Hankus bent and retied his shoe.

"But we shodn stop here. We shod—"

Irritably, Hankus straightened up. "Take that out of your mouth, will you?"

Teddy spit the jawbreaker into his hand. "Let's do what Dad and Mom always say, okay? Hurry away and don't look around."

Shifting his books, Hankus set off, but walking. Teddy lurched after him, sneaking a glance downward at the wet candy in his palm. Although the green layer was nearly sucked off and the purple one was next, the orb still looked the size of a golf ball. Hankus's jawbreaker was already down to marble size—the pink layer. It was that small bump in Hank's side pocket; he'd wrapped it up in tinfoil. But Teddy didn't want to stop to get out his own tinfoil now.

A second snowball slammed onto the brick sidewalk with such force, it bounced up again. Hankus muttered, "Stone inside, Teddy." Without turning about, he yelled, "Hey, no aim!"

"Stop," Teddy hissed. "Be above fighting. Dad says."

"You want better aim, kikes?"

"Whose voice? Can you tell?" Hankus stepped over the shattered, stone-centered snowball without breaking stride.

Teddy was trying to keep up, but his legs were shorter. "How would I know? But they must have been waiting back near the rhododendron bush."

Hankus laughed. "Rhododendron? You're amazing sometimes, you know?"

"You think so? Really? Because I knew the plant's name?"

"Quiet. Listen."

Both boys strained. They were four houses from the end of the block. If they got to the corner, they'd be on Lee and heading to its commercial center. Chances were they wouldn't get pounded on Lee, not with adults out and about. And not with so many of the glass-doored shops being owned by Jews.

Teddy heard footsteps—felt them, actually. "Let's run. I don't want to fight. Dad and Mom say—" Just then something sharp smacked against his temple. With a cry, he leaped back. Caught for a second, the black fountain pen rolled slowly from the wire sidebar of his glasses. The brassy metal nib, lined up from its tip with a vein of blue ink, was uncapped.

Hankus shouted: "What are you doing?" Whipping about, he saw two blond, beef-shouldered boys with innocent round faces. They had to be in at least the tenth grade. The shorter one broke into an angelic smile and stopped right where he was. From this distance his smile looked perfect, square and white. It struck Hankus that the boy looked exactly, but exactly, how he pictured Jack Armstrong. It flustered him, to see how a pale shadow stretched from the boy's boots now. He'd heard him, hadn't he, walk a thousand times across the front room, heard him open the big door? He'd heard his voice! Heard not only his jokes, but everything—the most private thoughts, his quickly whispered plans and prayers. Maybe he hadn't thrown the pen. He couldn't have done it. Then Jack's buddy pursed his lips as if for a kiss, and aimed it right at him. The gob of spit fell short, sinking into the slush on the pavement. That's when Hankus started toward them. But the very moment he took his first step, fists clenched, the two boys started whooping: "He throws like a girl! Look at that girl!"

Hankus wrenched around and saw Teddy. Squinting in fear, Taffy Teddy had drawn his arm back, but the jawbreaker was stuck to his palm. So he stopped the throw from his elbow, not only once but—and this was awful, Hankus saw it, too—*twice*. And he'd let his wrist fall forward, like a girl would. Probably so the sweet would dribble into his fingers. If it was just going to land on the sidewalk and not hit its target, then he didn't want to lose it entirely. Greedy. But what was Taffy thinking of, trying to throw candy? And with his eyes almost shut?

The high school boys were hysterical with laughter. "Kid. Hey, Yid kid," Jack called, his grin gorgeously full of light. "Your pal is a girl." The two high school boys turned then. They sauntered away, hands in their pockets. Across the back of their blue wool jackets were the yellow letters that spelled out the name of a school Hankus hadn't even heard of, under an arc of five yellow stars.

Teddy said in a low voice, "I knew they wouldn't follow us

past the corner. Not onto Lee." He wedged his books between his thighs, the leather bookstrap dangling, and dug his left hand into the back pocket of his knickers for the tinfoil. His right palm was smeared green and purple. In it the candy rose like a welt, a lumpish round bruise.

Hankus was quiet. He was shaking a little and didn't know what to think. Was he glad the boys were gone or not? Did he want to run after them? Did he want to pound them on their lettered backs? He wanted to kill them.

"You want the pen?" Teddy asked. He shoved the silvered jawbreaker, that sparkling miniature planet, into his pocket. He began to lick the stickiness from his fingers.

Hankus shrugged. "Might as well. They probably don't even know how to write with it."

"Probably not. Not if they're stupid enough to throw it away. Who throws away pens?"

But when Hankus bent down for it, he drew his hand back. "It's got teeth marks all the way up the shaft."

"Oh." Teddy paused. "Well, I don't want it. Germs."

"I don't want it either."

They started walking toward the corner.

"I don't know why I acted like that. I really don't throw like a girl, Hankus."

Hankus eyed the black leafless hedge bordering the yard ahead. Its meshed twigs were dotted by smooth white berries; though natural, the effect seemed decorative, like ornaments. "You don't, I know. Not like a girl."

Teddy sighed. "Nope, I throw like a Yid." He gave a quick laugh.

Hankus laughed too, a snow-cold burst, and hit Teddy on the shoulder.

Teddy looked up. "Hey. That was too hard."

Hankus hit him again in the same place. "Wise guy," he said, laughing. "Like a Yid, you say? Yiddo kiddo? A Yid can't fight?"

Teddy laughed uncertainly.

Under his fingers Hankus felt the good wool cloth of his brother's jacket. It was identical to his own, of course, because it was from their parents' store. It was long and straight, not the kind to snap at the waist, not the kind that was supposed to have yellow stars and letters stitched onto it. He dropped his hand a bit and rubbed the stiff nap, pushing his brother backward with each longer stroke.

"Hey." Teddy was still grinning. "Don't." He pushed Hankus away.

"You don't like it?" Coming forward again, a little thrilled, Hankus pinched the cloth and rubbed it. "You don't like this?" He laughed.

"This what?"

"Hmm, very goot material, dis is," said Hankus. "Da best. You don't put strain on it, it von't vear out for you for a long time. You get it, Mister Yid-Can't-Fight?"

Teddy said, straight-arming him, "Come on."

"No, Theodore, you come on. Come on, okay? Okay?" He shoved him harder. "Come on, Theodore."

Teddy said, "Oh, I get it." He gave a little laugh.

"Come on, really? You do?" Hankus shoved him again.

Teddy pushed him back. They were like bright toys set in motion, windup keys agitated in their backs. By the time they reached the corner and hurried across Lee, they were both laughing. Laughing silly and so hard that tears pricked their eyes. They paused at the fire hydrant. There, instead of gasping out their good-byes, they waved, and gave each other a last little shove of air.

Application to Sponsor

𝔘𝔫𝔦𝔱𝔢𝔡 𝔖𝔱𝔞𝔱𝔢𝔰 𝔬𝔣 𝔄𝔪𝔢𝔯𝔦𝔠𝔞

State of ___Ohio___
City of ___Cleveland___
County of ___Cuyahoga___

I, ___Evan Eichenbaum___,
age __36__, being duly sworn, depose and say:
I reside at ___2602 East Trainor Road, Cleveland, Ohio___

I am a __XXXXXXXXXX__ or Naturalized Citizen of the United States (indicate which)

as evidenced by my __XXXXXX__ Naturalization Certificate No. 108464 issued on April 14, 1928 by U.S. Circuit Court at Cleveland, Ohio.

I am married and dependent on me for support are wife and three children.
(married or single)

I am owner of Buckeye Shopping Center, located at 1623 Buckeye Road, Cleveland, Ohio and earn approximately $3,000.00 per annum.
(state fully business or occupation, location, earnings)

In addition I have assets consisting of Life insurance, cash surrender value of $10,000.00, bank savings of $6,000.
(state investments, savings, life insurance, real property, bonds, etc.)

I am the brother of Sol Eichenbaum, born September 13, 1909, Nagymihály, Czechoslovakia, whom I wish to aid in his efforts to come to the United States and join our family here. now residing at 26 Lobkowitzstr., Nagymihály, Czechoslovakia
(state relationship) (give names and ages of persons abroad)

who desire(s) to come to the United States to join me and others the family, and whom I am most anxious to bring over.

I do hereby promise and guarantee that I will receive and take care of my brother who is applying for an immigration visa, and will at no time allow him to become public charges to any community or municipality. I do further promise and agree that those of my relatives covered by this affidavit within school age will attend public school, and will not be permitted to work until they are of age.

I make this affidavit for the purpose of inducing the United States Consular authorities to grant the visa to my said relative, and herewith submit corroborative proof as to my personal standing.

Sworn to before me this 29th day of December 1935.

Harry Albert

Harry Albert_____ , notary public.

my commission expires January 15, 1939.

Evan Eichenbaum

Evan Eichenbaum_____
(signature)

The Letters

Szacsur, 12th May 1936

Dearest Sister and Ivan!

We were excited to learn that finally you have received official notification. To think that our applications for visas are now stamped as *received* in Washington! Everyone here thinks this is a very good sign. We of course understand also that the quota is full, and that we must be put at the end of the list. We have decided to be hopeful. Even Mama is hopeful for us, although as you know she doesn't like remembering that this will result in her two granddaughters leaving her. "Become invisible" she calls our emigrating, when she has to talk about it directly: "I know Miriam and Lily will behave and be good, even when they become invisible to me. I am so used to having their darling faces always in my eyes." She says this with a slow shake of her head. You remember how she does that, Verushka? How that is the way she quiets something in her?

The past weeks have been very hectic. I was told I must have three times the money I now have, in order to pay the State a fee upon our leaving. So I have taken a second job at nights as assistant to Doctor Francz, who because of the quota on those now allowed to practice medicine, has taken to working part-time and after hours. Last night he told me that Karl Leibling has emigrated and is in New York City working as a hotel porter! Can that be possible?

Karl was a dear friend of Andras's—I tell you this because now I think you were already gone before he set up his medical practice here. Well, after eleven good, happy years in Kassa, he decided to move to Prague to join his brother's practice. He left six weeks or so before Andras's arrest. Now Karl is in New York City carrying people's bags, and my Andras is gone. Life changes too much, these days.

Miriam and Lily question me all the time about their little cousins. If you can, do send fresh pictures so my girls can know their faces. The girls have such imaginations they make up stories about how strange all Americans are. Please send pictures of yourselves too. The ones I have are some few years old.

Is there more I should know about gathering all my character references and so forth? I have been tending to my financial affairs, as you advised, and will update the records every six weeks (along with the other files), since it is required. I am sick of requirements, although I am getting to be quite an expert concerning them.

Everyone in the family is fine. Margret sends her love. Did you hear of her terrible bout with pneumonia? She is very much better now. Her eldest, Emek, is talking about going to America by himself to be a "big ball player." What incredible nerve he has! He's a smart boy and makes us all laugh. He says he'll stay with the girls and me in Cleveland, and will chew tobacco and spit it on the floor, like ballplayers do. Who knows? Maybe he *will* do all this. The past couple of years have taught me how little anyone can predict about what's to come.

I hope I've made at least some sense in this letter! I'm certain I've gone on with much stuttering and stammering. I'm so different from my Verushka in this way! But please do understand me—I'm grateful to you, my family, more than I will ever be able to express.

Sending many hugs and kisses,
and much love,

Irina

———

Nagymihály, 18 February 1937

Our dear son and brother! Our dear Verushka!

Mother asks me to write for her, so I am her secretary. To make this more of a challenge for myself, I'll translate immediately her Yiddish into Hungarian. So, all then will be written to you in your old Magyar's tongue. The final translation into English, I leave to you. At least until I too am in Cleveland and study English. I promise I'll learn quickly and well. Ah, Mother is getting impatient, so I'll erase myself now. All of that which follows are Mother's words.

Dearest children!

I kiss you and my grandchildren a thousand times. I still ask you to come here and visit. I so want to talk to you, Ivan, to talk and look at your face. I want to say to you that Sol should stay in Nagymihály and be xxxxxxxxxxx. XXXXXXXXXXXXXX. (This is Solly: Mother believes I am writing her words, but they're entirely painful. So, I'm cheating her. Should I? She calls me her sweetest, the last of her darlings, her youngest, the final sweetness, the one who toddled after Artur, Imre, Oszkar, Rosa, Paula . . . Oh, on and on she goes. In front of her now I only am making my hand move. Is it wrong to deceive her this way?

To let her think I am still *darling*? But you understand, Ivan. You remember what it is to see yourself with no place to go, to get shut out in a town that is supposed to be *home*. Now it is much, much worse. The Silver Shirts have no shame. Artur says I'm too much the pessimist. I don't believe so—only what I see gives me no hope. None for myself here, and not for any of us; no hope. Not any good to come at all. No one wants to hear this. Wait. How can I do this? I'm deceiving Mother too long, pretending to record her words.)

(In truth this is Mother!). . . Here, we live our lives among our own kind. Nagymihály is a fine place for Jews, no different than always. I hear in letters from my friend Marie Belakoczi that you still aren't observing Shabbat, Ivan, the same as her Sandor. Because the Americans like it, you keep open the store on Shabbat and handle money from them. America is too much a hungry country. Can I allow it to eat the last of my sons? How are your little ones? Kiss them for me. I love them. If I could know them, if they would visit, I know I would love them with my whole heart, through and through! Kisses. Kisses. Many kisses to you, dear ones.

(This is Solly. I told Mother I would add my own words, last. Dear brother! Dear sister-in-law! I'm glad to hear from you that my application has been received by the right bureau. More than a year since we began this long process—it's gone! Don't worry, I'm collecting my affidavits; every six weeks I go beg friends for new ones. I've been to the police, too, asking each time for the records to prove I haven't engaged in criminal activity. The consul here said it's likely I won't get approved by your government for "at the very earliest" two and a half years. Do you think if I went to another country, it might speed things along? Please, would you see about this idea? What of Verushka's sister and her two girls? You say already they have been put on the wait list. Lucky for them!)

Mother sends her love, she says again. She wants of course to thank you for the money you wired her. She needs it so much—(this I am writing in, on my own). Well, when I get to America I will better you—and send her double!

Your loving brother,

Sol

P.S. What are the range of opportunities for me there? Tell me again, if only a note. That would be fine. But don't write to me here, where Mother will see it. Address

the envelope to me in care of Rosen, as before, 26 Heidel-
bergstr.

———

                          Szacsur, 11 November 1938
Dear Cousin Hankus,

   Thanking you for your letters. You are a good letter-
writer. Now write back right away again, even if only a
note. We want to know what you want from home. What shall
we bring you? Tell us immediately!! Please!!! Also, we
will bring it for Teddy and Joy. Think of something special, but small. We can't take so much to Portugal, and
then later when we get on a boat, we can bring for luggage
only a little, Mother says, unless we pay extra. But we
hope to hear before it's too late.
   Please write what you want to have from us! We are
waiting. See you soon!
   Your loving cousins,

        Miriam T. Osvat
        Lily Eva Osvat

———

            SERVIÇO DE EMIGRAÇÃO DA
        COMISSÃO PORTUGUESA DE ASSISTÊNCIA
              AOS JUDEUS REFUGIADOS

              RUA ROSA ARAUJO, 12, 1.º
                 LISBOA / PORTUGAL

AIR MAIL   16 February 1939

Copy sent by ordinary mail

                              Re: Irina Osvat,
                      Miriam Osvat, Lily Osvat

Hebrew Aid Society
10 Euclid Avenue
Cleveland, Ohio, USA

Dear Sirs:
   This will acknowledge receipt of your letter of 18 January, 1939, regarding the above-named.
   We hasten to inform you that this case has our attention and that we are assisting Mrs. Osvat and her children
in their proceedings with the American Consulate. Unfortu-

nately, Mrs. Osvat has started her proceedings here in the wrong direction, namely, she has requested a political visa, citing specifically the death of her husband by suspicious causes in a labor camp. She said that she did not know what else to try at this late stage. We have induced her, however, to make a new application, since a political visa will, we expect, set her and her children much further back in the process. Consequently she requires new affidavits made out by relatives, letters from American citizens stating that Mrs. Osvat is an honorable woman without any political aims whatsoever and having no ideas contrary to the American laws. Furthermore, in order to facilitate the proceedings, she would require a blocked account with a bank of approximately $2,500–$3,500 for her and her two dependents, payable at a rate of $100–150 per month.

If Mrs. Osvat could obtain all the foregoing, we would like to be hopeful that she would be able to get the immigration visas in due time.

Yours very truly,

Augusto Sedacca

Augusto Sedacca

Buckeye Shopping Center

Vera unlocked the metal grating over the front door of the store. Two factory workers stood back by the lamppost, waiting to be let in; they avoided looking at the somber-faced Negro who paced a few feet to their right; against his chest he held a hand-lettered sign: HUNGRY. WILL TAKE ANY JOB.

Vera began to push the grillwork overhead.

"Let me, missus." The taller of the two factory workers ambled over. "Georgie," he said, handing his lunch pail over to his pal, "do a little work, ya bum."

Out of the corner of her eye Vera saw one of the salesgirls hurrying toward her. Paulina, squinting into the glare from the snow-melt, let a truck rumble past before she waved, calling, "Mrs. Eichenbaum! I'm not late, am I?"

In reply, she smiled, shaking her head.

The main light switches were in the very rear of the large dark room. Vera didn't even pause at the entrance. Briskly she cut between the sales racks of pants and dresses that soon would be set out on the pavement in order to turn passersby into customers. At the side counter where boys' undershirts and undershorts were folded twelve to a cardboard box, she stopped to flick on a goosenecked lamp. Now anyone could see there were stacks of pants, each stack stratified like the earth into colors: gray, black, brown, blue, each pile sized and taking up somewhat more space than the one to its left; anyone could see there were cardboard boxes where each pair of argyle socks lay flat, the boomerang shape of the foot holding—as it never would again after a single wearing and washing—to a precise outline; anyone could see there were small cardboard boxes containing the folded squares of cotton handkerchiefs. Ties and bow ties, these the one circle of light didn't hit, nor did this light open on the girls', men's, women's sections beyond. But in those sections, also, everything was neatly laid out for purchase. She felt such pride, that they had so much to offer.

"One minute," she called to the silhouettes shifting inside the blazing white of the doorway, "I'll have on the lights."

Paulina said, "They're looking for work gloves."

"Well, we have very good ones. And see if that man outside wants a job clearing the front sidewalk of snow. Twenty cents, tell him."

Vera pulled the switches, and now the sun was nothing against the illumination for which she and Evan were billed by the electric company. Though she knew the men wouldn't come to the back alcove where the display rods ruffled with five different kinds of curtains for the home, she pulled on the fourth overhead, too. She had to pass through this alcove to get to the small business office.

A mouse skittered away. If she looked, she knew she'd find its droppings. Just the sound of its nails on the floorboards meant the traps long set out weren't working. Probably they'd have to set traps in their second store, too—that is, *if* Evan got the mortgage application for its purchase approved this morning. Vermin could get in anywhere. One hole missed and you had guests you freed yourself of only by killing. She hated the process: finding, enticing, trapping, disposing. But that's what you had to do to get rid of the filthy creatures.

She went into the back office. Its one window looked into the alley. There was, beside the one big desk, a makeshift kitchen area: on a card table were pots, a teakettle, some silverware, a hot plate, and in the center the typewriter. The black heavy-bodied Royal she'd partly draped with a dishcloth. She didn't like looking at it. By now Helen Schneider had come in with her thin fingers to type the same immigration-support sheets on it how many times?

"Mrs. Eichenbaum?" Paulina popped her head around the doorjamb. "Mary's in now, too. She wants to know if we can give any more credit to Mrs. Esterhaus—Esterhaus from East Eighty-sixth. She wants to buy her little girl a Communion dress and says before she starts looking, she needs to know. Because if she can't get credit, well—" Paulina shrugged.

Vera pushed back in the desk drawer containing last week's collection of bills. She stood up with a sigh. "I suppose the little girl is with her?"

It was another forty minutes before Evan came in. His cheeks were ruddy from the lake moisture sluicing into the wind; his lower lip was chapped as it often was during the long winter—bitten in the cold. The moment he entered the heated space he shivered and immediately took off his hat, pressed back his hair. There was gray in it, a silvery dullness amid the brown strands. One day it would all be silver. But not yet, not at age thirty-nine; now it was just enough of a new gleam not to be ignored. He nodded at one of the salesgirls. There were three milling customers. Enough; not a crowd, but at least something.

Evan saw Vera from the back. She was looping the strings of white price tags around the collar buttons of men's good shirts. Very deftly she worked her way along the low rack. It struck him how many times the human body bent over something as simple as a shirt, bent itself for the making and selling of one single item.

Despite how he'd hurried to get back from his meeting at the bank, he stopped now to watch. Vera's movements were quick; the weight she'd gained hadn't changed that. The phrase struck him: *grown woman.* That's what Vera had become. Faintly from the other side of the store came a brassy spurt of notes from the Philco radio. That new swing music. Only kids could dance to it.

Evan took off his navy-blue wool coat and folded it over his arm. He began walking toward his wife.

When she turned to him, she was already smiling. "A dollar forty-nine I'm marking them. So? Did we get the money for the loan?"

Evan kissed her, right on the lips, not something he did in the store or anywhere in public.

She said in a low voice, "What is it?" Dully, she moved back a step. "We didn't qualify for it, did we?" Then she drew a breath. "The bastards! Why? We aren't making enough in sales here, is that it?"

"No, no, we might get the loan." He tried to smile. "The banker might accept this store put up as collateral for the second one. He said it might be possible. Tomorrow, I'm to go in again. But—"

She touched the lapel of the coat hanging over his arm. "What? Tell me."

"But there's other news. It's not good news." His heart began beating rapidly. "Hitler went into Czechoslovakia, Vera."

She touched her hair, the tags still swinging from her fingers. She shook her head as if not understanding. "In? How *in*?"

"His army crossed the border. Hitler proclaimed a protectorate. Not just the Sudetenland now, the whole country. Miller, the banker, he told me. I was explaining how Irina and her girls' papers could be in order anytime, very soon, but meanwhile we must send money not only to her in Portugal but also to Nagymihály and Szacsur for the family there. I was asking him for more cash, extra. Above the mortgage. That's when he told me. The invasion came last night. What he meant was," Evan paused, "early morning. Only over here was it dark when the Germans crossed in."

"*Sha*—" she held up a hand. "Quiet a minute."

"You're all right, yes?"

Where are they? she was thinking. *Mother. Mother, where—where's Margret? Etel! Rose! Sara! Where are the children! Where are the husbands! And little Emek!* and then aloud said: "We got the loan? We're buying the new store?"

Wincing, he took her arm. "We need to decide now, if we should." He looked at the shelves. After so long, such a nice store. And the second one—he'd been working for the second one from the very moment he put one foot right onto America. With two places, no one could say he hadn't made it all the way over. Finally, he would be standing away from the edge.

He said: "I think we'll buy it. Janowitz agreed to the price, didn't he? If we say we need to wait a bit to see how things are going first for the family, well, he'll wait too. He won't let us slip away from him. And you know why?" he said, warming. "Because if he doesn't help us, he also loses. The banker too will help out, so he can make the loan. If he goes ahead and lowers the rate so we can borrow the extra we need, it's better for him, yes? More money in interest. It comes down to business, Vera. Everyone should help out everyone else. You want to help everyone." He looked at the rack of shirts. They would surely sell at this price. His was a good store.

"Always do you?" she asked quietly.

"Always what?" He glanced at her sidelong.

She was dry mouthed. "Do you want to help?"

"Yes," he replied sharply, almost under his breath, "of course." He took her arm in his and pressed it against his side so she wouldn't ask him anything more right now.

But she pulled away. "Evan, please." Trembling, she worked the price tags off her fingers. The last loop caught on the pronged setting of her wedding ring; finally, she was able to set them all aside in a small pile. "*Tateleh,*" she whispered hoarsely, "now let's go." She laid her hand on his arm.

From behind, where Mary and Paulina stood near the front cash register, it looked like Evan and Vera were taking a little stroll. Just a well-dressed man, a lively solid woman walking away down a wide aisle. The salesgirls grinned at each other, tickled by the unusual show of affection. Their bosses were acting as if they were in the world all by themselves. At the men's overcoat rack, the couple picked up the pace; leaning on each other, walking just slightly faster toward the back office. Yes, sweethearts—as if in the world only the two of them.

Public Classrooms

The schools made no special announcement that day, so the incursion kept its distance from the students for a while longer. Hitler already had annexed Austria, and that act also had occasioned no official break in the daily routine of the Cleveland schools. This morning what would Hankus gain by having his geometry class canceled? By forgoing the curiously sweet tension that came from his sitting next to Lesley Rubin with her slow grin and springy reddish curls, her chewing-gum-scented breath as she asked, as she almost always did, to borrow something from him? Didn't he enjoy learning that she looked to him for supplies and answers?

He was no longer the boy he had been, day after endless day in his first quick-running years. He was four-squared: sixteen— nearly seventeen; his jaw prickled with stubble, his smile was ready, his shoulders were surprising because the breadth of their bony unbookishness pleased even him. It seemed to Hankus that he was nearly worthy of his hands, worthy of their grip, and all they might one day do.

He was already playing with time, looking ahead to three-thirty, to the satisfactions and teamwork of practice; to running and sweating; the thud of a hardball snagged in his mitt, the thunk of it off his bat; the whoosh of air, the suck of his lungs; the full sit-down weight of his butt on the bench as crouched over he cheered on his buddies' heroic efforts. All around him and endless: young bodies in motion, dark churned-up dirt, a huge sky. At five o'clock would come the walk home with Harvey, Buddy, and Stu, with one boy after the other turning off; then he'd be there: standing on his own doorstep. For that split-second he'd let himself turn solitary again, let himself think about all he'd done in those hours with their straightforward demands for his mental and physical exertion. He could put that all behind him, and he could put his hand on the door of his own family's house and call out triumphantly: "I'm back, I'm home!"

But at this moment in the school day, the victor's threshold at two-six-oh-two East Trainor was still far off. Hankus had twenty-five minutes more of hypotenuse angles and proofs, then hours more of English, speech, lunch, American history, and all the rest of it.

Nor, in the junior high school, had the day's instructions been interrupted by announcements of the invasion for Teddy, sitting in row five, almost as scrawny at fourteen as he'd been at twelve. Between him and his older brother there was now too much that was different for him to even risk making comparisons. Teddy was furiously glad to have Hankus in high school and out of his sight for nine hours, so he wouldn't have to keep measuring himself. Too often he still came up short. That would change in the future; he'd make a bet on it.

But now he didn't want to think of anything besides this one moment, here. It was better for him to be off on his own. To be off, pure and separate; to be keeping away, apart. All himself, and completely independent. That way he didn't have to keep looking ahead or peering over his shoulder. Stuck, stuck, stuck. That's how Teddy felt when they were all home together, a family. Stuck between Joy the Baby and Hankus the first son; he was just *filler*.

"Psst, Ted, what'd you get for problem four, or how about five?"

Quickly he glanced back down. On his test numbers four and five were among those still left blank. "You don't know?" he whispered in clearly evident astonishment.

"Help me out."

"Don't talk. Not supposed to. Rules. Figure it out yourself."

Shaking his head at Marcus Katz, Teddy guarded the only three answers he did manage to get on the test. He bent his left arm around the sheet of notebook paper. The metal stems of his glasses cut into the tender backs of his ears.

Nor that morning were the lesson plans disturbed in elementary classroom 4-B, where at a small desk, hands folded, turning her face toward the front, Joy was waiting, with a mix of anxiety and excitement, for the teacher's eyes to light on her.

Joy was right then hearing the rudiments of long division from Miss Stepley, the fourth-grade teacher with the swanlike neck and languid gestures, the only one in the whole elementary school who (many of the girls decided) could have been a ballerina just like they themselves wanted, a fantasy that changed as they grew older to the possibilities of becoming a movie star, a nurse, a wife and mother, or finally, if need be, quietly, simply a teacher. Miss Stepley stood at the blackboard, a piece of chalk pinched between her long fingers. She was speaking to her rapt charges for the very first time completely in the language of long division. *There is a remainder now,* she was saying, her gaze sweeping closer and closer. *A two is left over. Before anything else, you have to carry the two upward again.*

It would be a good long while before Joy would begin to fathom why what had happened that night in Czechoslovakia could consume her parents' attention for years. It was such a small country; and it was divided too many times, like a blackboard problem that only starts out being simple. Even later, at the age of sixty-four, when Joy found herself waking in an alcove and staring past the sprawled exhaustion of her two grown children, both grievously silent and heads bent, next to her, she still thought of Czechoslovakia as something impenetrable and persistent, where after a certain point, despite all the care and instruction, nothing added up.

Two-six-oh-two East Trainor

"The man took my money," Vera said at the dinner table. "He said the telegrams would go."

"The one to your mother. Despite the changes. Despite the yelling of the other governments, the telegram will get there?"

"He said they would go, all of them."

"And she'll get it? Your mother?"

"He said so."

"And to my mother also you sent a telegram, like we discussed?"

"*Yes*, I told you. And I sent to the others. To all of them, not to some—all."

"You wired Solly special, what I asked?"

The three children were quiet around the kitchen table. The oilcloth grazed their thighs, their napkins covered their laps. Two weeks of schooldays gone, they knew about the broken border; they knew how the area containing Nagymihály and Szacsur had been given through diplomatic channels over to Hungary. What frightened them into silence, however, while cutting their chicken, forking it, chewing it dry, swallowing it down, was how their parents were talking in front of them.

"I'm not dumb," said Vera. "In care of Rosen, yes."

They were being ignored. And talked past. By them flew details they hadn't heard discussed out in the open before. The radio stayed on in the front room, but the volume was set too low; the voices hissed in a sputtering stream of static. It should be turned off if it couldn't be understood. It wasn't the usual routine to have the radio on while they ate, anyway. No announcer was going to crackle into life, clearly and finally announcing any changes that might have occurred in Europe that day, changes specifically in Czechoslovakia, changes specifically in Hungary.

Though no one had stated it aloud, they'd been sitting in the front room before to hear William Shirer's urgently flat voice reporting to them from over the radio console. But the fifteen minutes of national news came to a close without his report. They'd heard nothing, only domestic news and a proposal in Congress for a new trade bill with England, and of course some sports scores. As soon as the local announcer, Harry Webber, came back on with the lowdown on the city's activities, Joy reached to turn off the dial. "Leave it alone," Vera had said tersely, already up from her chair. "Come in for dinner. Everyone."

Joy turned, confused. Her brown hair, shorn of its false curls and so both short and stick-straight, wouldn't stay in place; the weight of it pushed the one pale ear slightly forward. "What did she tell me—?"

"Don't touch it," Teddy muttered, and went back to the pages of the *Saturday Evening Post*. All the time they'd been gathered in there with the darn radio blaring, he'd tried to keep reading.

"Let it be, Joysie, yes?" Evan interrupted. He pushed up from his own chair. "Mommy wants it on, then let it be on."

"But how come if we're about to eat," she began, and saw Hankus quickly shake his head at her and widen his eyes. Her cheeks were already flushed; she could feel the heat in them. Putting a finger against his lips, Hankus was telling her it was better to just let the subject drop; trust him. As quickly, she nodded back.

You're fine, he mouthed. And twisted around to look into the kitchen as a cupboard door slammed shut a bit too loudly.

Now at the table they all heard the static behind them.

"I don't know why everything is taking so long," Evan was saying. "As soon as we hear from Solly, I'll wire over to him the extra money, first thing. Maybe in the black market he'll find a way to buy his passage to Portugal. Maybe he can get to Irina and they can wait together."

"And what about all the others? My sisters. My mother, and yours?"

"We'll see what they ask us. So far they're not writing that they want to leave, only that they want to get through this changeover. So the town belongs now to Hungary. Hungary isn't the same as Germany. They say things will settle down, yes?"

"Things won't settle. You know it too. But instead of saving our money in preparation, you're getting ready to give over to your brother everything."

"Why not? He's the only one who's asked. But has he taken from us one dollar extra yet? I gave up the new store when Janowitz wouldn't wait, yes? Instead of a mortgage, I took out a personal loan for bringing over the family. And our own store, that I put up as collateral." His voice cracked. "Didn't I do all that?"

Vera paused. "You did. That's all good."

"I know what I'm doing here. Let me handle things."

"But you're giving it all to that Solly. A selfish boy. Worse than that, secretive. Hiding things, not telling things."

"No, he only doesn't want Mother to know his plans before it's necessary, that's all."

"Why?" she demanded. "Because if your mother knows he's leaving, she might want to go too? He thinks she'll be a burden to him? He'll have to take care of her?"

Evan put down his fork and knife and stared at her.

"I know about taking care," she said. "About feeding mouths and providing for others. It must frighten him, poor boy, not ever having done that."

"Why do you make up arguments against him? It's not the government's choice but yours, yes? You think you get to decide who comes to America, Vera? You're the big shot? So you choose to leave behind the one you don't know to take in the others? Solly's the sacrifice. Is this how you're mistaken? Like those big *macher* politicians with their *farshtinkener* Munich Pact, you think you can sign away people you don't know in order to keep safe some you do? That's what the *machers* think they can do."

Vera shuddered a little. "I don't know why I don't let go of it. You're right, I know what you're saying." She paused. "I have nothing I can say, *tateleh*."

"Nothing to say to the real big shots, only to me."

Vera ducked her head. That's when she saw Hankus. Every time she turned around these days, he was watching, it seemed.

Now his face was red, as if trying to hold something back.

"Okay," she said, "what are you doing, Mr. Wise Guy, just sitting here? Drink up your milk. To be healthy, you have to keep your bones strong."

"Ma—"

Just then the static on the radio gave way. A trio burst through: young women singing in angelic bebop harmony the jingle for Griffin's Shoe Polish: *Shine your shoes and you'll wear a smile. . . .* Hankus bit his lips.

"Oh," she said, seeing his grin, "you think what I said is funny? It's not a joke what I said—none of it is, Hankus."

"I wasn't laughing at you, Ma, I promise. In fact, I think it's terrible. I think there should be some way we can think of to help you out."

"Oh? You think that?"

He nodded.

"And what is it you think there is to do?"

He hesitated. "I don't know."

"I see, and you're not smiling? That isn't a grin on your face? A big joke this trouble is, wise guy, for you?"

Embarrassed for him, Teddy and Joy shifted their eyes to their own plates. Very quietly they both kept on chewing.

"What you and Dad were saying wasn't the joke, Ma. It was the radio; that's what made me laugh. Really, you can believe me. It was the way the girls started singing that ad."

Pulling her gaze away, she said after a moment, "I just want you to drink up your milk, please, Hankus."

He reached without another word for the cold glass. He downed the liquid in two gulps, his Adam's apple moving violently in his arched throat. He set the white-washed glass back on the table. Then he took aim at it, flicking his fingernail at a single point on the top edge. The contact made a sharp *clink*.

"I love my brother," Evan's voice shook. "And I love your sisters."

"You see what this is," Vera said fiercely, all of a sudden including the three children in their conversation. "You see what it means to have family?"

THREE

Like Birds

(1940 forward)

Two-six-oh-two East Trainor

She never loved one of her children, Vera once said, any more than the others. Look at her hand; here is the reason, right here. You see, if she cuts off this finger, or this one, or this, what does it matter? It hurts just the same.

There was a back stairwell in two-six-oh-two. Thirteen bare, narrow steps descended straight from the second-story hall, between the bathroom and linen closet, right down to the small vestibule at the rear of the kitchen. Hankus made certain to keep himself quick and light running down them. Just as rapidly he crossed the kitchen. The food smelled great. His mother had been cooking on and off for the past couple of days and for much of last night. In the dead times she'd leave the store and run home, worried that maybe she should cook a little more paprikash, maybe an apple strudel too? It was going to be a wonderful party. There was something to celebrate. Teddy's birthday, sure, but more than that. There was some hope finally to move everyone forward. Tonight there'd be laughter, the family surrounded by friends.

He wished he could celebrate, too, but when else could he sneak away without the absence getting noticed right away? His parents were like that, wanting to know their kids' whereabouts. No, he'd made his decision. He was going to move forward on his own, even if it meant those left behind got frightened by it. His aunt and two cousins were moving forward now. And hadn't his parents crossed all kinds of borders in their day?

He found the small gym bag he'd hidden in back of the front hall closet. Which one should he—? Maybe not his team jacket—just kid stuff. The good coat. The long formal kind he'd always disliked. Yet for someone all on his own, it might lend a certain adult stride and authority. Well, some things do change, don't they? You wise guy. Grinning into the hangers, Hankus pushed aside Vera's short jacket and tugged out his long dark wool by its notched lapel. The gloves were on the shelf; he stuck them into his pocket.

His fingertips brushed the roll of cherry LifeSavers he'd bought yesterday at Rivchin's, when he was worried a sore throat was coming on. But didn't he feel fine now? He felt great! He didn't need LifeSavers, not anything. He broke the roll in two. One half of it slipped into Teddy's coat pocket, the other down into Joysie's. A brother's last little gift. Would either of them figure it out? Maybe if they put the two halves together. He'd have to remember to ask later if they even wondered how they'd gotten the candy. Would he remember?

No one saw Hankus behind the closet door. In eight, maybe ten more seconds, he'd be out on the porch, down the five steps, and with two deep breaths more: through the front yard and on the pavement. By then if the curtains parted in one of the front upstairs windows, say, Joy's, as she peered out to catch a first glimpse of any early-arriving guests, he would already have become a shape of darker darkness—just someone out in the night and hurrying to cross the street; and as Joy continued to gaze downward with that same high, casual, no-more-than-neighborly glance, his five-foot-ten-and-a-half-inch frame would be foreshortened, perhaps look distorted; also: he would disappear and reappear through the black, sectoring branches of the leafless elms; it would be hard of course to tell just who *he* was, hard to distinguish just what *he* was about.

On the front porch of two-six-oh-two, Hankus shrugged on his long coat. The gym bag was in his left hand. He moved at a good clip. In less than ten seconds he'd crossed the Kleinmans' driveway.

A streetlamp illuminated the pavement there for some distance.

Quick, look. You don't always get a last chance.

Possible? From upstairs, Joy pressed close to the glass. Hankus?

At the corner, he almost hesitated. Almost looked back.

But, no, it was too dark. Just shapes, weren't they—and too far away now.

So: leaving takes no time at all.

Upstairs Evan lifted the camera from the top of his bureau and put the black strap around his neck. When the boxy metal Kodak slipped against his stomach, it pulled the thin leather tight as a nerve. On the bureau were two photos: one, the formal portrait of Vera and him—both smiling down at the letter she held to the light of the white window; the other, a picture of his brother, Solly—but this one was unframed. It had come last week with the most recent letter from Nagymihály, where he still waited. Rosen, Solly's friend on Heidelbergstrasse, had emigrated some months before, supposedly to second cousins sponsoring him in New Jersey; so, the return address on the envelope was their mother's. Solly wrote now only of despair: the six refugee boarders to whom they'd given over two of their three rooms and with whom they shared use of the kitchen; the "economic reforms" that meant even Artur, the eldest, the only one of the siblings left with a job, was out scrounging with the rest of them; the lines, standing all the day long at the doors of municipal and emigration offices.

"But," Solly added, filling the margins lengthwise and upside down and around in an ever-tighter and smaller scrawl, "our countries are not enemies, yours and mine. As long as the peace is kept between the two—as long as America does not join in directly—I can write my letters and get your replies. If America gives up her neutrality, then what will happen? All communication between us will then be cut off. But here, Ivan, is what I'm writing to tell you—yesterday, as soon as Hungary signed the friendship pact with Germany, Italy, and Japan, Mother said she decided to leave Nagymihály with me, if I do get the chance. But it seems every other Jew has suddenly understood the same thing, that such friendship pacts will not prove so friendly. I am gathering the new applications for Mother, though it's probably useless. Ivan, you must apply right away to sponsor Mother from your end. Let me know how it is going! I hear Verushka's sister Etel is filling out the same forms, and the rest are trying to figure out what they can do. Maybe soon everybody will be lucky, like Irina. Do you think so? Or maybe the world will change back. All doors get shut in our faces. Why?" Solly's photo was of a chin-lifted, sweetly smiling, sad-eyed young man with curling black hair who Evan couldn't quite recognize. The face was very nearly a stranger's.

But it was from the letters themselves where Evan without any doubt identified his brother. Over the years he'd kept watch over Solly by following the inky dots and lines on the page. *I went to the theater last night and saw a play by Henrik Lenkei, "The Great Prelude." You shouldn't tell Mother, since you know what she thinks of such activities . . . The other night Artur came by to educate me. He points out we've had hard times before, and so we'll survive these too, now; why shouldn't we? He may well be correct, but can it matter so much if this stretch is not quite the worst or is the very worst or is only slightly terrible, if I still want to leave? And must he always be right, totally? . . . I have taken to swimming, of all things, with a great feeling of happiness . . .* Yes, the scrawl of Sol's voice on pieces of paper, its loops and spires reaching in absolute silence from hope to need to stubborn rage and back again—Evan recognized and claimed this immediately as *brother.*

The date penciled on the back of the photograph was October 1940. The picture was recent then, not even two months old. Why had Solly had it professionally taken? Why bother now, with all the rest there was for him to do? And when it must have cost him also simply to send it?

"Better get dressed," Vera warned. "Anytime soon people are going to come, and you'll still be standing half-naked in only a shirt and shorts." Balancing on one foot, she twisted behind herself to straighten the seam in her stocking.

"You should sit to do that." He shot her a glance.

"I'm fine, all done. We have film and flashbulbs? I don't want to be left with nothing. This is a big night."

"I'm loading the roll I bought on sale from Rivchin's." He wound the silver knob until it balked against his thumb. Lightly, he pressed it once more to be sure. Then he cupped his hand around the top and gazed down at the square of smoky glass where soon he'd have to find everyone, center them, and fix them in place. He wasn't a natural, so he refused to be rushed. Elbows out, head down, slowly moving the camera in ever-smaller circles, he would fish for Vera and the kids until their tiny forms—each face-forward and smiling—slid across the dark glossy surface. Then he moved only his thumb. Then he was done. Then he began again to breathe. As soon as he looked up from that, nothing was the same. Loud and unpredictable, his subjects were going off in any direction they wanted. Nothing like the posed images he had caught, taken down into the glass and metal box, and secretly somewhere in the workings of the mechanism released.

"I'm so happy, *tateleh*." Vera shoved her dresser drawer closed with her hip.

From the hallway Joy shouted from the other side of the door, "Can I come in? I need to get buttoned up the back."

"Just a minute." Evan put down the camera. Now that Joysie was nearly eleven, he didn't like to be undressed in front of her. He took his slacks from the bed and shook them once before stepping into them.

"When are the people coming?" she called.

He zipped up. "Soon." He slipped his black lizard belt through the pant loops.

As she went to the door, Vera gave him a quick kiss on a freshly shaven cheek. "Okay, Joy," she said, opening up. "I'll fasten you."

Standing tall, Teddy welcomed in the Belaks and the Pressers. He was in his new brown wool suit, and he'd knotted his tie in a fat Windsor. He'd also tucked the tie's longer end into the waistband of his pants to hold it down, but no one would see that because he would keep the jacket buttoned.

"Sixteen?" Lili Belak handed over her coat. "I don't know if I can truly believe that about you, Teddy. Of course, you are filling out nicely. Sandor? Sandor, look at him."

"Looks about like he did when we visited the last time," said Sandor. "Only better dressed." Taking off his fedora, he turned it over and peered speculatively into the crown. "I don't know if they're right about the hat making the man. I think it's got to be what's under the hat." At that, he plopped his fedora squarely on Teddy's head. "Eh? You got a smart *Yiddishe kop* under there?"

Teddy went rigid with embarrassment as Sandor tugged the wide front brim heavily forward.

Joy called, "Can I get the doorbell this time?"

"Oh yes, very debonair," said Mrs. Presser a moment later when, stiff-backed, hatted, his arms full of coats, Teddy turned.

It's nice to have so many things to celebrate, he heard his mother say, with our friends.

Things. Our friends.

Deep down, Teddy had known the party wasn't really for him. It was really for Irina's telegram—only his parents were afraid to celebrate that too early. His parents still believed in the evil eye from the old country, although they always laughed at it, pooh-poohing when they saw someone spitting over his shoulder to ward off the bad luck. They were so sure about being modern, but he knew the truth. Giving a party for him felt safer than blatantly celebrating Irina's news, he'd bet. After all, his turning sixteen would happen tomorrow morning, no matter what.

He dumped the coats on the chair next to the hall closet. He lifted Sandor Belak's fedora from his head and noticed that the inside of its high black-felt dome was flecked with dandruff and the leather band darkened and oil-stained. Sniffing it quickly, he cringed. It was another one of those things that only looked good from the outside.

The telegram from Irina, well, from what he gathered from the papers and newsreels, he knew no one could tell how the message would finally turn out. The *Luftwaffe* bombed all kinds of ships in the middle of the ocean. And the RAF couldn't be everywhere, even if they had a lot of moxie. Hankus said the Brits were the only stand-up guys. Standing up when Poland was threatened, and again now, with France gone. The Brits are the ones mixing it up, he said, when really it's our fight too.

But who said it's our fight? That's what Teddy wanted to know. No one was picking a fight with him over here.

Joy staggered over, her arms gawkily encircling a bundle of what seemed to be mostly swaying sleeves. "Mommy says to put our coats up on her bed, so we can hang more of the guests' stuff in the downstairs closet."

"I should do it? Tonight? Me?" He glared at her staring, squinched-up face; she was probably going to start sweating, all dressed up. "Damn. And don't tell her I said that." He tossed Sandor's hat onto the top shelf of the closet. The doorbell rang in a half burst. *Welcome! Come in, come in.*

They're on the boat—on their way to Cuba, I hear, Evan. That's one step closer to us. God bless them. So they'll wait for approval from there.

God's watching over them, Vera. I know it will turn out a good thing they couldn't stay longer in that Portugal.

"Leave the hangers," Joy whispered at his back. "We need them down here."

He grabbed as many coats as he could. He had to unbutton his new jacket in order to get his arms around the pile. He had to feel his way up the stairs by knocking the toes of his good shoes into each of the stairs. On the second trip up, with the smaller load crushed against his chest and filling his arms, his shirt slowly stuck to his skin.

"Pretty noisy," Teddy greeted his mother as she lifted a tray of small cookies from the oven. He'd come down the back stairwell so he wouldn't have to help Joy at the front door.

Vera said, "Louie and Bernie are here. They told me Ira wasn't coming, Teddy. He's not feeling well."

"Oh, thanks."

"I know you invited only the three friends."

He shrugged. "Where's Hankus?"

"What do you mean," she said, smile fading, "where's Hankus?" She put down the tin sheet; thin lines of heat shimmered up from the centers of each red-raspberry-dabbed cookie.

"He's not in our bedroom. I was wondering where he is, I haven't seen him since we started getting ready."

"He's not on the toilet?"

"Uh-uh, I just used the bathroom. He isn't upstairs."

His mother's face stopped working, just froze. Then she raised her chin. She said with an edge, nothing overmuch, "This is a party. I have guests."

"Yeah," he said, relieved by the familiarity of only her normal anger. "I know it. Me, too, Mom. My birthday party."

"He knows not to go anywhere without telling us, we taught him." She slid a knife under a cookie to jiggle the small pastry up from the metal sheet. "Your brother has to be a wise guy. Maybe he's making an extra surprise for you. Go ask Daddy where he is."

But after he waited while his father gave Mr. Oppenheim's glass another spritz from the towel-wrapped seltzer bottle, he learned his father didn't know either. "Here," his father said, handing over the seltzer bottle and an extra CO_2 cartridge, "see if anyone needs some more." His father met his mother coming out of the kitchen with a tray.

Joy touched his elbow. "Where's Hankus, Teddy? We bet on how many men would wear solid-colored neckties tonight. I said ten, and he said everyone. But I just counted. You know how many? Eight. That's so far."

He saw Bernie and Lou standing by the Victrola. Bernie gestured to him to come over to the console and put on a new record.

You change it, Teddy mouthed back. *Swing. Make it swing.*

Joy said, "We put out the ashtrays and candy dishes together, then went upstairs to get dressed. He didn't say he was going out. Do you know where he went?"

"No." He almost pointed the nozzle of the seltzer bottle down at her nose, but suddenly he didn't know why he wanted to be so mean. She was his sister; she wasn't really trying to bother him. "What kind of stunt does he think he's pulling, disappearing for this long? It isn't funny. Someone needs to—someone should go out to find him."

"Should I?" Joy nodded, eyes opened wide. "If you want me to, I'll go right now. Are you going, too?"

"I can't." His voice cracked and went down nearly an octave. "I don't know, I don't get it at all. This is my party."

Five hours later when the two policemen arrived, it wasn't because the neighbors had complained of the noise from the celebration, because except for Sandor and Lili Belak and the Pressers, who'd brought them by in their DeSoto, everyone else had gone. Some guests promised to drive around and try to find Hankus, others who'd come on foot said they'd wander a bit to look as long as they could or they'd go straight home to pray that all would end well. Hankus, the guests all said, was a good boy. A strong, good boy. No harm could come to him, or, they said, no harm could he do. He was probably making a surprise for the party, like his mother said. Just like she said.

Some surprise, Teddy cried—and hated himself for the sting of salt in his mouth. He smeared his brown wool sleeve across his eyes. Some damn surprise. He could have said it would end up jinxed; he predicted it.

Vera sat rigidly in Hankus's chair at the kitchen table. She lit a cigarette and puffed on it twice, then forgot it. She wouldn't go into the front of the house. Little by little, the other women had brought back the hardly picked-at trays and plates, the filled bowls, the cups and saucers, the glasses. "Don't," she'd said, not turning once to see how the kitchen was filling up around her. "I don't want anything put away. It's not right for you to work, you're guests." The women didn't know what else they could do for her then—they could see she didn't want to talk, didn't want to be touched, was determined not to see the dismantling around her. Then one of them—coming in to say good-bye, she and her husband were going, they'd keep an eye out for the boy—brought in all the napkins. The small napkins—crushed, palmed—Vera had nothing to say about; for as long as they could, Marti Grossman and Helen Weiss stood behind her at the counter, smoothing out the white squares, refolding them. But there were only so many to pile.

At each shake of the wind, chug of a motor, voice out-of-doors, those left in two-six-oh-two fell silent.

Once Joy wandered into the kitchen and saw her mother sitting, back to her, at the table, looked at her mother's friends standing about, their hands too loose, their dresses too fancy, their powdered faces too eager at her approach, and she started to cry. She turned right around. For a while she stood in the hallway alone, staring at the cut-glass vase full of a mix of red, white, and purplish blue flowers. When one of the ladies walked out of the kitchen, she had to busy herself with the stems, moving the thin green stalks this way or that. The smell of the blooms, wide-open, narrow-petaled, deep-centered, was sickly sweet, and as soon as Joy was alone again, she drew back her hand.

Her father was talking. He was in the front foyer. Going over to him, standing as closely behind him as she could without touching, she didn't say a word. He didn't look around, but he paused, breaking off his words for a second—and in that pause, Joy knew he'd just felt her presence. Then he continued saying to Mr. Presser, who stood wide-legged in his open overcoat, jingling his car keys, "What if he's hurt somewhere? Why didn't he stay in the house? His brother's birthday, Sam. What if he's hurt?"

"He's not a drinker, a *shikker*, is he? Wild?"

"Don't be crazy. You know him, yes?"

"It could be a girl," Mr. Presser said, his long chin jutting forward. "I don't mean normal, but maybe, you know, she's the one in trouble. She might need him for, well, to help her do something. The wives might know about that, if they've ever had to—I mean, there are things that happen with a girl. He could be with her now, one way or the other."

"No, he's not like that."

"I'm not saying Hankus isn't a good boy. Did you call his friends?"

"They say they don't know where he is. I called Buddy and then Harvey. There are others I could call, but not as close to him."

"The girlfriend, Evan, he has one or not? You can't deny a boy's urges. Why should Hankus be any different? It could be he's with her, right now."

"I said he isn't like—he doesn't have one like that." Evan turned abruptly. "Joy," he said, "go to your brother." He was surprised to see his daughter's face quite so near to his own; the top of her head was level with the middle of his upper arm or, if he turned a bit more, with his heart. But the face was only a child's; the expression in the eyes blankly confused. He paused. Hadn't he used English with her?

"Teddy," Evan said then. "I meant Teddy, yes? Go on, Joy."

"He doesn't want me around. I make him mad."

"Don't be foolish," he spoke tersely. "He's your brother who loves you. Go sit with him in the living room. Time with a brother," he had to stop, to swallow. "Being with a brother, it's one of the best things in the world." He rested his hand lightly atop her head, smoothing the brown hair that once, not too long ago, was soft with long curls.

She nodded, just the slightest dropping forward of her chin, almost like she was shivering.

"I need to talk with Mr. Presser about Hankus. Alone."

She paused and glanced sideways at him, her eyes sleepily half-lidded. She whispered, "Is Hankus coming home?"

"Of course he is. Don't you worry." He was startled by how quickly Joy's smile sprang up; and then, like Solly's caught in the photo, how frightened it stayed.

What the two officers assured them after making them sort through their memories, bureaus, and closets, their fears and the pile of family coats on the big double bed, is that in their opinion, given the number of personal items missing, nobody but nobody had sneaked into two-six-oh-two and snatched this kid away like the Lindbergh baby. The young man either was going to show up sooner or later with his tail between his legs— crying and begging to be let in—or he was going to write or call or get some message to them to explain where he was, how he got there, what he was doing, and why. So far no reports of foul play or accidents had come into the station tonight. They should remember that a boy like him, from a family like theirs, didn't just up and leave, at least not for long. It's also a sad fact of life that some wild ones do run off. Then again, it wasn't that many hours since he'd left. It was almost Christmas break from school; maybe Hankus had decided to take himself on a little vacation? They should try their best to keep their spirits up and do the things they usually did. At six tomorrow night, if it was necessary, they could file a formal report. Then, when information came in to the police or maybe his status changed, they'd be informed immediately. Meanwhile, they should find a current photo of the young man to give the authorities. Once the case began to move through official channels, a picture for identification could speed things along. Any good likeness would do.

Winding Streets

Days dragged by. Nights passed, finally.

Evan edged the car through the neighborhood streets. The snow was changing them; white, the roads seemed to him too dark, their familiar turns now icy and unreliable, full of threat. He had the window rolled down; at one time he would have been embarrassed to lean out, calling *Hankus!* when no one was there or past those who'd already looked up and clearly were not who he was looking for: *Hankus! Hankus!* He drove past the State Theater when its marquee was lit, past the tall temple, the school yards. He passed the store. He drove down to the city, down Euclid Avenue, down Carnegie. He passed restaurants, hospitals, bars, libraries, gas stations, parks, the five big department stores, fountains, churches with ornate turnip-top spires like back in the old country, statues of soldiers, the municipal stadium. Calling, he drove into the flats near the Cuyahoga and past the steel mills during a change of shifts. The great whistles blew. He called, *Hankus, where are you? It's Dad. You're breaking my heart.*

He drove past the State Theater, its marquee dark. Past pharmacies, butcher shops, cobblers, barbers. Past the store. The block's business association's red-white-and-blue banner, strung from lampposts, flapped over the center of the street. BUCKEYE RD. MERCHANTS THANK YOU! He glanced back at his store, bothered by something in the rearview mirror. He backed up. He parked and got out. He knew Hankus wouldn't be inside, but he was uneasy. Something was loose, it looked like to him, in the store's protection. He rattled the metal grillwork pulled over the front. He poked his fingers through the open lattice and tried to reach the door's big brass handle. Nothing seemed loose there. Nothing gave way.

Still, Evan couldn't shake the feeling that something very small in the system must have broken and fallen, something he actually didn't quite know how to identify, so now this one tiny part was lost all the way. He shook the grille again. Somewhere one of the links made a weak jingling sound. With a wave of nausea, he understood how foolish he'd been. Too trusting, yes? for too long: counting on big locks to keep everything safe.

Two-six-oh-two East Trainor

"Like birds."

"What does that mean, like birds?"

Slowly Vera shook her head. "How should I know?"

"You just said it, Mommy."

"Did I say it? I did?"

Joy was turned about on the couch, a book upended beside her; what she'd really been doing in the long stretch of tingling silence was watching her mother sit listless and still. "You said, like birds."

Vera sat for a moment. "I don't know about it." Her hand fluttered stupidly in her lap. She put it palm-down on the thick red upholstered arm of the chair. "It flew from me, that's all." The air smelled of onions; sometime she'd gotten back from the store, cooked dinner, and they'd eaten their meal together, the four of them. She didn't know what she was doing anymore. She only did what she had to. Everything went from her. Where was her boy?

"Want me to read aloud, Mommy? It's about the War for Independence."

"No, thank you."

"Another name for it is the Revolution," Joy offered, as if that tag might be more fetching.

Teddy was hunched over the desk at the front window. Snow was piling up on the outside sill. "I'm trying to study, I have a test tomorrow. Mrs. Fleisher says it's going to count one-quarter of our grade. I think she's expecting me to get a pretty high mark."

Vera said, dry-mouthed, "And what subject is this?"

"Science. We're on plants—that's xylem, phloem, phototropism. It's okay. I like it well enough."

"Good," she said with effort.

"Where's Daddy?" asked Joy, still in the same position.

"Looking. Time for bed now."

The girl shook her head. "I don't want to go up yet. I want to wait down here with everyone else. Please? I want to know if something happens."

"Teddy, go upstairs with her. I don't want her sitting here all night for no reason."

"But I'm studying and I'm not done. Joy's not a baby anymore. Why can't she go without me?"

"Take her upstairs," Vera said, like steel. "You can work in your bedroom."

"I don't like working in that stupid room alone. Besides, it's not *my* room, only half of it is, okay? Why can't I stay down here? If I'm working, why can't I stay?"

"I don't want to argue. Go upstairs and take Joy."

The telephone rang.

"Sit still! It's not anyone." Vera ran to the hallway, to the small dark stand that the manufacturer's shiny label pasted underneath identified as an occasional table.

An operator said the call was international.

"Hi, Ma," he said, a voice in a fog.

She thought she was saying something aloud. She said, "Where—?"

The other two were suddenly bumping against her. "Where is he? It's Hankus! It's him, on the phone!"

"I'm in Canada, Ma."

"Not really."

He laughed. "Really! I took a bus to Buffalo. Then I put out my thumb and hitched in about three, four hours to Toronto. It's not that far from us, you'd be surprised."

"I'm surprised, Hankus, sure." Angrily she batted away the others. "It's enough now. The surprises are over, Mr. Wise Guy. Okay? Done."

"I'd like to talk to Dad, please, Ma."

"Come home now."

"I need to talk to Dad. Is he there?"

"Why are you doing this, Hankus?" Vera turned to the wall. "You tell me why." She waited. "You can't talk to him. Daddy's out looking for you. Four nights he's gone."

The buzz through the line was too loud.

Again he said, "I've enlisted here. I've volunteered for the British Commonwealth Army. They took me, I'm going to be trained. I'm going to fight. I bet it'll be Europe, Ma."

"What's he saying?" Joy tugged at her.

Vera's head swiveled. "*Sha!* Quiet! Be quiet.

"Hear me? I won't let you do this." She was squeezing the phone receiver as if she could change the way he would understand her words. "Hear me, Hankus? I'm telling you, you come home. We'll wire you money. Take the bus to Cleveland tonight."

Evan stopped the car, midstreet. That was Vera; she was standing ankle-deep in the snow at the end of their driveway; she looked like a refugee: tilted forward at the waist, arms about herself, coat collar hiding her chin. For some reason, instead of driving closer, he kept this little bit of distance between them. From the rolled-down window he called, "What is it?"

She didn't come over to him; it couldn't be good news. He waved her out of the way. Carefully he began to pull the car in. Upstairs it looked like only one light was on. The small bathroom window. The kids then, the two, were in their beds. Good. He turned the steering wheel; in the sudden gap as his coat sleeve slid down from his wrist, he saw the thin watch hands praying together against the pale face and the gold twitching wand that jerked over them, and then went on to the numeral twelve. And past twelve, to the one.

The Chevrolet came to a stop a few feet in front of the wood-shed filled with his garden tools. He set the car's brake and was about to roll up the window when Vera bent in, still hugging herself. Her eyes were glistening, whitely dark. "He called and I talked to him."

"Safe?" His breath left with the word.

She nodded.

"Where is he?"

Then as he sat there, not touching the steering wheel, the long black hood pointed at the small storage shed before it, she tried her best to tell him the rest of it.

He was still arguing, later. Not against Vera, but against the absence she was pushing toward him with those two words, *he says*. He says this. He says that. He says he wanted them to be proud of him. He says he had to do something. He says they all know the rumors about the Jews in Poland and Russia. Those rumors about starvation, firing squads—he says he knows his parents talked about them. Something from all that, he says, has to be real.

Evan wiped his face with the red towel. "Hungary isn't like Poland. It has a treaty, not an invasion. In Hungary they don't put Jews in a ghetto. Besides, what does he know from Poland? He knows what has to happen now? He can solve everything, that's what he thinks? An American boy. A Jewish boy from America—eighteen years old. Still with a semester left of high school! He should be at home."

"He says—"

"Just a few months eighteen."

"He says the Hungarian government will follow the examples of the German Nazis. Once bad things start, he says, they go on till they end. He's heard us whispering about such things all his life."

"He misunderstood." Evan passed behind her as she sat at the vanity. He shut the closet door. "Instead of this, he should be out with a girlfriend."

"He says America should help Britain fight."

"Then that will be the end of hearing from our family, if the countries are enemies, yes? Stop," he mumbled, "I can't think anymore tonight."

Her reddened eyes followed him in the mirror until the angle let go of him. She slowly tied a black hairnet around her head, flattening the fading brown curls in place. She pushed in a few bobby pins.

"Come to bed, Vera. I can't do this."

"Wait." Her voice was spent, dry as smoke, yet she was unwilling to let go of its sound. If she were to lie next to him and close her eyes, she would be saying: *This part is done, this part of the change in our lives I will have to rest with.* "He's been thinking about the family, he says. Our sisters and brothers. Our mothers and—and the young ones, the eight cousins his age. He wanted to do something, after all the time hearing us talk. Of course I understand how he could want this, how could I not, but I—"

"Listen, we can't stop him now." Shivering, Evan pulled the covers over his shoulder. For a few moments it was quiet. His breath rebounded from the pillow back into his face. Everything felt cold. He shifted his legs along the white sheet; there was a slight dip in the center of the mattress where his knees might be more comfortable. Such bony knobs, bent as if for running, although he was lying on his side. When had he run last? Years ago it had to be. Chasing after some little one in a game of tag, probably—or maybe the child, frightened, was dangerously tottering?

He lifted his head. "How did he get the idea?"

"A boy in his school ran off last month. Katz, I think the name was, or Barton. Maybe he said it was Barton Katz. There's already a whole British squadron full of only American boys. One does it, you know, and then they all get the idea. I'm proud of him, I am, but—"

"Yes, fine. I see what will be now with him."

"Oh?" At her elbow sat a shiny white, oval cardboard box, filled only with the fragile tissue paper that was used to protect a favorite brown hat. This week, agitated, she'd left the hat somewhere. It hadn't been returned to her. Still, she refused to get rid of the box. It was good, wasn't it? If need be, it could just as well hold something else.

"You don't see what will be with him, too?"

She didn't move, then with a bitter airless sob, shook her head. She whispered after a moment, "Teddy won't get the idea."

He turned on his back and didn't reply. Finally, the mattress tilted under her weight. Vera didn't lie down but sat half-propped against the headboard. He made no move toward her. Reaching over, she clicked off the bedside lamp. She, too, was on her back. She didn't like the silence, the strain of her breath, and his; then the silence again. "More letters to Europe," she said. When he didn't reply, she laughed dryly. "It's so funny, we're trying to get everyone out, and he decides to go in. Our Mr. Wise Guy."

"Stop, Vera!" He pounded the bedcovers. "You know that we lost him."

The Letters

```
4 JANUARY 1941
CENTRO ISRAELITA DE CUBA
JEWISH CENTER OF CUBA
HABANA, CUBA
CABLE: "CENTISCUB"—HABANA
TELEFONO M-1448
```

IMPORTANT:
DEAR ONES! STOP. SAFE ARRIVAL. STOP. JEWISH CENTER HERE WILL ADVISE. STOP. HAVE FEW U.S. DOLLARS LEFT. STOP. MONEY IMP. IN CASE U.S. VISAS APPROVED. STOP. WIRE FULL FUNDS: "BANCO UNITAS"—HABANA. STOP. TEMPORARY STAY ALLOWED HERE SIX MONTHS. STOP. GIRLS SEND KISSES! STOP.

LOVE, IRINA. END.

━━━━━

23 December 1940

Dearest Verushka!

Have you heard yet any word from Irina? Would you let me know when you do? Some of her letters from Portugal didn't get through to me. I am an old mother hen—checking on my little chicks while they try to fly from the coop! Now Etel says she's thinking to leave for America with her family too. I understand why she and Bela worry. But no one knows which way things might yet fall here, and then of course distance is terrible.

On the other hand, if I can think of you three girls together again, that would please me so much! What else can I tell you? I am busy with tasks, as we all must be these days. Still I do have my own time in my rooms where I can think of you. That is my pleasure, to give myself over to my daydreams! Darling, how is business? Is Ivan well? How are my grandchildren? Tell them the Grandmother wants them to do well! One day, we will all gather—you and I again, and the children and I—oh, can it be it will be for us just the first time? (Should I tell them tales about little Verushka—all the times she got into trouble! Childish trouble! Nothing too serious. How easy it is to laugh about those little pranks now.)

Let me know what news you have about Irina.
All is very well with me.
Many kisses and hugs to Ivan and children,
and many to you, my dear daughter—

Mother

Immigration Department
Affiliated With
Hias-New York
Hias-Ica. Paris
Hilfsverein-Berlin

Centro Israelita de Cuba
Jewish Center of Cuba

Egido No. 504 ::: Telf. M-1448

Cable: Centisc
Habana

Case No. *OSVAT, Irina, Miriam, Lily;*
HOTEL MANHATTAN,
Calle San Lazaro 673.
Apto. 312, Habana, Cuba

January 7, 1941

HIAS OF AMERICA
Cleveland branch

Gentlemen:

On behalf of the above named who arrived in Havana on January 4, 1941, on board of the Spanish boat MARQUES DE COMILLAS, and were met by us, we are pleased to ask your cooperation to interview the following relatives and friends in order to convey them the following message:

Mrs. OSVAT's sister: Mrs. Vera Eichenbaum, of 2602 East Trainor Rd., your city, who should endeavor to obtain a copy of the Certificate 575 issued by the Department of Justice, Washington, D.C., because the original one was mailed directly to the Lisbon American Consulate, and same did not arrive there until our clients' departure there-from—December 14, 1940—and same is badly needed now here in Havana.

Mrs. Eichenbaum's husband, Ivan Eichenbaum, (also known as EVAN Eichenbaum) must be induced to mail as promptly as possible a new Affidavit of Support *with full financial evidences* to our care. Kindly pay exceptional attention to this matter as he has already sent affidavits to the Consulate of Lisbon, Portugal, and failed to attach thereto the corresponding financial evidences, thus having hindered the visa issuance to our clients.

Further, we request that Mr. Sandor Belakoczi (also known as Sandor BELAK), of 77890 Euclid Heights Blvd., your city, mail immediately a new (more current) deposition stating the circumstances whereby he can confirm the relationship between Mrs. Vera EICHENBAUM and Mrs. Irina OSVAT, to be that as sisters. (A logical deduction made of that fact will be conclusive that MIRIAM and LILY OSVAT are nieces to Mrs. Eichenbaum.)

We thank you in advance for your valuable cooperation and are awaiting your early action.

Sincerely yours,

J. M. Kravitz

J.M. Kravitz
General Secretary

━━━━━━

Jan. 12, 1941

Dear Dad, Ma, Teddy, Joysie,

Thanks for writing. It's great hearing from you. You never know how much you can look forward to reading letters until you're away. The Canucks are good guys, and there are four other Yanks in my outfit. One of my best pals is from Detroit, Frank Weiler. Another—Robby Binkowitz, or Bink—is a Buffalo NY boy, born and bred. See, Dad? I'm not the only hothead, as you call me, not by a long shot.

We won't be shipping out until training's done. Since that's not now, I don't know the answer to Ma's question about where I'm going. But I can tell you I'm getting good

at scrambling over walls, saluting, and running for miles
with a forty pound pack on my back. It's not much different than baseball practice! Teddy, you're right—part of me
does wish I'd tried for the RAF, but when it came down to
it, I decided not to sign. After all, I've never been up
in an airplane, right?, but I've been walking forever. I
figured that I'd be better off just staying on land.
That's why I switched from my original plan at the last
minute, and chose Infantry.

Joysie (of course I'd get to you, kiddo), you asked
about the food. The *grub* is O.K. But it's not like Ma's,
not in any taste, shape, or form. Also there's nobody to
keep asking if you're eating everything on your plate. And
nobody tells you to drink up your milk. Remember how we
always used to complain about things like that? Listen,
you better eat up everything on your plate for me now,
kiddo. But I'm just kidding, really.

O.K. Write and tell me what's going on in old Cleve-
town. It feels pretty far away. But I don't want anyone to
worry about me. I'm part of a big effort now and part of a
great group, too. I'm right where I want to be. I know for
sure that I'm one lucky guy.

God save the queen!

Love to *all*,

Your son and brother,

Hankus your Yankus

(or, as the Canucks call me: Hank the Yank!)

━━━━━━

Buckeye Shopping Center

On the horsehair sofa in Buckeye Shopping Center's back
office, with the striped brown, red, and yellow afghan sliding
after each slow breath another eighth of an inch off her
upturned right shoulder, side, hip, thigh; with her right arm
shivery and bare of all but the green wool cap sleeve of her dress
and the black elastic-strapped wristwatch, Vera dreamed of her
mother waving to her. Inside her eyes she could watch how care-

fully she and one of her sisters—*Irina!* it was Irina—dropped the luggage they were carrying; could watch how they righted the bags atop the wet bricks of the street; how slowly together they turned to watch the lady running behind them, far in the distance. Oh, Mother was so small now. She was no more than a stick figure in the middle of a black smudge. Wasn't that her black dress? Mother was running after them, her own girls, and her voice was lost in the clatter of birds and leaves. She ran with her arms over her head, moving the hands together and apart, together and apart. The gesture was so stunted by distance, it seemed trivial. But she was able to disturb some air. They must have felt the ripples against their skin, because Vera heard herself mutter, "Cold, cold."

No one else was on the wet street—only small Mother running at one end, and she and Irina, watching from where they'd stopped. Of course once they'd turned, their destination slid behind their backs. Couldn't Vera, as the dreamer, somehow still see it? That sun still spilling down, the dry road still continuing widely to a horizon that like a curtain softly waved green and blue and gold and rose-pink? But between them and Mother? Only a reedy river off to the side and low boarded-up buildings that lined a street lying rain-slick and empty. From the empty interiors, the broken windows, the wind moaned like a congregation rising in sorrow.

"Wave good-bye," Irina mouthed. How happy she looked at that moment. She must have believed she'd spoken aloud.

Vera glanced over to Mother. How was it that those back-and-forth jerks of that stick-arm, even viewed from such a distance, seemed so familiar? So instantly recognizable?

"Soon she'll be too tiny to see."

Vera watched Irina's mouth form those words, though no sound came out. Irina's lips next made these shapes: "If we wave now, later we won't have regrets."

Suddenly Vera seized her sister's arm. Wrenching it upward, she shoved it this way and that. "Talk to me out loud," she heard herself screaming. "Rina, you know what's coming from you?

Nothing. It's all caught up on the inside now. I can't hear you! Rina, please, I can't hear you.

"Mother," she cried to the running stick. "I can't hear you either." A great bell began to toll.

Then Vera saw that she herself was running. Her own shoes were blurring. She was racing ahead of her mother, in the same direction. She heard Irina running too, between her and Mother, but why? Why were they running like that, far apart, in a silent line? The horizon changed, and there was the shore. Pulling away from it: an immense metal-gray ship.

Vera began waving arms overhead. She had to know his name. What was his name? She had to shout to him. There was his face, that white speck among all the others, the hundreds massed as one single body at the deck's rail. That one dot, her whole boy. She wanted him to come back to her now. The boy, he had to listen. Running, waving, Vera had to call with all her might. She opened her mouth, screamed for him once, and sobbed. It was wrong. She tried again, but all she could make was that same useless whisper: "Mother!" And again her cry kept streaming out: "Mother. Mother. Mother! Mother!"

Vera made quick work of folding up the afghan. With a pat, she placed it back against the couch. She didn't remember anything about her dream, and she didn't want to. What for? She had to search for ideas to fill up her time? Weary, she'd lain down for a nap; now it was done. The knot in her stomach and the tension streaking along her limbs, they told her all she wanted to know about the pain deep inside. Yes, of course, things hurt. But the twist of physical fear and the crazy veins of jitteriness also spoke to her of other, more useful truths: *Vera, better to be working, not resting.* And: *You know what matters: Verushka, you keep moving.* And: *You see what comes from lying down?*

She went over to the telephone. One ring. Two. Three. On the fourth, Joy answered. Vera felt a protective tug somewhere inside her, at hearing how high and young her daughter's voice sounded.

She'd just gotten back from school around fifteen minutes ago. No, Teddy wasn't back yet, but she did see him through the window at Rivchin's. He and his friend Ira were sitting at the side counter. He'd probably ordered a soda pop, she guessed. She didn't go into the pharmacy; she was walking with Sukie, who had to get home to practice piano. Yes, she had homework to do. She was going to have a snack first, sure. It was quiet now, good for getting homework done. No, no, she was okay. No, there wasn't any mail delivered, no letters. How's the day going on your end, Mommy?

Vera smiled. Maybe the voice sounded quick and girlish, but with this last question Joy was trying to act older, more adult.

"Oh," she said, her fingers working up and down the black cloth cord, "we're having a good day. We sold a lot."

That's good, Mommy.

Vera laughed, back to herself again. She could almost hear her girl standing up straighter, for her approval. "Everything's fine," she said, comforted by the repetition of it all. She picked up the pile of manufacturers' bills from the desk and shuffled through them. "Daddy and I will be home at seven o'clock, so begin heating up the paprikash a little before."

Okay.

"When Teddy comes in, tell him to telephone the store so we know he's back safe."

On her end of the connection, Joy paused, staring down the silent hall to the closed front door. She was flooded with the familiar desire of trying to pull her mother toward her even as she knew she was hurrying away. "I'm going to finish all my homework," she said.

Good, she heard. Then in the background came a rustle of papers. That would be the next task, claiming her attention already. Joy rushed ahead, "But I won't forget to have Teddy call. Don't worry, Mommy. I'll start the paprikash. Everything's okay."

"You're a good girl." Making a small smacking kiss into the receiver and hearing Joy's kiss in return, Vera hung up the phone. Her step brisk, she walked through the alcove between the curtain displays, then stood a second or two surveying the big room before her. Evan was showing a man a blue serge suit; Paulina was ringing up purchases at the front desk; Mary was setting out new stock in the special sales section. And there, looking up hopefully, was someone waiting for her to approach: a girl, maybe eighteen, nineteen years old, balancing a sleeping toddler in the crook of her left arm and with her right hand picking up ladies' half-slips and attempting, by dangling them midair, to size them.

Vera lifted her chin. "Is there something I can get for you?" she asked, nodding. "I would be very happy to show you anything I can."

Copy of Deposition

HEBREW SHELTERING AND IMMIGRANT AID SOCIETY OF AMERICA

UNITED STATES OF AMERICA
State of Ohio
City of Cleveland
County of Cuyahoga

I, Sandor Belak, being duly sworn depose and say:
That I reside at 77890 Euclid Heights Boulevard, Cleveland Heights, Ohio.
That I was present at the marriage of Vera Korach to Evan (Ivan) Eichenbaum which took place on April 5, 1920, in Szacsur, Czechoslovakia.
That I vividly remember the wedding took place on that date because I gave a ceremonial toast to the couple and also played my violin in a small impromptu instrumental group that aided in the festivities.
That Vera's sister, Irina Korach (later: OSVAT), also played violin in this same group for the wedding. Although this was the first and only time this group played, I knew Irina Korach from the many times before we had met more casually.
That I partook of the feasting and festivities which ensued after the wedding and vividly recall the details of being there, as I had previously been a frequent visitor to the house but this was the first time I attended a wedding there, and the first and only time I played violin with Irina Korach (later: OSVAT), known to me then, as before, as the younger sister of Vera Korach (EICHENBAUM).
That I hereby certify that I was present at the lawful

marriage of Vera and Evan Eichenbaum which took place on
April 5, 1920, in Szacsur, Czechoslovakia, and that Irina
Korach (later: OSVAT) was announced publicly at this gath-
ering as the sister of the bride, Vera Eichenbaum.

Sandor Belak
(Belakoczi)

_____

Sandor Belak (also known as Belakoczi)
Sworn to before me this 1st day of February, 1941.

Helen Altman

_____

Helen Altman
NOTARY PUBLIC

The Decorated Gym

The joint was jumping. The joint was the high school gymnasium, and during the Washington's Birthday Dance it was going
wild in a completely new way. Gone was the cold echoing space
where at sixth period he'd wait shiver-armed and -legged, shifting from foot to foot, until a ball—volley or basket—came in his
direction. That ball would magnetize the other boys about him,
each one smacking his palms and shouting: *Ted, here! Give it!* He
got sweated up more from passing it off, the snap decision of
Who should get it? When? than from any running or dribbling he
had to do. Sometimes, dribbling, hearing the pounding feet
behind him, his brother's old name for him, *Taffy,* floated into
his mind. The moment before he was overtaken, he'd spin
around, looking, looking for some quick way to get rid of the
damn thing in his hands but knowing he was likely to get stuck
before he'd make the decision. Jump? Feint? Bend? Twist? Pass?
To whom? How? When?

"Ted, here!"

He turned. Ira Margolin headed toward him, cutting around
two jitterbuggers and carrying three glasses of punch. The glass
in the center, sloshing slowly over his stubby fingers, was slipping

by inches. "Here, take it," Ira said, reduced to shuffling as the band's trumpets tickled the final high note in the steamy chorus of "Polka Dots."

"Sorry, not for me." Teddy smoothed his tie. "I'm going to dance."

"Sure, in your dreams. Here, buddy." Ira pushed his full hands at him. "You know you asked me to get it for you."

"Is it spiked?"

"That's swell. In your dreams, yeah. Come on, I'm getting wet."

"Oh," Teddy said out of the side of his mouth. "I guess you're doing the dreaming then, Margolin. Better wake up and wash." He slipped the slick center glass away, laughing as Ira's round face turned the thin red of the punch. Ira looked like a large astonished baby, with his soft curly blond hair and lightly lashed eyes. Teddy felt a surge of energy. The panic he usually felt in the gym left him; he'd just passed it off to his buddy.

Ira made a beeline over to John Caldwell, standing with a group of six other gentile boys, and handed him a drink. That was odd in a way. The two groups didn't usually mingle, not unless they were assigned to in class. Teddy waited, but Ira stayed there. Obviously he had something to talk about.

From the makeshift stage, Earl Rowanski and the Five Alivers burst brassily into a hot version of "I Got It Bad and That Ain't Good." Teddy glanced up at the wall clock, its face protected by a metal grid from wayward balls, and for some reason, he recalled putting on this jacket and overhearing his father say into the phone: *Proud he's going? We're very proud, yes. But we made him too modern. That's why he thinks he can stop everything bad*; how Dad then laughed, but with a rusty edge. So, Teddy knew right away he'd meant Hankus, not him. Which was wrong. He was every bit as modern as Hank the Yank. More, probably. His father just didn't know how to tell.

Teddy ducked his head and quickly licked around the wet glass, hoping no one would see. Then he took an elaborately slow sip. Over by the equipment wall, the freshman and sopho-more girls were standing in a sort of long dotted line, all talking with great animation. What would it be like to ask one of them to dance? He studied the clock again. Was anybody looking, even that very second, at him?

He heard from behind: "Eichenbaum!"

John Caldwell was waving him over. "The word is your brother's a fightin' man now."

Ira was grinning and nodding.

Slowly, Teddy joined the huddle. "Well, he's at boot camp."

John arched a black eyebrow. Nothing else in his taut, handsome face seemed to move. "But in Canada, right? Not here?"

"The Canadian forces, right, in combination with the Brits."

"A goofball," Vince Abuza laughed. "He didn't know enough to join up with his own country."

Teddy flushed. "What's wrong with you? He wants to fight Hitler, okay?"

"Know what I think?" Vince elbowed the others. "I think the guy's one of those pushy hebes Lucky Lindy talks about who can't wait to get us into a war. Those guys don't care about America first. They're strictly M.O.T.s—strictly members of the tribe. Listen, Eichenbaum, I hope your brother gets to fight. Let him do it. Otherwise, FDR's just crazy enough to get the U.S. mixed up in that mess."

"You don't like our president?" Teddy demanded. "Elected to a third term, first time in history, and you don't like him?"

"Nope. He sticks his nose into everyone else's business. You know, like Hankus."

"What're you teasing the kid for, Abuza?" John said lightly. "Maybe his brother will end up a hero."

He shook his head. "If that guy was really true-blue, he'd have signed up over here. I mean, didn't old Henry Stimson put on a blindfold to draw conscription numbers from a hamper, or what?"

Teddy tried to laugh. "Oh, Hankus said that draft isn't going to lead to anything. It's only a bunch of baloney. Just another load of paperwork, like with—" He stopped. He didn't complete the sentence, which would have been: *like with visa approval and sponsorship.* These boys surrounding him didn't have to know anything about that.

Furious at being dragged out in the open, he glared at Ira, who got him here in the first place.

"Baloney," John Caldwell persisted, "like with what?"

Grudgingly he said, "Paperwork. Having your number picked doesn't mean anything will change. What if Hankus had volunteered here, okay, and then just ended up in an army that sits at home on its duff? He knew what he wanted to do, and he did it." Teddy paused, then pushed forward. "He's some brave guy."

John lifted his glass. "To an ace! May brother Hank get a chestful of medals and kill himself a thousand Krauts."

"But no Italians," Vince muttered. "We got cousins back there."

"What about you, Eichenbaum?" Chip Waters asked. "You going to volunteer in Canada, too?"

"Come on, I'm only sixteen."

"In another year I bet they'd take you. You could always lie, too."

"Don't be a jerk." Teddy gulped down his punch. Pretending there was more of it left, he kept swilling only a moist, overly sweet scent.

"What, you afraid? Look, he is. Don't you want to be a hero one day like your brother?"

He lowered the glass. He realized his hands were sweating badly.

Ira said, "I stopped him from dancing. He was about to ask someone before I came over here."

"Yeah?" said one of the others in a low voice. "No kidding?"

Barely breathing, Teddy pivoted away. He could hear the silence holding behind him as he headed toward the equipment wall where the girls stood—most still talking with great animation. He wavered a moment. But he was getting watched from both sides. Anxiously he glanced up at the girded clock, then back down to the line beneath it, spying to his right the one girl who looked open to his approach.

Middle Bedroom: Two-six-oh-two East Trainor

He flicked off the switch. Even in the dark, the room didn't feel like only his. Hankus's twin bed took up space in a disturbing way. The absence of Hank's body in it, that affected everything. Nothing was disturbed with his Mom's and Dad's bedroom; both of them were still there; and Joy was used to having a single, so she didn't miss anyone. But things were different for him.

In the dark Teddy navigated forward in bare feet and pajamas until his fingers touched on the two butted-together bureaus. He put his pair of horn-rimmed glasses down atop the one on the right, then he edged over to the left. He knew exactly where he was, only his eyes weren't yet fully adjusted to the sudden change. Shimmering out of the blackness were the grayish rectangles that were their—his—beds. Teddy moved toward the only one of the two in which he'd ever slept. When he felt the bottom hem of the chenille coverlet brushing his toes, he bent over, patting the mattress's flat surface once to get the true edge of it, then he jumped in. He gave a huge sigh.

No breath but his.

Though he'd washed, he still felt sweated-up from dancing. He threw off the covers, and the airy chill felt good enough on his skin to make him greedy. He slipped off his pajama bottoms and left them in a tangle against his right ankle. He took himself in hand. The first pump, lying on his back, covers off, was so exhilarating, he murmured aloud to the unlit square of the ceiling, "Big enough, aren't you?"

The door drifted open, and stopped. From the angle, his mother said, "Did you have a nice time, honey?"

If she'd opened the door all the way, it would have been something they would have had to recall all of their lives. There would always be that sharp image of one lying naked atop sheets, and the other standing, face forward, in the full angle of light from the hall; but because Vera had hesitated, calling, "Did you have a nice time, honey?" and the door stopped opening, the long moment could now stay simple, a surprise that would gracefully fade beneath the dozens of other starts and half-gestures that would run to completion—most of them benign—by the middle of the next afternoon. Months later, decades later, neither Vera nor Teddy, still uncertain of the outcome of this moment—her hand on the doorknob, his hand on himself—would recall it had taken place, that they'd been so threatened, that the very next moment would free them from the pressure of a memory neither would want.

Teddy was making himself move slowly, as though just sleepy and shifting about; with the tips of his fingers he was pulling up the blanket. "What?" he said. "Better come in, Mom." And with a clearer to-do, he sat up emphatically against the headboard, sheets and covers bunched over his wilting erection.

She came in, almost to the foot of the bed, all the light behind her falling from the tall rectangle that was the unjambed hall. She was dark and featureless. Only the side folds of her nightgown filmed and filtered the two extremes: neither lit in yellow nor shadowed black, but the blur of both. "You had a nice time?"

"Yeah." His voice came out normal. This pleased him so much he took the risk and added, his palms pressing down on the covers, "I danced. And I'm not bad at it."

"You had fun? You met a girl?"

Under his bare back, the maple headboard pressed in a cool smooth slab. He was sweating like crazy now. "Of course a girl. Who else would I ask?" He snickered. "A boy?"

"Teddy, Dad will be so happy! He wants you to do these things and enjoy yourself." Vera laughed with uncommon delight. She shook her head a little, from side to side. "You should enjoy yourself, do nice things, you know?"

Out of the balance of shadow, her features reappeared for a second as almost her own. But Teddy didn't strain his eyes to try to study them. If somehow another black veil lifted from her face so her features came clear, fine, but he knew from lying a few feet away from Hankus for all the sixteen years of his life that when it was dark you couldn't see anyone—no matter how familiar—*as* familiar. You could still hear them breathing, or very quietly whacking off, or floating a whisper: *You awake?*

or now, just like his mother was doing, just laughing, but you couldn't really see anyone doing any one of these actions, except in the most general and sort of distorted way.

"What's her name, darling, the girl?"

He said, "Janet."

"Janet?" She waited.

"Oh. Rosen," he said, picking a name he realized a moment too late he must have gotten from his parents' arguments about Uncle Solly.

"Do I know her?"

"Probably not." He paused. "I mean, I just met her myself."

She laughed and said, "A nice girl?"

He slid down a bit. "Oh, sure. Yeah."

"We also had a nice night. We were at the Pressers. Four couples. We played some rummy, had a little kuchen and coffee, and talked—well, sure, that you would expect, the talking! A wonderful time. It's nice to have these kind of nights, Teddy. Going to someone's house, close by. Daddy and I like our friends very much. We don't feel like we need to go off and find new ones, far away."

"Good. Well," he said, pretending to yawn, "good night, Mom."

"Only sweet dreams for you." With a suddenness born of the dark, her lips were on his forehead. She kissed him by his left temple, a little into his hairline. *Gey shlofen, tateleh.*

"Thanks. You sleep well, too."

Corner of Lee

In the next few weeks he began walking Janet home from school. He'd wait in the hall outside room three-seventeen as she finished washing the frog-dissection trays from the biology labs. Though a girl, she was a member of the Future Scientists Club, and often volunteered after class for cleanup. She was full of all kinds of energy, he could feel it.

Janet Blackwood seemed to be in on some secret. Teddy was eager to find out what it was. Was he going to know something special that no one else did, because he was with her? Or was he finally going to know everything that everyone already did and stupidly thought common? He was on the verge of learning whatever it was, that was sure, and he could hardly contain himself.

Janet had a pale, smiling face, a delicately hooked nose, and thick, dark brown hair that fell in soft full waves. She looked more Jewish than he did. But she wasn't at all; she was not an M.O.T. That was the thrilling part. Because if he wasn't asked about her last name again, she could pass, and neither of his parents would be the wiser. Then at least some part of his life could be his own and not only theirs.

Her family, she said that first time they'd walked out of school together, had come to this country on the *Mayflower*. Janet had stopped at the bottom of the outside steps to give him her books so she could tug on red mittens. "As far as I can tell," she said, tossing her hair back, "no one in my family has ever really gotten off that stupid ship. It's ridiculous. I tell my mother the *Mayflower* wasn't the only boat that brought people here. To hear her talk, you'd think it was. How does she think everyone else in America got over?" She was walking backward in order to face him. "On *air*planes?"

Teddy laughed, but with a guilty twinge: actually, the *Mayflower* was the only boat to take to America. Certainly it was the one passenger ship that the schools told him he had to identify; that said something important, didn't it? He couldn't remember if he ever knew the name of the boat his parents took over. Of course, they couldn't wait to get off it, they'd conveyed that much. Besides the *Mayflower,* the only other passenger-ship name he'd had to memorize was the one stenciled on the bow of the *Titanic.*

He also had to admit that he knew about the *Saint Louis,* a name he hadn't been taught in class—for good reason; he hated thinking about it; what it seemed to mean frightened him. But Hankus used to keep talking about it. Sometimes Hank would whisper from the other bed, like he was telling a ghost story he felt meanly compelled to make up night after night just to give

Teddy the willies. Except the *Saint Louis*'s story was real. The ship was in newspapers last year when Cuba, after letting it sail all the way over from Europe, suddenly wouldn't open its port, saying the boat should head back to the open sea. No other country, including America, would allow any of the distraught passengers onto its shores—although many of them were supposed to end up in the U.S., where they had relatives waiting. The newspaper articles Hankus showed him became progressively more hysterical in tone. It was clear the captain of the *Saint Louis* would have to sail the ship back to Germany. At the last hour, England, Belgium, Holland, and France each agreed to take in a portion of the nine hundred passengers—all of them Jewish, except for one unlucky salesman who had boarded by mistake back in Europe. That would have been funny about that one man who got caught up in a mess that wasn't really his, except for how the story turned out: only those few hundred passengers that England took in found a secure harbor; Germany invaded the other three countries. All those people thinking they were going to be safe one way or the other, and what happened to them?

There was one more ship name Teddy knew. That was the S.S. *Laurentia* or *Lorraine,* or maybe the S.S. *Saint Lawrence,* on which Aunt Irina and his cousins successfully traveled from Portugal to Cuba. Well, that was something.

Silently, he and Janet walked on a little farther. They stopped at the curb just as an oil truck roared past.

"Your ancestors came here," she shouted over the reverberation, "on a boat, right?" Then she had to jump backward as slush arced heavily out from the huge tires.

He turned his head from her in the force of the wake. "My parents did. They came on one."

"What? You mean you're that recent?"

The air stopped vibrating. Teddy glanced down. Across his pants zipper were splatters of dirty gray ice. Face hot, casually shifting her stack of books to his other arm, he unobtrusively swiped at his pleats. "I'm not recent, okay? They are. I was born here." He stepped off the curb and into the bricked street. "We can go now, there's no traffic." He waved a loose arm.

But she didn't move from the pavement. She seemed a little surprised, her eyes narrowed.

Teddy hesitated, almost sick to see her standing up there. He couldn't tell what she wanted him to do. Should he go across now or go back to wait on the curb? A line of cars was starting up at the light, two blocks away. Would she even come with him now? "Want to get something with me?"

She pressed her mitten against her lips. He saw how her fingers were rubbing against each other inside the yarn—a series of nervy red lumps. Her eyes didn't move from his face. Did she think he was some greenhorn immigrant? He wasn't, not at all. But what did she want him to be?

He tried to draw a steady breath. "How about a Coca-Cola?" he offered. "Can I buy you one, a cherry Coke, Janet? My treat."

She brought her hand down and broke into a loopy smile. "Oh, I would love that. This is really nice."

Perimeter: Lower School Playground

As Joy watched, Mildred Siegel whispered into Sukie's ear. "No, no," Sukie shrieked, laughing, shaking her black curls, "that didn't happen."

Joy said, casual as possible, "What's the joke?" She rested her hand atop the stone wall that lined the perimeter of the elementary school playground and, even though it was cold, kept it there.

"Oh, it's not something for Joy Eichenbaum to hear, is it, Sukie?"

Pressing her lips together to stop from exploding again into laughter, Sukie looked only at Mildred, to whom she hardly ever spoke, and avoided Joy. Joy, her best friend in the world.

So, it was about her then, just as she feared. She knew of course that something like this had to come toward her. During the math test, she'd looked across the row just as Mildred was about to steal a glance at Roy Talbert's paper. And Mildred saw her looking—the worst thing that could happen, because this was a girl who could cheat at more than tests; she could be dishonest in a hundred different ways; she would always come out on top. All this was clear in the girl's cold blue-eyed stare back across the row.

To her shame, Joy looked immediately down at her own test. That's when she heard the scratch-scratch-scratch of the class's pencils. Like some whispering about her, that she had a duty to uphold the honor system, one of the codes of behavior she knew Hankus was fighting for. What good was she as a sister, if she betrayed him in something this simple?

Quickly she peered to the side: Mildred wasn't looking now. Red pigtails bobbing, she was bent over her own test. Maybe Joy'd been wrong about what she'd observed; maybe she could push out of her mind the fury she'd seen directed at her in the other girl's expression. Maybe the anger was because Mildred had thought Joy was cheating?

"Ten minutes, class," Miss Patterson said. The teacher stepped out from behind her desk. She began to walk up the first aisle. Every few steps she'd pause, checking to see how far a student had gotten. The thud of her thick-heeled black shoes came closer.

Joy tried to shake herself back to what she needed to do: finish the second-to-the-last problem, get to number ten, and then go back up the page and guess at the one she'd temporarily left blank. She was scribbling numbers in the margin when Miss Patterson's bony knuckles rapped on her desk. Feverish, she looked up.

Miss Patterson gazed calmly back. With her sleek small head perched high away on her long narrow body, her nose, eyes, and mouth cruelly overdrawn, she was a homely woman, but when she smiled, gentleness blurred what otherwise appeared grotesque and comic. "Panic," the teacher said quietly, "is how you make mistakes."

Flustered to be addressed in the middle of the test, and uncertain whether the teacher was saying she'd noticed the tense exchange with Mildred, Joy didn't dare to blink. She could almost hear everyone else listening in to learn what she'd gotten caught for.

Miss Patterson whispered, "Figure out one problem all the way and get it right. That's worth more in the end than hurrying out of panic and solving everything incorrectly. Understand?" She straightened the edge of the test page.

The seconds were ticking by. Joy opened her mouth. "Okay," she said, and stopped.

"Good."

The teacher continued walking. She passed Mildred. "Good," she whispered. And later at Roy's desk, "Good." And again, further along, "Good.

"Seven minutes left, class."

Joy raised her hand. "Miss Patterson?"

Faces turned; the teacher instantly came striding back to her. Bending her long body, Miss Patterson kneeled next to her small desk, the drab brown skirt spilling onto the floorboards. She turned her face fully to her student's. "What's wrong?"

Her big dark eyes were so liquidly close, Joy saw herself shrunken inside them.

"It's about the honor code, Miss Patterson."

The teacher said, nodding, "You're cheating?"

Joy's mouth fell open; she could hardly find her voice.

"I see. Someone else is, you mean?"

Slowly, she answered, *Yes.*

"Don't tell me anything more." Miss Patterson's features turned ugly as a stranger's.

"I dislike that part of the code. It's up to me to watch things. You children shouldn't have to inform on each other. That's what the fascists make children do." Miss Patterson unfolded herself and rose again. Briefly she touched Joy's shoulder. "Be concerned with your own actions. Honor thyself, Joy." She paused. "Do you understand?"

Stunned, Joy forced herself to nod. The word, *fascist*, had wiped nearly everything else from her mind.

"Good." In the old familiar way, Miss Patterson smiled back down at her from her lofty height, then hurried to the front of the room. She muttered once more, glancing at another student's paper, "Good."

Joy's face burned; no, how ignorant she was. Why had she done that? If you saw someone doing something wrong, you should keep quiet and concern yourself with your own actions. Is that it, it's what Hankus would want? Where was her mistake? Where was it? What if she couldn't ever figure out what American honor demanded of her?

"Four minutes, class."

Joy stared haplessly down at her exam. She had to work through to get just one answer, without panicking. Now.

The dividend Society Savings had to pay to Mr. Brown of Mayfield Heights on the first of April? A total of seven dollars, twenty-three cents.

Good, she said to herself.

Good. On Thursday, Mr. White had to travel from Ashtabula to Akron, a distance of seventy-five miles. He had to arrive by one in the afternoon for a business meeting with a client. If he left Ashtabula by bus at 7:30 A.M. and the bus made eight scheduled stops of fifteen minutes each while maintaining an average speed between the stops of . . .

Miss Patterson clapped her hollowed palms together. "Pencils down."

The entire class groaned. And a second later burst into sheepish laughter to have revealed themselves that easily.

"Papers forward." Miss Patterson watched carefully as the tests were passed in, desk by desk. "No talking, please. Please pay attention."

One hour later, Joy felt a shiver traveling up her arm from the cold stones of the playground wall. "Well, is the story about me?" she asked, though she dreaded the answer, dreaded being shoved out.

Again both girls laughed. "Oh," gasped Sukie, "I'm going to have to tell your mother on you, Joysie Eichenbaum."

Miserably, for now the two were grinning like twins, she said, "Listen, I can keep a secret."

Mildred kept her hand on Sukie's jacket sleeve. "How can I be sure you won't tell anyone else?" She flicked her pigtail away from her pink cheek as the wind whipped her red glinting hair around her. "It's a nasty story, isn't it, Sukie?"

Sukie said cheerfully, blinking her brown eyes, "It's very dirty."

"And whoever you tell will think I'm nasty too."

Joy paused, taking her time. "But I won't tell anyone, I'm not going to. I mean, I'm concerned with my own actions now. I'm not concerned about yours. I'm really not."

Mildred nodded slowly, pondering.

You're fine, Joy mouthed, as Hankus used to say to her.

A freckled grin slanted on Mildred's sweetly innocent face. "Okay," she agreed, and pushed Sukie forward as if giving her back. "Tell."

Sukie pressed, cupped a hand around Joy's ear and whispered: *You know Mussolini? Mussolini bit Hitler's weenie.* She took a breath: *Know what happened after he bit it?*

But Joy was already laughing; something terrible seemed over. Impulsively she grabbed her friend's hand and squeezed. She couldn't believe how happy she was that this was it. Not in a hundred years could this story ever have any connection to her.

"Remember," Mildred lowered her voice, "what you promised to say about my part, right?"

Open Line: Two-six-oh-two East Trainor

"I'll get it," Joy shouted, running through the front door.

"You get, yes," called the new hired girl from somewhere above.

"Hello?" she said, breathlessly.

"Hello, Joy. When did you get in?"

"Just did, Mommy." She put down her books. "I don't know if Teddy's home yet. Do you want me to ask Sofia?"

"Sure, ask. And ask also if we got any mail."

Joy put down the receiver.

Midway up the front staircase, Sofia was kneeling as she dusted the backboards with lax wide swipes of her plump arm.

She looked over her shoulder. What? Eh, no, the boy is not here, and it was only the one piece of mail she took in from the postman.

Joy found a long white envelope on the foyer table and hurried back.

"From the government, you say?" her mother whispered through the telephone. "*Gottenyu*. From Immigration it says, you sure?"

"Yes. Of the United States."

"Open it right away, darling. Maybe it's some news for us."

Excited, Joy tucked the phone receiver under her chin and began to tear away the glued-down flap.

"Do it right!" her mother commanded faintly into her shoulder blade. "Don't rip what's inside!" Carefully Joy slid out the letter, then put the empty envelope onto the dark little occasional table. From the front of the house, Sofia's humming got louder.

Done yet? Joy? She unfolded the stiff sheet, then lifted the receiver. "Okay, done."

"So," her mother said, her voice again strong. "Now read it to me. Slow."

"Dear Mr. and Mrs. Eichenbaum—"

"Wait, who signed it?"

Joy glanced down the page. "Thomas C. Wardston, Esquire."

"Schmesquire," she grumbled. "Who knows from him? Okay, what else? Go on, read."

Joy took a breath. "The Interdepartmental Visa Review Committee requests that you appear before its representatives at the federal court building in Cleveland on March sixteenth, 1941, at two-thirty in the afternoon, for a hearing on the visa application of one Irina Osvat and her—"

"Evan!" her mother shouted, pulling away, "come fast, *tateleh*. We have some news! Good news!"

Joy pressed the black receiver to her ear. Out of the store's spacious air, its clicks of nonsilence, its random murmurs, came the definite sound of her father's footfalls. Next she heard: "Good news? Vera?"

Her mother, clearer in tone: "They want to talk to us about Irina."

"Who wants to talk?"

"The government. For the visas."

"*Here* they want to talk to us?"

"What do you think. Yes, here! We don't have to go to Cuba to talk and not even to Washington. She is reading the letter out loud now, our daughter. The government is coming to us in Cleveland. They sent us a letter to talk with them downtown."

"Only to talk about Irina?"

"Wait, I didn't let her finish." Her mother came back on the phone. "Does it say Miriam and Lily also?"

Joy checked the paragraph. Her heart was thudding with each small inky name she saw. "Yep, they're here, Mommy! Miriam and Lily Osvat. Osvat, right?"

"See! Good news." Her mother was triumphant.

"No more names?" her father then asked. "No one else we have to talk about? That's all, you're sure?"

Her mother said more slowly into the phone, "Joy, anyone else it says in the letter? Maybe you skipped over them somehow?"

In one burst, Joy understood what was going on in the small back office of the store. Reluctantly she looked again at the paragraph. "No one else," she said. The answer echoed. She'd spoken it guiltily, as if she were the one to have left out the other names in some awful mistake. But she hadn't written the letter. She'd just opened it before anyone else had.

There was a long pause. Joy heard her mother say finally, "*Tateleh,* no. Evan, don't. We'll start with them, the three, all right? In the meeting we can ask about Solly and also—please, darling, no, we'll push now. We have to start where we are. At least we will be sitting face-to-face with someone from the government, true? Well, if you want, then you ask her. You'll only get the same answer."

Suddenly on the other end the telephone cracked against something hard. It was clear the receiver had only been fumbled and dropped, but Joy went rigid. With the first thud she saw her mother, who all of a sudden bent right down; who stood and held the receiver a moment, her palm placed so as to muffle whatever was getting said just then in the small office; whose fingers began to curl away from the horn, opening it up to sound again, as she passed it across, murmuring, "So if you have to be sure, you ask her."

Joy heard the voice she now dreaded.

"Joysie," he spoke very quietly into the telephone, very quietly into her ear. "Read, honey, to me. Be slow. I want to hear from you every word."

Afterward, he said in a lower voice, *Good, thank you.*

Yes. Welcome, Daddy.

Her mother came on. "We'll come home a little early tonight, Joy, if we can manage it. Six o'clock, maybe, Joy." There was a pause. "All right with you? Joy—?"

"Yes, Mommy. Bye."

She couldn't fold the letter into its envelope quickly enough. Never again would she be the first one home to get the mail. No one else's words would she then have to read and account for, as if simply by her pronouncing them, they became hers too. This was a promise: Never again.

Official Hearing Room

A few black threaded squares of the veil stuck to her mouth. Vera ducked her head and poked them out with her tongue, but a fresh gust of air blew the hat's netting inward again. "Chicago they call the Windy City?" she complained, clutching together the lapels of her coat.

Evan had one hand atop his hat; under his other arm he carried a cardboard portfolio, its flap tied with a soft brown string. "At least the wind's pushing out the cold front. Soon the whole winter will be gone."

"You like walking blind?"

A loose sheet of newsprint slapped against his legs; he slapped it off. "It will work out. Don't worry."

She snorted, glancing quickly at him. "What will work out?"

"It will go all right with the appointment. We're meeting with our own government."

They both ducked their heads. With two city blocks to go, they couldn't lift their eyes for too long to see what was being carried toward them. Mostly just little things, scraps that weren't weighted down: litter, refuse.

In the white echoing stone foyer of the Federal Building, ten minutes later, they shook off their coats. Vera rolled the veil up over the brim of her hat and without taking off her leather gloves, pushed her waves back in place. Evan took out a fresh handkerchief and blew his nose. Grit, belched from huge, distant smokestacks and pummeled finely enough to be considered ash and nearly invisible, had been driven into the pores of their skin and the weave of their outer clothes; but without soap and water, you couldn't get truly clean. Besides, in this section of town such particles peppered everyone who stepped into the path of the wind.

Refolding his hankie so the damp spot lay inside and centermost, Evan said, "If you're not ready, I'll go ahead and find out what room." He slid the soft white square into his breast pocket.

"No, no, I'll come. I don't need to fix myself more."

The waiting room was small and painted green, the circular brass ashtrays filled with cigarette butts, ashes, and crumpled candy wrappers.

"Eichenbaum, on time," said the secretary, checking a column in the appointment ledger. "I'll inform Captain MacKenna."

Evan turned to Vera and raised an eyebrow. Quietly he said to her, "Why a captain? For citizens?"

She shrugged, keeping her face impassive. "A big shot, that's all."

They took two of the chairs beneath a half-finished portrait of George Washington and sat, their coats still on. Evan balanced the cardboard folder across his knees, his fingers plucking lightly at the string. Under his breath he asked, "You think Sandor is still here? Maybe he's talking to the same man."

Again, Vera shrugged. "I don't know why they want him too."

"He's smart, that Sandor," said Evan, nodding encouragingly. "He always knows what to say. He will vouch for Irina."

Vera's lips tightened and she closed her eyes. She placed red-gloved hands atop the scrolled clasp of her pocketbook.

They waited.

In the hearing room, with a dirty window to the captain's back, they took off their coats and hung them on the pegs behind the door.

Captain MacKenna introduced a somber, much decorated Lieutenant Ladd as from Naval Intelligence; MacKenna himself, likewise beribboned, but older, taller, and sternly thick of neck, was Army Intelligence. Both he and Lieutenant Ladd were being served by Private First Class Gillespie of the army, who would function as secretary, recording all the questions and answers during the interview. Mr. and Mrs. Eichenbaum should make themselves comfortable. Also, since this was a legal proceeding, they would be put under oath.

"Answer only what you know to be true," said the captain, standing on the other side of the wide table, hands clasped behind his back. "If you're unsure about your answer in any way, then say that; otherwise, you perjure yourself. You understand what I mean by perjury?" The canvas shade floated away from the window for a second as the wind hurtled past.

Yes, they both answered.

The captain nodded at the secretary. "Proceed."

"Please raise your right hands, sir, madam," said Private Gillespie. He slid a Bible onto the table between them. Bound in dark leather, the face of it was embossed with a thin gold cross. "Please place your left hands on the cover."

Vera had to reach across herself to put the tips of her fingers on the thick spine of the book. She glanced straight ahead. Evan touched just the edge of the right side.

A moment later, they were told they could sit.

"The file of Irina Osvat, nee Korach," said Lieutenant Ladd, in a low, dry voice. He didn't look up as he read from a sheet of onionskin stationery clipped to the front of a file. "Formerly of Czechoslovakia and of Hungary. Now of Cuba, following a temporary residency in Portugal."

He and Captain MacKenna opened their folders at the same moment.

Evan shoved forward the cardboard portfolio. "I have brought some papers, some photographs and letters, for you."

"Mr. Eichenbaum," said Lieutenant Ladd, without looking up, "only if requested. Potential sponsors usually bring in information that's not pertinent. We'll ask when we want to see anything, sir."

Evan sat back, his face frozen. Quickly, Vera put her hand on the portfolio.

"Irina Osvat is your sibling, I take it?" Captain MacKenna asked.

Vera nodded, pulling Evan's file in from the center of the table.

"And when, madam, did you last see her?"

"When I left, you know, to come here, to America. That was in 1920."

"When in 1920 did you see her last? Exactly."

Evan turned to her. "September, yes? At the picnic?"

"Sir!" said Captain MacKenna, his voice a ruler slapping wood. "My question is directed to the lady. Do you understand the process here?" He turned to the secretary. "Private Gillespie, strike this last exchange, please. If at all possible, let's try to keep the record clean."

Vera couldn't look at Evan, who leaned stiffly forward, his breath nowhere, as she said, with impossible containment, "I saw my sister Irina at the picnic in September."

"Where was that, madam?" asked Lieutenent Ladd.

"In Szacsur, at my mother's house." She spoke tightly, so no anger would slip out. She directed her gaze right to his eyes. She didn't care to see his medals. "Everyone came to eat, to say good-bye. It was sad and happy, both."

"Yes." The lieutenant's green eyes stared back. "Could you tell me if a Mr. Sandor Belak was also at this picnic?"

"You want to know about Sandor?" Her forehead wrinkled. "I think he was already gone. *To here* gone, I mean. Can I ask my husband, please?" She bit her lower lip and gave a small smile. The slanting bottom edges of her front teeth wore a thin waxy red line of smudged lipstick. "Sometimes he remembers the things I forget. After you're together a long time, you have habits this way, you know?"

"Sir," Captain MacKenna said brusquely, "was Mr. Sandor Belak at this picnic in September of 1920?"

Evan didn't move more than a muscle. "No. He was over already. He was here."

"You're certain."

"He was in New York City already, working. Younger he came over. He is a good friend. That's why she forgets he wasn't always with us." Evan massaged his upper left arm.

The captain nodded curtly.

"What about the husband?" Lieutenent Ladd said, flipping a sheet of paper. "Was he there too, madam?"

"Who? My husband?"

"No. Andras Osvat." The lieutenant spoke the name as separate syllables, as if otherwise he'd be lost in a whirl of long, ungovernable sibilance. "Was your sister's husband at the picnic in September?"

"Andras Osvat," Vera stated, "he was not, no. Irina knew him only a little back then. They didn't get married until later, when we were over here."

"Is it logical to say, madam, that you knew Mr. Osvat even less than did your sister? After all, you said that your sister herself knew him then 'only a little.'"

Under the table, Evan touched her hip. Vera said, "I knew him, Andras. He was a smart boy, so everyone knew him. You are proud to know such people."

"But would you know anything about him, say, in regard to his political views and activities?"

"He wasn't that interested, I'm sure."

"But how are you sure? Do you know his beliefs for a fact?"

"My sister wrote me, always."

"Did she share his political beliefs, madam? Mr. Osvat was arrested, wasn't he? And he died not long after, serving time in a concentration camp"—the lieutenant checked a sheet in the file—"in 1935? Was it because he was involved in some political activity?"

She held still. "What do you mean, 'activity'? They said what they wanted about him, the fascists, so they could take him away. But all he was was Jewish."

"A teacher," Evan muttered.

"Sir. We are not questioning you."

Vera sat up. "Listen, sir, you think I don't know my brother-in-law was a teacher of biology at the *gymnasium*—at the high school? My sister wrote me everything. We are close." As she'd raised her hand for the oath, now she raised it again, but with the index and second digits crossed. Voice shaking, she said, "We are like this. Understand? Close like this, since we were little babies together. This close. You have to break my fingers off if you want to try to make me speak against her. You see how it is? With us, it's exactly like this, the very same. That's how our mother taught us."

"Please put your hand down, madam," Captain MacKenna said, the gold thread on his epaulets catching the light from the window. "No more histrionics, please. We don't care for such extremes of behavior. It doesn't play here."

Vera glanced at Evan and hurriedly buried both her hands in her lap.

"Strike that last exchange, private," said the lieutenant.

"Beginning where, sir?" The secretary looked up from the ruled pad.

"From where she talks about her fingers." Lieutenant Ladd shook his head. "Captain?"

Captain MacKenna leaned an inch forward and said, "Madam, your sister's application for temporary residency in Portugal was denied. We are led to understand it was because she applied for a political visa for herself and her two daughters. Do you realize that she also filed a visa application from Lisbon on those same political terms with the United States Consulate, and then pulled that application, apparently upon advice from an immigrant agency?" He waited. "Madam, do you have specific knowledge of that application as well as her rejection by the Portuguese government?"

Vera bit her tongue. In her lap, her fingers were still crossed. Her legs trembled under the folds of her dress and she pressed with the heels of her hands, trying to still them. She couldn't bring herself to look up; on the other side of the table were the men who had just shown even her how she was trying to fool her own government. She could hear from the older man's tone what he thought of her.

"Sir," the captain said next, "do you have specific knowledge of the Portuguese visa which Irina Osvat applied for on political grounds?"

"I have knowledge." Evan tried to keep everything in himself quiet. "A mistake."

"Really? How is that?"

"She only thought it would help. She thought, Irina, it would make the process go faster. Since 1936 she and the little ones are waiting on the quota list to enter America. She is trying hard to help her little girls. But the quota limits for Czechoslovaks, or Hungarians—"

"We know about the quotas, sir," said the captain, tucking his chin down against his jowls. "Is that how you're explaining the political orientation of her first Portuguese applications? Is it possible Mrs. Osvat shares her late husband's political persuasion and beliefs?"

"What beliefs?" he cried, voice breaking. "Suddenly you take fascist words about a Jew as true? There are not even any words on him for you to take! These three girls, yes? they are being chased for no reason. They are not criminals." He pulled at the string on his folder, "Let me show you, please. I have pictures, letters."

"Personal items aren't useful in this instance, Mr. Eichenbaum. Thank you."

"But, you will see—"

"Thank you, sir," said Captain MacKenna firmly. "Now, if you will excuse us, Lieutenant Ladd and I need to confer for a few minutes. Private, we're going off record."

The scratching of the pencil stopped. The young man sat, his hands still.

"Do you want—" asked Evan abruptly, "you want for us to leave the room?"

"Not necessary." The captain tapped the lieutenant twice on the back of his hand. Turning their chairs around, the two military intelligence officers leaned together, their backs curved only slightly. After a moment, they began whispering together.

In that pause, Vera and Evan exchanged furtive glances. Each showed a face haggard and lost. They might as well have been wearing nightclothes and sitting bolt upright in bed, caught wordless at the end of a long shared dream that, though already fading, gripped them still. They looked away from each other, unable to shake out of themselves the words they knew.

The officers pulled their chairs back around. "On record, Private Gillespie," said Captain MacKenna.

"Is there anything," he asked the couple before him, "you'd like to add to the proceedings?"

Vera roused herself. "Yes, sir." Under the table, she squeezed her fingers. "Please, think of her girls. The political application Irina made, it was because she was scared and was trying everything to come to America, in any way possible. If you let them come, we promise to the government to take financial responsibility. They will never for one day become what is called 'public charges.' We will provide for them, everything. We have a store. Do you know that, that we have a nice store on Buckeye Road?"

Captain MacKenna said, "Thank you, madam." He turned to Evan. "Do you have something pertinent to add, sir?"

"I want to ask," Evan said slowly, "for my brother. His name is Solomon Eichenbaum. With my mother he applied already several times because of the time limits on the affidavits. They are in Czechoslovakia, which is now Hungary. For a long time they are on the quota list. Too, we have another of Vera's sisters, Etel and her family, asking about the possibility—but this is a much newer application. Solly is waiting since from 1936. If you could tell me anything good, so I can write it to him. If you know one good thing for me to write—"

"Sir," the captain said, grimacing. "Our hearing today concerns only the specific application before us. Neither Lieutenant Ladd nor I are privy to information you request from us. I can't help you here, sir.

"Off record, private." Scraping his chair back, Captain MacKenna stood; then the lieutenant rose from his seat. Both officers extended their hands across the broad shiny table.

Two-six-oh-two East Trainor

"Let me explain it again," Hankus said over the telephone.

Evan held up his palm, signaling *silence* in the back half of the hallway. He nodded permission to continue, though of course Hankus couldn't see that. Aloud he said: "Explain again, yes."

"Usually the soldiers get—*I'd* get a pass before shipping out. But because of the bad weather forecast and the way things are going, they want to have the troops board ship early—the day after tomorrow. So, they'll be giving us—*me*—a special pass later, over there. I can't see making it back and forth to Cleveland in time. Some of the Canadian guys are luckier. Their families live closer."

"Over *where* are you getting the special pass?" Evan's palm was still raised toward the others, so they wouldn't press in on him with their questions.

"Overseas."

"Where overseas? This isn't good. Which country?"

"Dad, you really think the brass is about to tell the unit where it's—where I'm—being sent? If I knew where I was going, honest, I'd tell you. I mean, if I had permission to. The thing is, Dad, well, I'm a soldier now, not a son."

Slowly Evan shook his head.

"What does he say?" Vera stood to his right, next to the telephone table.

He held out the receiver. "He's leaving without coming back here. You talk to him. "

Joy cried, "He's not coming home first? In the movies they do, they always come home first."

"Shut up," said Teddy, scowling. "You want him to hear you sounding like a baby?"

She stepped back in agitation, a terrible desperate feeling in her stomach. "But I miss him, I want to see him. Are you so stuck on yourself you don't care whether or not we can tell him good-bye in a real way?"

"I want to see him, stupid, yes."

"Quiet." Evan waved a hand. "Don't talk to each other like that. I don't like to hear it."

Vera said, taking the receiver, "Fine. I'll talk.

"Hello, Hankus," she said.

"Ma, hi. I'm sorry." His voice started out pure and ended up prickled with static.

"Tell me what is happening."

The moment he started to tell her, she interrupted. "Stop a minute, no more of this *chazeray*." Turning, she addressed everyone, all the four, all at once, though she spoke clearly into the telephone. "All right, we are driving to Buffalo. If you can be a hero, so can we. We'll start from here soon. We will get in the automobile at ten o'clock, tonight."

Cries went up everywhere. With a wave of her hand, Vera continued, "We will meet each other halfway. Hankus, from the camp you can get to Toronto and across to Buffalo?"

"Ma, I don't know if I can really do that."

"You don't know. Really?"

"Well—"

She laughed; the three faces in front of her were so astonished, each seemed pulled back a good inch on its neck. Then, all of a sudden, there was a charge of electricity. Evan mouthed: *Buffalo?* Joy began dancing in place, hugging herself in her red angora sweater. Teddy threw his head back and whooped like a wild man. She nodded at them, which meant: Enough sitting quiet and waiting for nothing!

"Listen, Mr. Wise Guy," Vera teased her eldest, "if you did it so easy going in one direction, you can do it just the same in the other."

He said, "But we're not talking about a whole lot of time, Ma. And we're being shipped out before dawn. I'd have to be back before then."

"So? We'll be together for an hour."

Evan's lips were still pursed; he raised his brows quizzically.

"Okay, in one half hour we're going to leave to meet you. Daddy is good at driving at night. Aren't you, *tateleh*?" She smiled at Evan encouragingly. "When will we see you, Hankus? Ten hours? How many? Twelve? Is it more? I don't know about the distance. I haven't been to Buffalo before."

"Ma," he said. "Don't get into the car."

"No, don't? What are you telling me?"

"Don't drive to Buffalo."

"Why not, don't?"

"Because. Just don't."

Levelly she repeated, "Why not, don't."

With a groan, Teddy turned away, shaking his head.

"It's not enough time, really. As soon as I'd get there, I'd have to turn around, you know? And there's something else."

"Why," she said, plaintive, hunching her shoulders, "*why* is there?"

"See, I know it seems bad, sort of—but when I heard there was only this day and a half's leave before shipping out, I promised someone that I'd—that we'd spend the time together. It's my last chance for that kind of thing for a while. Do you know what I mean?"

"So that's it." Vera felt Joy and Evan come inching forward together toward her, and she pulled herself protectively closer around the telephone. Teddy had one foot on the stairs, as if any moment he would run up them, get away from this. Vera waited. The room was perfectly silent around her.

Hankus started to cry. "Ma, listen. I just think it's best not to try to squeeze everything dry. You know there's not really time. I'd only get to see all of you for just a few minutes, then I'd have to get back on a bus. It'd be awful. I don't know that I can do it."

"Stop this, you hear me?" Vera took the receiver from her ear.

"What's wrong?" Joy whispered hurriedly, face drained. "Is something wrong with Hankus?"

Vera said to Evan, "It's a girl. You wanted that for him so he'd stay put; well, now he has one. She gets to see him tomorrow, not us." She shrugged. "He goes and does just what he wants, like always. A lost cause." She gave a sharp, bitter laugh. "He's good as gone, isn't he?"

Evan put up his hand to ward off her words.

"No, Ma, that's not what I want to say. It's not about a girl. That's not really what I was trying to tell you. Didn't I explain it right?" Hankus said, a faint strangled voice as she held the receiver out in the air, away from her. "Hey! Hey, you there?"

"Who wants to talk next?" she asked coolly, furious at him, that she couldn't stop him. "Who," she said, "wants to tell Hankus good-bye?"

"Ma, wait!" they all heard from the telephone. "Wait, Ma!"

Suddenly, the fury went out of Vera and her face seemed to collapse, become very sad and small. As if moving against gravity and hoping to breach some large distance, she lifted the telephone a ways over her head, signaling to the other two children, only one of them turned toward her.

"Ma? You still there?"

Vera forced out her breath, the words barely audible: "Teddy? Joy? Joy, you say good-bye to your brother. He's going. He's getting on a boat, you see. He's going, day after tomorrow."

Kitchen: Two-six-oh-two East Trainor

Joy was busy setting the table for dinner when Teddy came back late from school. Under his arm he carried something long and rolled up, carefully wrapped in brown paper. He walked into the kitchen and put the tube down on the drainboard, where it rolled against a lunch pail.

"It's a gift," he said.

Silverware in hand, she looked up, surprised.

Shaking his head, he smiled. "It's mine."

"Oh." As she'd been taught, Joy turned the blade of the knife in and set it beneath the rim of the plate. She said finally, "Who gave you a present?"

"Janet."

"Is that your girlfriend, Teddy?"

Looking right at her, he laughed. "Is that what you think, Joysie? Come on, you think some girls can like me enough to give me presents?"

"Well—"

He tilted his head. "Well, what do you say?"

She felt strangely embarrassed. It was as if Teddy were asking if she *herself* could like him. But she was so used to his being sullen, she didn't know what to say. The boy now in front of her wasn't anyone she actually knew. His face was too open and happily naked—almost prideful. As he nodded encouragingly at her to just go ahead and answer, she felt her cheeks flushing as hot as they ever did. She moved carefully around the table to the chair that was Hankus's.

"So?" he pressed. "Is that what you think?"

Reaching out, Joy smoothed out the oilcloth so it lay perfectly flat. "Maybe I do. I guess that girls can like you enough."

He laughed again. "You can see that, huh? That they could like me?" He looked at her, eyes wide with delight behind his glasses. He was entirely shining with expectation.

She couldn't believe Teddy was waiting for her opinion.

"Well?"

"Well—"

"Here, Joy, look," he said and put up his arms in a he-man pose, flexing his arm muscles, really poking fun at himself. "This help you decide? Do girls like me at all, you think?"

She laughed. "Sure. Sure, they do."

"Think so, huh?"

She nodded vigorously. "I do. But what do you think, Teddy? I mean, think about me?"

He threw up his hands. "Come on, what are you asking?"

She smiled awkwardly. "Well," she said, and paused. "I mean, I guess, do you like—I guess, do you think someone could like me, too? Enough, I mean?"

"How would I know?"

She stood stock-still.

"You won't make a guess?" she said finally.

He shrugged.

"You don't know, or—"

"Are they back yet?" Turning, he started out the kitchen.

It was over. The stranger who'd stood here for a few clear seconds—he was gone. It surprised Joy just how much it hurt now to have seen him at all. Teddy—he could be nice, he could be charming! Whenever he wanted, he could make people like him; and make them want to *be* liked by him.

Joy wanted to cry. She hadn't seen this nice way he had about him before. Or, she'd thought it was something he used to compete for Hankus's approval. But now without Hankus around, Teddy was free to act toward her just as he wished.

She watched him moving away from her.

"Anyone home?" he mumbled over his shoulder.

Joy bit her lip to stop herself from shouting: *I am! I want you to talk with me.* But did it matter what she told him? All that had ever been between them was what he wanted from her. And what was it that he'd want now?

The answer popped into her head: nothing. The rightness of the reply struck so deeply that both question and answer dissolved the moment they formed. She'd gotten it so wrong. For whatever awful reason, Teddy didn't want to have to think about her, not one bit. He simply saw no use for *Joysie*. For the first time, detachment edged over the old hopeful disappointment she had always felt about herself—that somehow she might yet figure out how she could please her own brother.

Still, she didn't quite turn away. But this small moment when she was eleven would return in various guises over the

years. It would be that vague *something* that would always hold
the girl, the young lady, the mature woman back from asking
any more from her nearest-in-age brother than his own self-
interest.

"Mom!" Teddy shouted, snatching up his gift. "Dad! You
home?"

Joy listened for the sound of his footsteps to fade; Teddy went
through the hall and up the stairs—his weight settling, as always,
just a bit more on the left. Then she put a shiny spoon, fork, knife,
at his place, and continued laying out the rest of the settings.

When he unwrapped his present for everyone to see at the dinner table, it turned out to be a map of the world and two small
boxes of thumb tacks, one of green-headed tacks, the other
plain metal. There was also a short red ribbon crossed over itself
in a simple one-loop decoration, a safety pin keeping it together
where it might more normally knot.

Teddy stood holding the map in front of his chest the same
way that on street corners unemployed men held up signs asking
for work—though with the economy moving, such men were visible less frequently now. "As soon as we hear from Hankus, see,
we stick on the red ribbon to symbolize where he is, his location.
We use tacks for the armies' positions and for important skir-
mishes and battles. It's like a game, but we can keep track of
Hank. I think this should go in the front room because of the
radio, okay? Then when we hear news reports we can move the
tacks to the right position."

Evan finished buttering his bread. He tore the soft slice of
challah in half—keeping his movements slow in response to his
son's excitement. "Your girl gave you this war map?"

Above the United States of America, colored green and situ-
ated in the exact center of the yard-long sheet spread with the
earth's flattened globe, Teddy grinned. For a moment, the
lenses in his spectacles caught the reflection from the bulb overhead. "Janet gave it to me. I wouldn't say she's my girl. Well,
maybe she is. Anyway, she knows about Hank's shipping out. Can
I put this up in the front room by the radio?"

Vera said edgily, "Put it away, we see it already. Your food's getting cold, sit down and eat." She turned to Evan. "I don't want it in the front. We have company there."

"Fine, Vera."

"How about in the kitchen?" Joy offered, drawn to the map, despite herself.

Vera shrugged. "I'm not so excited about having it anywhere, to tell you the truth. Who wants to get pins sticking in the eyes every time you turn around? You want to see pins in the wall when you get food or when you have people over?"

"I told you," said Teddy, "the red ribbon means Hankus! And those are attack tacks, not just pins."

"Don't shout," Evan said tersely.

"I know. Anyway, it's mine. I'm only trying to explain to you how it works."

Evan studied him. "You like seeing it, honey, how the armies go?"

"Sure. I like looking at maps." He plopped down in his chair. "This one's a swell gift, and I want to use it. It could be, you know, that FDR is going to bring us into the war soon."

"Why? Is that what your teachers say?"

He nodded. "Miss Ammons says the Brits might need more from us than just our goods."

"Take bread." Evan passed the plate with the challah. The rounded golden crust was indented where he'd held it securely under the knife.

"You like the map, Teddy," Vera said, "then you put it up in your bedroom."

"Okay. But I bet you change your minds and want me to bring it downstairs." He shifted forward and leaned his elbows on the table. "Don't forget I've got this. Anytime you want to, you can come in—all of you—to see it. You don't have to ask me. Just come in, I'll have it up there."

"We'll see," said Evan. "Now please pass the bread to your sister for her gravy."

Vera saw Teddy's face darken and his mouth turn down in a scowl. A moment before he had sounded so happy. Her good boy. She felt a flash of anger over his disappointment in them. Why should they want to have visible all the time that which to him seemed like a wonderful gift but to Evan and her showed a region too pricked with holes and cut sharp? A small crossed red ribbon means Hankus!

Joy held the challah plate. "Mom? For you?"

Shaking her head, she turned to her son. "I want to meet this Janet. Darling, should we have her to dinner? You want to do that, Teddy? Invite her over?"

His expression froze. "Oh, I don't think so. I mean, it's just one gift."

She laughed. "Only if there's a second present, we feed her, huh? You tell me when that happens, okay?" Amused, she glanced at Evan. But he was twisted around, looking over his shoulder at the rolled-up map, the long cannon of the world swiveled and pointing out from the dish drainer; the small paper boxes of tacks open on either side.

Front Room: Two-six-oh-two East Trainor

Vera sat down at the bright window and held the letter up to the light. Evan, standing slightly behind her, reached over her shoulder; his fingertips almost touched the single thin sheet of paper. Together like that they read the judgment of the State Department of the United States concerning Irina Osvat (nee Korach) and her two nonadult dependents, Lily Eva Osvat and Miriam T. Osvat, who were petitioning to immigrate; all three petitioners actually residing in Havana, Cuba: *Entry Denied.* The following sentence said that, as provided by law, applicants who wished to reapply could do so after six months had passed from the date of the notification letter. Further: Re-applications had to be completed in full; and: All forms and affidavits submitted must be brought up to date; and: No explanations would be given in regard to the current decision.

They stared at the letter, forgetting themselves. They were the more silent and sadder versions of the selves caught and stilled in the sepia photograph balanced on top of Evan's bedroom bureau. "Well," said Vera, the moment the window darkened and the white sheet of stationery dulled, for outside in the spring sky clouds full of cotton swabbed up the sun, "we knew it, didn't we? Those bastards."

Evan brought his hand back from the page and straightened up. Dry-mouthed, he said, "We told them it was wrong about the politics. We said we'd take care of the family. It makes no sense."

"No sense!" She shook the letter. "Just when we're done working like crazy on the Easter sale—the best Easter in years. All the *goyim* buying new clothes. Do the bastards know we reordered from our suppliers three times already? Suddenly everybody is eager to buy, they're done with making do. For the first time ever, even Negroes are working the line jobs in the factories—*that's* how good it's getting. Everything is running full speed. And the big shots don't know? Instead, they think the good times are passing by only our store? Why would they think that?"

"They don't understand."

"With profits like these, we can bring everyone."

"That's right."

"We can bring not only Irina. We can bring your mother"—Vera took a breath to try to slow herself down—"and Solly. Someday, not so far away maybe, also Etel. Oh, we were so happy the store was turning a profit. We were clicking our heels and dancing!" She couldn't bring herself to laugh, even bitterly. "What, *tateleh?* I didn't hear." She waited. "What did you say?"

Trying again, he forced his voice above a whisper. "They made a mistake, maybe. They sent the wrong letter."

She shook her head. "No. I don't think so."

As she crumpled the paper in her fist, she thought she heard Evan mutter, *Now what?*

The Letters

Nagymihály, 28 April 1941

Dearest Ivan and Verushka!

I'm writing you for the fourth time. It is a challenge now to complete a letter, since I am always getting called away in the middle and the paper gets put somewhere or other (with our belongings now squeezed into just the two rooms organization is difficult)—and so three times already my letter to you is lost, half-finished. It is better, I have learned, not to find and then reread it. But I am writing now to thank you for the parcel. Mother and I were watching out for it once we read from you it was coming. We think of you when we put on our plates all that you send—thank you, it's very much appreciated. We have a tin of meat nicely hidden away, still.

This can't be a long letter, because it is almost ten in the morning and if I'm not in line at eleven o'clock, then the only other time we are allowed to shop for food is at three. Since I have finally gotten a small clerical job at the Molnar Center I must be there, not in the line. The new rationing laws are in effect. Everything (for us) is allowed for purchase but fruit, poultry, pork, venison, fish, vegetables, onions, garlic—the list is very nearly complete. It even includes shaving soap. The officials are quite benevolent to us in all ways. Again, many thanks for the package.

I ask that you do all you can to help Mother and me come to you soon. I've learned that boat tickets can be sent by wire and that the consulate in Vienna will notify us. The help, we hear, has to come from elsewhere, so I must ask you once again to do your utmost. No need for me to detail again the many steps I wrote down in my last letter. Yes, I have written to Vienna to see what is possible. We are well. We try to get by.

Mother says to send you and the children all her kisses and love. But I must end now. I must hurry to shop. Please forgive these few words for not holding news of the rest of the family. But I must leave off now or miss the cutoff on the line. Or keep this back to finish later, and risk this page too not sent.

When I am with you in Cleveland, I promise to repay you a thousandfold for everything.

Your loving brother,

Sol

They are well. The family—My silence here is made of haste only—) I must shop.

Read by Military Censors

May 22, 1941

Dear Dad, Ma, Teddy, Joysie—

Sorry it's taken me a while to write back to you. I *have* been receiving your letters. The army's very good about getting mail to us. I've gotten five letters from you so far—three from all the family at once, one from Joysie alone, and one from Ted. Thanks. The letters are great. They really mean a lot to me.

I'm not allowed to say where my unit is, but you probably figured out by now I didn't make it to ████████████ I wish I was nearer to ██████████████████████████, but maybe it's for the best. They want to keep our unit jumping. Where we first landed, things didn't go our way, so as you maybe could tell from news reports, my battalion was one of those evacuated from ██████████████████████████████

██ Now they've got hold of the region, at least for a while. I've seen things happen. One of my friends, Bink, from Buffalo, New York, I lost him.

████████████████████████████████████

████████████████████████████████████

████████████████████████████████████

I know it's not my fault I couldn't get help to him when it counted. I do know that, but I saw him hurting and still alive. But I was stuck on the far side of the bunker. Both of us were pinned down by the line of fire. Only he got the bullets, not me. When it's quiet sometimes, you know, it's hard to stop thinking of ways I might have saved him.

But you can't beat yourself up over the things you tried to do and couldn't pull off—especially if there really was no way to pull it off. You can't win 'em all, that's what they say. I'm over here with a bunch of great guys. Really great guys. Sometimes you can learn a lot about people. The good ones mean everything to you.

I guess I didn't tell you yet how it was coming over. I guess that's not so important anymore, because here I am. The details of the crossing will have to wait for another letter or maybe till I get home. I *will* say I'm glad I didn't join the Royal Navy. That would have been a big mistake, because I found out that I'm one of those guys who gets pea-green seasick. Sick to my stomach all the time. Too much up-and-down motion. The entire way over I kept thinking what a miracle it was, Ma and Dad, that you reached America on a ship. I know now, really, how much

you really must have wanted to come. I take my helmet off
to you for that.
    Don't forget to write to me.

love from your very own,

Hank

Two-six-oh-two East Trainor

Unlike Vera, lying on her stomach, arms tossed up and out from
her sides, Evan couldn't sleep. It wasn't the sultriness of the late
June night or the sudden burst of insects in it that kept him
awake, it was the news that had come on the radio: FDR said he
was ordering the German and Japanese embassies in Washington closed down. It was the end of formal relations with the Axis
nations. For the past two weeks, America had been in a state of
unlimited national emergency. Although the president tried not
to spell it out, it was clear the country was rolling toward war.
Business kept booming. There was that. That was good.

Who knew what would come of what.

For a while Evan stood at the door he'd opened to Teddy's
bedroom, straining to see through the dark to where the war
map with its tacks and pinprick holes glowered on the wall, but
he couldn't make out much more than its overall shape, not
unless he was willing to go in farther. It was better not to risk
waking up the boy. Teddy had come home late after going to the
movies with Janet, and he'd gone right to bed without stopping
by their bedroom to say if he'd had a good time.

With her prompt way of answering and her good manners, at
least the girl seemed to be nice. Vera and he had met her only for
three very short conversations—no dinner yet. Maybe it wasn't
going to be serious with her. So there was nothing to think about,
only to enjoy. Evan himself hadn't known romance when he was
young and innocent as Teddy. Not romance! Only when he
already had dreams and plans for it—when the emotion already
was *love* because it was attached to a further destination: Vera and
he would be wife and husband and move to America—did he

know something about romance. But the feeling didn't linger; it came into the world already expecting to turn toward its work.

Evan pulled Teddy's door shut. He resisted all but a quick peek into the dark edging Joy's room. He wouldn't go in; she slept quietly enough to stop his heart—not one breath audible. Unless he went right up to the bed and waited, he couldn't be sure about her. The little moaning sounds most people made she swallowed behind her closed lips. Over the years he'd learned not to mistake this inertness of hers for catastrophe. *Joy will be okay,* is what Vera said. *She's not the one trouble will find; see,* tateleh, *I promise, about her you won't have to worry.* But uncertain whether or not he could trust stillness as sleep, he used to bend and pat her thin shoulders. Even then, she didn't stir. She just seemed to close herself down.

He might not ever get to know her. He hadn't, until this moment, understood that he didn't know her. Or that, on these nights, he actually was looking for the secret place where his own little Joysie hid herself so firmly and securely away. How could he not have known this—not any of this—until right now?

Evan turned abruptly. All at once he feared being awake. He was not used to these loud feelings; everything in the hall was too silent.

Barefoot, he went down the stairs; they creaked.

Maybe it was romance or love pushing Irina. *A marriage proposal came,* she cabled. *Stop. I agreed. Stop. Civil ceremony set here for 1 July 1941. Stop.* She didn't have to add that, on July 5, she and the girls would otherwise have to leave Cuba to try to get in some other country. Until they received the telegram this morning, they expected Irina was trying to get into Brazil, from where she planned to reapply to the U.S. He and Vera would try again to sponsor her. They had already sent money for her to purchase boat tickets. *Details follow by regular mail. Stop. Love—Rina. End.*

He didn't want to think about her situation. Maybe he wouldn't need to, not after the marriage. Irina was nice-looking; she could have found a good man. It was silly to be thinking about love. And it was better for the girls, yes? to not always have to be running.

If a native Cuban, the man might be Catholic. She might have agreed to be with him from desperation.

At the base of the steps, he hesitated. He wasn't hungry. Instead of the kitchen, he turned to the front room and a few moments later clicked on the brass lamp. In the sudden circle his hand didn't look like it belonged to him. A yellow hand ridged with veins and bony-knuckled. Annoyed, he decided not to give any of this a second thought. His father, who hadn't lived one day beyond his thirty-three years, had never reached out with a grip that looked as age-loose as his son's now did. Simon Eichenbaum had been wound in a linen shroud and laid in the ground when the flesh still fit his bones. He'd had a strong body, yes? It looked as if it should protect him from everything. But whether an attack comes from within or without, death can come at any moment.

This thought startled him also. Evan raised his head like an animal suddenly sniffing the storm on the way.

Strange, too, the horsehair couch looked, and the long pale swagged drapes at the black window, and the chair and cleared clean desk, and when he turned to the dimness behind him— the polished cabinet of the radio. This was his home. Upstairs slept his wife and two of his three children. But everyone else of his blood was on the other side of the world. What were they doing? Where was his Hankus? What sounds were flooding his ears? Was it the day or the night where he stood or sat? Was his boy walking or sleeping? Was he talking? Evan decided that he was. He was talking, Hankus was, to him. The boy had been caught in a too-quiet moment somewhere, and under his breath, he said, very clearly: *Dad.* Then, like when a little boy, he covered his mouth with his hand, hiding the already dead shape of the word on his lips; he crouched down, behind a big rock at the bottom of a hill, maybe, and hid himself all the way. Suddenly— gone; but just for a moment! Behind that boulder, he was still staring at his Dad, yes? with his clear green eyes? Evan had only to be patient and he'd poke his head up again. Hankus was like that, their Mr. Wise Guy, their pop-out-of-the-box joker. Not yet? Then soon. A father could hold still if he wanted to outwait the child.

When later Evan finally glanced down, he was surprised to find his own feet visible. Naked, his toes were long and articulate, almost like fingers, and on each one of the ten a nail gleamed with a square-clipped milkiness. Even the bones were insistent, like the strings pulled tight over the fret of a violin—but here under the skin. When Evan saw what he rose up from—so mortal, so beautiful—he didn't ever want to see such a thing again.

Nothing was what it was. He couldn't recognize even the parts of his body, or keep them from changing.

Suddenly, he didn't know next where to go. Why was he down in the front room? Why not in bed next to Vera who turned and threw her arms out and squeezed the pillow and sometimes moaned, but always in her sleeping soothed him? He barely had to touch her and she would stir and say, "What?" She would repeat it until she got an answer. "What? Evan? *Tateleh*, what? What?"

He would face her. But if his mouth opened, he just wouldn't—*War is uncontrollable. I won't be able to save anyone*—he wouldn't know how to say it. All was lost inside him.

Evan took a step, his heart thudding. "Too quiet here," he said aloud to steady himself. Then: "It is wrong to think this way. Nobody needs it." Slowly he tilted his head. He held still a moment, then looked across the dim space as if searching for someone who wasn't there. "So," aloud he said, "so don't think."

The lamp he'd turned on was calmly burning its little light on the table and onto a few swirls of rug, and onto his naked feet.

The Letters

Read by Military Censors

September 2, 1941

Dear Ma, Dad, Ted, Joy—

Sorry this will be short. I got a bunch of your letters. Thanks. That's weight I don't mind toting in my pack. By the time you get this it'll be Labor Day. (Or is it already gone?) Are you taking a picnic somewhere, like

always? Eat extra for me. When I shut my eyes, I can just
about see all of you forking up the potato salad, a huge
bowl of spuds, eggy-yellow, really thick with mayonnaise.
I love how you make it, Ma.

Glad we're done with the ████████████████████████████
███
███ Word
here is that Uncle Sam *has* to come over, but no matter
what, I'm sticking with my buddies. Especially on ██████████
████████████████████████████████████ no one else I'd trust.

███
██████████████████████████ They're like family.

It's strange to think Teddy is going to be a junior in
high school and Joysie's starting junior high. By the time
I get back, they'll probably be unrecognizable, both of
them real smoothies against an old guy like me. But isn't
that nuts? Really, I'm only kidding.

How's everything going on Buckeye Road? I keep thinking
about people coming into the store and trying on new
clothes in those small rooms with the drapes, where no one
can see them. I hope the line of your customers never
stops.

Think of me.

Love,

Hank

━━━━━━━━━

14 October 1941

Dearest Ivan and Verushka!

Mother received your letter of 27 August with the package of food (many thanks!). Then in the very next delivery
came your letter to me of 19 September, saying Irina was
married now to a Catholic, to the man whose house she
cleaned illegally, since she could not get a work permit.
No one knows what to feel. Telephones are no longer
allowed (for us), so we have not spoken for some time to
Verushka's mother or sisters. Mail (for us) is still supposed to be legal between towns, which is why Artur
insists that soon we'll get word from Szacsur telling *how
everyone is*. But the joke going around Nagymihály is that
it's one week quicker to write to you in America and get
the Szacsur news that way. Of course, everyone here hopes

for Irina the best. Also, everyone is happy for her girls.
Perhaps this is happening so they can put their feet up
for a while and not have to run?

Each month America requires something different for its
immigration regulations. If you can get the information
easily, please write me what is now current. Also, please
write again to the Vienna consulate to say that Mother and
I have our new affidavits prepared. Also, we are about to
secure boat tickets, although we've been told not to
expect leaving until at the very earliest the first of the
new year. If you can, please try to buy the passage from
America—it will cost many times more to buy it from here.
The boat tickets will determine when we might go. By 15
January would be best, before the current affidavits
expire. I have to believe that any time now our numbers
will be called! The Weisses were lucky and left Nagymihály
on 4 September. We've heard nothing from them since, so
all must be well. The "stars" are coming out now—not very
far away, and always at least a little bit visible to
those who are watching from here all the time. But maybe
this is a rumor and it is "heaven" shining on us.

I'm sorry not to write more, but my day has been long.
The "boarders" are finally quiet (we have gained two addi-
tional young girls from Ungvar), so I should be able to
get some sleep. Mother is already dreaming or she would
urge me to put down how much she loves you. Isn't it true
that she would dictate with deep feeling, making me labor
over this poor page, and saying more in a way than either
you or I want? (Now you see truly why I'm awake and writing this so late at night! But of course I say this only
to make you laugh!) Ivan, everybody thanks you and
Verushka for the package of food. We divided it up among
the family. Mother and I are saving the dried beans for
winter, just in case. Out of everything, they will keep
best.

I hope you receive this letter much sooner than most
likely you will. How long did it take to reach you? Three
weeks? Somewhat more, or less? Let me know please, if you
can. Communication, like prayer, is lifeline these days.
Both travel into the Unknown while—here we sit.

My sincere prayers go to you in America. With love once
again from

Your own brother,

Sol

The State Theater

When she looked into the line of shadow-splashed blank faces, Joy realized this wasn't her row. The dark slope of the State's aisle and the patter and flicker on the bright screen must have misled her. But how lost could she be? The screen was set above a rise of three stairs, and on it Veronica Lake and Ray Milland were too tall and airy—and too loudly witty—for Joy to just all of a sudden crash into the picture. As for the rest of the theater, the darkness was not only populated, but it also kept to bounds. Perfectly safe for her, wasn't it, getting lost in the State Theater's Saturday matinee?

Joy began a slow walk down the aisle. If she missed her vacant seat or Sukie who was sitting alongside it, then she'd go straight back to the exit and head down again, counting. Going out to the rest room to readjust and check the first sanitary napkin she ever had to wear, in fact she had counted the rows, tapping each seat back much as a hiker in woods marks trees. Only on her return, eager to catch up with the plot, she fixed all her attention on the movie. A common error, to ignore the pull of downward momentum, to pretend instinct alone will stop you.

If her father had been in the State, he would have been looking out for her; if she didn't halt while wandering past, he'd have whispered, *Here!* and: *Don't you know to count the rows, honey, so I won't have to signal you?*

I meant to, Daddy.

So next time, instead of getting yourself lost, you will—

Her mother: *Stop talking! You think it's my job to always tell you the parts of the story you're missing?*

From the big speaker behind her, a full orchestra of violins swooned. Before the chord ended—as it was yet hanging on for all it was worth—Veronica Lake said to Ray Milland, "I won't let you go. I don't want you to fly away like that. No, don't say that I'm silly! Don't, darling. I know we have no choice now, but, oh—oh, my darling, I swear this hurts. I can't let you leave me." Tears filled Joy's eyes. Maybe someone that beautiful was saying the very same thing to Hankus before he had to go off on his missions. Oh, oh wouldn't that be wonderful?

In his last letter—which he wrote to her alone, in response to one of hers, he said he was proud of all he was doing, but that's right, he didn't really want to tell her the stories now. He'd save them for when he got home. Hankus said her latest letter made him feel so good that he even read it aloud to a few of his buddies who didn't have sisters. "I'm lucky," he'd written, "to have a pen pal like you."

Joy stumbled as the toe of her oxford snagged on an open seam in the carpet. Right away the woman in the aisle seat leapt up as though to catch her. "The film's on fire," she shouted. Suddenly throughout the vast box of shadows, the audience was leaning forward. People were pointing to the screen behind Joy, as if it were on that white rectangle where the flames burned, just as many could see in pinholes on their wall maps at home the actual flapping of ripped flags and the chaos of battle. From every direction, voices cried, "Fire!"

What Joy saw as she swiveled in the aisle, just four rows away from Sukie and the plush seat that, resilient, had lost by now the warm impression of her body, wasn't the original mishap but its effect. Ray Milland, no longer able to talk, had already dissolved around a brown hole that leapt out of nowhere and covered his face; his knees had gone in the same way, though he still stood for a second, for those were his boots climbing and raising him onto the wing of the plane. Veronica Lake was also splattered, pools of her gone into a mottled background composed of the same stuff as she. In a flash, catastrophe turned liquid. People, no longer solid, flooded inward, into the scenery. *Hot.* Hot to the eye.

The audience fell silent. After a moment, the house lights rose to full strength. No one moved. Joy saw Sukie in three-quarters profile, blinking at the dead screen. She looked windblown; the collar of her plaid blouse was unbuttoned and pushed back; her black hair was mussed.

Then someone laughed. Then somebody else did, farther

away. Row by row, the ripple spread. Audience members twisted about to gaze up at the projectionist's booth. A blurry cone of smoke drifted from it as the projectionist appeared, waving an arm. "Folks?" he called. "Sorry. Won't be but ten minutes more, I'll have it spliced back together."

The lady in the aisle settled back in her seat and looked over at Joy. "You lost, sweetie?"

Joy shook her head.

"What a day, eh?"

Joy tried to shift her weight a little from one leg to the other, still awkward with wearing the thick Kotex. She gave a small nod. "Oh. Yes."

As though speaking to another adult, the fat lady sighed. "You're right, dear. A day. Why does it always have to end up like this? So disappointing. And when all we came in looking for was a little entertainment. Just a little something to brighten things up. Makes me tired, you know?"

"But wasn't it," said Joy, thrilled by her daring in continuing the conversation, "a *little* entertaining anyway, ma'am?"

"How do you mean?"

"Well, I mean, well—the fire. I mean, I've always worried what I'd do if something bad happened, and I was caught in the middle of it. Well, I guess," Joy hesitated, but the lady was still listening, "I know maybe a little bit more now. After this, I mean. I think that's good."

"Why, aren't you something?" The woman smiled up at her from beneath a corona of peroxide-yellow curls, the strong lines of fatigue in her face deepening. "You sound so bright, dear."

Joy broke into a grin.

Sukie waved at her. "What're you doing? Over here!"

"I'll have to remember this conversation." From out of her pocketbook the lady withdrew a fresh pack of Lucky Strikes. For a second it looked as if she were going to offer Joy a smoke, too. "We need to take whatever we can get from our movies, you mean?"

"That's right," she nodded. Signaling Sukie: *One second!* "That's how to do it."

• • •

Despite the projectionist's assurances, the show finished not ten minutes late but nearly twenty-five. For a while the girls were part of the slow surge shuffling toward the lobby; then they decided it would be faster to get out of line and duck under the ropes. Holding hands, Joy and Sukie began to work a path through the center of the room where the crowd for the next show was waiting. The new patrons had the early-December wind still on their overcoats. They stood in queues, four lines across, at the refreshments counter.

"Excuse us, please," Joy said.

The dark man in the tailored brown coat took no notice. "I'm telling you," he said to his friend, "you can smell the ghetto on 'em. One whiff and all you want is send them right back."

"Jesus, Howie, not everyone can be Albert Einstein."

The dark man laughed. "Think I consider my father an Einstein? But the people coming in now—the lowest of the low. When my parents came over, it was different. But these people— they're just not making life any easier for those of us who're already settled in. No wonder that blowhard Coughlin keeps yelling about the Jews."

"Excuse me." Joy's face tightened. "Excuse me? May we cut through?"

He looked down, blank-eyed. "What say, little miss?"

"Cut through," she repeated, louder.

"Can we get past you, please?" Sukie pulled a black curl stuck Betty Boop–style from the corner of her nervous mouth. "We just want to slip by."

He laughed. "You girls go 'round the back, like you're sup- posed to." He turned his wide chest in its beautiful brown but- toned-up coat flush to them. "You think you can disturb every- one else? We're waiting in line for the refreshments."

"You're a creep, mister."

"What's that?" he said, jaw hardening.

"You're a creep," Joy repeated. She felt her eyes widen with surprise at what she'd said aloud. "My Aunt Irina is going to come here, and my cousins, too. And also you're"—Joy plunged on—"you're glue. Everything's rubber and glue. Whatever you say bounces backward and sticks right onto *you*."

She grabbed Sukie, and the two of them worked their way back behind the velvet rope. Wordlessly, they rejoined the crowd filing slowly next to the long wall where the posters for the next four *Soon-to-be-at-the-State* features boasted about their stars— CAGNEY! LOMBARD! HOLLIDAY! ASTAIRE! AND MORE!—from behind the protective glass cases.

The moment the girls got out of doors, the line before them broke apart and people began heading off into the cold afternoon air. In the first clear spot, Sukie spun in a circle, blue mittens flying out widely from the loop of yarn around her neck. "You talked so fresh to that man!"

"I know, I can't believe I said those things."

"You were positively dripping dis*dain*. You sounded like a movie star. Like Joan Crawford, like Bette Davis. And that old rhyme was perfect."

Joy flushed under her olive skin. She quickly started buttoning the front of her red stadium jacket. "He was a creep. I hate people who pretend they're better than everyone else. Don't you, I mean, hate that?"

With a moan, Sukie hugged herself under the ribs. "I'm such a baby compared to you, Joysie. You're so lucky. I wish I had my 'friend' too. It's changed you already."

Joy looked around, embarrassed. "Not so loud."

They were walking toward the ticket booth, where Mrs. Greenwald bent over her small towers of sorted change, her fingers, long as a pianist's, flicking out the silver coins as required. Even from ten feet away, Joy could hear the tune of *ping ping, ping: Ping!* as nickels, quarter, and thin dimes swirled into the shallow metal basin set beneath the partition glass. A woman in a dyed-blue fox neck piece—her tickets purchased—snapped up the change; she called over her furred shoulder in a husky voice, "Hilda, Jasper! Starting!"

"No one heard," whispered Sukie, hooking her arm into Joy's. "Not about your 'friend.' If I don't get mine soon, though, I'm going to die."

"Don't be silly. All it means is, well, that you can have babies when you're married."

"Do you want to have babies?" Sukie turned giggly.

Joy shot her an uneasy glance. "I haven't thought about it. It's too strange."

"Well, I think you're going to have a big family. I bet that'll be your fate. You'll have a circle of kids around you all the time. You and your husband, Isaac Dubow."

"Not him!" Joy shrieked.

"Him and your four sons!"

"Oh, pish! I already have brothers."

"Too bad. Because one of your sons is going to be a doctor, just to make you happy. Two"—Sukie held up her fingers—"will become lawyers. Double—double the pleasure. And the fourth is going to be a rabbi. Not an Orthodox one, though; that's too much. With four, you cover the bases."

"All boys?" she moaned, and felt the special belt and hooked-on sanitary pad shift. There was some real stickiness now. "Can't I have a girl?"

"If you give up one of the sons, sure. But it can't be the rabbi. He has to stay. You have to keep him."

"Why?" Laughing, she let Sukie just keep pulling her along the pavement. "And Isaac Dubow, too? Do I really have to keep him? He always cocks his head to the side. Like he can't hear? And he's sneaky. When he thinks no one's looking, he takes things at recess; I've heard that."

"Sorry, he's your fate. What can I do about it?"

That's when Joy saw Vera standing two stores away, at the street corner. Her mother was staring at her, tight-lipped with anger, as if—impossibly—she'd heard every word. A stream of air whistled coolly against the nape of Joy's neck; she had her hair up in two pigtails, like Sukie sometimes wore hers. Just then, two grade-school boys, chasing each other, cut around them. The second boy's elbow caught Joy on the left side.

"'Scuse me," he shouted and kept running, didn't so much as turn his head about to see her response.

"Say, don't you mention it," Sukie yelled. To Joy, she said in a more reasonable tone, "Wasn't that Ruthie's cousin? That shorter one? He's getting really cute."

"My mother's here," whispered Joy. She was frightened without knowing why, knowing only that the glare Vera sent toward her wasn't breaking off.

"Didn't they want you to go to the matinee?" Sukie whispered.

"I asked last night at dinner. I thought she said yes."

Vera took a deep breath. She stood just to the right of the green metal postal-storage box. Without calling, she reached one arm toward her daughter, walking so fresh-cheeked and in her bright red jacket; and then she reached with the other one.

Joy broke into a run, but only on the inside of herself. Outside, her steps hardly quickened; with her elbow still hooked into Sukie's, each stride of hers stayed short. After a few yards she called, "Hi, Mommy."

Vera saw her daughter hesitating, five pavement squares away, as if the space between these raised arms couldn't be meant for her. As if she—her mother—wasn't showing her how much she wanted her to come close. How much she, waiting, needed her now. Vera's fingers burned from the blood surging through them; her arms tingled in the effort of staying up, shoulder height.

"What's wrong?" Joy asked apprehensively.

The other—the Horowitz girl—disentangled herself, but all the while looking down. Tugging on her mittens, she mumbled, "Hello, Mrs. Eichenbaum. Well, bye, Joysie—see you."

"Come here, Joy." Vera opened her arms a few inches wider, as a signal that her own girl could find room.

Against her, Joy smelled faintly of popcorn and sweat. She was old enough now to have to be diligent about washing away body odor. Quickly, Vera said in a low voice into her daughter's ear, "Do you know where Teddy is?"

Joy shook her head once but didn't pull away. "Usually he doesn't tell me," she said against her mother's collar.

"How to—but I have to, now," Vera murmured, and again caught herself.

"Mommy, is something wrong with him?"

Vera stared down the length of the block, to the brightly lit marquee. STATE THEATER flashed every few seconds. She shut her eyes. She was not going to let herself start crying. In a wave of dizziness, she gripped the girl pressed against her.

"Joy," she whispered, her hands shifting position on her daughter's back, "a telegram came to the house. We have to go now, go right to the store, to tell Daddy about it. The two of us, you and me, we'll do it. See, Hankus is missing in action. You see, that's what the message says." Vera stiffened as Joy lurched once in her arms and gave a little cry. The girl's moist breath burst warmly on her neck. Vera didn't move.

Her own breath came fast then—shallow and sick with fear. She counted to five: "So. All right now?" Still holding on to Joy, she stared ahead to the dark marquee for just another moment; in that moment STATE THEATER pulsed out, bright. "So"—Vera forced out the next words—"let's go, all right. We'll tell Daddy now."

Joy nodded. The embrace broke apart. The damp air rushed between them. By keeping always half a stride behind, Joy managed to follow her mother. Her mother always knew what to do. She was telling Joy to cross the street now, telling her to stay close, telling her to cross again here at the north corner, and soon again at the crosswalk, and there—no, quick! Go fast, go back that way to get that taxi at the far stoplight. Joy, run and get him. Get him! You get there, you get him. Get him before he leaves.

It was the first time for Joy that history spun on its heel and changed her sense of direction. When the next morning Japanese pilots flew above the American fleet docked at Pearl Harbor and opened their bomb bays, she took in this news as the logical extension of what had been targeted and exploded on her neighborhood streets at four o'clock on the afternoon before. To the end of their lives, the majority of Americans would remember December seventh with unnerving clarity. Few would recall any of the events that demanded their attention on Saturday, the sixth.

That wasn't so for this family.

Winding Streets

"Our boy will come out of this all right," Evan said, slipping the telegram quickly back into its yellow envelope. "Soon we'll be notified he's safe. Or if the—if they captured him, it won't mean that he is—it's not the other." Sucking in his lower lip, he nodded deliberately, up and down, looking with each nod into Vera's dulled face. They'd stood, the three of them—the two adults, the adolescent—in the store's back office, and when of a moment it seemed Evan's knees were bending weak, he slapped a hand against a chair back, making them all jump. He steadied himself then. He said, "Mary or Paulina will have to close the store. We're going now."

He packed them into the long black Chevy parked not directly in front of their own store but by the curb near Rivchin's Pharmacy, where Mark was stacking brown glass bottles of peroxide and blue paper boxes of antiseptic cotton gauze in his father's display window. The boy looked up and loosely and silently waved his free hand. Evan, barely aware of it, nodded back. He slammed the car door closed on the passenger side and went around to his side, the driver's side. He was sourmouthed; and his hands shook when he gripped the steering wheel, but he could manage. Numbly he turned the key in the ignition. He released the hand brake.

"I hope we— I need to go home now, Daddy."

Evan caught his own eyes widening in the rearview mirror, then his daughter's face coming toward him, blocking his view of any traffic. "Sit down," he said. "Sit still, Joy." Shifting into first, he stared at the two-lane street ahead through the faintly grit-scarred windshield and, giving the motor a little gas, pulled out. "We're not heading right home."

A horn blatted from behind them.

"*Tateleh,*" Vera said, her voice thin from stretching over her emotions, "where is there to go?"

He glanced at the rearview again. "That man is far enough in back of me. I was careful. He had no reason to disturb the peace that way." Not until after they passed Heller's Kosher Butchery did he say more loudly, "Is Teddy at his girl's?"

"Maybe."

"What do you say, Joy?" Evan stared ahead, to the slapping back doors of a small truck; inside, lead pipes and plumbing supplies rolled back and forth. The speed limit was twenty-five miles an hour.

"I don't know. I mean, I think he's with Janet more than with his boyfriends. On a Saturday afternoon I guess he could be anywhere."

"Take from my jacket pocket on this side, Vera, a piece of paper with a street name. I think I put it there."

She slid closer to him along the cold seat.

Glancing backward, he muttered, "Such a face. So full of anger, that one behind me. A monster." And when Joy twisted about, lifting herself off the seat, he snapped furiously, "You don't need to see him! He's the kind who owns the whole road. Don't give him the satisfaction."

Joy squeezed her legs together and faced forward. She bit back her tears. She didn't know what to do.

Signaling, Evan turned onto East 116th and sighed, "If you can't find the paper, Vera, don't worry, it's fine. I remember the street name."

"Good. Where are we going?"

"To Rockwell Street." He sped up. "We're getting our son. Teddy said Janet lives on Rockwell, off from Fairmount Boulevard. It's not a long street, maybe two or three blocks. The neighbors will know which house. So, we'll knock on a door and ask whoever answers where the Rosens live, yes?"

He pulled the Chevy over in front of the corner house, number one hundred, a massive two-story brick structure with a white-columned portico, hunter-green shutters, and a facade veined by cold-withered ivy. The lawn leading to it was close-cropped, like for a golf course, and edged by bushes that seemed to have taken root a good generation or so earlier. The bushes were already bundled in burlap, in expectation of big snows.

"Very fancy," Vera muttered, under her breath. "They're all fancy, the whole area."

Evan looked in the rearview. "See if they know where the Rosen family lives, Joy, so we can get Teddy. He should come home."

"Do I have to? I can't."

"Joy."

"I don't want to. Please?"

He still gripped the steering wheel, which vibrated. He dropped his forehead down against it, the top of the cold curve. The thwarted power of the idling engine shook into his body. "Go ask."

The back door opened, then slammed.

"So, that's why," Vera said quietly. "Look at the backseat. A stain."

He twisted about. "Blood? From her?"

"From who else? No one."

Together they watched how Joy walked oddly up the front path, with her legs like sticks, her hands pulling at the back of her dark blue skirt.

From the lady of the house Joy heard that no Rosens lived on this side of Rockwell, especially not if Rosen was a name, as the lady said she thought it would have to be, please excuse her, of Hebrew origin. The name didn't strike a bell, she had to admit. Not one tinkle.

Joy apologized, and because the lady was still watching and didn't close the front door on her, she backed away as long as she could. Then at the porch steps, she had to turn around.

Crying, she ran toward the car. She saw the small white terry towel her father used for cleaning the windshield lying across the backseat and burst out, "I'm sorry! I said I had to go home. I said it."

"Enough, it's nothing. A little blood will wash out," Vera said shortly. "Where are Rosens? Which house?"

She choked, "No Jews live here, the lady told me. It's restricted."

"But Teddy said Rockwell." Evan quickly pulled away from the curb. "I wrote it down, in case."

"Who cares about Teddy?" Joy was crying in earnest, sitting on the crumpled towel. "I don't care about Teddy. Why are we looking for Teddy?"

"Don't talk about your brother that way," Evan said, and louder, "Control yourself. Teddy said Rockwell. He said that."

Vera muttered, "He said! From now on, he wants a map, he should put up Cleveland. I should stick the pins in him, after this."

"He said she lives on Rockwell. Why would he lie?" Evan rolled his window open a half crank. "Maybe that lady is new living here. Sometimes people lie when they don't know how to answer, yes?"

The automobile glided along under the tall barren-branched elms. The house numbers climbed by increments of a hundred. On only a few of the mailboxes nailed to posts by the curb were family names stenciled.

Vera said, "Stop here. Not at this one, Blackwood, but at the next; Tyler, it says. I'll see there about Rosen."

The car came to a halt in front of a slate-roofed, stone-fronted house, set with narrow windows and white gingerbread trim. Without a word, Vera got out and walked toward the door. Not two minutes later, she was back.

"A restricted area," she said. "No Rosens." And faced forward. "You want to keep looking?"

"Home," Joy sobbed. "I have to change this thing. I'm flowing. I can't sit here in the back of you all the time. I don't understand why we're doing this. Why are we looking for Teddy? Why shouldn't he come home? He lives in our house, he's not the one missing. It's Hankus. Can't I say it right? It's Hankus now."

Two-six-oh-two East Trainor

Rarely were the doors bolted at two-six-oh-two. The safety latch on the front door hadn't been locked, only closed on that sixth day in December. Vera, home from work to bake a sponge cake and cinnamon-sprinkled *rugelach* for the Belaks' twenty-third anniversary party, had just begun sifting the flour when the front bell rang. Flour had fallen dryly from her fingers as she stood outside on the stoop and ripped open the sharp yellow envelope; some ghost grains rolled down the thin slip of paper and into the bottom fold of the envelope she wouldn't bring the slip out of completely; one glance and she shoved her son's name back inside. *No* she said in Hungarian; *Nem*—and nothing more. The messenger, a boy with Brylcreemed black hair and shined brown shoes, mumbled something and ran back down the path. She hadn't heard him hop on his bicycle or pedal away, though she'd stood in the open doorway, watching him as he rose up and down on his shiny shoes, with each full revolution getting a bit smaller and a bit smaller and a bit smaller and a bit smaller. So small that boy got, and so easily, she wanted to scream. She ran back inside and shook her hands free of the rest of the flour, and shaking still, went for her red wool coat, which was hanging with too much space around it in the front closet.

Now when Teddy came back in the late afternoon, it was to an empty house. He walked in through the back door and saw the kitchen left as if quickly abandoned. Tiny bottles of vanilla extract, almond extract, and rum stood uncapped; the paper sacks of sugar and flour were untied. On the newspaper spread on the counter to wrap the garbage were the cleaned-out halves of six white eggshells; four others, ovoid and full, rested under the curve of the large metal mixing bowl. He peered into it, at the raw mucous whites, blotted with unbroken yolks. His mother didn't tolerate tasks left undone. But was it his place to put the bowl in the icebox? Getting it wrong, something mistaken like that, could bring down her wrath.

He walked to the front foyer. "Anyone here? Mom," he called, "Dad?" He listened for a second, trying to catch a sound from upstairs, maybe a hasty footfall or a squeaking mattress spring. Nope. They wouldn't have stopped work midday to come home to do *that.* He'd never heard anything wild like that happening between them during the day. Maybe he had heard them together in the middle of the night, but those sounds were unattached to any visible certainty, and after a while they slipped away easily. Those muted, night things.

He grinned. In broad daylight, from two-thirty until maybe a half hour ago, Janet and he had been necking. Well, petting actually, which was more serious. John Caldwell had been doing the same thing with Trish DeVries. John had maneuvered his gleaming, hand-waxed DeSoto to the farthest edge of the parking lot in Cain Park and pulled on the hand brake. It set with a delicious grinding sound. Then he slung an arm over the top of the front seat, asking, "How's this? You want to be here, ace?" There were cars clustered at the other end of the lot, as close to the start of the hiking trail as possible; they were mostly family cars, parked where it was practical. Families!

The pine boughs draped moodily across the windows. Teddy turned to Janet, who nodded and flicked back a curl of dark hair from her forehead. On her wrist was the identification bracelet he'd just bought, right before his seventeenth birthday. Its curved silver plate was engraved: *TED*. Some people had initials on theirs, but *T.D.E.* looked silly, like a misspelling of who he wanted to be, first and foremost. He didn't like to think of himself as Theodore David Eichenbaum, and the family diminutive of Teddy was something he'd always been wild to outgrow. With Janet dangling three letters on her right wrist he became Ted—a clean name, simple. A name like the salt of the earth.

He whispered to Janet. "Want to?" Under her coat, she was wearing a cashmere sweater. He slipped his hand up beneath it and felt the front cup of her brassiere. Then a few moments later as they were kissing, he freed the full swell of her breast from the cone of stiffly stitched cotton. Their mouths were open and they were touching tongues. Ted got her new red lipstick all over his face like a badge of honor. When he moved her right hand to his belt, she didn't pull away, like he'd heard Jewish girls had to do. She was just wonderful. She was the best part of his world. He was too excited to feel it, but he knew the links of the ID chain were swaying just above his zipper; if she would only come down a bit more, the *TED* plate would be resting on him. He was almost bursting toward it.

• • •

At the heavy slam of a car door outside, Teddy looked up. He walked into the front room and glanced out one of the two side windows. The Chevy was stopped before the storage shed. Joy was already out and running, head down, across the driveway; his mother and father just sat in the car. Then, almost at the same time, they opened the black doors and stood up, both facing the house. Neither seemed to notice him, though he should have been perfectly visible, there in the window. Teddy was about to rap on the glass when he saw their expressions. He just turned away with a sick feeling.

Joy came through the front door. Hunched over, she ran up the stairs without stopping.

"Joysie?"

Apparently someone was coming through the back entry. "What's going on?" he said nervously, walking toward the kitchen. Overhead, the pipes clanged a few times as water began to rush through them.

His mother stood in the middle of the room, arms down, staring at the cluttered counter. She didn't move to take off her coat. Then she looked up and saw him. Her face was cold as stone. "Why didn't you help?" she snapped. "You have eyes and hands, don't you? You have feet."

He shrugged. "How could I know if you—"

"You couldn't see it would spoil? A half dozen eggs cracked in a bowl and sitting out in the air? You couldn't move to help me a little by putting it in the icebox."

"Mom, I just got home, too." Apprehensive because she was moving too rapidly even for her, he looked toward the rear entry. "What's Dad doing? What's going on?"

Turning, she dumped the raw eggs into the sink. Two long clear strands clung from the metal lip of the container. She shook the bowl again. "Probably ruined. No use trying to save them."

"Sorry." His palms were sweating.

She ran the faucet into the bowl. "Where were you till now?"

His father came in, his beautiful overcoat buttoned unevenly, one button off from the breast down. "Mom and your sister and I went looking for you." He said, even more quietly, "She lives on Rockwell, yes? Janet?"

Slowly Teddy nodded.

"Rockwell, yes? We drove up and down Rockwell. Do you know what? The street is restricted from Jews."

Again, just once, he nodded.

Frowning, his father came close to him. He gave off a sour smell, not the faint clean whiff of talc, which he applied after bathing in the morning and usually seemed to stay with him all day, despite his long hours at work. He said, "Why did you lie to us, darling?"

His mother turned off the tap, and the pipes in the ceiling clanked. All the water rushing inside two-six-oh-two's walls was surging up to the second floor now. Joy had to be filling the tub. The sound was like wind but murkier, and every so often it came in a pounding.

Teddy said, "Everybody is acting nuts here. Why's Joy taking a bath in the middle of the day?"

Still not looking at him, Vera picked up the metal flour sifter and smacked it with the palm of her left hand. She gave it a shake; a few of the wire-webbed grains dropped out.

Teddy said, "Come on, did Joy fall in a mud puddle or something?"

"So you don't want to say what the truth is," said Evan.

He shrugged. "Maybe the truth is you made a mistake. I'm not sure I ever said what street she lives on." He shoved his hands in his pants pockets. His hands had been full of her only a half hour ago. He had been part of some other world.

"It's your brother." Vera finally turned to him.

"No," he said flatly. "It's not."

"Yes, your brother is missing in action." She walked over to the table and pulled out her chair. She sank down, the oilcloth tugging a way with her. "They don't know what happened to him," she said wearily.

He burst into giggles. He saw his father's shocked expression and could only roll his eyes upward, laughing, breathless. The giggles of a kid. It was awful, like the sound and surge of the water that wouldn't stop. "Do they think he's dead?" he gasped.

Evan's arm whipped around. And slapped him. Across the face.

"Is he? Dad, is—is Hank—?"

His left cheek burned, struck—a second time. Evan had never raised a hand to any of them, not to his three children. Teddy heard: "You can talk like that about your brother? You throw your lies up to us now?"

He heard his mother cry: "What are you doing, the both of you!"

He cringed, couldn't get away from the blows. He tried to swallow, he tried to stop laughing. "Don't. Don't, Dad. Please don't hit me." He doubled over, sick with his laughter.

And overhead, the sound of water rushing loudly in its circuit as Joy, tears stinging, threw her stained underpants, slip, and skirt into the open-drained tub and, punching them down until they were soaked, washed and washed.

Just after dawn the next morning, his body aching all over from the unnatural landing of blows on his son, Evan got stiffly out of bed. Vera seemed to be sleeping turned on her side, away from him. Quiet as a mouse he opened the closet. He patted his suit jacket and then from the breast pocket pulled out the overseas letter; it had arrived yesterday at the store. In the terrible troubles of the afternoon and evening, he'd forgotten about it entirely. Now, again, he read over that part, the one following: *You must, Ivan.* And grew just as cold as he had before—before Vera and Joy came in with their news.

"For myself," Mother wrote in Yiddish (or rather, since she didn't know how, she'd dictated to Artur), "I am too much a part of Nagymihály, even as the life here is changed, but the boy must leave. Each day he wakes up tired like an old man. Now, there is no work at all for" (Artur had written something, then censored it, crossed it out), "and everything is rationed since" (again: crossed out) "or if available, then too terribly expensive to buy. So, he runs in circles all day. He is only a boy. He tries and tries, but he has not the power to make what is not there *there*. Please, I am asking you, Ivan, do everything in your power to take my Solly to you. I bless your home."

At the bottom of the page, beneath where Artur had written out squarely in his steady hand: *Mother*, stood a black *X*, tilted and faint, about half an inch high. The legal mark was almost the worst part of the message.

X—his mother, petitioning him as if he was someone with authority! *X*—trying to prove in this way she had a singular and real existence. With this sign, the distance between the two of them—no, between him and all his family in Nagymihály—stretched out so thin and far that he might as well be up on the moon, for all they knew of his life. Or—and here he shivered—for all he knew of theirs.

Suddenly, Evan wanted to rip everything into ten thousand pieces. He wanted it with all his heart. To never again have to hear from overseas—to not hear from his family or Vera's. If only that could happen some way or another!

Some people made it happen. They decided to forget and get on with their own lives. Maybe they mourned in secret, maybe they did; but in the bustle of the day-to-day, they thrived. Those who lived outside of America, well, they became part of the old dream. They didn't exist in the here and now. And America was about the here and now. It had little to do with the past, except as something to throw off. Didn't Schecter at the shoe store act that way? Softly pushing away all talk when asked about his childhood or where he'd come from? A shrug. A wave of the hand. Or what about Abramowitz, angrier, who'd answer by arguing: He'd come over on his own thirty years ago, without the Nazis to push him. He was sorry about it, but these people had made their beds, they'd have to sleep in them.

Those two were no longer pulled in every direction, without knowing which way to turn. If their sons were missing in the fighting in Europe, they wouldn't be distracted by other obligations. If Hankus was a son of one of theirs—if his Hankus was . . .

Evan stared into the right shoulders of his hanging suits.

Vera rustled in bed. "What is that you have, *tateleh*?" Her voice was bleak.

Folding the sheet into its thin envelope, he stood still a second. "Just a bill," he said. He gazed for a moment at the return address and slipped it back into his suit pocket.

A door creaked open down the hall; footsteps. A moment later the bathroom door hinge squeaked; water was turned on.

"You brought home a bill?" Disturbed, she turned about, the covers twisting tightly about her body. "Why? How much is it?"

"No, no, it's nothing."

"But who do we owe?"

"We don't owe." Evan paused. "I didn't say the right thing. It's a letter, Vera." He sat down on the edge of the bed. "A letter from my mother." Pulling back the covers, he got back in. "Artur wrote it. I'll show you after breakfast. It can wait."

Wearily she just nodded, the back of her head against the pillow.

"Rest a bit more, Verushka. You were tossing all night."

"So," she said grimly, "you didn't sleep either?"

The bathroom hinge again. A door shutting in the hall.

"A little I slept, I think."

"And how many nights, Evan, did we sleep while our Hankus was in trouble? Four, maybe? Seven? Two dozen? But no one told us and so we slept like babies. You know what? I curse those nights. Every minute I didn't pay attention and he was calling for me."

"You don't know that." He lay down next to her and waited. "You want to call Canada again and check on him? We have that special number from last night. I know the clerk said we would be told right away if something changes. But time's passed now. Also maybe she didn't have all the rules right. The military is complicated."

Vera turned her head. The drapes weren't more than halfway shut. She thought she always pulled them tight against the neighbors' eyes, no matter what. Through the vertical gash, the sky was brightening, not a bird flying in it, not one cloud. The sky would remain clear overhead all that day and also all that night in Cleveland. The next day's sky would prove fair, too. The fierce plumes of oily black Pearl Harbor smoke, still five and a quarter hours away from inception, would take quite a long time to disperse and drift. In any case, they were half a world away. As were all the smaller explosions, each one rising, spinning, darkening, scattering, blocking out everything.

"Vera, you want to make another call now?"

"No," she spoke without hesitation. "No, what for? They'll only tell us the same thing. Gondar, Italian East Africa. Italian East Africa is where Hankus was—*is.*" She sat up, the strap of her nightgown slipping smoothly off her right shoulder. "I'm getting the children. Both of them. We're going to temple. I don't care if it's too early and there are no services yet.

"Teddy!" she shouted, moving briskly away from Evan who lay still under the sheet. She went into the hall toward the closed doors. "Joy!"

Teddy had been awake. It was Joy who, startled by her mother's shout, lifted her head from the pillow. Something pleasant was fading inside her. Greedily, eyes still closed, she tried to hold onto the sweetness for just a moment more. Somehow she knew that she was already forgetting the world and people she was seeing.

"Enough, Joy!" she heard again after what seemed like hours—followed another few hours later by the command, quiet but clearly impatient now, "Darling, you have to get up."

Joy opened her eyes. She saw she was in her own shuttered bedroom. So it hadn't been true then, that other place, and all the rest of it. Was it Hankus she'd left there? His wide, open face, his shining eyes, his lips caught in a smile and then suddenly forming the words: *You're fine.* His arms stretched out? Sideways, his feet almost running? Left him spinning and spinning without her; wasn't it him back there—where it was all so splendid?

Her mother nodded grim-lipped at her and turned away, keeping the door partway open; *there* her mother walked, along the dim hall, in her blue cotton housecoat. With a gasp, Joy started to cry. She couldn't believe it, that this all around her was the real light.

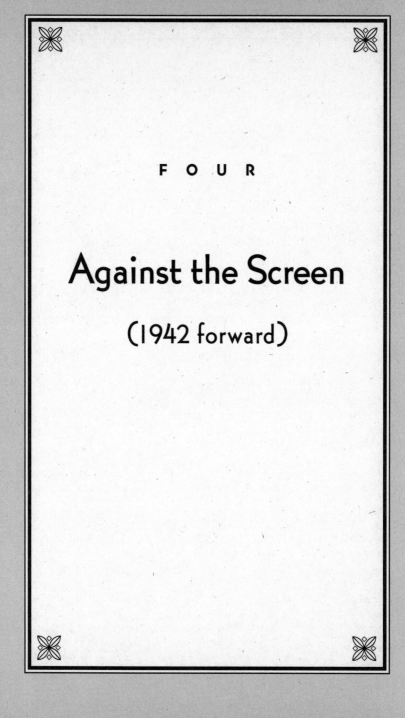

FOUR

Against the Screen

(1942 forward)

Winding Streets

Damage in a shirt, Vera once said, means mending, same as in anything else. You quick get a needle; make the stitches almost invisible, pull them tight, close together. Otherwise—and this you don't want—even that small wound will one day open up.

Fifty-eight days after the Japanese forces attacked the American naval fleet at Pearl Harbor, the Chevy still had four good rubber tires, many of its replacement parts were still in stock, and gasoline ration coupons were still two months away from national implementation. True, automobile manufacturers already had announced they wouldn't be concerned with passenger cars for the duration, having given over their booming factories to defense work, but that didn't mean that a six-year-old 1936 black hardtop sedan wouldn't be driven away from the center of Cleveland and out to the countryside far beyond Solon, in a trip that took up nearly two hours.

The ride wasn't supposed to take that long, and Evan knew it. It wasn't that there were that many roads or hidden turns from Kinsman to East 116th, to Miles, to Northfield, on and on to Aurora, and on from there; they were all straight-laid roads, which in the two decades immediately after the war and in the two after the end of Evan's own lifetime would be widened many times and many times asphalted over; would be used differently; would be changed. The stretch of East 116th south of Kinsman one day would be called Dr. Martin Luther King Boulevard; and State Route 43—also known as Aurora—would be wildly overshadowed by the arcing double spans of Interstate 271. For now, though, in this midwinter day in '42, the roads were as they were. The only alteration that befell them was abstract, the consequence of Evan's unfamiliarity with his destination; he was too watchful for a road's end: the routes seemed to stretch longer than they should; perhaps they had already misled him?

Yet where the handwritten, penciled directions indicated there would be a gray farmhouse, an unpainted barn, a stand of elms, and a mailbox declaring the occupant as *Russell*, in fact there had been. The dirt road rutted by farm machinery, supposed to exit east off of Aurora, finally that, too, had appeared. Evan turned onto it, one foot lightly riding the brake, noticing ahead the more irregular grade of the surface.

Seven minutes later, he would have just turned off *Russell*'s east-shooting utility road. He was traveling north on a road much the same as its neighbor: rough, pocked with dark ice, the now barren fields on either side a hard cloth of winter-coarsened and paled dirt. Still, these flat acres of turned clumps gave him heart. There'd been some harvest. Someone had either the hope or the discipline to keep on working, preparing the ground for what he believed he should next put in it.

The second utility road was to carry Evan past a *pond with a diving board, a small "nothing" roadside fruit stand, a mailbox ("The Gordons")—This Is It!!!* He was to *turn onto private road, go up to house, key stored above door sill (top right corner). VERY IMPORTANT: Before leaving, lock up and replace key in exact same place. Don't forget: Look at root cellar (very dry). Also big pluses: Toolshed, chicken coop—both in good condition, both open. (Tools go to the lucky new property owner. Gordon ate all the chickens. Ha! Ha!)*

As instructed, Evan turned after the mailbox, drove in a fifth of a mile over a couple of gray hillocks, and stopped the car by a low wall of whitewashed stones. Leaving the key in the ignition, he got out. The air was still and quiet and cold. Once, and then again, Evan stretched his arms above his head, enough to force a jaw-snapping yawn. He put his hands on his hips and bent a little forward from the waist. All the while his gaze didn't leave the front of the small farmhouse, taking in the two tar patches on the roof, the slight tilt to the chimney, the pulled blinds behind the five windows (three up, two down, and behind them *twelve hundred feet total—the two floors, not including crawlspace/attic*), the scrofulous white paint of the clapboards, the hand-carved design of a sunflower in the unpainted wood door, the small rectangular rocking-chair porch.

He was up the three wood steps and running his bare fingertips along the high lintel when the door gave way. The toe of his right wingtip had prodded it. The last person to be here maybe hadn't locked up?

"Who is home?" he called. Overhead, his fingers touched on the cold key. Quickly he claimed it, dropped it into his pocket. "Hello, anyone?" He stepped into the musty dim interior.

The more he went from room to room and then from inside to outside, inside to outside, and inside to outside of the three structures—house, toolshed, chicken coop, and the more he looked off to a horizon that seemed placid and undulating, cut into only by two groves of trees, the more sure he became. This was *it*, just as the penciled directions declared.

This certitude was enough to carry Evan through the drive back to Cleveland, the secret complex transactions of the next two and a half weeks, and a ride back out to the farm on the weekend, with Vera on the wide front seat next to him and Teddy and Joy silent on either end of the one behind. The others didn't know he was certain about anything, nor that there was anything as definite as a destination in front of them. They thought—he'd been leading them to believe—they were just on a *drive* after temple. Since the day of Pearl Harbor, Vera insisted they attend a weekly service as a family; and this morning, while coming down the temple's wide stone steps to the street, Evan had proposed the drive. As a family, he said. A-ride together, to talk, to look at something new. We need that, he said, yes?

So now when he coughed nervously and jerked the steering wheel, pulling the Chevy off the second utility road onto what clearly was someone's property, Vera said excitedly, "What is it, what's wrong?" She slid over and placed her palm against his chest.

Another cough and he cleared his throat.

"Daddy?" Joy leaned forward abruptly. "Are we lost?"

Evan's eyes went to the rearview. He saw his daughter's anxiety from there. Then he leaned a little forward to see in the left corner how his son's eyes quickly shifted away from his own mirrored gaze—an act of avoidance repeated endlessly it seemed since that awful, awful fight. Sighing, he saw the front brim of his fedora and the distinct shadow it cast over the upper half of his face.

"Careful, Joy, sit back the way you're supposed to," he muttered. "The surface gets rough soon."

"You know this road?" Vera said, surprised. Her hand suddenly pressed hard against his chest; then she lifted it away. He nodded, silent. He was waiting for the house to appear, so he could add: *I do. It's ours.*

East Utility Road: The Gordons

They sat in the stilled car after he told them.

"So?" he finally had to ask.

"What," said Vera slowly, "did you do? What are you saying to me, we have a farm?"

"We own it," he said, "that's right. Get out, I'll show you."

"How do we have a farm?" She didn't move for the door handle. Behind, the two kids didn't make a peep.

He said, "We have it the way anyone would have it. I went to a realtor." Evan paused and gave her a little smile. He saw that he'd been expecting her anger. Of course, he should have said something to her before, but instead he convinced himself that it wouldn't matter, or that it was better if the farm stayed a surprise. His silence hadn't come from a desire to shut her out, and not from greediness, exactly. It was that something dull and painful was driving him, something that brought about a shortness of breath. Could he carry out his plan on his own? Could he complete it, by himself?

Cranking his window down just an inch, he inhaled a good slow breath from the thin line of cold air. "I went to Manny Schnabel and asked about farms. He told me about this one. I came out, looked at it, and I decided it would make a good place to raise chickens. We can sell the eggs. And maybe also have a vegetable garden—but that's just for us, not to sell. The rest of the land we can rent out to others to work." He spoke quietly, flatly, insistently. "You know, in Nagymihály, I always thought about such a place. Maybe we can get a horse for Joy to learn to ride. Would you like that, Joy? For the Fourth of July when it's hot, a swimming hole. But that is already here. Did you see the pond, back by the road we just left? Maybe we can have Fourth of July picnics, invite friends to come from the city. Everyone can share rides if gas rationing—"

"Are you *meshugge*?" Vera said in disbelief. She turned only her head to him; her spine was pressed against the seat back, as though the car were still going somewhere. "A second store, something to bring in money—the store we've been working so hard for—*that* would be worth the struggle."

"Listen to me—"

"We don't have this kind of money to throw around, Evan."

Teddy mumbled something under his breath. Joy hissed: "Shut up, it's not funny."

"We have the money," he said. "I couldn't get another mortgage on the store, because we owe already for the personal loan. But now, since there can be no communication with the family in Europe—" his voice trailed and he glanced away. "So, I took money from that loan. But I didn't use all of it for this. I kept some in the account, in case things change and we hear something."

Vera made a little strangled sound. "So," Evan continued quickly, "to get the remainder we needed, I cashed in my life insurance. Sandor took back the policy. Also the insurance on our house I canceled. He sent that in and got me the cash left on that, too. Enough to make a forty-percent down payment for a mortgage from another bank. They don't ask where the up-front money comes from; they see I had enough to secure the loan for the farm."

"Sandor? He did this?"

"I told him to do it. He's our agent."

Vera said, "I don't—" She stopped. Unsnapping her pocketbook, she dug out a tube of lipstick, twisted the case, then without opening it, quickly dropped it back. "I don't understand."

"You don't see?"

"What should I see?" She glanced bitterly out the window. "A farmhouse? Well, I see nothing. I see everything gone."

Joy said, "Are we moving way out here now?"

Grateful for the interruption—and the tremor in a voice that he knew he could soothe with the right answer—he replied, "Oh no, no, you'll be staying at home."

"But how can I—I mean because you said it that way, Daddy—it sounds like you're not going to be with us."

"Let's get out of the car, yes? I'll explain. Get out of the car, please. Teddy, you also."

The doors swung open and the family stood, two on each side of the car, the ground frozen under their feet, the long curved black roof between them—a kind of too-tall kitchen table, cutting them off at shoulder height. Out of nowhere, a whip of wind snapped at their coat collars.

"Okay, good," Vera muttered, "explain."

Evan said very quietly, with calm control, "Here is what it is. Only Teddy will live here, weekends for now and then full-time starting in summer. In the fall, he'll change schools and stay here to work. He'll take care of the chickens and the—"

"I'm not going to be hired help."

"Evan, what you're saying's cuckoo, it's *meshugge*."

"Daddy, that's silly."

"Let me explain, yes?"

"*Meshugge*, Evan."

"I'm *not* living here by myself. In fact, I'm not living here at all."

Evan raised a hand. "I don't want to shout over everyone. Please, quiet."

"I am not staying on a farm. I'm no rube, okay?"

"If you will please listen a minute—"

"This's some stupid joke, isn't it? Well, it's really nuts." Teddy's speech was so agitated that a spray of spit landed on top of the car; the tiny circles immediately began freezing.

Evan said, voice shaking, "I know what I am doing."

Vera turned and walked toward the blank-windowed house. Joy looked back and forth between her mother's rigid back, her father's stiffened profile, then ran after her mother. She couldn't

look at Teddy, whose face was terrible, so obviously was he frightened by where a simple country drive had brought him. Leaning
over the car roof, Teddy stared straight into Evan's face. If he
didn't turn around and look at the house, it might as well not
exist.

"I won't see Janet," he said abruptly, though he was supposed
to not be seeing her anyway, since it had become clear she wasn't
Jewish. "Janet and I are over, okay? I promise, we're history.
That's why you're punishing me. I know that's it, Dad. Okay,
swell, I give her up, who cares. But I'm not staying out here."

Quietly Evan said, "I'm not punishing you on her. It's
because of the war."

"Because of our war?" The round lenses, fogged from his
breath, made Teddy's narrow face appear even more flushed.

Impatiently, Evan said, "Because of the fighting, the war
going on over the world."

Vera came stomping back with Joy trailing, eyes down,
behind. She stood again by the closed passenger door. "All right,
explain to me."

He paused. "Boys who do essential labor, part of the war
effort, yes? the draft board doesn't have to take them. Agricul-
ture is considered essential, because it means food. If we
already—you see, if already we have with Hankus—Hankus and
all the rest. Our family—" he stopped, swallowing with difficulty.
"You see, Vera? This is already legal. Teddy can be on a farm. We
can keep him this way."

"I never thought—" she said. "We can keep him?"

"I read in the newspaper about the exemptions."

"You think he'll be all right?"

"No!" Teddy exploded. "No, you're acting like I'm just a kid,
like I can't know my own mind. I can't believe this. Everybody I
know always talks about going. My country, Dad. America. What
will my friends say? They're all going to fight. When we turn
eighteen, we all said we're going to register, become aces—"

"When they register, you'll already be working. Essential
labor." Evan's arm swept out, his fingers flicking at the air, the
house, the chicken coop, the land—the full eighty-five acres

fenced along its last inch by a single strand of barbed wire. "You'll be in one piece."

"I'll be a chicken farmer? You want me to become that?" Teddy choked back a sob. His voice dropped. "I *can't* be that. I really can't be that. What'll I tell my—everyone? If I stay here, they'll think I'm a chicken."

"Teddy," Joy whispered, mesmerized by the image he'd drawn, "the *chicken* farmer."

"Yeah, that's right. That's what they'll say about me." He looked up with a sickened, loopy grin. He took off his glasses. "You want to give people the chance to call me those kind of names, Dad?" His eyes were small and pleading.

All the times in the past weeks he wanted Teddy to look at him again, and now he couldn't meet the boy's gaze.

"Dad, you want people to see me like that?"

Evan's heart was thudding so hard, it felt like it was beating him. What could he do? He couldn't spare the boy in all ways. He just wanted to keep him whole. After that, everything else could come to him. "It won't matter about any names. You'll see, one day you'll thank me."

"I won't."

He took a breath. "Yes, one day when you find a girl who's right for you and you're happy to be alive, and with a good future ahead—"

"Who's going to want me," Teddy cried, "if I don't fight? I'm always different from everyone else! I'm never the same. I'll never be the same."

"That's not true," Vera said fiercely.

"Sure it is, okay, Mom? I'm not really good enough at anything. I know that. I'm a fake. I'm afraid all the time to be found out. Not only by you, either. And Hankus—" He stopped, frightened by what he was hearing himself admit, his face registering that shock and pain. "I know I can't do any of the things Hank does." He looked up at Evan. "I still think about the day you hit me for asking if he was dead. I was ducking you, you know? I was more afraid of your discovering I was with Janet that afternoon than I was of anything else—than I was about learning about Hank, okay? Got that? God, Dad."

"Teddy, please—"

He choked. "A fake about everything. Whenever I think about Hank—"

"No, honey, stop—"

"I don't want to get killed, too."

"Enough!" Vera slapped the car hood. "No one's killed."

"You listen, honey." Evan pressed against his closed door. "I bought this for you. The farm is yours, you can stay here and not have to worry the way—the way you're telling me now that you do."

Teddy's jaw jerked wildly. He looked at his parents, at how they were looking at him, directly at him, to help them out now. All he had to do was give himself up to staying, just give himself over to their fears and his own. If he did that, then maybe there'd be less pain for them. He hated it, how his family could never ever be thoughtless and happy. "You think I can stay?" he ventured. "With the names and all?"

"What are you talking about? Wait a minute!" Joy rose onto her toes, though she could see everybody perfectly from where she stood. Her voice went high and thin. "Teddy, what you just said about Hankus—"

"Don't be so stupid," he snapped. "If Hank's a prisoner, they have to tell us; it's a rule of war. But no one's told us, okay? Got it, little Miss Stupid? You want to believe reciting those old prayers at temple will help, well, go on." Slowly he twisted his neck, the short nape hairs riffled in the wind.

Joy was trembling. Why didn't their parents stop him? But she was furious now at even herself, for the part of her that wanted to believe him so she could stop thinking about Hankus, just stop all the worrying. "You're the biggest chicken there is, Teddy," she whispered, "saying something like that. You only think about yourself."

"Shut up, okay?"

"We have to keep hoping for Hankus, don't we, Mommy?"

Vera nodded, stricken.

"See, Teddy? And, you don't know who has him now, do you, or if those people even obey the rules. I mean, how could you? But you just want to give up all the way anyway?"

"What do you know? You'll never have to fight a war. You're a girl. You have no say in any of it. You're so full of it, Joysie."

She swallowed down the sick feeling inside her. "You don't know anything about me," she said, finally. "You're the one who's full."

Glancing at his parents, Teddy bit his lip and turned. Nodding, he took a few steps toward the house; then hesitated and crossed halfway to the stone wall. "Hell." He laughed and threw up his hands.

He turned about in a little half circle, going only to the point where he could still keep his back to them. He abruptly repeated the arc. He was like some awful, unnecessary toy stuck on a pavement crack, yet there was nothing, not on the frozen, flattened dirt, that could trip him. After a moment, Evan called to him. They watched as his shoulders began to shake.

The wind was slight and they could hear Teddy sobbing. "Don't let me go. I couldn't make it. I'm not like him."

"Honey—"

"I don't want to fight, okay? I never did want to—you're right, it was just a lie, I was lying again."

Evan's heart was pounding. He had to do it, he had to snatch one of his own out of danger. Teddy, safe, their good boy. Evan stepped away from the driver's side of the Chevy. Vera gave a sharp cry. She spun around and went toward her son.

"Let me stay, okay?" he was sobbing. "It's okay, I want it."

"No," said Joy. "Wait a minute, Dad!" Her voice was so bitter that Evan looked up, startled. She was watching him from under her hooded eyes.

He gave her an unsteady smile. "What, darling?" he said, and saw her shiver and hunch forward slightly like some old woman. Her face was pinched.

"Daddy." Her arms went about herself. "This can't be right."

"No, no," he said, trying to wave her concerns away. "Don't you worry, he's going to be fine, you'll see. He'll be with us, like always. He's safe now, yes? Same as you. Please, you shouldn't worry." He glanced down at his chest and brushed at a gray smear on the lapel of his overcoat. "Teddy? First you want to walk and see the outside or go right into the house? We'll fix it up for you the way you want, honey, everything."

The Letters

15 June 1942

Dear Cousin Verushka,

I am writing you from Argentina. I am your mother's second cousin's daughter (Cousin Rose's daughter). I was Rose's third-born. Maybe you recall me, the one with red hair? My eldest child Josef and I are now in Rio de Janeiro. I regret to have to tell you my husband is not with us; he was arrested and taken away to Poland to work; for a while he used to teach in the *gymnasium* in Kassa with your brother-in-law Andras Osvat. His subject was music. Our two girls disappeared; they were on a simple errand for me—they were just going to the pharmacy! (Their names are Malka and Eva. Both young, born after you left for America.)

Your sister (my cousin) Irina gave me your address when I went to speak with her before she left for Portugal with little Miriam and Lily. But perhaps she is with you in Cleveland? If so, I hope to be seeing her again soon. I have saved your address up until now, as you can tell. After many troubles, my son and I arrived in Argentina three months ago and have nothing left.

Would you sponsor us? (Josef is thirteen and can do many things. I can sew, keep ledger accounts, do housecleaning, etc.) And, if you are able to, would you be able to send us some amount of money? Anything will be helpful. If this is too hard, let it go. I enclose some information from the agency advising us on the back of this sheet.

I hope this letter finds you, your husband, Ivan, and your four children in good health. If Irina and her girls are with you, please give them my love. If Irina is still

in Portugal, then I hope you can remember me. Besides the
red hair, I used to make jokes. Often I would sing "Hinta,
Polinta" and do a little dance at big family gatherings.
However, I don't mean to insult you with my rendition of
the past. I am certain your memory is much finer than
mine.

With many thanks for your kind attention to this letter, I remain—

Elsa Honig (Gellert)

Yours sincerely,
—Excuse me, but it occurs to me you must want to know
about your mother and sisters. All I can tell you is that
when I was able to leave, things were hard. But my
mother's second cousin Frieda in Szacsur, I heard, was
managing as best she could; the same with her daughters
(my cousins) and their families. All, fine. This is of 16
February; after that, I was gone from there. I'm sorry I
don't have anything more now I am able to give to you.

Utility Road: Eichenbaums

From the farmhouse's upstairs bedroom window, Teddy watched
the caravan coming toward him. The lead car, his father's, ahead
by forty or so feet, crested each rise in the dirt road slowly, as if
the four sedans trailing might otherwise lose sight of him. But
which of the drivers was going to break from the column? Which
at the slightest signal was ready to veer off the road and race
across the uneven field like a renegade tank?

He watched the two Chevrolets, the two newer Buicks, and
the DeSoto, front grilles gently rising and falling, move through
the dust. When a horn honked, three short taps, one long, he
stepped back from the window. With a certain nervousness, he
picked up the comb from the bureau and stuck it in his back
pocket. The only mirror was in the bathroom.

The rumble of the engines was getting louder. He suddenly
caught a snatch of a song. God, he couldn't believe what he was
hearing, they were singing!

Mares eat oats! The motors drowned out the rest of it, how they were singing the nonsense words with exaggerated enunciation. Then, like a slap: *eat ivy. A kid will—* The wind carried the voices away. Among them would be the Belaks, the Pressers—his parents' friends. And a car with his friends, though not Janet of course—he'd broken it off with her; but probably Bernie was driving with Lou and Ira. And Joy's little friends had to be in one of the cars.

Aloud, he said, "Get out of here, go back home."

He didn't want them here, not for the Fourth of July picnic, not for the weekend after, nor for any of the days following. He didn't want any visitors.

More quickly than he could have imagined, he'd come to recognize everything on the farm as his. The backward tilt to the porch steps; the slow cat's-eye marble spin to the north-most corner of all the planked floors; the smell of iron that rushed from the tap and into a bathtub supported by four delicate clawed feet, the grit left on the porcelain bottom as he lifted himself, dripping, from the warmish water.

And the chickens in their coop, female and scratching at dirt. Scared stupid, to a one. Each time he'd approach, they'd squawk in fear, the whole lot spilling away from his feet and running in circles, running nowhere. Might as well have their heads cut off as have them still connected. They had no memory, no will, nothing at all resembling an ability to reason. Yet he recognized the hens as his in a way he wouldn't have believed possible: his disgust of them alternating with a sense of pity so familiar it was almost affection.

But the brainlessness of the brown-and-black rooster with its chest-first, military strut and bent tail feathers he hated purely. Its garbled cry curdling in the red air each dawn called up his one moment of clean rage. As soon as Teddy's eyes opened to the plastered-over cracks in the white ceiling above him, he'd vow, "Today I eat him."

When he'd get to the outer barbed-wire enclosure, the beady fowl would be pacing right at the gate, its head jerking rapidly on a glossy neck that swelled, ruff bristling, the nearer Teddy approached. With a silent hiss, the bird lifted its wings slightly away from its body.

"Want me, *Il Duce?* Come on, okay? Come get me."

The rooster grabbed on to the barbed wire with its beak and bit down, the wire jerking with its head, back and forth. The only eyes that fixed right on Teddy each morning were these two hostile, ringed yellow disks. Despite his dislike of the bird, Teddy would toss it a couple fistfuls of cracked corn. Which the rooster fell to. Pecking at this meal in the dirt, it was unable to stop, even as Teddy walked past.

In the dark low-roofed coop, his work shoes pressed down the newest layer of feathers and scattershot pellets of dung. The air was acrid, warm, almost smothering, no matter the weather outside. It had something to do with the oven-heat nature of the chickens themselves. Now the hens were flapping, fearful at his presence among them. Poor helpless idiots. They couldn't remember: he was the one who fed them. And if he was also the one who cleared their nests of their cushioned, fecal-spotted eggs, well, what did it matter? They had no specific attachment to the chicks that would hatch, or those that wouldn't. Every day the hens' movements just dumbly repeated. And if they didn't lay and only ate, he was likewise the one who tagged them; then the one who crated and loaded them, who drove a cargo of beaks poking through slats, of wings bent but not flapping, off to Bill Abbott whose business depended on being quick with the axe.

Teddy hated the ride over the rutted back road to deliver the hens. He hated it as he did every task that had to go from start to finish on the farm. The thriving farm. The greater acreage bringing up rows of beans, higher rows of corn, and the cow pasture—all rented and tended by others: the Barden family, the old bachelor Markham brothers, people who wanted to make use of what they couldn't own outright. They'd wave to Teddy and bend again to their tasks. They probably considered him to be just like them.

And they were right. He wasn't different. He was finally the same. All of them, rubes. Teddy could imagine Hankus suddenly surprising him one day at the farm. He could imagine Hankus's amazement to see how his younger brother was working, just like some yokel. He could imagine Hank's teasing—*Hey, Farmer Ted!*; how Hank would call him one of those rinky-dink names he always liked to make up. Hankus—one foot on the fence, the other on the ground, his elbows leaning on the top rail, his chin atop his folded hands—and a wide grin on his fine face. No, forget it. Hankus wasn't here. And he, Ted, couldn't imagine any of that. He just wouldn't; he refused to. His big brother laughing right out loud, a miraculously sparkling full embrace of a sound. *Eddy-tay! Taffy! Yid-kid! Chicken-boy! Yokel!* Teasing him about the names he really deserved to be called, because he'd made the decision finally and all the way to be scared. It was true, okay? That's who he was. By giving in to his fear—and to his parents' also—he'd given himself up. And inside of himself he had no fight left. Okay, fine. He didn't care. Contest over.

Standing now at the bureau in the upstairs bedroom, Teddy heard three long blasts of a car horn. He wasn't ready to see any of them. Couldn't he just be left alone?

He was down the stairwell and shut up in the one bathroom before the car doors began slamming and the picnickers began climbing out. Stalling, he shoved on the tap over the tub. The curved rim was damp from the bath he'd taken less than an hour ago.

"Teddy?" he heard his mother shout. Couldn't hear her quick step or where exactly anyone was in the house. Then suddenly a whole army invaded. Bursts of laughter, voices. The floorboards shook as boxes of food and picnic supplies heavily dropped.

He was bending over, stripping off his clean clothes. Over his shoulder he shouted as if surprised, "You're here?"

He put one leg over the side. Tepid. The hairs raised on his body. The water heater must have been emptied out by his real bath. "What time is it? I didn't hear you arriving, it's early. I'm just washing up!"

Behind him, someone opened the door.

He crouched defensively. He didn't know who was seeing his long pale backside. "Shut it!" Awkwardly, he drew his other foot into the high-walled, curved tub. He sank down without turning.

Two-six-oh-two East Trainor

Two-six-oh-two was a big house for three people. That's why it struck Joy as funny that now when she and her parents were inside it, they all seemed more aware of one another than they ever had—everyone more alert to where in all that space the others might be. She'd have thought it'd be the reverse. After all, no longer did anybody have to share anything. There was no line in front of her if she came home from school and wanted to play a certain Frank Sinatra or Andrew Sisters record on the Victrola; no one from whom she was blocking the hallway if she wanted to slide around in her rolled anklet socks, trying out dance steps—*the lindy, the Jersey bounce, jig walk, flea hop,* all the while smiling, right arm held out toward the open door of the closet where her partner, the dustless full-length mirror, smiled right back at her while the coats and jackets made a crowd, just off to the side.

With only the three people in it, two-six-oh-two was pretty quiet. There used to be a lot of conversations around where you could look up and toss in your two cents. Well, that was no longer true. These days when Joy entered some room where her parents were talking, they'd pause. One of them would look over and ask if she wanted something. If they'd been talking in, say, the front room, usually she'd shake her head and answer, "I'm going to read." Then she'd hold up a book. Often it was one of her *Five Little Peppers* books; though too old for the series now, she still liked revisiting certain chapters where the eldest sister was so kind to everyone. Or perhaps she had a book to get through for school: *Great Expectations, Uncle Tom's Cabin,* or, sadly, because no one in the class seemed to like it, not even the teacher, *Silas Marner.*

Reading downstairs for her own pleasure, Joy would make a space for herself on the horsehair sofa; if the book was assigned as part of her education, she'd cross to the desk facing the front window. This was where Teddy had worked, for as long as she could remember. But now when she tugged on it, the walnut chair with the straight back slid toward her easily. Hankus: the sofa was his regal throne—his legs sprawled lengthwise along the seat, his back bouncing against the cushioned arm; he seemed to be able to command everything from that position without ever standing. So, Teddy—at the desk, back to them; Hankus—stretched like a raj on the sofa.

Funny how Joy couldn't remember exactly where in here in all those noisy crowded chaotic now gone years she herself had been positioned. She could call up only where her brothers had been. She had the feeling that as a little girl she kept hovering about the edges. In her own memory she was never sitting down; she was instead quietly inching forward, attention focused on the others, perhaps waiting for the permission to come on, yes, into the very center. As if everyone understood that *here* was her brothers' domain; as if she didn't really belong.

But she belonged in here. She was the hub of a crucial new ritual that she couldn't quite explain, not yet.

Her parents always stopped talking now when she crossed the front room. They'd start up again the moment she bent her head over her pages. It didn't take many times for Joy to figure out that when they weren't really concerned about her overhearing their conversation, they would lower their voices just enough to maintain the veneer of continuity, which meant *normalcy,* but of course then she couldn't really hear the unimportant things they were saying, no matter how much she strained. But if it was something significant she'd interrupted, well, they'd change topics completely and swiftly raise their voices to a lucid, louder-than-usual level. Then Joy could hear not only the words, but more specifically some sort of relief and gaiety springing up behind them. Gratitude pumped through her parents' voices for these few moments she'd thrown them off their secret course.

In this way, without any of the three speaking about what they were doing, they annoyed and comforted one another.

•   •   •

Joy turned on the lamp at the end of the couch and settled back against the pillow.

"Billie Oppenheim told me something," her mother said in a loud-enough voice, obviously switching subjects from something Joy shouldn't hear to something innocuous. "Oh, you'll laugh at it, Evan. See, with business so good now—all the big spenders coming to eat and drink, workers with money, GI's with their dates—she's put up a new sign up in the cafe. Know what it says? BE POLITE TO THE HELP, PLEASE—CUSTOMERS WE CAN ALWAYS GET."

"She's something," he said, in as clear a tone. "Well, good for her, yes?"

The overstuffed chair gave a muffled creak as her mother leaned forward to catch what it was he truly wanted to tell her.

Joy turned the page. Did he whisper *Malta*, the name of an island always in the newspaper now because of the fighting? She couldn't tell. Was it *Malka*, a girl's name? Did they have some relative named that? That old-country name? It might be *malted*; Daddy could want one; and so the two grown-ups might soon stand, announcing a little walk out into the balmy night air and down to Rivchin's Pharmacy where, if their daughter didn't join them, the two of them could continue their original conversation. A talk they'd break off only to suck at the white paper straws, drawing thin cold lines of ice cream—sweetly grainy vanilla—up over their tongues.

At these times Joy was aware of being the youngest. The discontinuous youngest. And aware of her parents as suddenly seeming very much older. Without Hankus and Teddy to connect them, the distance between herself and them seemed confusingly clear and yet somehow a relief. It was as if she and they lived on opposite sides of a chasm; but when her parents looked over at her, they wanted her only to wave happily at them. Clearly, she was expected to stay just exactly where she was; she wasn't to cross over yet. Clearly, she was of otherwise little use to them. Otherwise they'd be explaining to her the deep danger, the causes of the silence that fell off so steeply between them, wouldn't they?

Joy tried to pick up what she could. She kept her ears and

eyes open. But they wouldn't let her in on anything of real importance. After that one awful outburst the first time they saw the farm, no one spoke directly about Hankus, although the three of them kept going to temple to pray for his safe return. Joy hesitated to ask her parents when they thought they might be told he was being held as a prisoner. They couldn't believe he wasn't going to return, could they really?

But she wasn't supposed to ask, she could tell. She looked across the chasm, smiled and waved.

Each morning she watched how they checked the newspaper for the list of local boys reported as killed in the fighting. She heard them note sadly but with some pride in their voices: "A Jewish name. A Jewish boy, may his memory be blessed."

Was it only Teddy then, out on the farm, whom they cared about?

She didn't ask. She knew not to.

And the family in the old country? Joy knew their countries were enemies now, but couldn't the families find some way to contact each other and claim they were blood relations?

She didn't risk asking about it. Her mother didn't phone from the store and ask her to check the mail, first thing. There weren't any more letters from Europe.

When she looked through the newspapers on her own, she could find hardly a mention about the situation and fate of the Jews overseas. The few articles she did find were brief, three or four paragraphs at most, usually placed in the back sections.

She didn't dare ask either of her parents why.

And in terms of movie newsreels, for all the footage of bomber planes, exploded cities, Allied soldiers running across quick-flashing ground or kicking back muddy-faced in trenches, or of ordinary Brits chin-upping it for the roving camera, none of it seemed like the war her parents weren't explaining to her. The screen was exciting. It wasn't tricky or unclear or too quiet, which was the way the war felt when she was back home.

Without saying anything to anybody, Joy made herself keep looking for Hankus in the newsreels; still, she was frightened that she might find him sitting on the dirt, head bowed, behind barbed wire—a prisoner, too long held, of the enemy. She wanted to see him again—she wanted this more than anything. Where else but on that screen could she look for the evidence of her brother's existence in the world?

She scrutinized the newsreels for her distant relatives also. About their faces of course she was much less certain. But wouldn't there be something recognizable, some resemblance or gesture that would pull her gaze immediately to them—center her on her family alone, out all of the masses? Wouldn't there be a connection that could never be mistaken?

Joy might have asked her parents, but she didn't, somehow.

She shuddered whenever Hitler raised his arm—*Sieg Heil!*—on the screen. Sometimes, booing with the rest of the audience at his hateful flickers of light, she closed her eyes and booed simply to drown out his image. She didn't want *der Führer* to step any closer. Then, outside the theater, with the streetcar rumbling familiarly and automobiles passing and stopping and honking, Joy saw how impossible it would be for him to exist here. What he was seemed too terrible. He belonged on the screen, on the radio, on a map. Was he really and truly alive anywhere else?

She didn't ask her parents.

Instead, with friends and classmates, she participated in salvage drives, collecting tin cans and aluminum and rubber and paper. In place of cherry Cokes, she bought war stamps and filled up whole books with them. She participated in a Clean Plate campaign and distributed anti-black-market pledge cards. She collected library books for servicemen. Joy did what Vera and Evan Eichenbaum's only daughter, their last child at home, their youngest, was supposed to do: participate in the energy and optimism of America. She'd make it her contribution for the duration.

Sitting in the front room, book in lap, Joy heard her father whisper for the second time: *Malka,* or an odd word that sounded much like it. Just slightly, she lifted her head.

"*Sha,* Evan," warned her mother, voice low. "Wait."

Immediately they both glanced over at her.

"Do you want something, Joy?" Vera cleared her throat.

Joy brought her hand up, almost a little wave, and said, "No, I'm okay."

They both smiled in return.

They turned back to each other, and Joy looked down at her book. The lines to which her index finger went read: "Then she laughed again. 'What a start that gave me! Thank goodness, Peter, you're only *you* and I don't have to rush about shouting, "Oh, help! Help!" as I first thought! Aren't you a rascal, stepping out of the shadows by our garden wall like that. I feared it was someone who meant to attack me. But now I see it was you, you scamp!'" Joy grinned. Oblivious to the live voices across the room, she read to the bottom of the page and on to the next. And then the next, her imagination totally immersed in the delicious slow honey of the story's sentimentality.

Well, she would be reading a telegram soon enough, one that arrived on a weekday midafternoon with the name, *Evan Eichenbaum,* typed in block letters next to the red-inked *Urgent* on the front of the envelope. Joy was the only family member home to receive that, of course. She answered the doorbell and saw the messenger, then she stood with the thin envelope in the hallway, wondering whether to read the message to herself first or to telephone her father and mother at the store and say a telegram of some sort had arrived. And when she did open it before phoning, and did read the message silently to herself: *Wire five hundred dollars for my safe passage, fast. Stop. Love from your brother, Solomon.* And next, the return wire: *Auschwitz,* a name that still meant nothing, but paired with: *Poland,* a place name she did recognize, Joy was caught between the excitement that her father had heard finally from Uncle Solly—that they might be able now to bring him over—and the fear that she wasn't fully certain what the message meant. Still, she lifted the telephone receiver. She had to tell them—this she knew—that some news had come.

Joy read the words aloud over the telephone to her mother.

Done, she paused a half moment, wondering if she should ask now—break their long trio of silence? She almost cleared her throat.

But Vera immediately said, "Okay, Joy," and hung up the phone. Trembling still, Vera hurried from the back office to find Evan. Then not two minutes later, she and Evan ran out of their store and across Buckeye Road. Then Evan was running ahead of her, to the bank. He ran to the oak counter, shaking, his voice quieter than ever she'd heard it. Then he withdrew five hundred dollars from what remained in their personal-loan account and made himself count out twice the bills he'd received. Vera placed both her hands on his upper back as he bent over, counting. Then he turned his face half around to her: "Now. Let's go." They ran four streets over to the Red Cross office. They told the woman there about the telegram, showed her the cash, told her they wanted the agency to wire it, as instructed—*fast*. And the woman, she smiled sadly at them, or perhaps she winced. Then she led them through the office to a dim hallway and then to a frosted glass door. Then she turned the knob. There, on the tables, on the shelves, on the floor, were hundreds of telegrams, each with the same message: *You can save me*. She said then to Evan, "Your brother is already dead. The Nazis make people write to their families over here before they take them for good. We won't wire anything for you. Not now, and also not if more telegrams come to you later, from your brother or from anyone else over there. You want to feed Hitler's troops? Because that's where your money will go. It will go right into the Germans' bellies."

But this was a routine and peaceful night at home, and Joy, at age fourteen, having succeeded in ignoring the murmurous conversation of her parents close by, was rereading—simply for pleasure—the sixth chapter from one of her favorite childhood novels. How she enjoyed it! Vera and Evan sat together comfortably across the living room. They were talking in low voices about almost anything in these few moments their girl was near—anything but the losses that they'd always expected and now sensed were almost upon them.

Entry: Two-six-oh-two East Trainor

From the hallway Vera saw Evan shut the white wooden door to their bedroom. The inch of space under the jamb immediately went dark. She heard him pad across the floor, then the mattress springs—but these she was pleased she couldn't hear, not from the hall. Joy's door also was closed and quiet. "Too early for me," Vera muttered. She was still dressed. She went downstairs and opened the front door. From nowhere, small moths flew forward, their papery wings beating furiously as they traced the square screen mesh for some way to reach the lamp glowing in the foyer.

Vera flicked her thumbnail at the taut wires. For a few moments, that's all, she wanted to stand undisturbed. Have a nice breeze in her face.

It was too hot. Tomorrow the family was going out to the farm, as they did on most Sundays. Often she couldn't wait to get there and see her boy, but tonight once again the telephone conversation with him hadn't been good. He'd told them not to come. Of course he said it in that snide joking manner he now had. The way he said things sounded like he thought the person he was talking to was beneath him. Don't come, he said, unless you want the hens to get in a tizzy and go off their laying. They don't like strangers.

They'd had the farm for just over two years. Maybe Teddy had gotten too used to his own company. Sitting back in one of the farm chairs, his eyes never quite on you as he spoke, he'd joke that his standards were exceptionally high. Maybe that's why he couldn't live with anyone but himself. He knew—and here he'd nod—what was top-drawer. Not many people did. Most people gave up their standards too quickly. They were shirkers.

She felt sorry for him. And angry at him. And glad with

every breath that he was alive. She didn't forget the fear of losing him, and forgave him everything he was becoming.

Still young, Vera told herself; and that's what she repeated to Evan. Teddy would get over his easy disappointments. Though she knew he was afraid to be involved in the fighting, it bothered him to have to face the truth that he wasn't at risk. He was left out of his *generational challenge*. She'd heard him tell this to Sandor at the picnic they had at the farm two Sundays ago. To Sandor, sitting in black bathing trunks, his bald head covered by a hat, his narrow pale feet dangling in the warm water of the pond, Teddy could say such a stupid and heartsore thing. But to his own parents, he said only: Don't come, okay? Or: Got any nice girls for me? At this point, you shouldn't care if she's a shiksa, I live like a monk. You know what a miracle it is to be the only Jewish monk chicken farmer in America? And then, leaning back in his chair so it was balanced on its rear legs, he'd laugh. And laugh.

At such times she wanted to strike him. But she held back. Because he wasn't Hankus. Because Hankus was not writing to them, still; still each day so perfectly silent. Her Mr. Wise Guy. She dreaded how deeply she understood that this *nothing* was all that would be coming to them from Hankus now, forever, from now on. Though she wouldn't for any amount of money admit this to anyone. That's why every time she wanted to smack that smirk off Teddy's face to stop him from saying such stupid things, she caught her fingers in her other hand and squeezed them, hard. See, every hour Teddy was working on the farm, his brother was being silent to him too.

There was too much silence in the world. It existed even in the middle of the noise. The world had always had many loud noises. Worst of all was silence's clear slap. Its dead slap. So let Teddy laugh with his head tilted back in that terrible way. And let him speak to Evan and her as if they were two dummies with no idea of what, or who, he was laughing at. Let him make whatever little selfish noises he could now. He was young. What he had to bear wasn't so bad.

No generational challenge! She struck the screen. The moths bounced into the dark and surged back, beating in the same breath to fray their wings on the wire grid. They climbed up the strained air, not far from her face. Futilely they pushed themselves—and only little insects with eyes too small and wings puffing away a chalklike powder. But only insects.

Behind her was the letter table with nothing personal on it. Only bills for money due. Not one letter from Mother, or Sara, or Margret, or Rose, or even Etel, for two and a half years. Not a letter from Solly. Or from Artur. Not one letter dictated by her poor, aggrieved mother-in-law. Where were they? She stared at the moths, too small to have eyes she could find.

From Irina she heard every four weeks. In the last letter Rina wrote that her face and hands were now the color of honey; the tender pink skin of Kassa—gone. It seemed silly to even mention it, but Rina was surprised at herself for only just noticing what Cuba's strong island sunlight had done. Miriam and Lily were accompanying their stepfather to morning mass every Sunday; he'd always been pious, devoted. They went with him, Rina wrote, only to please him. Umberto Alonzo was a very kind man, and he cared about them all. He tried to make them feel at home, as if they belonged. And they did, she wrote, feel safe.

Vera thought about a sun so potent and wily it could make Irina, her fairest sister, slow to notice that she'd turned darker. She thought about her nieces kneeling on a stone floor in a small church with Señor Alonzo nodding approval.

All wars got over. Surely, the girls weren't in danger of forgetting the religion and people they came from? Surely, the three would come to live in Cleveland when the opportunity finally arose, even if they were doing well where they were now? Especially if the cousin in Argentina and her boy got their American visas approved too, wouldn't they come? Join the family?

The moths moved so fast, they were just pale blurs. How long, she wondered, could they live if they kept ruining their wings, scraping them against a closed door.

With a fierceness she couldn't explain, Vera suddenly loved

her house. Well-kept. Clean. Familiar. Her daughter, her husband, both sleeping in the too-warm air upstairs. Loved even the screen and the door she stood behind.

She glanced at the lamp lighting the bare little table behind her, hoping to see the letters that she knew weren't there. Her dear sisters—all of them once as close to one another as Rina's young girls now had to be. Girls who surely said prayers.

Teddy had no idea what a generational challenge could do. Let him not know. Not ever. Not like Hankus knew. Let Hankus please not have—but Vera stopped herself. What was the good of it, reciting a long list of her private worries?

Her big talker. Teddy hadn't stepped one foot off the farm more than a few times, had he? No, he just kept working there, laughing at them, and staying. If he was that unhappy, he could sneak away on his own. He could go anywhere. Though she didn't want that. She didn't want that at all. It had to be better for him to be safe. Surely, he could grow in the place they'd made for him and be happy one day, her last boy. They could all be happy where they were. The five—the four of them.

"Get away," she said, and rattled the outer door. Not a sound but they were beating themselves against the screen. Senseless moths. "Go away," said Vera, raising her voice. "Go on out of here, go!"

Upstairs Shower: Two-six-oh-two East Trainor

As soon as he wiped the beveled mirror clear with the towel, it fogged up again in no time at all. To shave by touch, you'd think he could do it, but after all these years the most Evan did was turn from the glass for a moment, the razor traveling a short lathered path he'd already thought out. Leaning back from the sink, he'd call through the slightly cracked door, "Yes, what do you want from me?"

This time when he called, he heard only how the showerhead dripped, although he'd yanked the lever well beyond its normal position. The drops fell separately, each one thirsty for the drain opened below.

"What do you want from me?" he repeated.

But, nothing, yes? So from the narrow ledge tiled black and celadon green, Evan took his cup full of lather and the soft-bristled barber's brush. Soaping his face, he methodically made himself look like an old man, as he did at the start of every morning.

"You're being too slow," said Vera, entering the steamy room. She was in bra and half-slip, her stockings not yet on.

He worked the blade in small spurts over his chin. "Not any slower than yesterday, I'm sure."

"Don't be so sure," she muttered, and continued to tug at the waistband of her half-slip, untwisting the yellowed silk that was bunched around the elastic. "You don't remember we have to open the store early? The Pittsburg Wear man is making a special trip to show us his samples. It's navy middies this season, he told me. A new craze. Everyone wants a uniform. Epaulets on everything."

"Epaulets?" He tensed. "I didn't forget the appointment."

"You know how much time we have left?"

He held the straight-edge still. "I'm getting handsome for you. So, if you would please give me two more minutes?"

"I'll give you one." Suddenly, she smiled into the mirror, so he could see her face, then bent to give him a quick kiss on his elbow. She left the door ajar. From the bedroom came the sudden stutter of the radio. The lilt of a big orchestra leaning into the long chords of "Sleepy Lagoon." It had the sound of another melody he'd heard played before in the background of those ballrooms where everything is a big to-do, food, friends, talk—the whirling going to your head, an intoxication. The type of song that played just when you were trying to decide whether or not to stand up and dance or to finally take your leave.

Evan stared through the mirror's fog to the image of his own nearly naked face. He studied the strands of graying hair wetly combed back from a high forehead, the cleft chin and narrow cheeks scraped smooth. Who looked like him? Joy maybe came closest, but not the boys. He, Hankus, where was he? He wasn't anywhere in these features. Evan lost his breath. Why shouldn't a father grow to look like his son, to hold him that way? Why should it only be that a son inherited characteristics from the father? He wanted to see in his face something physical, something that told him that he and Hankus were really part of each other. Lucky sons, who could see before them their long lineage!

Plunging the stubble-flecked lathery blade into the sink water, Evan called, "You'll see, Vera. Today, everything will go right, right from the start."

The agitated warm water splashed up from his fingertips. Who looked like him? Maybe in Nagymihály. Was there a face still in that town—one that he could bring alongside his on the glass and compare? Was it still possible? That one of his brothers was aging? Solly could be. Please, let him be. He could be changing surprisingly as he got older. It could be possible, despite everything, the articles that said nothing, the rumors quoted in the Jewish papers. Artur, maybe? He was looking all right still? Artur was always meticulous, like him.

No, better not to think. Better to just silently take care of what you have in front of you, yes? The face, the body. You don't study them, you care for them. You make yourself clean. You shave your beard, you trim your nails, you sprinkle on talc; you get everything out from your closet and the drawers of the bureau; you put on nice clothes. You go out in the world. Do what you can! Go where you can! And if you're lucky, you find yourself moving among others who look enough like your own kind.

Leaning forward against the cold edge of the sink, Evan made ready to finish. He squinted through the blur of condensation, then thought: *Careful.* And swiftly wiped his left palm across the glass, clearing it of breath and mist again.

"Vera, yes? You heard me say everything will go fine?" He spoke into the mirror.

"Sure, I hear you! Thirty seconds left, then out of there. I can see your watch lying on top of your bureau. Now it says twenty-five seconds. Joy, you wake up. Or don't you go to school anymore?"

"I'm awake, Mommy! I'm going to school."

"I don't want you to give me any trouble. I need you to be good. Smart but good too, you know?"

"Okay, I'll try."

Evan smiled, hearing Joy's first outburst, her energy.

The work left to do right under his nose was the most delicate. Evan shook the last slipping drops off the blade. The song kept hanging on to its last chord. He didn't care about the name of the song this one sounded like. It didn't matter whatever connection there was or there wasn't. The melody, even if it was all alone, was doing what it should. Which was making of itself something useful and pleasant.

"Ten seconds, *tateleh*," Vera called.

"I'll be ready." As soon as he spoke, his smile faded. For a moment he held still. Cleanly he drew the razor against his upper lip; again and again he felt the edge, until he was bloodlessly done.

Entry: Two-six-oh-two East Trainor

Joy was alone in two-six-oh-two. At the bell's ringing, she hurried, shoeless, in rolled socks from dancing, down the hall and opened the door. A messenger stood on the front porch, back near the glider. "Yes?" Joy placed her hands flat against the screen, pushed it open a ways.

"Western Union." In two strides the man was in front of her, fiddling with a leather satchel strapped to his belt.

Joy quickly glanced across to the houses of her neighbors. Quiet—the same as always. A pink handball bounced into the middle of East Trainor. No one came rushing after it. Joy watched the ball dribble to the curb, bump against it, and slowly keep rolling. Then she heard the messenger's annoyance: "I repeat—is Evan Eichenbaum home, miss? Telegram."

"He's working, he's at our store. I can take it, I'm his daughter." She added hopefully, "And let me get you something for your trouble, all right?"

"Oh, it's no trouble." The messenger shrugged, though now he was smiling.

Joy was pleased by the adult phrase she used. She'd heard her mother use it, so she'd been eager to try it when the situation seemed right. Here, where she was certain that the man was in fact only doing his job, it was perfect. He could gallantly deny expending any great effort, and she could repay him quite easily. After real trouble, nothing could compensate.

"One minute, please." Joy hurried over to the small fruit-wood table and opened the drawer. A tiny china bowl filled with coins sat atop some old overseas letters.

"Thanks so much." She handed the messenger a dime.

As his boots pounded down the outdoor steps, Joy glanced at the envelope. The front flap said in red ink: *Urgent!*

After a moment's hesitation, Joy tore open the yellow envelope; she carefully worked out the thin sheet. She read the first line, and doubled over.

"Hankus." Her arms flew away and wrapped about her middle. She could hold only herself. The telegram, forgotten, floated downward.

Joy was screaming, "Hankus! Come back. You can't be— Please, Hankus. Please, don't leave."

No. Wait. She was not shouting.

Joy was not shouting. She was breathless. She was not shouting. The telegram was on the floor now, upside down; the envelope was near the edge of the rug. Stepping around it, trying not to see it, she—Joy, Joysie—then moved toward the telephone. She put her narrow hand, shaking, on the thick receiver; it dropped to the floor. She couldn't hold on to it. Bending for it, crouched down, she saw the telegram in her peripheral vision. It was yellow. She wasn't sure; maybe it said something different. Maybe she'd panicked and misread it. Maybe she'd made a mistake. She's made mistakes before. She's gotten things wrong. He couldn't have died. He couldn't really be dead. Not her brother. For as long as she could remember, he's been full of life. Hasn't he always been? Full of life?

The girl who was Hankus Eichenbaum's sister turned toward the fallen slip of paper.

Soon Vera and Evan will come out the front door of Buckeye

Shopping Center. They'll be stunned, not touching each other—they won't touch each other until the moment passes where they've taken hold of that square of paper—cool, almost transparently thin, a piece of dead *nothing*. Hurrying along the pavement on their journey, neither speaks.

They're moving in disbelief toward the Chevy, parked as always in front of Rivchin's Pharmacy; they're almost there. Evan gets out his keys, drops them near the tire. Vera shakes the locked handle on her side though she knows it won't open to her. She curses at it, tugging with both hands.

Teddy will hear last. He'll answer the telephone at the farm and hear Evan asking him to come home right now, yes? Get in the truck and drive—but go slow. Honey, be careful.

Back on East Trainor, Teddy opens two-six-oh-two's front door and pauses in the foyer as though lost. He sees them in the front room waiting for him, sees the day's tears dried on their faces, sees the fresh tears springing and flooding their eyes, and he fists up his hands. He turns away with a groan: *Shut up, okay? I don't want to hear, I know what it is!* He turns his face to the wall and stands there, as if posture alone will shrug everything off.

But Joy had only just dropped the phone. Socks slipping on the floorboards and still moving toward the telegram, she was telling herself that she had to be wrong, that the mistake had to be hers, that *dead* was only an error she'd made in a single word of her reading. She believed the true message might possibly turn out now to be something else. She didn't yet understand. She's so awfully, perfectly young.

Stretching out her hand, and crying, Joysie Eichenbaum bent in the entry to pick up the thin slip, again.

FIVE

In the Alcove

(1993)

Nnone of them ever stepped foot in the house their mother grew up in. Of course they could have. They could have gone and knocked on the front door, explained who they were to the most recent owners, and asked to have a peek inside. But they didn't do that. And no one ever suggested they should, although their own house—a roomy suburban semi-Colonial set smack in the center of a wide weedless lawn—stood only five miles away.

"The house on East Trainor" was how Joy's children knew it. For them, the verbal designation was reality enough. Like many children, they didn't really want to imagine their mother as a child and they wanted even less to put her in a house where they themselves had no quarter. Walls and roof, five loud wooden stairs of a porch, the slam and lock-click of a screen door—these would take little-Mom even further away. In such a structure their Nan and Pop would be concerned not fully with them but with only their first, real kids: Hankus, Teddy, Joy. And just as Abby, Hal, and Ricky didn't want their mother living anywhere but home at Eight-hundred-and-three South Hampshire, so too they didn't want their grandparents anywhere but that one place they'd always themselves found them: in a green-shuttered red-brick apartment building where they could rush through the main lobby, loudly vying for the privilege of punching elevator buttons.

How majestic that old elevator seemed to them. They stood in the cage while slow, gray, ponderous as an elephant, it rose from massive wrinkled knees to lift them all the way up to the third floor. There in the mirrored foyer their grandmother was waiting. Her hair gray, her body solid and broad, Vera had an energy that felt both in use and pent up. The moment she saw them, she grinned and her arms opened wide. "Nan!" Running from Joy, the children jostled one another for her embrace. The four walked all crunched together (Joy took a breather by trail-

246 • MARCIE HERSHMAN

ing behind), on toward the apartment that Vera and Evan moved into in the summer of 1950. They'd sold the house on East Trainor one month after Joy had moved out, nearly giddy with laughter to find herself included in the popular surge of young postwar brides. Both of them were happy about Leo Buckland, a bright guy with a big smile and black curly hair who'd just put himself through business college on the GI Bill. Oh, they could tell he was ready and able this boy to make his own luck. He was prepared to get right to work for the good life—and this everyone could see, yes?—now lying ahead.

Crossing the threshold in Vera's embrace, the children would catch first sight of their grandfather. "Pop!" With his long silver hair combed back from his high forehead, his face looked distinctively handsome, avuncular. Evan was always just standing up from some chair. Coffee cup and saucer in hand, he greeted them with the mixture of good manners and pleased reticence that one finds these days only in old black-and-white movies on TV.

That was their simplest home, really, their Nan and Pop's apartment. There they were given cakes and stories and told wonderful secrets. *In my eyes, you're beautiful. In my eyes, you're the smartest little one ever. In my eyes, oh you! You're a vision.*

One thing they understood was that their grandparents had seen a lot. So if Vera and Evan spied in them virtues that others just couldn't, well, they knew whom to trust. Whether their grandparents recognized in them bits of their futures or fragments of personalities and gestures resurfacing from their own pasts, it's now too late to say. But back then in Vera and Evan's eyes, the children found some of themselves.

When Hal was about six he lost his baby fat. As his face narrowed and the dark brown of his eyes took on new prominence, the adults were quick to say how he might one day come to look—well, not like his namesake—not Hankus, no, this wasn't mentioned and wasn't there anyway, why pretend, why borrow, why try to see who wasn't there—but yes, truly, and one could know this with the whole heart: Hal looked like Evan. It wasn't just the firming jawline or the subtly lengthening and aristocratic hook to his nose, it was also that Hal was starting to hold himself differently. No longer did his head bob childishly and eagerly about, nor would he race into whatever activity anyone else suggested. Instead, he often seemed already engaged; he'd begun the process of tilting inward. He knew how to keep, at that early age, his own watchful counsel.

Abby, a boisterous child, couldn't understand his new reticence and so teased him without pity. Ricky was a round little toddler then and warranted only a passing, though affectionate, interest. As eldest, Abby wanted Hal, her best playmate, back. But after a while it was clear that her cause was lost; Hal was going to become himself in ways in which even a sibling wouldn't always have a say. So, with the brother's first turn inward the sister found herself launched too.

Both were too young to see that these times of edgy distance and solitary pursuits could become the basis of their later becoming good friends to each other. Joy, watching intently, hoped for the best for them. For the first time she found herself to be part of an elaborate system of silent communication as she, Leo, Vera, and Evan signaled one another over the children's heads when Hal and Abby played their *Come near—No! Go away* games, and Ricky, alternately oblivious to or aggrieved by his siblings' benign exclusion, knocked down the towers of wooden alphabet blocks he'd built (going always, always one letter—*A? E? C?*—too high) alongside the main action. "Little ones," Vera called, peacemaking during these contests, "you want some cake? Pop's at the table already, and you see how nicely he sits? But he's lonely without you. Kids, can't you keep him company?"

Was it true that Hal responded to the others' enticements back then as he would years later, by continuing for a few deliberate moments in the activity he was already pursuing? That only then, in this solitude, would he make his next move? Whenever he did refuse, it's so that he did it nicely and at a slight remove; and that after this no one could budge him—unless it was Pop. They always did have a special, quiet bond.

There were of course no photographs of Evan as a child in Nagymihály, so even when he was still with them, they couldn't directly compare the two, they could only surmise. And since it was difficult to regress Evan, everyone instead had to progress Hal. "How he holds his shoulders . . ." they'd say. Or, "Maybe his walk . . ." Or: "If he combs his hair back . . ." But after a comment or two the kids would get bored and move off, seeking new games. Like many children, they found most compelling their own presentness, their own endless minute, and didn't care to tug for very long on the pulls of the future or the past.

As the years went on, none of them ever turned away from the gifts put in their hands. The first pleasures of Davy Crockett raccoon caps with ersatz fur tails and Betsy-Wetsy dolls that wetted the water poured into them gave way to ten-dollar bills, which they deposited into bank accounts toward their futures; gave way to modish new clothing, which without being urged they hung up in their closets; gave way to the heft of seriously small-typefaced reference books, which they paged through, challenging the adults to recite the facts they themselves were finally ready and eager to learn.

"Nan," Abby might say as she flipped open the new dictionary, "of course you know what *epidermis* means."

Vera put down her mending and leaned heavily back against the couch. After a moment, she shook her head.

"What? You don't, really? You're sure?"

"No, you tell me."

"Skin. It's the outer nonsensitive layer of skin. That layer covering and protecting the true skin or corium." Abby kept twirling a strand of blond hair about her finger. "Gross! I can't believe I've got some kind of a 'true skin' somewhere under this top one, can you? Want me to read the full definition aloud, so you'll know it, Nan?"

"Sure." Vera waved a wrinkly hand, gracious as the queen of England. "Read to me all you want, *mameleh.*"

Or Hal might say, leaning over the text, "Okay. What about *abrasion?*"

"Easy as pie. A boo-boo."

"Nan, that's not funny." The corners of his mouth tightened, his whole face seemed to darken. "You're making fun of me by answering in baby talk."

"Oh, I am, Mr. Wise Guy—Mr. Handsome Guy—you think so? When you were just a little *shmendrick* and you'd fall down, you'd come running to me, crying and shouting, *Wah-wah, wah-wah! Kiss my boo-boo. Nan, please kiss my boo-boo.* You asked—and I kissed. Boo-boo abrasion all gone! You think I make fun of what works?" She gave a slight grimace. Brushing the bodice of her blue dress of invisible dust, she stood up. "Well, enough for me with these words, I'm going to help Mom in the kitchen, making dinner. I want to eat later. Abby, you come too, so you learn. And you"—she looked at Hal—"shouldn't be upset with me."

"I'm not mad." Protesting her assessment, he snapped his fingers. "All done."

"Good. You want to test words, ask your Dad when he comes out of the den. Or better, you should go outside and find Pop. He's out back in your Mom's vegetable garden, tying up the tomato plants. The littlest one is there too; he's holding in place the sticks. Go be in the sunlight with them, darling."

"Okay, Nan, I'm making bye-bye!" Hal waved and flashed a smile perfect in potential, the white teeth sheathed in silver orthodontic wires. "I'll ask Pop what it means to depose. You think he knows what that is, to *depose?*"

It was during the children's charge into adolescence that Evan died. Though his death didn't come tragically early by conventional standards, nor was it due to large-scale violence or hatred, he was the first family member Joy's children had to mourn. Abby was fourteen, Hal a preteen, Rick still a giggling boy; each took the blow of his death differently. Out of her own green-black haze of grief, Joy saw how Abby sobbed, giving out a deeply guilty woe at her own inadequacy, still naive enough to believe that somehow she should have been able to save him; saw how with a sharp intake of silence Hal turned away his face whenever he was addressed; how he went on long walks by himself, which everyone (Joy included) willingly mistook as stoicism rather than what it truly was—a solitary embrace of his heartache; saw how Ricky, by imagining his grandfather's profile in the swirled oak grain of his bedroom door, saw a vision so silent he was terrified to shut his eyes, lest the shape leap into life and attack him.

The three of them missed their grandfather much more than they could then fully understand. But it wasn't their own feelings, Joy saw with a start, that the children sought to examine in the emptied months following Evan's death. It was their grandmother's feelings. And it was her own. Vera and Joy were before them now as the essential witnesses to loss. The children were frightened but also eager to see how the two of them would change.

What lesson would mother and grandmother impart by their mourning? Or by their persistence in eating, speaking, touching, sleeping, waking? Underneath it all, perhaps the children understood from their long-ago, night-soaked, adult-voiced retellings of fairy tales that when one of the characters in a tale dies, a second, a third, and a fourth remain to pick up the narrative.

Perhaps they understood, too, that although entire groups might be lost—a whole town, say, or a family, or a circling ship, or an indeterminate number of like-minded, affectionate travelers—taken off by some terrible magic, there is always a safer shore somewhere in the story. And someone waiting there—who turns and cries out.

Joy could feel her children watching, preparing themselves for the moment when surely their grandmother or mother would begin to speak to them of everything.

Yet, for the life of her, she really couldn't have said what she'd want to impart to them other than this: *Be happy! Thrive! Don't worry!* Words that, like her parents' to her so long ago, were hinged to the promise of the future. And why shouldn't she speak hopefully to her own children? Her evasion of old and difficult matters wasn't pernicious. It was, well, more of a kindness all around. Joy was in the midst of her own best years, years blurred and filled by the ordinary stainless-steel sunniness of daily suburban life. She was in charge of a household: three active children to raise, a husband whose business (Buckland Electrical Supply) kept growing and prospering. Their lives were moving ahead faster and more solidly than anyone would have had a right to expect. She felt the family had finally *arrived*.

Unlike some of her friends, Joy regarded herself and her children as being more or less in constant communication. Of course, it was usually about when Hal would be done with the film-club meeting (vice president), when she'd be at the field to pick up Ricky from baseball (center field), at what hour Abby should phone from the party if she had to be late (member, planning committee: social council). Joy spoke often too with Leo and Vera about small but persistent problems: whether Ricky would grow out of his stutter (should they get him a tutor?); why Hal was unwilling to get his hair cut (the brown locks fell almost to his shoulders and made him look wild and messy, a repudiation of his usually thoughtful demeanor); how to get Abby, with her sharpening wit, slender figure and that newly rebellious tilt to her chin, disinterested in Marty Bauder (a boy rumored to smoke marijuana). Did Joy have, really, any time to look back? Any desire? Their lives together were happy and also for all of them a strong source of pride.

Yet horribly now, sitting here, Joy couldn't stop the repetition of a phrase in her head: *It's like back then.*

The phrase wouldn't leave. A tough, incongruously sharp echo. What her mother Vera once said, wasn't that it? The words stitched themselves in and out of her thoughts. When she spoke them, propelling them only barely into sound, and still under her breath, something in the back of her throat, some muscle she never thought anything about, tightened in spasm. *It's like back then, Vera said. And put her hand on the cool doorknob.*

Going into a small white room to see Dad—Evan, her husband, her friend, tateleh, in this very hospital. But some other floor in this hospital than this one; clearly it must have been a different floor. But Joy couldn't remember, nor did she even expect herself to remember where the cardiac intensive-care ward was back then—how many years ago? Twenty-five, twenty-six. Almost thirty years ago. Already.

And now, in so many ways she can barely enumerate, she is sitting very nearly—surely this is implausible and clearly to everyone in the family unexpected—almost exactly where her own strong mother had sat. No one wanted to believe this new situation could overtake them— although maybe that's what her mother was trying to say to her nearly thirty years ago, with her plain, sad words. Of course, "back then" Joy'd thought Vera was talking only about the losses suffered thirty years before. She'd thought the sentence being uttered stretched only backward, only in her mother's lifetime, and went no further. But maybe her mother was saying: Joy, Joy, I am frightened. Look how easily, you see?, Now *might turn about and remind of* Then.

It's like back then—*how simply and slightly a story will break off and mutate? How life's projected course loops back to a beginning one thought has been not only escaped but superseded? But when her father was here, perhaps on this floor of the hospital, Joy had still been too young—though nearing forty—to understand in a deep way what her own mother was getting at. Instead, she now remembers, she'd told her mother to remember how "lucky" they always were. She remembers how she'd stood awkwardly next to lanky Marky Rivchin—Richards, Doctor Mark Richards—stood there waiting with him until he mumbled something about "other duties" and pressed her hand in his dry steady one, blinked at her once with surprisingly full, compassionate eyes, and strode away, the back panel of his white jacket swinging, the stethoscope looping out of his pocket, leaving Joy alone in the overheated hall. She wanted suddenly to bring him back, the childhood companion and stranger, but it was* Now *now, and she had no way to go back again and ask Mark who he was, really (was it true what everyone whispered) or what he ever saw about her family that she herself missed (if there was something she could help change). She wanted to go back, because in those quick ticking moments, so caught up in her dull fear for her father, she'd only been able to think:* I forgive my mother for her fatalism. *Because for her mother—Vera—loss rolled. For her, for Vera and Evan and their generation—forward-facing, backward-glancing immigrants to this shore—for them alone, for them only, a fresh loss would always call up the original "back then"; they had a past that they could never quite outrun. But for Joy's generation, life was supposed to be different. That was even more clearly the case for her children. They were truly born to America, each an individual spelled with a capital* I, *and weren't supposed to get*

caught in a harsh impersonal net of epidemic proportions. The children,
especially, were supposed to be secure.

Now, with her fingertips pressing lightly against her lips, though
she has no desire to utter a sound, Joy Eichenbaum Buckland,
sitting upright in a green vinyl chair in the hospital alcove,
watches Abby and Ricky sleeping as if they're still truly hers, her
own babies, curled sweetly there under her protection, trusting
that she'd do what was right and good for them. But her daughter is nearing forty now and, slouched in a matching chair, looks
sad and exhausted, even in sleep, all her attractively bright animation tucked inward. Maybe she's dreaming—though Joy
doubts many images Abby has right now, even in dreams, could
be pleasant. Rick, stretched out on the long cushion of the
couch, which he'd dragged onto the floor, seems utterly closed
down; his head is on his arms, face turned away; there's a bald
spot visible on his crown that she's never noticed before. He
must take pains to comb over it. Her baby. Who has a toddler
and infant now of his own.

It hurts Joy suddenly to see her children in this light, so
exposed in their aging weariness. Though she's glad—*very*
glad—to have them with her. Two out of the three are well. And
so close by, she can reach over and touch them. Abby. Ricky.

She exhales their names quietly, so she won't focus on the
one name she is maddened and disheartened and frightened
by—by how much she keeps shouting it, inside and silently: Hal.
Sweet darling her boy her dear son her Hal. Her Hal. First son.
Lucky son. Brilliant boy. Books the films for a big theater chain.
A sensitive, warm, good-looking man. His special joke with her:
thumping his chest and then a teasing Tarzan-like yodel. But
also quiet, well-spoken. Deep brown eyes and a steady focus.
How long does he have left?

She winces at how the question comes forward although it
was unbidden, unsought. She does not want to be curious about
something like that. She does not want to get news of a change
in his status.

She looks down again at her watch. Made it to 4:30 A.M. Leo

is, she hopes, getting some rest in the motel room they rented a few streets away from the hospital. Abby was supposed to go; it had been her turn for a shower, a nap, whatever would serve, but she insisted on staying in the alcove. Abby wanted to be near in case Hal asked for her. She said so in a sharply emphatic way, the same way she announced her divorce four years ago: quickly, with no room for argument, to cover herself and to halt her parents from finding the pain that wells up from too much probing. Joy couldn't dissuade her. *I promise, nothing's going to happen now.* Couldn't convince the older, worried version of the thin sweet girl who years ago stood in the living room window to watch (and, Joy thought, bless) her parents' car racing up the neighborhood street to help her grandfather Evan. Couldn't convince her to leave, to take an hour away from this alcove for herself, not a half hour.

Abby just bit an unlipsticked bottom lip and shook her head; the brownish permed curls swayed a half-beat after. *I'll wait,* she said, and settled back in the uncomfortable chair, crossing her long blue-jeaned legs, the laces of her sneakers double-knotted, as if she expected to suddenly sprint forward in some race. The distance between Hal and her was dwindled down now to a matter of yards, no longer the thousands of miles between San Francisco and Chicago they'd grown used to—the distance that for years they'd managed to bridge by lengthy, twice-weekly telephone calls.

Rick glanced over at his sister's profile. She didn't notice, still gazing down the hallway leading to Hal's room, vacant for the past hour, since an orderly had wheeled him elsewhere for tests and procedures. Rick hitched his shoulders and said loudly, Know what? He'd stay, too.

You use the motel room then, Joy said to her husband, putting her palms lightly against his chest. Leo was breathing quickly, as if he'd been chasing something. But he hadn't been doing anything physical at all; he'd been sitting against the couch, eyes closed, a Walkman softly hissing a tape of swing music into his ears. Leo hated hospitals. *If we get any news, any at all,* she promised, the old words thick on her tongue, *I'll get to the phone and call you.*

Leo gazed at her. For a moment she thought he was going to protest angrily; instead, the rims of his eyes reddened. Without speaking, he slipped off the headphones, and from the black foam of the earpieces she could hear a tiny, eager voice singing without any pause, *Pardon me, boy*— and going on with a lilt to inquire, even for the millionth time and with a curiosity still fresh, when would the train he's been waiting for finally arrive? Immediately the horns blared a response full of warning: *Clear the rails, move back!* At the familiar chugga-chugga power of Glenn Miller's orchestra, a thin flare of pleasure sprang up in Joy's throat. Astonishingly, terribly, she wanted to laugh. Everything in her swerved toward the music. She wanted to step into Leo's arms, have the two of them begin twirling thrillingly down the endless, sterile hospital hallway—yes, let him spin her!— even at the same moment he was saying tonelessly above the bright tune: "I don't want to leave you here, Joy."

Against Leo's chest, her hands trembled. Pulling back, she looked down, ashamed. So that simply, if she wished, she might yet ignore grief!

"Go on, Dad," said one of the children; Joy wasn't paying attention to bother thinking which. Only a familiar, beloved voice. But she made herself speak up, to concur with the opinion that someone should act clearheaded enough to get a few hours of sleep and store up some energy.

Leo hefted the blue duffle. It sagged in the middle, and he shifted it over to his other hand. He stood before her, as if waiting for something more. Clearly, they were both exhausted.

She could only repeat, "I'll phone."

He was sixty-eight now, Lucky Leo. He was wearing a sporty white cardigan, a blue-and-white-striped Izod T-shirt, and beige cotton slacks. He was missing only his golf cap pulled over his thinning curling white hair. He tried to smile, as if to mirror some slight mutual agreement. Was she doing that for her husband, smiling?

A faint bridge of notes from the headphones stretched between them. He leaned over and quickly pressed his lips to hers. "I'll be back by dawn. Unless he—you need me before."

Leo walked backward a few steps, then lightly thumped his hand over his heart. He didn't need to say their son's name to her before he turned and kept going, his stride heavier and slower than he would have wanted her to see it.

Hal's feet, naked—that's what she was thinking about now, in the alcove—the "now" after Leo left, and Abby and Rick let their eyes close. Hal's feet, naked, mature, and strangely beautiful. In that way too he's come to resemble her father. One memory Joy has of the years of her own early motherhood is how her infant son, her first son, wiggled his toes in the air while she and her husband and her mother and father leaned over the bassinet. All of the adults were laughing, really laughing. The tiny red heels had not yet born any weight; they were rounded and soft. One by one she, Leo, Vera, and Evan put their lips to the baby's soles and kissed them. Hal loved it, holding still, gazing up distantly beneath all the attention.

Vera turned her head and whispered, her red-coral lips quietly shaping the words, "The little girl's watching."

"Abby?" Joy looked around. "Do you feel left out?"

Sitting at her tiny wooden desk set with its stick-on decals of violets, roses, and giant yellow bumblebees, Abby pretended she hadn't heard. Frowning, she kept right on turning the big stiff sheets of her book, although with each flip, she peeked up at the adults. Abby's determination to maintain the charade of reading twisted Joy's heart, even as she suppressed a smile.

"*Mameleh,*" Vera called, stepping in front of Joy, "you want a bite of him, too?"

"A bite of who, Nan?" Abby asked, immediately eager. She looked at her grandmother with wide thrilled eyes.

"Of your little brother. Want a bite of his feet?"

She ran over, her cheeks flushed. She was inconceivably golden-haired and fair-skinned. *Like Irina's coloring, at least back home,* Vera said, only once.

"If I bite, I won't hurt him?"

Vera waved a dismissive hand. "Oh no, *mameleh*, no." She whispered something to Evan, and he winked at Abby.

"Watch, darling." Evan bent over the railing and carefully cradled one tiny heel; he pretended to nibble on the toes. *Too lovely*, he breathed out next, eyes closed.

Hal emitted a moist gurgle.

"You see? Look how delicious. Pop loves to eat the baby's feet."

"I can't hurt him, Mommy?"

Joy assured her she couldn't. It was all really pretend. The bites were really kisses, the eating was really just touching. Understand? It was only that they loved Hal so much, the same as they loved her. Didn't she want to come closer now?

Leo swooped Abby up. Buzzing like an airplane, he lifted her over the edge of the bassinet and, straight-armed, droning louder, flew her back and forth, with each pass coming lower. The little girl hovered, concentrating, pursing her lips to kiss her brother on his perfect toes.

Joy shivers now, remembering that Hal hasn't had the strength to stand for some time. As he lies on his back in room ten-eighteen, his feet point up under the hospital bed's single white sheet and mark his length, once his *height*, like an end bracket.

Her son's fighting; he's hanging on. When she's allowed back in, she might ask if he'd like her to massage the arches. She saw how much this had helped John two years before. Hal's partner John was hospitalized back then, and it seemed that nothing could bring him comfort. Eyes swollen shut, skin blotched with Kaposi's sarcoma lesions, John was so feverish he could barely talk. The Hickman catheter, the antibiotic intravenous, the two long clear plastic tubes of the waste catheters made even his slightest movement difficult.

Joy was appalled. Though she'd read newspapers, seen some brief reports on TV, she hadn't truly known that this was what AIDS looked like. For years she and Leo hadn't really wanted to know; Hal was living in Chicago, and he was healthy and well;

and it appeared that John was healthy and well; and so Joy and Leo managed for a long time not to ask much and to keep their distance. It seemed too difficult for them to have to get used to the possibility of anything this dire affecting anyone they loved; too difficult for them, especially after the jolts of loss and anger she and Leo already had felt when Hal told them back in college that he was gay. It didn't mean that Joy or Leo—he promised—had made mistakes; they were good parents, they had to know that. Yet he was who he was; was how he felt; was all right. But at the start of the process of when he came out, Joy could only think: *Hal is gay. Our son is different.*

And now, she would say to herself in those first years when news of a "new plague" began trickling into the public consciousness, *and now*—but immediately tossing the thought away as soon as she'd think it in the middle of the night, waking in the morning, when driving to go shopping or waiting in line for a movie, when climbing into bed next to Leo—*now this. This exists.* This terrible net, opening wider, might fall suddenly upon her son. This she knew, too, but wished not to remember: outside of a very few circles, not many would care.

Then one night, watching television in the den, she stood up to answer the phone ringing in the hall and it was Hal, calling from Chicago. He said simply, "John's ill."

Holding that receiver, Joy raised her hand above her head, her mouth open, crying in such silence that it stretched her whole body. She didn't want him to hear her crying, wanted nothing to stop her son from talking to her, wanted to signal her second son Rick, sitting with Leo in front of the TV set, to race over to her—he was strong, he was young—to somehow help her keep going. Hal was explaining to her about John's examination, what the tests meant. She tried to hear at least some of it, but her mouth was painfully open with that terrible shout of silence that was filled with the question: *And you? And you, Hal? How will you be? If he's in trouble, if he gets taken, what of you?*

So, clearly, she'd try to wait until nearly the last opportunity to go and see John. John: finally and suddenly ill in that extreme, final way, in that white-sheeted hospital bed, in rain-driven midtown Chicago.

Hal, that afternoon, sat down on the edge of that bed. Waiting a moment, he looked at the patient in it, as though not seeing the symptoms and marks of the disease inexorably overtaking John (as it'd overtaken, what had he told her, twenty-four, forty-four? of their friends and colleagues) but somehow he saw only the man beneath it: John Elliott, his partner of the past eight years—a sandy-haired, once-burly, sweet-tempered North Carolina boy he'd met a few years after college—and in these moments too: still here with him. Joy saw Hal study John. He didn't turn to his mother with a conspiratorial glance of: *Oh no, he's worse!* or: *Should we pretend not to see what we see?* or: *I can't handle this anymore; you take over.* Instead, he was quiet, as he used to be as a boy, considering what to do next.

For a few minutes, no one spoke. The machinery blinked, the tubes dripped. Then: "Will this help?" she heard Hal ask. He went around and stood at the bottom of the bed. Gently he picked up one cold, shaking, high-arched, blue-veined white foot between his two palms. John was mostly bones, and Hal seemed to want to cushion him with his own warmth. After a while, talking quietly, now and then letting there be silence, her son took his partner's other foot between his hands. Whispering "Is this better?" Hal applied to the arch what seemed the lightest of pressure. Joy saw that John wanted to answer, but with his breath so strangled by phlegm, speech was impossible. The fingers of his right hand lifted a few inches up off the mattress. Hal nodded, the long brown hair falling across his high forehead, and continued. "I'm glad," he said. "It feels good like this to me, too."

Overhead, the fluorescent tubes flicker a half second too long. Using the tips of three fingers, Joy combs at her hair, dyed a vague blondish tone, a hue she's been assured is kinder to an aging face than a naked, dry gray—something youthful, but still not too blatantly false. She doesn't want to feel that pang of betrayal; it's about Hal, how ill, how poorly he looks.

Silently Abby watches her mother patting at herself: Joy's eyes are focused seemingly on nothing as she moves her hands about the halo of hair. There's a kind of absence of attention in her mother's gestures, which Abby, who's been awake for a while, preferring to keep her breathing slow and rhythmic and to watch from beneath lowered lashes, finds infuriating. She thinks of it as willed ignorance on Joy's part, probably a vestige from the fifties, when women were supposed to act as if they saw or knew nothing. Most likely it's about self-protection.

That's why it's startling when Joy turns and says as if seeing through her charade of being asleep, "Sit next to me, Abby? I want to hear what you're thinking."

"Mom, what?" she replies, but too quickly. Then goes on to say that she wasn't thinking about anything.

Slowly her mother nods, as if she knows that her daughter has been seeking refuge somewhere else. Certainly, Joy can't know that it's their old house she's been drifting through—all those years when they all lived together in the split-level on South Hampshire. That Abby's been watching herself again going about opening bureau drawers and quietly lifting the others' neatly folded hankies and socks to see what might be hidden there. What was it, Abby mused, wavering, disturbed between the filmy half layers of sleep; what was she looking for all those times when she was young? She was searching so intently for *some*thing.

"Can't you still sit next to me, honey, even if we don't talk?"

Abby unbends herself. The muscles in her shoulders and the backs of her calves are stiff; she's no longer able to sleep just anywhere. Rick's lying on the long single bottom cushion taken off the alcove couch and put directly on the floor as a mattress. Back to them, he's curled on his side, a swath of pinkened skin visible between the waistband of his jeans and where his sweatshirt has hiked up. He doesn't look too comfortable. Under his shoulders and hips the green cushion is compressed to one airless inch from the floor; his feet hang off the pad's more buoyant edge; he's kept on his running shoes.

Of the three of them, only Rick's chosen to live where they grew up. Within a fifteen-minute drive of South Hampshire, and twenty minutes from East Trainor, he and Jill are raising a family. In the early seventies, when Abby was studying painting at Berkeley and planning a postgraduate move to San Francisco (sure, she'd take a job as a secretary if it'd help support her art—well, it did; and, yes, it does), she laughed at doing something so safe and limiting as returning to live in one's hometown. Now, though she'd never admit it, she's grateful in a way that Rick has stayed close, working in their father's business. Something of them can remain in Cleveland; in this not-too-large but complex-enough Midwestern city where their grandparents wanted to put down deep roots, the generations can turn again.

Abby drops quickly, reaching for her toes in the attempt to loosen up her body. Now that she's finally out of the chair, she can head for any number of places: she can go down the corridor to the nurses' station to ask if anything's changed with Hal's status. She can continue past the station to the very end of the hallway to his door, number ten-eighteen, to try and overhear what the medical staff inside might be saying. She can put a hand on the doorknob. She can turn it and lean in: "Hal, hurry, get dressed! I mean it, no more fooling around, Zorro. Get your cape and mask. I've got your horse, I'm getting you out of here. Let's go."

Instead, she sinks into the chair next to her mother's. The armrests are too high—awkwardly angled, as if to prepare the sitter for immediate takeoff and flight. Her mother looks exhausted; every line in her face appears worn and rubbed. The delicate olive shading seems no longer a sign of windy afternoons spent on a golf course but of something stronger, some richer color, being leached slowly away. Nan was darker than she. As a freckled, blond-haired girl, Abby often watched how her mother and grandmother placed their arms next to each other, as though comparing tans; but it wasn't what was temporary that they were measuring.

"Tell me"—she shifts her weight in the chair—"what you're thinking about, Mom?"

Joy lets go of hardly any breath at all, so as not to wake Ricky: "My brother."

Damnit. His name's still not on the visitor's list; she meant to add it last night. Should she go to the nurses' station and do it right now? She's sorry she forgot.

"Teddy?" Her mother gazes at her. The corners of her mouth have tightened as precisely as if the skin has twisted about two tiny screws. "Teddy won't come," she says coolly, probably meaning it to sound neutral; she almost succeeds.

"No, he might. Hal asked for him, so I phoned yesterday, didn't I mention it? I thought I told Rick to tell you too, but maybe I forgot to tell him in the first place. Well. Anyway, I left the message on their answering machine."

"We'll see." Joy passes her hand over her eyes and for a bare second lets her head drop, half-brushed, half-cradled into her palm. Across the way, a door opens and a nurse comes out. Briskly the woman peels off the thin yellow plastic gloves and with a paper towel pushes them into the special waste container marked: BE ALERT! CONTAMINATED ARTICLES ONLY. CONTAGIOUS BODY FLUIDS. BLOOD PRODUCTS. DANGER. She walks off swiftly.

"I wish I'd had a chance to know Hankus," Abby says with a slow shake of her curls. "Uncle Hankus, I mean. I think about him sometimes, but I don't know much. I really can't imagine, Mom—I can't think what it was like. For you to lose him, I mean." Her voice trails away. "How does a person get through it, losing a brother? I mean, when other people aren't—" Abby hates how she's wheezing. But it's what she's asking for that she hates most. What kind of daughter would ask such a thing, and of a mother like hers? And keep asking now? "It seems we're always—I mean, everybody in our family—Nan and Pop, Uncle Ted, you, has always had to face, each time, with a sibling—"

"Enough," Joy says sharply.

Abby doesn't mean to reach for her mother's hand.

Joy pulls herself stiffly upright. "No one has to lose."

Pressed against each other, each one of their fingers feels too warm-skinned. Suddenly neither woman knows where to look. Not at Rick's broad curved back or the dirtless white soles of his running shoes. Not at their own clasped hands, the wrists bent and awkwardly positioned. Where? The label on the waste container is a bright pink rectangle with black letters. The container itself is the same yellow as the protective gloves now stuffed inside with the paper towels, used syringes, the soiled disposable gowns. The hallway walls are pale yellow.

Dr. James, says the loudspeaker, *Dr. Eileen James, room eight-oh-five. Doctor Eileen James, please.*

"Not an emergency," Abby says, as they carefully disengage their hands. "Not a STAT, I mean, with everybody racing madly over." She swallows, dry-mouthed. "That's lucky, right?"

The gray-black door the nurse exited stays stone-still. Outside Hal's door, also dark, stands an identical yellow container. All the rooms in this wing are guarded by waste barrels that are periodically loaded onto a dolly and wheeled away. They aren't relieved of their contents right in the hall.

"Abby," Joy takes a deep breath, "I'm sorry. I shouldn't have spoken that way. I meant to reassure you."

Her daughter puts on a smile. With a shock, Joy realizes she expects Abby to wave to her cheerfully from across the chasm. But that was she, Joysie, who would do that, not her own child.

Rick mutters some kind of garbled phrase. Instinctively, Joy looks over to where he's facing the wall. The sweatshirt rucks across his back, his shoulders twitch; then it's clear that it's sorrow he's trying to gulp back down.

"If he's awake," Abby leans in closer, whispering, furious, "why won't he turn? Doesn't he think we might want to talk with him?"

"You can ask him to—"

"No. I'm not coddling him like you and Dad do. You always want to protect him."

"We don't," Joy replies lamely.

Her daughter shrugs, one finger twirling a strand of hair.

"He'll be all right, sweetie, you'll see." But she doesn't know if she means it, nor about whom she's really talking. Quickly she looks at her watch.

Made it to 5:17 A.M.

• • •

When Leo can't sleep he comes back to the alcove to find his wife gone, his daughter sitting, eyes closed, in a chair, his son lying like a log on a strained thin cushion facing the wall.

Abby says Joy's gone to wash in the ladies room.

Ridiculous, her father answers. Then complains this place could use air freshener. And the circulation's lousy, too. It's a hospital, for godssake. There has to be all kinds of crap in the air that's no good to breathe. Doesn't she notice it? No? Then she's been breathing it in too long. He wants her to find her mother and wants the two of them to get out of here for a while, at least go take a shower in the motel. Clean up and you feel better. He feels better.

Swinging the blue duffle down on the one empty chair left in the alcove, Leo goes over and with the toe of his right Reebok prods the cushion where his younger son lies. Rick stirs, his voice muffled: *Don't kick me, I'm up, Dad.*

Good boy. All right, here's the story, here's what's what: Abby and Mom will be at the motel, maybe forty-five minutes, an hour, and when they come back, it's his turn to leave, hey? Abby's going to tell Mom, isn't she, that he's just talked to one of Hal's doctors, that's right, and he said there's only the X rays left to do. They've put the new Hickman in and are set with the other catheters. He's stabilized. Anyway, Hal's third in line up there. Unbelievable, that someone in Hal's situation, let alone at this hour, has to wait lying on a gurney in some kind of line. He doesn't like to think about it. Anyway, when the technicians finish they'll wheel Hal back to his room and clean his feeding tube there. The staff shift changes over at seven o'clock. He bets rather than rush and squeeze him in, they'll wait for the new nurses to do it. Cleaning the feeding tube, hey? They're allowed to see him after that. That's it. Another hour and a quarter at most, till they're back together.

Leo stands awkwardly, grinding his fist into his other palm; he seems unwilling to sit, as if once down, he'll have to go silent. The sound of his own voice now, instructing, complaining, ordering, is familiar and comforting to him.

Not much longer—he's been promised. Then Hal will be brought back. They'll all be able to see him.

Intersection

Abby goes to find Joy, meets her coming out of the rest room, and tells her Leo's story of what's next. The moment they exit the wide, glass-fronted main door of the hospital, the air snaps around them like a sheet on the line.

It's hateful, isn't it, how much Joy loves feeling it strike? As her daughter does, she turns her face toward it, and all the time she hears herself thinking that it isn't right. The world is so fresh. Hal should have this wide air. Her son needs it. She and Abby are moving through it, moving away from him, but only for a short time.

They're walking so quickly down the deserted city sidewalk that something about the gait doesn't look quite normal. To the light, passing traffic of factory workers and eager-beaver stockbrokers heading into Cleveland, they probably look like two women hoping not to call attention to themselves but still trying to make their escape. The great hospital rising at their backs refines that perception: *not escaping, but hurrying in order to get back to the place they just left; hurrying now before there's a reason for turning around and running flat-out.*

From the west, church bells begin ringing for six o'clock mass; from the greater distance, carried by the vagaries of wind, comes the low, one-note bellow of a freighter. Abby can hear her mother's fatigue; Joy's breathing is fast, shallow, dryly ragged. Well, she's fighting sixty-something, isn't she?

"Want to slow down, Mom?"

"No."

Their faces are beaded with sweat, and gray. From head to toe, they're dimmed by long shadow. Ahead of them, at the narrow end of the street, the sun is rising, flooding its watery light onto the asphalt, animating the cars coming toward them with a rosy, newborn glow. The bright orange orb is at the angle where their moving forward, heads high, is blinding, so Joy and Abby look down at their shoes, where the concrete is dull. The sun will need to get higher to warm these colorless slabs and make the glass splintered and left littered across them sparkle. And of course the sun will rise; it will do that in fewer than thirty minutes. The day will be clear and beautiful. Anyone can see that's the final outcome, even this early into the unthinkingly direct and natural process. It will be a nice day. Fresh as its first breeze.

"Let's cross at the next block, Mom."

Preoccupied, she barely nods. "I want you to look good when they let us see him," she says. "If you look like you've been sleeping in your clothes, he'll know that's how worried you are. My father always said appearances matter. Pop was meticulous about grooming as a matter of respect."

"I don't think appearances matter now."

Joy hesitates. "Well, of course you can think what you want. It mattered to him, though, even at the end. Mom told me once how in the hospital, Dad—" she breaks off.

"What did Nan say?" Abby asks. Between her brows appear two vertical wrinkles.

"Oh, well, nothing much. Silly to bring it up, it's just something that sticks with me, I guess. I wasn't there—maybe you don't know this, I guess you don't—I wasn't there at the end. And I wanted to be. So when Mom mentioned even a tiny detail, well, I held on to it, maybe more than I should have. Just look good for your brother, Abby, okay?" She turns and smiles hopefully.

"But what did Nan say? I'd like to hear."

"Oh!" Her mother waves a hand. "It wasn't anything, really."

"Tell me," she says, hearing the edge in her own voice.

"Well, just that he asked her to shave him. Dad was feeling like his face wasn't his, it was so rough after five days. He didn't want anyone to have to see him looking that way. He thought this kind of change in his appearance would disturb them. That's when it happened, for the second time—you know, with his heart—when Mom, Nan, I mean, was getting water to lather up the soap. Her back was turned; she was in the little bathroom off to the side; the water I guess was running and she didn't hear him when—" Again, she falters. After a few moments, she glances sidelong at her daughter; on Abby's face is a look of fierce concentration, almost an expression of anger, an *aha!* that this trailing away ends the story, this break in energy and will, this stuttering into silence is what she expected to learn from her all along. She walks with eyes lowered, the sleep-denied lids red and puffy, hands jammed like a kid's into the pockets of her jeans.

"Nan didn't hear him call out to her," says Joy. "I was downstairs in the cafeteria having a cup of coffee. Well. That was too bad. But I couldn't know what was happening right then. And I'd been there all the rest of the time! I told Mom later he might not have called out. She shouldn't punish herself for not hearing. It's possible Dad slipped away without a word."

From the corner of her eye, Joy catches a quick movement, a lifting of her daughter's head. "So, you try to care for each other. If you do that, then you can't keep beating yourself up over what happens in the very last seconds." Joy exhales slowly. She hardly knows what she is saying. "Because we don't have all the control. So, anyway."

But Abby prods her again, voice low, but clearly excited. "So, anyway?"

"So," she says, depleted. "Make yourself look as good for him as you can. Like Pop, he'll appreciate what you call just keeping up appearances."

They come to the corner opposite Dunkin' Donuts. Its pink neon sign has lost some of its illumination; sometime over the past twenty-one hours, the second *u* has gone dead. Every five beats, DON TS flashes out. Ahead lies a shoe-repair store—HEELS WHILE U WAIT, a florist, a blank-faced chain-store pharmacy, another florist shop: HOSPITAL DELIVERIES! FREE OF CHARGE, then an alley and the long white side of their motel, a modern concrete box, studded by faux balcony railings set inches in front of tall windows that don't open.

Joy steps into the crosswalk; Abby's a half stride behind. All of a sudden, a car swerves from the curb and drives right at them. From not quite fifty feet away, the driver gives a blast on the horn. The warning is amplified by the walls and windows of the silent buildings.

Their pace quickens. Joy skips forward, taking little rabbity steps. Abby holds her hand over her head, her middle finger raised in an obscene gesture at the driver. It's a one-way street with three lanes, and two of them are empty; what's he doing?

"Joysie!" they hear. "Hey, sis!"

Joy stops in the middle of the road.

"See?" Abby grabs for her hand. "All we had to do was ask."

"You think I need this?" Joy twists away, looks at her daughter with incredulity.

The red Chevy Camaro glides toward them and a few yards distant comes to an abrupt stop. The tinted front windshield is clean and dark.

"I recognized you from far off," he calls in a muffled way from the passenger side, not sticking his head out the window. "Want to get in? We'll take you wherever."

Joy goes over to the other side, the driver's side; its glass zips automatically down. "I'm so sorry," Abby hears her aunt say in her clipped accent. "How is Hal?"

Her mother winces, then leans toward the opening. "Well," she says, finally.

"He's well now?" Rosalie's voice shoots up. "It's possible?"

"Oh, God, no. No," says Joy. "I just . . . I didn't know how to answer, so I was pausing. You know."

Rosalie makes a furious sound, half a laugh, half a sob. Sometimes colloquialisms still did that to her, tripped her up. She emigrated from Romania after the war, at sixteen having survived two concentration camps, two refugee camps, and any number of viciously idiomatic foreign languages.

"I'm not thinking right, Joy. Please excuse my stupidness. Of course I know what you were meaning to say."

The passenger door swings open. Gripping the frame, Ted slowly climbs out, shaking his head. He's wearing a new-looking sky-blue nylon warm-up suit. Slight-shouldered, hair dyed an erased shade of black, for a few moments he stands with his face averted, as if drawn to the brightening glow of the sun rising behind him. A moment too long, though, to belie he's not stalling. Another breath, and he turns to his niece with a small, ready smile. In an overly hearty voice, he says, "Abby! Long time no see."

She stiffens at his tone.

"So," he rushes on in the same way, "how're you doing?"

She jerks her chin back at the hospital. "Not too great, actually."

He remains behind the opened door, still holding on to it. "When did you fly in? You should have called me, let my agency book this. We can get special emergency fares—most people don't know about them. Let me handle these flights in from now on, okay? For you, or if you're seeing someone, I can also—"

"Ted," Joy interrupts, "what are you saying?"

He gazes across the low roof of the car. He thumbs his plastic-framed glasses, settling them higher on the bridge of his nose, as though that will bring the thin blond woman opposite him into clearer focus. "Well, Joysie," he says from his side.

"Well, what?" Her voice is tight. "I don't have a lot of time right now. Hal's waiting."

"I was just telling Abby she should use my agency, okay?"

"Are you coming to the hospital, is that it? I guess she left a message on your answering machine that Hal asked to see you?"

"I got—we got the message." He blinks. "Thanks. You have good kids, all three of them."

Rosalie turns off the radio inside the car.

"They're good. They don't give up on anyone. Darn!" Joy slaps the metal roof. "Darn, I don't mean that the way it sounds. But I'm surprised at this, Ted. I didn't expect you'd come." She frowns, uncertain. "You never have before. Not even for Dad."

Beeping, a battered Ford Escort rattles past in the next lane. The stink from a dragging exhaust pipe fills the air.

"Too fast," he mutters, looking self-consciously over his shoulder. "Rush hour's starting. They're coming in off the freeway. Better get in."

"We only have a few blocks." Joy glances to her daughter standing by the bumper. Abby's half-turned, squinting off at something across the street, as if not at all interested in these goings-on. Another two cars whiz by.

"You want to get yourselves killed?" he says.

The Chevy's yellow hazard lights start to flash. Rosalie calls, "Everyone in, please. I can see in my mirror."

The oncoming cars begin dividing into either lane around them. Slowing, some drivers rubberneck, expecting an accident. A few rap on their horns. "Get outta the street," a man shouts. "What's the matta, ya stuck?"

Joy sees Abby run behind her uncle and duck down, disappearing into the Camaro. "Mom," her voice echoes. "Let's get moving."

Grinning nervously, Ted gives a thumbs-up and shrugs himself into the other side.

Rosalie leans forward to allow her sister-in-law to press behind and into the rear compartment. She says into the rearview, "I'm very sorry about this, Joy. It's no good." Her eyes, sad and baggy, dart away from contact. She stubs a mentholated cigarette into the ashtray, sending a cloud of minty smoke swirling backward. The immaculate black interior of the car is permeated by the smell of cigarettes, and of coffee. Wedged into the shallow space between the front bucket seats are two napkin-wrapped paper cups from Dunkin' Donuts; both have the protective plastic-lid tabs poked out for carefree roadway sipping.

Joy gives a weak shove to a suitcase on the backseat.

"That hurts." Abby pushes the luggage toward her again. "Watch it. You got my hip."

"Oh, for heaven's sake, I didn't mean it."

They wrestle the black canvas carry-on between them. It's heavy, and there's little room for maneuvering. They stand it on one end between them on the bump in the seat.

Ted pulls his door closed. "Rosie, put it into reverse and go backwards, okay? To where their motel is. Hey," he says sharply as she puts the car into gear, "what are you doing? Go for the entrance."

"I will, right after the cars pass. Don't get excited, *tateleh*." When she leans toward the steering wheel, a white hair, loose as a cobweb, floats from her head, sticking itself to the vinyl head-rest. Teddy bats it away.

Closing her eyes and sitting back, Joy says, "Thanks, both of you." She opens her eyes and smiles at Abby. "It almost feels ordinary, doesn't it, sitting in someone's car."

Blinkers clicking, Rosalie stares into the rearview, then begins to steer diagonally back across the road. Her soft, multi-ringed fingers tremble on the wheel, and she hardly accelerates at all. The car feels as if it's drifting. Abby pushes a button, low-ering the side window partway to bring in fresh air.

Joy says, "Abby and I are going to take quick showers. Would it be all right to ask if you'd wait and drive us back to the hospi-tal? That'd give Rick a little more time, too. You know, he and Leo are still back there. Hal's on the tenth floor. He's been in room ten-eighteen for five days." She sighs. "Oh God. Oh god-darn everything."

"Okay, Joy, listen."

"Listen to what?" his sister says.

Ted casts a swift glance across at his wife's profile just to reas-sure himself.

He's sitting rigidly in the sloped bucket seat, and the seat's angle presses the vinyl backing against Abby's shins. She can see how his ears where the glasses cut into them and the fleshy folds on the nape of his neck begin to turn red. Ted says: "We'll wait for you two if you don't take long in coming down. But I'm sorry, I can't go on up into the hospital, okay? No time now."

Abby bursts out, "*What?* None at all?"

"He's leaving," says Rosalie quickly, her hands still slowly turning the wheel, hardly turning it. "From here we're going out to Hopkins, to the airport." She peers into the mirror. "I think soon I'll make a U-turn. This is not good, going backward. When it's clear, I'll turn and drive the wrong direction."

"Business trip," says Ted, half under his breath. "I'm going to Tahoe."

"You weren't waiting?" says Abby. "What are you doing here, then? I don't get it."

"I stopped by the motel lobby first, okay? The desk clerk

said"—and here he mimics to keep it light—"'Mr. Buckland just left off the key. He said his wife and daughter will return shortly.' I guess you're all sharing a room, right?"

Joy doesn't say anything; she keeps gazing out the window, the buildings sliding by slowly, in reverse.

"That's my suitcase right there with you, okay? I'll be home in five days, flying back in late on the red-eye. But I thought I'd—" dryly he coughs, "I'd try to—I wanted to see someone in the family now, with all this, or at least leave a note. I kept thinking that Mom and Dad would expect me to—"

"What do you think this is all about, Ted?" Joy says.

"I knew it," he mumbles.

Mirthlessly she laughs, lifting her hand, "Oh, never mind! I don't have the energy. I somehow don't. I have other things now." With a *crack*, the suitcase jumps against her leg. Furiously, she slaps it again. "I didn't call you, Ted, I know better than that. It's not me you should see. I'll be all right. But Hal's in trouble. You can't see him? Is there really somewhere else you should be now?"

He says in a high, strained voice, "Make a U-turn already, for God's sake, Rosie. Cut in and get somewhere, can't you?"

"I am trying to do that."

He turns back around. "Okay, when I come back, I bet I can—"

"He might not be here then," Joy replies dully. "Hal probably wants to tell you good-bye. You do remember Hal, don't you? That boy, that young man, who listened to you so often at holiday dinners? The one who thought you were really part of his family—"

"Not fair, Joysie."

But she wouldn't be interrupted. "Listening to you, while you went on and on, talking about yourself all the time?"

"He was interested," he says flatly.

"Interested in your theories? About how Dad probably sold the farm too cheaply? Didn't ask enough from the developers when the boom came through? Well, you—you would have kept the farm and sold it for twice the amount, you think? Who knows what you would've done? It wasn't yours to sell." Her voice shakes. "Well. Dad did fine. Set you up in your business, didn't he? And Cousin Elsa and Joey, he brought them here, right? There was even enough left over for Mom too, at the end. But your theories had only you being right, is that what you think? That he made too many mistakes with his life? He lost his first son. He lost Hankus. And his whole other family. But what didn't he try—" she catches her breath. "Oh, why couldn't you have come last night to see him, or the day before, or the day before, sometime when there was time." She catches her breath. "Let me out here, Rosalie. I want out."

"Please, Joy, I promise, you're not being fair to him." Rosalie glances back over her shoulder. "He's trying to—"

"Stop!" he shouts. "Rosie, my God."

Everyone freezes as an oil truck roars past the front grille of the car. The huge tires bearing a single-hitched cylinder of gasoline stream just inches away. The wake—only air, only air!— thuds over them. Rosalie had almost shifted forward into its lane.

For a moment, no one speaks. Then shakily she starts up the Camaro again. "It isn't fair what you're saying about him, Joy." She is slowly turning the wheel. "Ted is not able to be here. He's not able to be."

"Mom," Abby's voice wavers, "I'm so sorry. I mean, I never knew all this. I thought—we thought—"

Joy faces her over the suitcase. "Done. Over and done, Abby. Well. For now, I guess."

"Please," Rosalie persists, "after I drop Ted off for his flight, I was hoping to go to the hospital. Our plan was for me to see Hal and, also, wait with the family."

The Camaro comes to rest, front tires butting against the curbstone.

"Well, thank you," says Joy, her face strained. "For the ride."

"I want to be with family." Rosalie's accent sharpens in her agitation. "I am able to do this, you won't let me? I want to sit with you."

Joy says, "He's in room ten-eighteen." Hunched over as she

gets out of the low car, she seems all of a sudden to have trouble with her footing. Her hip bangs into the door. She stumbles to the right.

Instinctively, Abby lunges toward her mother, stretching across the fallen suitcase, but she can't reach far enough. Joy's gripping the handle to steady herself, the door wobbling inward and back. Abby can't see her face, only her arms.

"Mom, you—?"

The heavy wing falls back against the dark interior of its own weight. The vibration shakes the car. Sealed in, Abby can see a slight, brightly sweatered torso through the side window; it's moving jerkily, stiffly, toward the back of the car.

"Always like that," Ted mutters. "Look at her. Never not like that. When we were young, okay?, she'd just—"

"Leave her alone!" Rosalie and Abby say at the same time. Abby almost keeps going on, out of fury: *Horrible. He doesn't behave as a brother should toward a grieving sister!* But she holds back, for her aunt's voice like a cautioning hand had overlaid hers, and because Ted's not her brother; he's hers, Joy's. Her only. Her mother said what she had to, and it's not Abby's place to take it any further. Besides, she needs to save her own energy now.

Ted turns awkwardly toward her, his nylon warm-up suit sliding dryly against the vinyl. He sees his niece as looking at him with great concern. "Tell Hal, okay?" He tries to offer a small smile in consolation, to show that he doesn't hold any of this against her. "Tell him I'm thinking of him."

Coldly comes back, "Sure."

It strikes him then, how thoroughly his niece now dislikes him—probably as much as his sister does. Of course Abby doesn't care that he made an effort. But he was stupid to have shown up. He's not given a place here; he's supposed to stay away. The odd guy out in the family, okay? She doesn't know? He reaches around the seat to squeeze her knee.

"You know, they can't run this conference without me. Travel-agency guys, I'm a big deal to them." He blinks a few times behind his plastic frames as he looks past her and on through the sloping back window of the car; Joy is no longer in view. Gone. His pulse pounds, one surging staccato of relief and dread. He did it, he sees, what might be expected. "We're doing all right with the time, Rosie?" He wipes his palms on his pants. "Rosie?" He looks down, then abruptly away from the damp streaks.

"A little late."

"We'll stay with our original plan, okay? You'll go to the hospital for me?"

The lighter pops out of the front dash. Pressing the red coils against the end of her new cigarette, Rosalie inhales. Without air in her voice, she says, "Tenth floor." A twinned stream of smoke leaves with the next breath: "I will be over there with you soon, Abby."

Abby puts a foot out of the car and pauses. Her uncle is facing forward and shaking his head as if trying to clear it of something. He'd saved her, that's what she remembers him saying long ago, back at one holiday gathering or another. She must have been young, because she couldn't quite understand the anger that edged the jovial tone. But he was talking to Hal and her; he had a full plate of food balanced on his knee. He was grinning tightly, waving a fork in the air. See your Aunt Rosie over there? he stage-whispered. Know who made her an American? No, not the president, come on, Hal, don't joke, okay? Know who? That's right, Abby! I did. No, by marrying her, okay? Gave her permanent citizenship. Your Uncle Ted's not useless, is he? At least he knew—I knew how to do something. Whadya say about that, Abby? Hal, how's about you? Not too bad, right, ace? Hal? Hal?

After Ted stood up to join the grown-ups, Hal's eyes had an expression she couldn't read. What was that about, she asked him. Hal shrugged, making a silly face, and then the corners of his mouth dropped like the mask of tragedy, exaggeratedly down. Plucking at her sleeve—taking a slight pinch of her skin with the cloth—he put his lips close to her ear, his breath rushing warm, and whispered: *Let's get out of here, Ab. Zzz-zip, like Zorro.*

From the driver's seat now, Rosalie says, "You don't have to lock the door when you leave, Abbushe, only just shut it. I am able to control it also from here."

Motel Room Three-two-nine

The sound of the shower overrides the television, bright but inaudible in the far corner of the room. "I'm back, Mom," Abby calls, clicking off the set.

No answer.

She goes into the bathroom. Half-submerged in the sink are a pair of Joy's panty hose with a tiny pink bar of motel soap dissolving atop them.

"Mom? Did you hear me?"

Behind the pebbled glass door, her mother's gray silhouette appears to be floating through the steam. Abby taps on the glass. Joy turns full-front, only her eyes and mouth prominent: three small darkish circles; lower, the pubic hair of her mons makes a similarly indistinct patch.

"I'm back."

Joy inches closer. The tight wet chamber catches her voice, and its echo. She needs another couple of minutes in here; it feels so good.

"If I know you, you'll use all the hot water. Try to remember to save me some." As soon as she says it, Abby cringes. What made her speak like that? With the derision of a suspicious adolescent, sure that whatever she asks for will instead get withheld? What was the matter with her? She'd meant to make an old joke. A joke from back when they all lived together. Meant to make them both laugh.

Her mother swipes a hand across the enclosure—perhaps waving *good, very funny*—and the gesture remains as a soapy arc. The white bubbles drip and dissolve as Joy steps back into the pounding spray, disappearing again.

Abby turns away. In the bedroom she clicks on the reading lamp over the nightstand. Her mother's outfit—brown knit skirt, suit jacket and blouse—is neatly laid out on the nearer of the two double beds. Abby goes over to the top drawer of the bureau that's not fully closed. She casts a quick glance over her shoulder, hears the *plop* of a washcloth, then the shift of beat in the spray as Joy bends down to retrieve it; she listens for the rhythm to become regular again.

Shaking, Abby pulls the drawer open fully and lifts up the single thin stack of clothing. It's her own stuff, packed hurriedly, thrown together without any consideration—*take this, need this, this, this, Ab, you need that, this*—in the half hour after her mother's deadly frightened call. At first, though, hanging up, she didn't know what to do. She tried to reach Greg, to tell him she couldn't make their date that night, to ask if he'd phone the airlines for her, find out the best connections she could make to get to Cleveland as fast as possible, but his line was busy. A minute later it was busy still. When she turned to the telephone again: busy. What the hell was she doing? She'd only gone out with him twice. What was she doing, leaning on him? A bad habit left over from her failed marriage? She started packing. His line was busy, a fourth time. She called her friend Sue. Who answered and said yes; and yes; and called back not ten minutes later to say that everything was set, she'd come by to pick up Abby in front of her apartment in about twenty minutes; possible? Yes, Abby said, possible.

She lifts a blue T-shirt out of the drawer: no good, it's the same as the one she's changing out of; a black silk blouse, no; no. An off-white linen top. Fine. That's a start. She must have packed more. Maybe still in her suitcase? She shoves the drawer back in, and something clicks against the wood. She hesitates, then searches behind the stack of clothing. Unbelievingly, she lifts it out: the smooth white plastic oystershell-shaped case that holds her powdered latex diaphragm, and beneath, in its perfect domed shadow, a foil-wrapped condom.

She gives a harsh laugh. But oh, yes, Abby, you'll need this, and need this, need this.

The water clanks off. The door pops open. Clear-voiced, Joy calls sharply: "Where are you?"

Special-Care Ward

"I don't want to talk about him," Joy says as they stand newly showered and in fresh outfits, in front of the hospital's lobby elevator. "He's not my brother, that's how I feel."

With a shrug, she faces Abby. Her lips are a valiant coral pink, waxy bright with color. "But if you could, at the nurses' station add Rosalie's name to the family list?"

Abby nods. They enter the elevator with the half dozen others who were waiting and ride silently until the third floor, where the door opens. Two passengers, one carrying a floral arrangement of tiny red-and-white carnations, hurry out. "I wish my mother were here," Joy says under her breath. "I wish she were still with us.

"I miss her." The door slides shut.

"I know," Abby whispers.

Everyone in the elevator is stone-silent again.

"But I'm very glad, honey, you're with me."

"Me, too," Abby says. "You."

"The taupe slacks go nicely with your top. I like that pin, too. You look good in that outfit."

"So do you, Mom. In yours."

Joy nods. "He'll take heart from it." She doesn't add what they both know: *If he can see.* If he can open his eyes, the lids distended, shiny purplish yellow, lids as swollen and as tightly sealed together as the two halves of a walnut with one midline seam.

On the hospital's tenth floor, a third of the way back toward the alcove, Rick is standing alone, slumped against the wall, his head down. Joy squeezes Abby's hand. "Add Rosalie's name." She goes toward him. Hurriedly Abby moves off to the nurses' station to amend the permitted-visitors list.

When she looks up, Joy has turned from Rick. She is rushing away to the far end of the hall. Her pocketbook swings from her left arm. In her haste to round the corner, she stumbles; she rights herself with one hand reaching out in front of her, grabbing on to nothing, onto the air.

"Mom!"

Joy looks back, her eyes not taking the time to find her as she calls: "Go to your brother!"

Suddenly Abby is half-running.

Rick takes two strides and stands dead-center in the corridor. He spreads his arms out as a block. "No, Abby," he says, hugging her to him.

"Rick!" She pounds his wide fleshy back.

"No, Abby," he says again. "No." And can't get beyond that.

She twists away, stands apart a few feet, heaving. "Hal's still here with us, isn't he?"

He says, as if he doesn't hear, "I phoned Jill. She was almost out the door with the kids. Last time Eli asked if Uncle's a hundred years old. He sees Hal now as—"

"Rick, is Hal still alive?"

"Oh," he says, bobbing, his arms around his gut, his sweatshirt soaked through. "Oh, maybe he—maybe. Something's got him, every part of him's jerking. Brain seizure, maybe. Dad's standing at the door, calling out, to hang on, to come back, he can do it. Abby, to hear him call—" he chokes. "Now Mom's there, too." He ducks his head, tries to get his breath. "The docs said to keep out."

"Let's go."

He looks up with a glare. "Not me. It's hopeless. You want to see him like this? He doesn't look like anyone I know." He laughs bleakly. "Unless we count the specials on TV about the camps. Remember how we'd search for relatives in them, in the piles? That's who's in that room now, but jumping. Out of control. If I really thought that guy jumping was Hal—" He starts sobbing.

Frozen, Abby tugs on his arm. "You have to come. He would want us there. To see him. To witness this for him." Abby, pulling on Rick's forearms, tries to walk backward, tries to pull him forward. Rick's face is furious: close, wet, lined by its years. He's shaking his head, as if unable to clear it of something.

"I'm not going. The three of you, you go for me."

"You don't want Hal to be without you now. Do you? Ricky,

do you want him to be without you now? Everyone's losing everyone, okay? Oh, shit. *Shit!*" She bursts into tears. "You can't act like this; it's too late. You have to help me get down this hall. Come with me. Come wait with me. Ricky. Rick, you're my brother. I need you, too."

Arms stretched in opposition between them, neither one is able to move. Then they're running past the alcove and on to where they believe their parents are waiting for them.

Room Ten-eighteen

There in the distance, near the end of the corridor, Leo and Joy stand with their backs turned to any and all passersby. They're facing the one slight opening left to them: that line of light where the door hasn't been fully shut in the staff's haste. It seems to Abby and Rick coming in from the distance that the dark door has swayed. It wasn't a full gesture, but a movement entirely meager—a tease, a mute, mimicking breath.

Rick and Abby edge in behind their parents. Coming from the other side of the wall:

Get the Hickman in. Now!

Don't elevate.

You hear me? Good, then draw it, use suction.

I need that to be—

Hold his head still!

"Here, kids," Joy says curtly. And she and Leo, just—without asking them whether they want this or not—move apart. Then as if in an old dream Joy raises her hand in front of her; she nudges the door a bit wider.

No one inside notices. They're working bent over, which blocks any view. The white top sheet of the bed has spilled onto the floor. The medical team keeps stepping on it. But a sheet was all Hal has had covering him for the past three days; there's no johnny, nor other clothing; his body has had to be immediately available to meet any emergency procedure that might occur. That's why the ward is kept so warm, because of the possibility of needing access.

There is no jumping.

"Hal," Joy says, and reaches behind herself for someone's hand. Leo's. Abby's. Rick's. Her hands are immediately grasped. Tethered, she inches forward, past the entry. Her son. Hal's face—oh, help him—lies pressed against the mattress, his mouth open in an O. Then as quickly the view is blocked again, as a doctor, cursing, kicks the bedsheet crumpled on the shined floor, shoving the tangled cloth out of her way. She walks toward them, her eyes fastened with each step on Joy's, her yellow gloves wet.

Think of it this way: Instead of the doctor's first words in the sudden stillness, it is Hal's voice. He's able to turn his head, and his lips, not blue at all, move. He's still with them for just a little time more, enough time for the family to come close, enough time for the circle around him to break apart—none of the staff needed now except to flap a fresh sheet over him, covering his body just up to the point where that new catheter exits his chest; someone scoops up the sheet they've been trampling and carries it outside the door to deposit in the yellow waste container. The sound of the staff's peeling off their gloves, taking off the various articles of their protective gear, continues until Hal asks Leo to shut the door to the hall.

Now it is just this one family in the white, huge-windowed room.

Hal smells of warm flesh after strenuous physical exertion and not of dripped medicines and his own leached fluids. The swollen eyelids part. His brown eyes are clear. His smile, though weak, exists. The strands of hair he has left after all the procedures and treatments are combed back from his forehead.

"Hi, Mom," he manages. Then slowly he names them all.

His mother stands at his left side, his father over at his right, his sister and brother are each holding one of his hands, exerting the lightest of pressures against his wrists. He can feel through these warm connections his pulse becoming fainter, more erratic.

We love you, Hal, they'd say.

And they would have the time, if you can imagine this, to tell him it's okay now. *We're here with you, Hal, and we love you. Let go.*

Instead of what happened. Instead of the commotion. The distance. The hallway. The wall. The just barely opened door. And the rest of it. You might want to imagine this. How it could be, instead. See? The family would get to agree on it: that this might be the best time, the best way, the only time their time together could end.

Nineteen-six-oh-six Van Deusen

"Let me show you something," Vera once said.

Joy, knitting a tennis sweater for Leo, looked up from the overstuffed chair in her mother's apartment. "What's that box, Mom?"

"Oh." Vera shrugged. "I was thinking I might show the little ones."

Hal and Abby turned from the mullioned window. They were watching the streetcar idling three stories below; one by one, passengers were disappearing inside. The rapid transit's long black roof wand was vibrating. The wand connected the yellow lozenge-shaped car to the electricity that coursed through the overhead wires. Every fifteen minutes, right on schedule, the shiny rapid transits pulled up. From here, they traveled in only one direction. The building at nineteen-six-oh-six Van Deusen marked the last stop on the line, the turnabout back into the heart of Cleveland. Seven people now waited for the next car; Abby and Hal had counted.

"What's that you're holding, Nan?" Hal said, scratching his arm. "What's inside the box?"

Ricky, who the older two hadn't let stand at *their* window because he wouldn't stop pestering them, began jumping up and down. "It's candy, right? It is, isn't it?"

"It's a pretty big box," Hal pointed out. "And it's round and fancy. Maybe a cake?"

"No, a whole lot of candy, right?" Ricky said.

"What's with you kids?" said Vera, indulgently. "You only want something sweet." She laughed, her dentures square and neat.

"No, we don't," Abby said. "Or I don't, at least. But the others, because they're so immature—"

"A gift?" guessed Hal, brow furrowed.

Ricky kept jumping. "Oh boy, yeah! Then, who's it for, which one of us? I think it's for me."

"You see, Joy, how your children are?"

"I see, Mom." Placidly, she kept knitting, the blue metal needles clicking.

"Is it a gift?" Hal demanded.

"Oh, a kind of gift, sure. But it's for all of you, not for one alone." Vera jiggled the shiny white oval cardboard box. The contents shifted dryly. "Enough. Come to the back and sit with me." Vera crossed to the bedroom and over to the bed, its expansiveness formed by two twin mattresses pushed right against each other. The covers on the left, the side nearer the bathroom, were rarely mussed now. That side used to be Evan's.

"Sit, darlings," she said, patting the blanket.

The kids sprawled atop only her half. Joy leaned against the edge of ash bureau; she didn't feel quite right about going into the room any farther. She'd keep to the sidelines. Hadn't her mother as much as said that this was for the children?

"No shoes," Vera ordered.

Three pairs of sneakers thudded onto the pink carpet.

Vera propped her feather pillow against the headboard and then lowered herself heavily, leaning so the pillow cushioned the small of her back. She placed the box on her lap.

"So," she said, hands on either side of the lid, fingers spread. She gazed at the children, her eyes fixing on each of their faces. When she breathed out, the air rushing against her lips made them flutter a little. The sudden looseness of her flesh scared Rick, and quickly he leaned away.

"Open it now, Nan," Hal encouraged her.

"Look at that. So nervous."

"Who's nervous?" Abby sounded worried. "You are, you mean?"

Vera didn't answer. She stared vacantly past them. Then all of a sudden, she slapped the box. A *smack*—just like that! Immediately, the children all did it. Wild and giggling, the three made that box into an echoing drum.

"Don't!" Vera wrenched it away. "Don't. My mother's picture's in there. And letters and snapshots, from everyone. From my son. Don't hit them more. Why would you want to do that?"

"They didn't know, Mom," Joy said quietly.

"Nan, sorry."

"Sorry."

"Sorry, Nan."

"See, I haven't looked at any of them in years. Not even one peek. That's how much I miss them, you see? How much because of love it can hurt." Lips tight, she didn't say any more.

The kids pulled their hands back and glanced anxiously over to Joy, who put her fingers against her lips and mimicked *silence, please!* to them. But smilingly, so they wouldn't get scared. She felt surprised though, perhaps even a bit put out. Her mother hadn't confided in her that she was keeping something like this. Joy just wouldn't have thought—well, she hadn't stopped to think about it, really, what her mother might or might not have salvaged from East Trainor and packed away in a closet here. She was really too busy keeping things straight in her own house now.

"I want to see the pictures, Nan," Abby whispered. "We all do."

Hal nodded. "We'll respect them."

"Me, too. I want to see, too."

"Or just read us one letter, okay?" Abby said. "We'll listen."

Blinking rapidly, Vera looked away to Evan's side of the bed. She seemed to be trying to imagine him there. As if he would look over and very quietly in his measured way tell her what to do next with the little ones, yes?

"Nan, I really want to see the family. I'm extremely curious." Abby plucked at her sleeve. "I'm old enough to see. Maybe the others aren't, but I am, Nan. I'm really ready."

"We are, too," the boys chorused, Ricky a half beat behind.

"Maybe, Mom, if it makes sense, just, well, if there's one thing now—"

"Enough with my long face, you mean, huh? Okay," she said feistily, lifting her chin. "You're right. Here goes."

Her grandchildren cheered, throwing their arms in the air. "We're right," crowed Hal. "We convinced Nan. Yay, Nan!"

"Yay, Nan!" The three kids, delighted, were grinning at one another. They bent closer, holding their breath.

"I've been saving them. So, little ones." Vera nodded at them, and then over to her daughter, who leaned forward a little.

"My darlings." Slowly, with both hands, she began to work off the lid. "Let's see what's in here for you."